Dear Reader:

It is an editor's greatest delight to discover a book by a new writer that is truly extraordinary, that sweeps the reader away to another world, that evokes powerful emotions which linger long after you've read the last page. SEIZE THE FIRE by Laura Kinsale was for me that exciting reading experience, and I am thrilled to share it with you.

Laura Kinsale has already won numerous awards for her first three historical romances, all published by Avon Books—*The Hidden Heart, Uncertain Magic,* and *Midsummer Moon.* In SEIZE THE FIRE, she surpasses her previous work by creating a hero and heroine who are unlike any in historical romances—and a love that will live in your hearts forever. Amusing and poignant, sensual and action-packed, SEIZE THE FIRE will make you laugh and cry. It is a love story to cherish.

I hope you enjoy SEIZE THE FIRE—a treasure of a novel from a very talented writer.

Warm wishes,

Ellen Edwards

Ellen Edwards
Editor, Avon Books

"SEIZE THE FIRE is intense, passionate, lovely . . .
Don't pass this one up."
Laura London

"A wonderful, captivating love story . . .
The characters were so fresh and alive.
This one will definitely become a keeper."
Julie Garwood
author of *The Bride*

Other Avon Books by
Laura Kinsale

THE HIDDEN HEART
MIDSUMMER MOON
UNCERTAIN MAGIC

Seize the Fire

Laura Kinsale

AVON BOOKS NEW YORK

SEIZE THE FIRE is an original publication of Avon Books. This work has never before appeared in book form. This work is a novel. Any similarity to actual persons or events is purely coincidental.

AVON BOOKS
A division of
The Hearst Corporation
105 Madison Avenue
New York, New York 10016

Cover illustration by Steve Assel
Inside cover author photograph by Constance Ashley, Inc., Photographer
Published by arrangement with the author
Library of Congress Catalog Card Number: 89-91197
ISBN: 0-380-75399-5

First Avon Books Printing: October 1989

Printed in the U.S.A.

K-R 10 9 8 7 6 5 4 3 2 1

'Tis in my head: 'tis in my heart: 'tis everywhere:
it rages like madness and I most wonder how my reason holds.

—Thomas Otway

Prologue

It was hell being a hero. With the guns crashing and the deck a blind chaos of powder smoke, Captain Sheridan Drake wiped his sleeve across his eyes to clear away a crust of Mediterranean sweat and battle-grime. He thought of his botched boyhood Latin lessons with profound regret.

Really, he ought to have listened to his schoolmaster, and gone into practicing law.

A barrister, now—there was a profession for an intelligent man. Sleep late, rise rested, hot coffee and fresh eggs for breakfast . . . but no—he'd best not think of fresh eggs; he'd start hallucinating after a hundred and thirty-seven days at sea without one. The guns roared and the deck beneath him trembled with the recoil. To starboard, a Turkish ship jibed, swinging bows around and peppering the deck with grapeshot and rifle-fire. Sheridan ducked behind the mizzenmast and squinted longingly at the closest hatch, calculating his chances of slipping below unnoticed. No sense getting himself killed in this sordid little squabble.

He shouldn't even have been aboard, but of course no one besides himself would give a thought to that—the British navy being more interested in gallantry than brains, and inclined to become maudlin over its heroes. For the past week the legendary Captain Sheridan Drake had suffered through the stultifying honor of dining here in the flagship, gazing gloomily into his wine and listening to officers of the British, French and Russian navies work themselves into a frenzy of indignation over the way the Turks were enslaving the Greeks.

Or was it the way the Egyptians were devastating the Morea? Whatever—it was just another dubious variation on the old and unpleasant theme of poking one's nose into other people's wars. The only saving thing about it was the way they toasted his health every five minutes, a common official practice which Sheridan approved as a harmless pastime and a cheap drunk.

His moody silence had been taken for a deep and painful case of martial ardor. Deep, because everyone was certain old Sherry was a firebrand for King and Country and Duty and Honor and various other high-flown sentiments—which he wasn't—and painful, because he was known to be a hell of a fellow when it came to a fight—which he was. A hell of a coward, not that any of them would believe it if he said so.

But he was forced to turn himself onshore, unlucky chap; he was leaving the fleet to pay his respects to his beloved father's fresh grave and take up permanent care of his dear invalided sister. It was a sad case, a sad end to a glorious naval career; anybody could see how poor Sherry was torn to pieces over giving up his command, and not a bit comforted by his nabob father's boundless fortune and estate.

It made no difference that poor Sherry himself had never voiced any of these sentiments. It was also immaterial that he would rather have been any number of places than trapped aboard a warship with a bunch of antique admirals who were itching for a fight. Nor did Sheridan bother to mention that he intended the imaginary invalid sister to be a fine sloe-eyed courtesan with a good education in the passionate arts, or that he had despised his father, his father had despised him, and the nabob fortune most probably had been left to a Home for Fallen Women in Spitalfields. Sheridan Drake had the gift of smiling darkly and keeping his mouth shut. He never lied without sufficient provocation.

Just now it was becoming unpleasantly hot on the quarterdeck, even for heroes. Vice Admiral Codrington didn't seem to notice—too busy pretending he was back twenty-two years ago still bellowing broadsides at the Battle of Trafalgar. The old fool apparently hadn't even realized that a bomb ketch behind the enemy line had managed to draw a damned accurate mark on his flagship. Sheridan sucked in an anxious breath as he heard the unearthly whistle of another falling rocket. He closed his eyes with a brief, private groan.

Below him the guns boomed again, covering the blessed *thwop* of a miss as the bomb hit water near enough to send the splash fountaining over his cuff. With an ardent oath, he flung off the drops that glistened against his dark blue coat. If one of those shells hit the deck and exploded over the powder magazine, the fact that he'd been relieved of his command with honors just this morning would be a point of academic debate. It certainly wouldn't make any difference to the tiny pieces of Sheridan Drake scattered all over the Bay of Navarino.

He'd had enough of this hellish nonsense. Like any sensible hero who wanted to live long enough to lay eyes on his laurel wreath, he hit upon a plan. It wasn't a first-rate plan. In fact, it was a damned shaky plan, but things were tight. He drew his sword for dramatic effect and took a step toward Codrington and the knot of flag officers, fabricating a fierce look and an obscure but frantic need to dispatch a boat back out of the action—a boat which Sheridan had every intention of being aboard. As he closed the space between them, the eerie shrill of another incoming bomb climbed to a screaming pitch. He spared a glance up past the mizzenmast.

In that numbing instant he saw his plan and his life and his future go for naught. The shell howled along its trajectory with nightmare clarity. In his panic the thought that pushed every other from his mind was that it was a terrible rotten practical joke. He hated practical jokes; it had been a vicious prank that had launched him into this abominable career, and now it was going to be a stupid black twist of humor that would take him out. Of all the days for Codrington to start a fight; of all the ships for

Sheridan to be on; of all the bombs that were plunging down on all sides, there had to be one with his name on it: Captain Sheridan Drake, Royal Navy—*Almost* Paid Off.

In that endless moment beneath the bomb's rising shriek his life seemed to vanish before him—just evaporate, like steam in thin air: no time for evasion; too far to the rail; too late to do anything but complete the step he'd already started that took him among the officers next to the admiral. He was going to die—right now—with his guts dissolving in fright and fury. It was outrageous; it was monstrous, and it was all Codrington's fault.

Noise blasted his ears, cracking thunder, drowning every other sound. The ship shuddered. Something snapped inside him, an instant of strangeness, as if the air had thickened into molasses and wouldn't fill his lungs, as if a wall in his mind wavered, slipped . . . and then dissolved. Murder howled through his brain and body. Amid the confusion and screams and squeal of splintering wood, he swung his sword and threw all his weight into a wild, vicious blow to the admiral's neck.

The ship heaved beneath him in mid-swing. Something caught Sheridan hard in the back. His sword went flying; he brought both hands up to save himself, sending Codrington sprawling amid the cascade of rigging and deafening smash of plummeting timber. Sheridan scrambled as the tangle of rigging that had fallen around him began to rise. On his knees, he looked over his shoulder, shoving at the wreckage from the downed mast that lay across the quarterdeck. The smolder of burning powder stung his nose. Just beyond his trailing leg lay the splintered end of a three-foot-diameter tree trunk that had been the mizzenmast, still vibrating in deep bass from the fall.

It took three fumbling attempts to make it to his feet, his muscles having gone to pudding. Codrington hadn't even gotten past the process of turning over. Sheridan stepped forward. His brain refused to make sense of the scene, consumed with a flaming urge to kill the old fool while he was down. Crewmen shouted. The tangle of rigging was still moving, pulled in a groaning mass by the mizzen, which trailed precariously over the stern. As a shattered spar lifted, it revealed a dark oblong shape that rolled erratically across the deck toward Codrington's feet, curling a thin black pencil-line of smoke.

Sheridan's mouth opened. For an instant a warning trembled on his lips, and then with the weird single-minded logic of extremity it came to him that any man stupid enough to have started this fight was too stupid to do the obvious thing. While Codrington and the others lay there like sapskulls waiting for the bomb to smash them all to atoms, Sheridan muttered a string of imprecations and moved. He stepped gingerly over the menace of sliding rigging and picked up the live shell.

It was heavier than he'd expected. The weight of it brought his mind out of shock and back to reality, and he found himself with a bomb and a burning fuse in his arms. He'd had one of those vague hysteria-notions of tossing it overboard, but he should have known they never worked. The rail was miles too far away. As that appalling realization struck him, his mind ceased to function at all. At the same moment a taut stay finally parted with a throbbing twang and the mizzenmast lost its last connection with the hull. The whole bulk of mast and rigging and canvas moved with a vast jerk. Sheridan had the bizarre sensation that he was suddenly floating above the ship's deck, that it was sliding slowly past him when it had no right to do so. A sharp pain closed on his ankle and he fell backward with a grunt, holding onto the bomb as if it were a baby. The pull on his ankle increased to agony and things began to move toward him—the stern anchors, the wheel, the railing—all flashed past in a bruising tangle until suddenly there was nothing underneath him but air, and then water that came up to burst into his eyes and fill his nose in a burning intrusion of choking salt.

For an interminable, confused moment he could think of nothing but that he must not breathe. He felt himself going down and down as his lungs burst. His fingers weakened and lost their desperate hold. He dropped the bomb, bracing himself for the inevitable explosion and pain, but all that happened was that he was suddenly buoyant, and his body was singing an electric agonizing song for air.

His consciousness seemed to have telescoped to a tiny pinprick of life. He hung onto that, rising. Something pushed down on his head, and he twisted in panic, clawing upward. He was dying; his whole body spasmed with the knowledge of it, but he would not open his mouth. He would not answer the killing demand of his lungs. He wouldn't give that donkey's ass Codrington the pleasure of drowning him when he'd already left the navy—with honors, hang 'em all.

His fingers dug into a mass of wreckage, too feeble to answer his mandate to pull him upward. Carried by water, his body rolled. Coolness hit his face. The noise in his ears changed.

He opened his eyes and his mouth at the same time, taking a gulp: half air, half seawater. A cough convulsed him as the blunt end of a spar rammed into his neck. He clutched at it and lost it as a swell rolled past. Ahead of him, the flagship and Turkish man-of-war sailed serenely on, still thundering away at one another, already a quarter mile downwind.

"Bastards," Sheridan croaked. He floundered onto a mass of floating rope, but it sank under his weight, tangling in his boots. He fought it off, bobbing and gasping. The sound of the guns echoed around the bay and a white haze hid the land and horizon. A piece of taffrail floated by. He lunged and missed it, wasting strength in a useless splash.

As a wave lifted him, he caught sight of a dead Turk drifting in the next trough, spreading a dark stain in the clear blue. While Sheridan watched, the dark stain seemed to grow and elongate. The body made a sudden twist, as if it were alive, and then disappeared, popping up and shuddering in a grotesque mimic of struggle before it was dragged down again for good, leaving a trail of blood.

Sheridan closed his eyes. Hysteria fluttered in his throat. He wanted to shout and curse and babble fear. Instead he only managed one pathetic oath before a wave slapped his mouth and filled it with seawater. He spat it out and sobbed for air.

The cannon still filled the sky with the crashing, uneven

sound of battle. He thought, with a kind of grief, of fresh eggs and hot coffee. Another wave hit him, washing furious tears off his face.

With sodden, sluggish strokes, he tried to swim. Something large and shadowy slid past beneath him in the water. His muscles went paralytic. He floated and prayed.

It was bloody hell being a hero.

NAVAL CHRONICLE
14 November 1827
Gazette Letters

Copy of a letter from Vice Admiral Sir Edward Codrington to His Royal Highness the Duke of Clarence, dated on Board of H.M.S. Asia, *the 21st October.*

Sir,

It is with regret and respect I must add to my formal report the following information regarding the conduct of Captain Sheridan Drake, formerly in command of H.M.S. *Century.* At eight o'clock yesterday morning Captain Drake carried out orders to transfer his command of the *Century.* As he was then honorably relieved of further duty, and in view of his history of gallant service to his King, I invited him to join me aboard the flagship. When His Majesty's forces were unexpectedly and dishonorably fired upon, precipitating the action I have described in my previous dispatch, I had personal reason to be deeply grateful that Captain Drake did so, for when the flagship was struck with a five-inch shell which dismasted the mizzen, he valiantly and selflessly threw himself forward into the path of the descending mast to save me from crushing. He then fell upon the bomb itself, which had struck the deck with fuse still burning not three feet from my person, and carried the live shell to the rail to dispatch it, thus risking his own life to save the lives, not only of myself, but of all on board. Although he accomplished his intention, I much regret to report that in the course of this noble action he was lost overboard and was not recovered. I respectfully beg to draw Your Royal Highness's attention to his unselfish conduct and sacrifice, which appears to me to be highly commendable.

I have the honor to be, with deepest respect,

Yr Obedient Servant,
Edw. Codrington

THE LONDON TIMES
15 November 1827

His Majesty the King has taken the unprecedented step of conferring upon the late Captain Sheridan Drake the Most Honorable Order of Knight of the Bath in a posthumous investiture which took place last evening. Captain Drake, readers will recall, courageously stepped beneath a falling mast to save the life of Vice Admiral Sir Edward Codrington and then sacrificed his own life to extinguish a bomb which threatened all aboard the Vice Admiral's flagship during the action which has come to be known as the Battle of Navarino in the Ionian Sea.

Although many here at home and in the government lament the conflict with our ancient Ottoman ally that this unfortunate and unnecessary battle represents, by His action, His Majesty very properly acknowledges once again the selfless and noble gallantry of the men of His Royal Navy, who have served so well in the cause of Great Britain.

NAVAL CHRONICLE
10 December 1827
Gazette Letters

Copy of a letter from Vice Admiral Sir Edward Codrington to His Royal Highness the Duke of Clarence, dated on Board of H.M.S. Asia, *the 1st instant.*

Sir,

It is with true pleasure I inform His Royal Highness of the recovery, alive and unharmed, of Captain Sheridan Drake, who was reported missing overboard and feared dead in the action at Navarino.

Captain Drake informs me that he succeeded in swimming ashore and was succored by a Greek fisherman and his daughter, who cared for him until he recovered amply to present himself again for duty.

I have instructed Captain Drake to proceed at once to Plymouth and thence to London bearing this dispatch, to place himself at the service of His Royal Highness.

I have the honor to be, with deepest respect,

Yr Obedient Servant,
Edw. Codrington

10 December. War Office to Office of the Lord Chamberlain.

Having considered as requested the matter of Captain Drake's K.B., we are sending him along to you directly. It is immaterial, I fear, that His Majesty finds the captain's unexpected appearance to be in a bit of bad taste—these things happen, and now we must follow through with it and get the fellow properly knighted or face a great deal of ridicule and questioning of motives.

With upmost respect, I hope it will comfort His Majesty to realize that this office does not yet consider Captain Drake's gallantry to be quite at the end of its usefulness.

Palmerston

One

As a princess, Her Serene Highness Olympia of Oriens felt she was unimpressive. She was quite a common height, not petite or lofty, too plump to be delicate but not substantial enough to be stately. She didn't live in a palace. She didn't even live in her own country. For that matter, she'd never actually seen her own country.

She had been born in England, and had lived as long as she could remember in a substantial brick house with ivy on the walls. Her home fronted on the main street of Wisbeach, facing the north brink of the River Nen. It possessed the same laconic, self-satisfied elegance as its neighbors, a little string of successful bankers, solicitors and gentleman farmers tucked deep among the canals and dikes and marshes of the misty fenlands, which Olympia supposed were about as different from the mountain passes of Oriens as it was possible for landscape to be.

She drank tea with her governess-companion, Mrs. Julia Plumb, and was dressed by an experienced lady's maid. She ate dishes provided by a German cook, had two housemaids and three men to keep the stable and the large garden behind. In a cottage at the back of the garden lived Mr. Stubbins, her language master, who had taught her French, Italian, German and Spanish, plus the Rights of Man and the truths held to be self-evident among enlightened thinkers like Mr. Jefferson, Monsieur Rousseau and, of course, Mr. Stubbins.

She dreamed, in her yellow chintz-hung bedroom above the river, of widening the boundaries of her life. She dreamed mostly of returning to Oriens—where she had never yet been—and leading her people to democracy.

Sometimes Olympia felt she had a great bubble of energy within her, a bubble that threatened to expand and explode in the quiet landscape of her life. She should be somewhere, accomplishing something. She should be making plans, executing agendas, fomenting rebellions. She should not be waiting, waiting, waiting for life to begin.

So she had read, and dreamed, and heard in her mind the crowds cheering and the bells ringing freedom through the streets of a city she had never seen. Until one week ago, when the letter had arrived, and real life had begun with an unpleasant jolt.

Now, amid the befogged and treeless desolation of the marsh a few miles beyond Wisbeach, Olympia stood on a set of sandstone steps, gazing reverently up at the snow-dusted walls of Hatherleigh Hall. He was in there somewhere, girded in this modern Gothic mansion that loomed up out of the fens in a dark jumble of spires, towers and gargoyle-infested flying buttresses. Captain Sir Sheridan Drake—descendant of Sir Francis; decorated veteran of the Napoleonic and Burmese wars, of battles in Canada and the Caribbean; celebrated naval tactician; and most recently, created Knight of the Most Honorable Order of the Bath for his valor and selfless heroism in the Battle of Navarino.

Olympia slipped her hand from her muff and adjusted the coverings on the potted fuchsia she was carrying as carefully as her cold fingers would allow. She hoped the plant hadn't frozen on the four-mile walk from town; it was the only one still alive of the five she'd carefully potted in honor of the naval victory at Navarino as soon as the Cambridge and Norwich papers had announced that Captain Sir Sheridan was coming home. A potted plant perhaps had not been a perfect choice of tributes, but she did not excel at needlework, so an embroidered banner had been out of the question. She'd fantasized about a presentation-sized oil painting of the glorious naval battle, but that was far beyond her pin money. So she'd settled for the plant, and a gift from the heart—her own small, leather-bound and gilded copy of Jean Jacques Rousseau's *The Social Contract* in the original French.

She knew just what Sir Sheridan would look like. Tall, of course—splendidly tall in his blue captain's uniform with immaculate white breeches, a white-plumed *chapeau bras* and gold epaulettes. But he wouldn't be handsome in the ordinary style. No; she envisioned a plain face, a dependable face, saved from homeliness by kind eyes and a noble brow, and perhaps even some freckles and a touching way of casting down his eyes and blushing when confronted with a lady's regard.

She'd pondered what to say to him for days. Mere words seemed inadequate to express her admiration each time she thought of how he had thrown himself beneath a falling mast in order to save the life of his commander and then boldly leapt overboard into shark-infested waters to prevent a live bomb from destroying the ship. She wished she had something more than a frozen fuchsia plant to honor him. And yet she'd dreamed, deep down in the depths of sleepless nights, when the house seemed very quiet and her life seemed very small, that he would smile and understand, and value a potted fuchsia as if it were a medal of royal gold.

But those were dreams. Now that she was here at his door, her heart beat a slow thud of self-conscious terror, confirming her worst suspicion about herself—that in spite of what she wished to be, and ought to be, and would need to be, she was a coward at the bone.

The bell sounded dully beyond the ornate door when she pulled the chain. The moment she let go of it, a quantity of heavy snow cascaded from the portico's roof, pouring over her shoulders and bonnet and landing on the stone with a muffled thump. The front door of Hatherleigh Hall opened just as she was wiping her face and peering out through the broken and bedraggled plume of a green-dyed hat feather.

A small brown man with bare feet and a red fez on his

shaved head stood in the doorway, trailing multitudes of blankets wrapped snugly around his body. The servant ignored Olympia's snow-damage and made a rakish bow, sweeping the step with the corner of a blanket. He looked up at her, blinking and squinting with dark eyes in a round face. "O Beloved," he said in a liquid soprano. "How may I serve thee?"

Olympia, standing with snow in small piles on her shoulders and a lump melting off the tip of her nose, wished she might sink through the stone. Finding that option closed, she forged ahead as if nothing had occurred and placed a slightly damp calling card in his shivering hand.

"Ah!" he said, tucking it beneath his fez and hitching up the blankets. Leaving the front door standing open, he led her through the vestibule and across the polished chessboard of pink-and-white marble into the looming depths of a great hall.

Olympia darted discreet glances at the shadowy cavern. Carved wood flowed up the walls in ornate rhythms, punctuated by dusty banners and dark glittering sunbursts of steel: broadswords and sabers, axes and pikes and pistols, all arranged so artistically that they seemed something else entirely until she looked twice.

With much nodding and bowing, the servant told her she must wait at the foot of the paneled staircase. Instead of walking up the stairs he mounted the banister, sliding himself to the top like a monkey up a palm tree, where he disappeared into the gloom above. Far off in the house she could hear the slap of his feet on smooth wood, and then his voice, awakening echoes in the huge hall. "Sheridan Pasha!" The name was followed by the little man's faint shriek. The sound of a scuffle drifted from the darkness. "Sheridan Pasha! No, no! I was not sleeping!"

"Lying dog." A distant male voice carried clearly on the cold air. "Give over those blankets."

The little man cried again, a sound that rose to a mournful ululation. "Sheridan Pasha—I beg you! My daughters, my wife! Who will send them money when I am a dead and frozen corpse?"

"Who sends them money now?" The unseen speaker gave a snort. "They only exist when it suits you anyway. What the duece would you do with a woman if you had one? Look here, you Egyptian donkey—there's a hole in this shirt I could poke a nine-pound cannon through, and I've got no shaving water."

The servant replied vigorously to that, a plaintive rise and fall of tones in a language foreign to Olympia, who spoke five fluently and could read and write in four more. The deeper voice answered in English, the thump of footsteps closer and clearer as the speaker moved down the corridor toward the stairs. "Well, send her to the devil! Damned if I'll be ambushed by another bombazine horror in a hideous hat." Disgust reverberated in the air. "Females! The streets ain't safe. Get her . . ."

In the midst of a curse he appeared in the shimmer of candlelight, half naked, a white towel slung over his shoulders and shadows tarnishing his bare chest. He carried the blankets bundled loosely in one hand. His fawn breeches and black boots blurred into the gloom at the top of the steps.

He saw her. He halted. A faint spark of dull gold flashed from a crescent-shaped pendant as it seemed to twist in the light and come to rest against his chest. He closed his fist over the towel on his shoulder, hiding the crescent in shadow. Olympia clutched her gifts tighter, peering through her hat feathers as he stared down at her in abrupt and heavy silence.

He wasn't at all what she had imagined.

Tall, yes—but not plain, not dependable, not kind. Not by any stretch of fancy.

The gray eyes that regarded her were as deep and subtle and light-tricked as smoke from a wildfire. The face belonged to an archangel from the shadows: a cool, sulky mouth and an aquiline profile, and Satan's own intelligence in the assessing look he gave her. The candles behind him lit a smoldering halo of reddish gold around his black hair and turned each faint, frosted breath to a brief glow.

He was not homely, He was utterly and appallingly

beautiful, in the way the gleaming steel blossoms of murder and mayhem adorning the walls of the great hall were beautiful.

"Who the dickens are you?" he asked.

Courage, she said to herself. It didn't help. She straightened her snow-crusted shoulders, attempting at least the image of composure. She dropped a slight curtsy. "Olympia St Leger. One of your new neighbors. I've come to welcome you to Hatherleigh."

He looked down at her from the landing with no sign of concern for his state of undress. "Good God," he said, and raised the towel to scrub at a spot under his chin. "I ain't worth the trouble, I promise you." He flipped the cloth over one shoulder and watched her a moment longer, his head tilted a little to one side, like a sleepy panther mildly intrigued by a mouse. Then he turned and bellowed over his shoulder, "Mustafa!"

"Sheridan Pasha!" the little servant cried. "I was not sleeping!"

"Yállah! Brother of vermin, do you see this? Miss . . . St Leger, was it? . . . has been soaked. Take her the blankets."

Mustafa appeared, catching the woolen bundle that his master tossed at him. He slid down the banister, his loose white trousers flashing in the dimness. Whispering under his breath, he placed the blankets over her, fussing about and smoothing the corners into place. Olympia noticed for the first time that he, too, wore around his neck a golden ornament shaped like a crescent moon, with a tiny star hung just above the lower point. She peeked up at Sir Sheridan, but could no longer see his pendant in the shadows and the way he held the shaving towel.

Mustafa stepped away when he was satisfied and bowed toward the top of the stairs. "You will have a tête-à-tête, yes? I bring refreshment."

Sir Sheridan made a sound, midway between a word and a groan, which didn't sound promising to Olympia—but Mustafa was already gone into the dark nether regions beneath the stair.

"I don't mean to impose upon you," she said quickly.

"Don't you?" He stepped onto the first stair, but instead of descending, he only sat down where he was, resting one boot on the top step and the other on the next level down. "What exactly do you mean to do?"

She controlled the urge to moisten her lips nervously. It wasn't going at all well. He wasn't dressed. She shouldn't have come. She ought to leave. She wished, rather desperately, that he'd turned out to be plain and freckled and shy after all. And wearing clothes.

She drew the blankets a little closer around her shoulders and disengaged the wrappings from the fuchsia plant. "Well—I've brought you . . . ah, a gift." Why did it seem like such a silly idea now? "It isn't much. That is—not as much as I would have liked." Unprotected by the muff, her cold fingers were stiff and clumsy. The wrappings fell away to the floor, and the plant drooped forlornly in the freezing air, its bright flowers gone limp and withered. "In honor of your arrival, and your selfless valor on behalf of your country." She bit her lip. "But I'm afraid it's dying."

"Is it?" he murmured. "Most appropriate."

She looked up, and pulled the copy of Rousseau from inside her muff. She lifted her skirt and started to step onto the first stair. "I also wished to give you—"

"Don't!" His command froze her in place as if her limbs didn't belong to her. "Don't come farther."

"Forgive me!" She backed up hastily. "I didn't mean—"

"Just stay there." He stood up and descended midway down the staircase. Then he hiked himself over the banister and pushed away, dropping a full six feet off the other side. His boots hit the marble. The great hall sent back a volley of echoes.

He came around the newel-post toward her. There was an efficient grace to his movement, a swing and balance that seemed to assess the ground beneath him, to interpret and exploit terrain instead of merely walk upon it.

"The first ten stairs can't be trusted," he told her. "They're meant to collapse under weight at random moments."

She looked from his impassive face to the stairs and back again. The feathers hanging in front of her face swayed as she turned her head.

"It's a joke," he said.

He was taller than she'd realized. She had seen paintings of red Indians that looked less intimidating.

He lifted his eyebrows. "What's the matter? No sense of humor, Miss St Leger?"

"Pardon me. I didn't realize it was meant to amuse." She paused uncertainly and then added, with more honesty, "I'm afraid I don't understand."

"Sadly overcivilized, I see. You've probably never understood the sport in pulling the wings off flies, either."

She thought of explaining that she was considered a humorless person by most of the residents of Wisbeach because she often failed to laugh at the proper subjects, such as a goat with its horns caught in a hedge, or a drunken tavern girl falling in a wet ditch. However, she decided to omit that particular information, unwilling to expose herself. Sir Sheridan was a stranger, relentlessly disconcerting, not the least because he was not dressed, and she had never before seen a man undressed at close range—or any range at all that she could remember, discounting marble statues. She found it beyond her ability to look only at his face; from behind the protection of the feathers, her glance kept skipping downward, to his shoulders, his chest, the base of his throat.

Observing him from the edge of her vision, she realized with a faint sense of confusion that there was no pendant resting on his chest after all, nothing but a curve of muscle that must have caught the light and created the illusion. His skin was dark and gold and smooth and mysterious. She wanted to touch him.

"My father," he said conversationally, "delighted in maiming flies. Did you know him?"

"Oh, no. Not at all, I'm afraid. He kept quite to himself after he moved here, you see."

She hoped that was a polite way to avoid saying that the elder Mr. Drake had lived in such isolation in this house built for him in the midst of a fog-ridden marsh that he hadn't even shown himself to his steward, but left the man notes of instruction. These missives told the steward precisely where to place each of the paintings, bronzes, medieval manuscripts, weapons and gemstones the reclusive owner ordered his agents to purchase. It had been the chief topic of conversation in Wisbeach for the first five years of Mr. Drake's peculiar residence, but after eight, it had again lost place to Lord Leicester's prize bulls and the weather—only to receive an enthusiastic revival recently at the news of the old man's death and of his famous son's imminent arrival.

"That's just as well," Sir Sheridan said. "He seems to have arranged for several entertaining pitfalls for the unwary when he built this place."

"Did he?" Olympia was trying, with limited success, to keep her eyes decently averted from his body. But she was cheating. As she peeked, he suddenly shuddered: an uncontrolled, startling move.

Sheridan crossed his arms and rubbed himself amid the shivers. "Deuced cold in here," he said between his teeth—which was certainly no lie, though he mentioned it chiefly as bait to draw this implausible creature out into the open about her motives. He had yet to determine what she wanted out of him, coming unchaperoned and uninvited as she had; whether it was money, blackmail, minor sin or complete seduction, or just a tale to boost her backwater status among the local gossips.

She looked up at him through the ridiculous mess of wet feathers on her hat, her face obscured by ostrich plumes except for the plump, winsome curve of her chin and one cheek. With the intense silence that seemed to characterize her conversation, she held out the blankets Mustafa had given her. As they slid from her shoulders, he had an intriguing closer view of her high, generous bosom, nicely adorned by moss-colored satin trimmed in black.

Sheridan had spent a sizable portion of his recent visit to London in observing the current state of feminine fashion—from both inside and out. He judged Miss St Leger's costume to be expensive and strictly in style, not to mention appealingly hourglass in shape. However, his concern with fashion being only a minor extension of his interest in what was underneath, he was well aware that the silhouette had little to do with the figure inside it. In this case, he felt, the initial inspection clearly warranted further investigation.

As a first step toward carrying out his dishonorable intentions, he made a brief, noble issue out of taking the blankets, gently refusing to accept them until she was practically begging him to leave her in the cold. The odd little chit became almost frantic over it, to the extent of offering him her redingote, too, and babbling on about how he must be unused to the climate, having just arrived from the Mediterranean. She actually began to unbutton her collar.

He watched in astonishment as she stripped off the coat. His suspicions heightened. He wondered if this weren't some ploy to get her undressed, in which event he could expect Outraged Papa through the door at any moment.

The awkward disrobing revealed an abundant figure in a stylish green gown, with a large diamond pendant at her throat. Sheridan glanced down at the offered redingote, mentally transforming the pearl buttons and expensive braided trim into shillings. He looked up hopefully. If Papa was this well padded, Sheridan hoped he'd hurry, and he needn't have gone to so much trouble, either.

"Miss St Leger," he said, as amiable as the spider to the fly, "it's far too cold for either of us to stand here. Won't you join me somewhere more comfortable?"

The feathers on her hat bobbled. It was like talking to a sheepdog. He resisted the urge to stoop down and peer up at her from below, instead throwing the blankets around his shoulders and drawing her firmly onto his arm.

He cast about quickly for a place to take her, and settled on the tiny study near the front door as the only suitable option. It had been used recently by the steward, which suggested it was relatively free of his father's vicious pranks. It also contained a sofa of convenient length for criminal conduct.

Mustafa appeared with a tea tray just as they were crossing the hall. While Sheridan settled Miss St Leger on the couch, Mustafa successfully re-created the din of a minor war with the coal scuttle. The skirmish, including full artillery, ended with Sheridan sending him to the devil—in Arabic, so as not to offend delicate feminine ears—and building the fire himself.

He sat down next to his guest. "May I take your hat, Miss St Leger?"

Her fingers curled. Behind her, a bank of tall windows painted with a collection of fictitious heraldry dyed the light gold and green, bringing out deeper colors in her dress. She fiddled with the corner of the leather book in her lap, saying nothing.

"Are you hiding under there?" he asked, careful to keep his tone light.

She hesitated, and then said, "Yes. I suppose I am."

He liked her voice. It made him think of sable pelts, husky and soft. Sheridan reached up and gave the green ribbons a gentle tug, pulling the bow free. "I'm afraid, Miss St Leger, that I must claim the right to actually see whom I'm entertaining. How do I know you aren't one of those *sthaga* fellows, come in disguise to assassinate me?"

A poor topic for levity, that, since it wasn't entirely out of the realm of possibility and thus no joking matter.

"No," she answered, very serious. "I understand you to mean the thuggee sect of India? Why would you think so?"

He ignored that piece of witlessness and lifted the huge, drooping mass of millinery from her head. She instantly lowered her face, staring at her lap, so that nothing was visible of her beyond the cluster of sunflower curls that framed the netted bun on top of her head. Intrigued by the curve of one plump cheek, he lifted her chin and made her look toward him, ignoring her flinch as he touched her.

His first impression was of green eyes, wide as a baby owl's and just as solemn. Dumpling cheeks, a straight nose, and a firm little mouth—all ordinary, and all in common female proportion. There was nothing notably strange about her features—and yet it was an odd face, the kind of face that looked out of burrows and tree-knots and hedgerows, unblinking, innocent and as old as time. If she'd had whiskers to twitch it wouldn't have surprised him, so strong was the impression of a small, prudent wild creature with dark brows like furry markings.

Strangely, she made him want to smile, as if he'd just pulled aside a branch and discovered a nightingale staring gravely back at him from its nest. He found himself reacting in the same way, consciously containing his moves and his voice, as if he might startle her away.

"Hullo," he said softly, giving her a light, suggestive chuck beneath her plump chin as he let her go. "Honored to meet you, Miss St Leger."

She held out the book. "This is for you."

Sheridan looked down at the small volume. He opened it in the middle, read a line of some French nonsense about the "social compact," and then a phrase asserting that when a prince told a citizen it was expedient he should die for the state, that citizen ought to die.

A nice idea. He hoped Monsieur Rousseau had been fortunate to experience the social gratification of perishing with a bullet in his belly and his legs torn off by cannon shot. Personally, having been invited to die more frequently than was polite in the interests of a bunch of blockheaded bureaucrats, Sheridan looked upon the sentiment with some skepticism.

He flipped back and paused at the flyleaf. In a careful hand, Miss St Leger had written something in Latin. Since Sheridan's formal schooling had ended at the age of ten, he could only frown at it and hum-hum and look wise, not wishing to tarnish her image of him, which was clearly exalted and ought to be taken advantage of before the new wore off.

"Thank you," he said, looking up at her. "I'll treasure this."

Her lips parted slightly. She managed to smile without smiling, her serious face ashine with pleasure—real pleasure, which was something he recognized only because he'd never seen it before, not on any of the hundreds of faces which had smirked vainly or proudly or coyly at him as he played out his hero farce.

It was Sheridan who looked away, feeling unexpectedly awkward. She was outlandish and yet curiously lovely in her sparrowish, humble way. It made him uncomfortable. He was partial to beautiful women; he liked prettiness as well as the next man. But this was something different. Something that touched him in obscure and half-forgotten places. In his soul, he might have said, if he'd thought he still had one to stir.

Which he didn't, as he proved to himself by lowering his eyelids and enjoying the deliberate and easy kindling of more familiar sensations. Her dress, cut in a modish horizontal line across her bosom, revealed quite enough to assure him that nothing artificial amplified the swell of her breasts. The straight neckline made an inviting path, starting low on her shoulders and crossing the opulent expanse of skin at a point that on most females would have been perfectly modest, but which on Miss St Leger clearly showed the shadowy prelude to a luxurious cleavage.

He shifted the blanket a little to hide his interest, which was rather more than intellectual, and bought some time by pouring for them both. Undecided on the best approach to achieving a considerably closer acquaintance, he found himself sitting next to her and sipping like a schoolboy at a charity tea.

Her motives still baffled him. It was beginning to look unlikely that Outraged Papa would appear. Possibly she was going to ask Sheridan for money for Distressed Needlewomen or something, but if so, she was taking her sweet time about it. He looked at her slantwise and saw her chew her lower lip, obviously working herself up to the point.

He sipped again and waited to see what it was. Watching her face, rolling sweetness on his tongue, savoring both after months of forced abstinence from every civilized pleasure, he slowly allowed himself to slide into tranquil sensuality. He appreciated simply existing, enjoying the cool air on his face and the warmth the blankets radiated back from his bare skin, the feel of his spine pressed up to the solid horsehair couch. His career had taught him one true thing amid the folly—there were few enough moments of peace in life. He took this one and treasured it with sincere gratitude, which was as close to religion as he came these days.

Miss St Leger stopped chewing her lip. She seemed content with the silence, sitting with the mute patience of a dog or a cat, staring pensively into the struggling fire. Her lowered profile emphasized her chubby chin, creating a picture that Sheridan found genuine and vulnerable to the point of painfulness. She should have known better than to display her little faults so conspicuously; any other woman he'd ever met would have. Spinsters whose beauty had gone to wattle still had the presence of mind to preen and maneuver themselves into presenting their best angle to a new acquaintance. He wondered if she had ever set out to seduce a man before.

He caught himself in that thought. Vain bastard he'd become, with all the misplaced glory and its agreeable effect on females—but for God's sake, what else could she possibly want from him? To call like this, alone, unchaperoned . . . he'd been out of the country for a long time, but not that long. Morals had not become so cavalier in his absence. The consequences for her were monstrous, and yet there she sat, asking nothing, hinting nothing. If she'd simply wished to bestow upon him a dead pot plant and seditious literature, she could have had them delivered. And certainly ought to have.

As he observed her in musing silence, a novel thought occurred to him. It slipped through his mind so subtly that it seemed to mingle like smoke with his physical perceptions, with the way the dim light through the stained-glass window fell across her hair in little iridescent rainbows, and the scent of old tobacco and dust lingered in the room. He wondered, absurdly, if this was what she had come for—simply to sit in the stillness and be alive and share it with him.

Something inside, some tiny something he hadn't even known was there, seemed to unfold, to spread tentative petals open like a desert flower sensing rain.

She turned and looked up at him, her great, unblinking eyes full of cryptic forest wisdom. He thought foolishly: *Let me stay here. I need this.*

"I've come to ask you a favor," she said.

If she'd dashed him in the face with her tea dregs, she could not have shattered the instant so effectively. He set his cup on the saucer. "Naturally." He smiled, aware of the way his mouth didn't quite manage humor, but caught at irony. "What is it, Miss St Leger?"

Olympia had been gathering herself piece by piece to get to this moment, amazed in every second at his tolerance and simple hospitality. It was immensely encouraging, far more than she'd expected, that he would sit so patiently while she dealt with her terror. Afraid now that her daring would collapse if she hesitated, she began to speak as quickly as possible.

"Of course I have no right to ask anything of you, I know," she said. "But I am desperate." She hesitated, saw one dark eyebrow begin to arch at that, and rushed on. "I must leave the country, and I don't know how to go about it, and I have no one I can ask to help me."

He put his cup on the side table. The sofa creaked as he stood up, pulling the blankets over his shoulders. At the hearth, he picked up the iron poker, rotating it in both hands for a moment, looking down at the brass handle. Then he turned to the fire and shifted some of the coals.

Facing away from her, he asked, "What have you done?"

"Oh, no," she exclaimed hastily. "You mustn't think that! I haven't explained myself well, of course—but please be assured there is no crime of any sort. I haven't *done* anything. I'm not fleeing, exactly. It is that I must get to Rome as soon as possible. The reason is . . . " She wrapped her fingers around themselves and squeezed. "Personal."

He looked sideways at her. "I see. Personal."

It seemed astonishingly rude to reserve her reasons, now that he'd pointed it out. But the whole thing was awful and outrageous anyway, almost unreal, so impossible did it seem that she'd actually come here, that her body had taken the steps her mind had only imagined.

He stood in stillness by the fire, The blankets had slipped off one shoulder to hang down his bare back. She stared at his arm, the long, relaxed curve of muscle down to his wrist and hand, where his fingers rested loosely around the poker. Behind him, amber light picked out the pattern on the stylish wallpaper in a dull sheen of gilt.

"It isn't completely personal," she added. She stared at her lap, and then forced herself to look up at him again. "It is in the cause of liberty, in a way. I suppose that must sound peculiar. But I . . . I seem to have some political significance, you see, and I am to be coerced into something that will be very detrimental for my . . . country."

"Miss St Leger, I'm afraid I don't understand a word of what you're saying."

"Perhaps you won't believe me," she said. "That's why I didn't tell you instantly, because I wouldn't blame you if you thought it was a hum. But I am not an Englishwoman. I'm actually—" She hesitated, and lowered her head. "I'm actually what the world is pleased to call a—a royal personage. King Nicolas of Oriens is my grandfather."

The poker clattered against the hearth.

"It's true," she said.

"Good God." He stood up straight. "Good God. Do you mean you're a bloody *princess?*"

Two

"Yes." Olympia sat up straight on the horsehair sofa and stared ahead, her hands tightened into fists. She pressed them tightly together. "And I have received a communication. My people wish me to return to Oriens."

It was a small lie, saying that her people wanted her. Actually, she hadn't meant to say that, but somehow to admit her complete impotence to a man of action like Sir Sheridan Drake was too painful. And as if that fib weren't shameful enough, with a kind of detached horror she heard herself expanding on it.

"I've been told that I am needed for the cause," she said. "To help lead the revolution which will bring them to freedom and establish democratic principles. So I must return."

Sir Sheridan blinked at her. "To lead a revolution?"

Olympia nodded.

"What a singular notion," he said.

She moistened her lips and hung her head. "You will think I'm the greenest of greenheads, of course. To ever hope that I could achieve such a noble end! But please, Sir Sheridan—if you can only conceive of what it is like. You've fought in the cause of freedom and human dignity; you've risked your life. But can you understand what it has been for me? To be kept here like a bird in a cage, in exile"—she lifted her head scornfully—"for my *safety*, they say, and so I'm coddled and nursed and hedged about while my people suffer oppression—and I, who am morally responsible because of my position alone, have done nothing to aid them!"

He cleared his throat, frowning at her as if she were a navigational chart that had proved to be grossly inaccurate. He started to say something, stopped, then shook his head. "You've floored me."

"I know it must seem quite mad."

He laughed. "Rather."

"I suppose you need not believe it, if only you will help me."

For a long moment he looked at her, and then shook his head again with another soft chuckle. He leaned one arm against the mantel and toyed with a misplaced inkstand, smoothing his forefinger down the fringe of a feather quill. "I believe it."

"Then you will help—"

"Ah—let's not proceed so fast, Miss St Leger. Or is that your real name?"

"Well, to be more precise, it's Olympia Francesca Marie Antonia Elizabeth. The St Legers have ruled in Oriens since Charlemagne."

He gave the quill another meditative stroke and slanted her a look, as a lazing wolf would cock an ear to a distant sound—not alarmed, but almost imperceptibly more intent. "Oriens lies in the French Alps, does it not? Why go to Rome if it's Oriens where you're wanted?"

Olympia kept her back straight. "The Alps of Oriens are not *French.*"

"Nevertheless," he said, "they're a considerable distance from Rome."

"I must pass through Rome for another reason. I told you, I am under coercion."

"What kind of coercion?"

She looked down at her lap. "Will you help me?"

In the long pause, the fire hissed softly.

"We are at an impasse, ma'am. I'm not in the habit of committing myself to dubious positions on questionable information."

She considered that, sorting the reproof from the important thing, which was that he wasn't dismissing her out of hand. Of course he would want to know everything. And it wasn't as if she couldn't trust him. He was a champion of freedom. He'd risked his life in the fight to rescue the Greeks from their degrading slavery under the Ottoman Empire. He'd proved his love of liberty by action under fire—which was far more than Olympia herself had ever done for the cause of democracy.

No—it wasn't his integrity that made her hesitate; it was her own cowardice. Her own miserable cowardice and shame that she could not cope alone with the disaster thrust upon her. And worse, the niggling fear that rose up in her throat when she looked at him and saw what he was—not the safe, freckled, boy-man hero of her dreams, but a man in fact: quietly sanguine, quietly confident, quietly asking real and pointed questions about an all-too-real situation.

It was that fear she shrank from most: the perverse dread that if he understood, he *would* be convinced to help—that events would be set in motion which she could not stop. And she would fail. She would find that she was inadequate to the role that destiny had set her.

"It's very complicated," she mumbled.

He snorted. "If it's anything to do with that mare's nest they call continental politics, I don't doubt the particulars will reduce my brain to a stupefied wreckage. But I'll endeavor to muddle through."

Under his steady, slightly impatient gaze, she ran out of evasions. "You know where Oriens is located?" she asked hesitantly.

"Between France and Savoy, is it not? A splotch on the map about the size of a tea stain." He waved his hand. "That was before Bonaparte, of course. God only knows where they've put it now."

"It's still where it has always been," she assured him. "The congress at Vienna left it intact, and restored my grandfather to the throne."

"Fortunate. Ah, but I had forgotten! You are to have a revolution shortly. Was that part of the plan proposed at Vienna, or is it in the nature of an extemporaneous uprising?"

"It is extemporaneous, as far as I am aware," Olympia said. "Do they plan such things in congress?"

He looked at her, and went back to studiously stroking the feather. "I daresay a parcel of drunken diplomats is capable of anything. But continue with your own story, please."

She twisted a fold of her gown around her finger. "Oriens controls the best passes between France and Italy, you see," she said. "They are open all year round, even in the worst of winters. And my grandfather has a treaty with Britain for their use."

"Mmm. In return for protection from overly friendly neighbors."

Olympia smoothed her dress and then folded it around her finger again. "I think that is putting it too nicely."

"Really?" He looked amused. "Then let us say that your country would rather whore for Britain than be raped by France. That's not putting it too nicely, is it?"

She looked at him, startled, and then felt herself turning crimson. She moistened her lips anxiously. "Is that meant to be a jest? I don't wish to offend you by not laughing," she said hurriedly, "but I don't often understand jokes."

"That doesn't bother me. I consider it a virtue. And I still know almost nothing of your problem."

"Well, you see—it—it's always been so with my country," she stammered. "We are small, and in constant danger of losing sovereignty. In some ways Bonaparte's aggression helped us, as it has made the greater states take an active interest in the balance of European power."

"Ah, yes." He sighed. "The god-awful Balance of Power."

She frowned at him. "You sound as if you resent it."

"I rank it slightly below Original Sin in the hierarchy of human ideas. A clever turn of phrase, but bloody hell in actual practice. It nearly blew me to Hades at Navarino." He made her a little bow. "But pardon me. I am a cynic."

She cleared her throat, wishing for another cup of tea. But Sir Sheridan was watching her so intently that she feared to take the time to pour. Taking a breath, she went on. "I was saying that my grandfather has allied us with your country. But he is very old. I've never met him, but he's written to me saying he has named his heir."

After a silence, he prompted, "Who is—?"

She shifted a little in her seat. "My father was the oldest son."

"And?"

"Both my parents died when I was an infant. I have one uncle. Prince Claude Nicolas. There is a body of principle which would make him the heir."

"Salic law." He rested one boot on the fireplace fender, still leaning against the mantel. The fire set a red glow to his bare skin, illuminating the smooth curve of his chest. "Do go on. I'm fascinated."

"Claude Nicolas is . . . not a favorite with my grandfather. Or the populace. He has become a Roman Catholic, while most of the country, particularly our guilds and merchants, follows Presbyterian precepts. And he is a monarchist, fiercely so. With his detachment of palace guard, he prevents any open discussion of political topics. Forcibly. Also, he has made many friends among the Russian embassy, and my grandfather is very unhappy with him for that."

"No doubt your British allies are a bit put out, too."

She nodded, looking down at her lap. "So my grandfather has proclaimed that another kind of law will dictate the succession. I think it is Neopolitan law, but I'm not entirely certain. He didn't go into the precedents in his letter. But there are some. Enough. The courts and his councillors support him fully."

"In other words, he declares for you."

She lifted her face and nodded.

He locked his fists behind his back, gazing thoughtfully at the floor. Then he asked in a dry tone, "Is he aware that you're contemplating civil war?"

"I'm not!" she said in horror.

"There was the small matter of a revolution."

"Yes—but that is something else entirely. At least, it isn't what I need help with."

"You don't? Then I'm sure I needn't point out the rather

glaring logical discrepancy in leading a revolution against yourself."

"Sir Sheridan," she said, with a touch of exasperation at his unaccountable slowness. "Obviously I wouldn't do so. I will never be on the throne, don't you see? If it were so simple as waiting for the succession and abdicating in favor of a constitutional democracy, I would do so gladly."

He drummed his fingers on the mantelpiece, then tilted his head and squinted at her. "You really are a radical."

"Yes!" She nodded vigorously. "But I can't delay until I'm handed the throne. My grandfather's declaration has done no good at all. My uncle is going to—"

She stopped. A blazing flush rose in her face. Sheridan gazed at her with interest as she turned pink over every bit of exposed skin. Her lower lip trembled for a fleeting instant, and then she caught it in her teeth and lowered her face.

"This is very hard," she said, with an obvious attempt to be resolute and a fetching little upward break in her husky voice.

Sheridan knew an opportunity when he saw one. The invitation was as clear as a lace handkerchief fluttering to the earth. Every immoral instinct urged him to go to her side, to rescue the hankie and offer solace—and reap the lush reward. But he stood where he was. It was odd and uncomfortable, leaving his brain to adjust his body's automatic and enthusiastic response. But there she sat in straight-backed misery, with that metaphorical bit of lace on the floor crying out for comfort, and never even knew she'd dropped it.

He wondered irritably if he had a fever. It seemed likely he was sickening for something, what with this sudden attack of scruples.

He drew an aimless pattern in the dust on the mantel, waiting. After a few moments, she lifted her chin.

"My uncle thinks to marry me," she said, with a trace of defiance. "He has sent to the pope for a dispensation to do it."

She was absolutely scarlet now, whether from disgust at

the idea of a closely consanguineous marriage or just at the idea of marriage in general, he couldn't tell.

"You will say I should refuse," she added in a rush. "Of course I should, and I will, but my grandfather is very weak, and my uncle has brought great pressure to bear on him by threatening to invite in Russian grenadiers to quell what he calls the 'disturbance' among the people. If my grandfather is made to agree, and the papal dispensation is granted, then I understand that—that in fact, my own consent is not very necessary."

Sheridan made a sympathetic noise in his throat and silently saluted Prince Claude Nicolas as a flash contender. The fellow had obvious style. From the chit's account, he'd nicely checkmated his father's move to bar him from the throne. Married to a figurehead queen, with both the Vatican and the Czar behind him, he'd be a formidable force in a two penny place like Oriens, as good as king any day and possibly better, since his wife would provide a convenient scapegoat for unpopular actions. Sheridan doubted he could have thought of a better plan himself—which made him highly reluctant to get on the wrong side of the man who had.

Besides, Oriens could do worse than have a ruthless, intelligent and astute politician at the reins. It could, for instance, have this pretty dumpling of a revolutionary nut for a ruler.

"Rome," he said. "You're going to appeal to the pope?"

She looked up at him, green eyes wide: ferocious and determined and about as intimidating as an oversized field mouse. "Yes. Perhaps, based only on my uncle's word, the pope can morally give a dispensation, but when I tell him how offensive it is to me to participate in a"—she began to turn red again—"a profanity of marriage, and that I will never convert to his faith, he'll understand that I'm being forced."

"An optimistic assumption."

"Am I not being reasonable?" she asked uncertainly.

He shrugged. If she couldn't predict that having Oriens added to the Roman Catholic fold would be a powerful antidote for any queasiness the Vatican felt about consanguinity, he saw no reason to argue the point with her. "And what is it you require from me in all this? Are you suggesting I accompany you?"

"No, no," she said—a rather feeble denial. "That would be asking far too much. I only hoped you could help me get started."

"Buy you a seat on the London coach, perhaps?"

"I thought—actually—that there would be more clandestine ways."

"There may well be. I can't say I know anything about them."

She fingered the diamond pendant. Sheridan wondered if that was meant to be a hint. Meeting her anxious eyes, he decided that, unfortunately, it probably wasn't.

"I was under the impression—" She looked embarrassed. "I supposed, from your reputation— Forgive me, but do you not have many contacts among the . . . ah . . . organizations?"

As the product of a hard school, Sheridan was wary of organizations. If they were clandestine and unmentionable, he didn't want anything to do with them at all. But she kept fingering that necklace, until he could just about feel his empty pockets burning.

He cleared his throat. "I'd like to help you," he said, as vaguely as possible. "But, uh—I've just arrived in the neighborhood." He paused, watching her and feeling his way. "I'm afraid any contacts of mine are far away." Nonexistently far away, but what difference did that make when she kept reminding him of the crown jewels in that pointed way?

"But that's what I need most," she said, dropping her hand from her throat and interlocking her fingers. "I can't travel openly—you understand that. I suppose I can begin well enough; I believe I could reach London on my own, but beyond that, I'm at a loss."

He leaned both shoulders against the mantel, toying with the corner of the blanket and calculating madly. The last thing he'd do was hie off to Italy, of course—too damned many bandits and petty despots loose about the place for his taste—but there were other considerations. Money, for one. To be vulgarly blunt about it.

He perused the diamond at her throat again, contemplating several alternatives for getting payment in advance and abandoning her on the docks at Blackwall. He could make it seem an accident—hire a couple of bullyboys to appear to overpower him in a dark alley—she couldn't demand her jewelry back if he'd made a reasonable effort to pop her off in the right direction, could she? Or better yet, he could lay information with her keepers—she was bound to have some; she was a princess, after all, or so she claimed, even if it was a pip-squeak country. She wouldn't have sneaked off to see him alone if she'd had someone official on her side.

His mouth flattened a little. The pay couldn't be much if she was in it all on her own. He wished he could get a closer view of the diamond. Three carats, at least.

If she had a few more of those tucked away, things might come right enough.

"I'd hoped to get a letter of introduction to the Carbonari," she said wistfully.

"The *Carbonari.*"

At his exclamation, she bit her lip and looked down. "Perhaps they would not wish to bother with me."

Sheridan sucked in a long breath. He saw what kind of clandestine organizations she was talking about now, the preposterous little piece. How the devil she came to think he'd be mixed up with a bunch of ravening Italian revolutionaries like the Carbonari, he couldn't conceive. God, the very thought of it made his palms sweat.

But he needn't ever go that far with the whole thing. And there was that diamond, winking at him, sending back prisms of color, a tiny concentration of all the hues in the stained-glass window behind her. He needed money; he needed it quite desperately, and he needed it now.

Máshallaah, as Mustafa would say. *What God wills is good.*

Good enough for gallant Sherry, at any rate.

"The Carbonari," he repeated thoughtfully. "Difficult . . ." He scratched his jaw for a long moment. Then finally, slowly, he nodded. "But I believe it could be done."

Her face took on that shine of silent joy again. She managed to look elated and terrified at the same time.

"It will be dangerous," he added. "You realize that."

She nodded, chewing at her lower lip in a nervous rhythm.

He allowed a long silence to pass before he finally straightened up with an air of decisiveness. "In point of fact," he said, "I think if you're determined to carry through with this, I'd best tag along myself."

Her lips stilled, parting a little.

He spread his hands in an imitation of self-conscious rue. "I doubt I'd sleep well, you see, knowing I'd sent you into the fray alone."

She came about and fell onto the proper tack like the sweetest ship in His Majesty's navy. "Sir Sheridan," she whispered, "you are a truly noble man."

A shrug and a faint smile were the only answer to that. "Line of duty, ma'am."

"No. It is not your duty." She looked at him for a moment and then dropped her eyes. "Your duty is to your own country—it is an act of generosity and kindness to trouble yourself on my account."

Considering that he didn't plan to go to much trouble at all, beyond peddling her stone to the highest bidder, it wasn't difficult to make light of the matter. Playing at hero wasn't always so easy; it required a fine hand to strike the right note between truth and fantasy, but Sheridan took a sinful delight in the game. He was his father's son after all, he reckoned—that it pleased him to make a fool of the world in general. And as far as he was concerned, there was nothing more blindly simpleminded than the world that had managed to find a hero in Sheridan Drake.

"Well," he said, shoving away briskly from the mantel, "we won't split hairs about duty when you and your country's freedom are at stake. After all, the brotherhood of liberty knows no national boundaries, does it?"

She made an incoherent exclamation of relief and concurrence, a sound that didn't have tears far behind it, if

Sheridan was any judge of female feeling, which he modestly fancied that he was. He sat beside her again, pouring out a lukewarm cup of tea and shoving it in her hands to forestall a spate of maidenly sniveling.

"Steady on," he said. "We won't get far if you're going to indulge in waterworks already."

She took hold of herself, tossing her chin up with a quick sniff. "Of course not," she said.

In spite of himself he wanted to smile. It fleetingly occurred to him to plant a quick kiss on the tip of her quivering mouse-nose. But that was out of the question now. He might run a minor swindle on a princess, but he certainly wasn't going to compromise one. He had no desire to get himself on her uncle's hanging list. Instead he said bracingly, "Good girl. Now—we must make some plans. I'll take care of the traveling arrangements beyond London, of course, but as far as this end—I'm afraid I haven't been here long enough to learn the coaching schedule, far less know of a clever way to spirit you off."

She took a deep, shaky breath. "I'd thought of walking to Upwell and asking Fish Stovall to take me on the river in his punt to King's Lynn."

"An excellent notion. But can this Fish Stovall be trusted not to talk?"

"Fish is a very, very good friend of mine," she said seriously. "I would trust him with my life."

Sheridan made no comment on the wisdom of trusting one's life to a man named Fish. "And—uh—forgive me; I don't wish to pry. But have you considered the"—he cleared his throat, looking pointedly away—"ah, finances?"

"Oh, of course!" She put down the teacup and fumbled at the diamond, searching for the clasp. "You must take this. I hadn't wanted to seem forward and press it upon you without knowing you truly wished to help me. Can you sell it? And I'll bring the rest of my personal jewelry along to provide for us on the way. This is only one of the smaller pieces."

The gold chain and setting flowed into Sheridan's palm. He glanced down at it, turned it over once and managed not to break into ecstatic smiles. He closed his fingers over the stone. "Princess," he said softly, taking her hand and pressing it against his fist, as if he could not bring himself to let her part with the jewel. "Are you quite sure?"

She bit her lip, hesitating, and for one awful moment he thought he had gone too far. Then she looked up and nodded.

He lifted her hand to his lips. "You are a brave and gallant lady."

He expected to melt her to a puddle with that. But instead of going pliable and moony, she straightened her back and set her jaw, staring into his eyes with a little shake of her head. "No," she said in a small, gruff voice. "Not yet. Don't say so yet."

He held her hand a second longer. Her fingers, enveloped in his, had a faint, rhythmic tremble. It might have been merely the cold. But her skin had gone dead white, her eyes were wide and her lower lip was not quite steady. It was a look that Sheridan knew. He'd seen it on the fixed faces of untried midshipmen watching their ship closing in to a first encounter, and on the dead-pale countenance of a man seized up for flogging. He'd recognized it in his own mirror and felt it freeze his own face times without number.

He let go of her. She sat still for a moment, gazing into space, seeing God-knew-what nightmares in store for her. Then at last her face came alive again and she looked up at him . . . and now there was adoration in her eyes, worship for the hero he was not and never had been.

He'd seen that before, too—as often as not on the faces of those same poor, fatuous midshipmen who thought he was going to carry them to glory, when all it would be was guns and noise and mangled limbs and hot-cold terror. It made him faintly sick, meeting that look here, on a female face—on her face, round and solemn—as if a sparrow expected to be a hawk and thought he could make her one.

He could not. And he would not have if he could.

With a flick of his wrist, he tossed the diamond into her lap. "Take it back," he said quietly.

Olympia looked down at it and up, bewildered. Sir Sheridan's expression had gone flat and uninterpretable, his mouth a straight line and his gray eyes shifting away from hers. He stood, leaving the blankets in a tumble on the couch.

"Take it back," he repeated. "Go home. I'm a bad egg, you know. Liar and a knave. I'll cheat you when I'm able, and leave you hanging when I'm not."

"Pardon me?" she said.

"You think I'm an honorable man. It so happens you're wrong." He slanted a strange smile in her direction, a tight upward curve of one corner of his mouth. "But you'd best keep the secret to yourself. I'd rather it wasn't spread about, and no one would believe you anyway."

She tilted her head. For a shocked moment, she'd thought he meant what he said, but that peculiar smile enlightened her. "I understand," she said, with a nervous curve of her own lips. "You're joking again."

The odd touch of humor faded from his face. He watched her without speaking. His hair was very black against the golden light, curling a little below his ear and at his neck. She felt a queer regret that she would never again see him like this. She wanted to memorize him, to put him in a book to take out and treasure in secret midnight moments—to survey at her leisure the shape of shoulder and chest, to imagine the texture of his skin, sun-touched and shadowed.

But those were thoughts for hidden places, thoughts to ponder in the safety of her own bed in the night. She lowered her lashes to hide them from him. When still he did not speak, she gathered the gold chain and pendant and laid it next to his teacup. Collecting her redingote, she stood up from the couch.

"I should go now."

He made no move to help her with her coat. She struggled into it by herself and looked up from buttoning.

"When you wish to contact me," she said, "leave a message with Fish at Upwell. I see him every day."

His brush of black lashes lowered. He stared at the teacup and the diamond that lay next to it. She could make nothing of his expression, and yet she was disturbed by it. She wet her lips and picked up her hat, rolling the brim in her fists. "I cannot—Sir Sheridan . . . you must know there are no words to thank you."

He looked up at her at that, a quick flash of gray, intensely cool in the warm light of window and coal fire. "Not yet," he said, with a lift of his brows and a ghost of that disturbing smile. "Take a page from your own book, Princess. Don't thank me yet."

The imperturbable Mrs. Plumb spread out a bolt of silver satin on the bed in Olympia's room and stood looking down at it with one of those sideways tilts of her chin which emphasized her elegant cheekbones.

"What do you think?" she asked. She was an extraordinarily handsome governess, with a statuesque figure, a tiny waist and an unerring fashion sense where Olympia's wardrobe was concerned, although Mrs. Julia Plumb herself was never seen in anything but the most modest of widow's weeds. "I believe it would make up into a lovely walking dress."

Mr. Stubbins wrote poetry about her. Mrs. Plumb laughed at it, and asked why a fellow barely out of leading strings should waste his time playing the flirt with an old woman—although Olympia thought secretly that Julia seemed to like it well enough. It had made Olympia wildly jealous years ago, when Mr. Stubbins' soft golden curls and brown eyes, aflame with revolutionary fervor, had been the focus of her sixteen-year-old dreams.

By now, at twenty-four, she'd long outgrown that infatuation. It was nothing but childish aristocratic vanity to care for such things. She poked unenthusiastically at the silver satin. "It seems overly pretentious to me," she said. "I prefer muslin."

Mrs. Plumb ignored that, except for a little sniff. It gave her a certain status, Olympia supposed, to have a position in the household of a princess, no matter how unexalted. Olympia and Mr. Stubbins deplored such conservative and ignorant sentiments, but neither of them had the nerve to face down that chill and beautiful gaze by stating their opinions out loud.

"The seamstress had the fashion illustrations I thought would suit you best," Julia said. "There are several that will compliment an excessively full figure very well, I think." She looked up from the bolt of satin, her fine blue eyes regarding Olympia with an opaque expression. "You took a lengthy walk this morning, for such a cold day."

After the smallest of hesitations, Olympia turned toward the window and said, "I left a card on Captain Drake."

She was annoyed to hear the words come out with a trace of defiance.

"Indeed," Julia said mildly. "That was very forward of you."

Knowing it was true only made Olympia more defensive. "He wasn't at home to me," she lied. "And it was not in the way of a social call at all. I think everyone in the neighborhood should pay him their respects, and I don't see anything 'forward' about being the first to do so. He is a very great hero."

Julia stroked the satin with her forefinger. "Yes, so they say. But it was most unbecoming of you to go alone to visit a bachelor, no matter how heroic. I hope you will avoid that mistake in the future."

Olympia felt herself turning crimson. "I only left my card."

"People will gossip about such things," Julia said. "You have the dignity of your position to consider."

"A pox on my position," Olympia cried. "It's good for nothing, to me or to anyone else."

A faint dry smile played at the corners of Julia's shapely mouth. "Nevertheless—" Her tone grew heavier. "You're not to call on Captain Drake alone again. I'll have your word on it."

Olympia raised her chin and inclined her head. "Very well," she said, choosing her words carefully. "I promise not to call on him at Hatherleigh Hall."

She didn't promise anything else.

"Thank you." Julia glanced at the ormolu clock on the

mantel. "Now, I must go out this evening for an hour, if you have no need of me or the carriage."

Olympia nodded, folding the fabric. After Julia had left, she remained staring out the window at the ice-crusted banks of the river, with the silver satin folded over her arm.

It was a familiar view. She had stared at it for twenty-four years.

Sometimes she wished she could offer her royal diadem to Julia, who would have made a much better princess anyway.

Three

Sheridan lay propped up on his elbow in the shadowy depths of his father's bed, watching the woman who had been his father's mistress for as long as he could remember. She tilted her chin, rebuttoning the last button at her throat and adjusting the tiny bows on her demure bodice in an elegant whore's gesture.

"Julia," he said lazily. "Charming as ever." He lay back, locking his hands behind his head. The chill air cooled him, playing over the perspiration on his chest and arms. He eyed the modest dress and virtuously simple hairstyle. "A true credit to Christian womanhood."

The single candle caught purple highlights in her black satin dress. She leaned near, tracing her forefinger around his mouth. Sheridan allowed his lips to part, tasting the salty tang of arousal and satisfaction that lingered on her hand. He stirred, turning toward her to catch her wrist, kissing the cup of her palm.

She pulled her hand away.

He dropped his head back with a sigh. "So," he said flatly. "Now we come to the point, do we?"

She drew her finger down the side of his face and jaw, ending in a light circling tease on his chest. He pushed her hand off and locked it in his fist.

"My dear," he murmured. "Let's omit the second round of compliments for the moment. Just what is it you want from me?"

"Sheridan," she said huskily, raising their entwined

arms and caressing his hand with her lips as if his hard grip on her were only a fondling hold.

"Looking to take up residence again?" He let her kiss the back of his hand. When she met his eyes, he deliberately ran an assessing look up and down her splendid figure. "I can't say you haven't got talent and experience, and you appear to have aged remarkably well. How old are you?"

Heat flashed in her eyes. She lowered her lashes and bit him lightly on the side of his palm.

Sheridan settled back and looked up at the canopy with a faint derisive smile. "I couldn't have been much under six years old when my father set you up for his doxy. You were no infant then, and that was nigh on three decades ago. How many years do you have on me? Eighteen? Twenty?" He pulled his hand away easily. "Sorry, m'love, the position's open, but I'm only considering applicants with a reasonable number of working years left in 'em."

"You're a bastard," she whispered. "You always were."

He stretched and sat up, kicking the blankets aside. "Runs in the family."

"Your father was good enough to me."

"Was he?" Sheridan reached for his clothes. "You're clearly a leg up on me, then." He pulled his shirt over his head. "Did he leave you any money?"

Her shoulders went still for an instant. Sheridan took note of that, and silently carried on with his dressing.

She ran slender fingers over the carved back of a chair. "Haven't you read the will?"

"Not that it's any of your business," he said mildly, buttoning his waistcoat and disdaining the crumpled neckcloth. "I've an appointment with the solicitor tomorrow. I can't say my hopes are very high. Pardon me, but I'd suggest you don't sit in that particular chair, unless you'd like a fountain of ice water applied to your magnificent derriere."

She straightened hastily and cast him a glance.

"Yes," he said, "yet another sample of my dear father's delightful sense of humor. The place is mined with 'em.

All the beds except this one are stuffed with horseshoe nails. The doorbell is rigged to dump snow on arriving guests. The wardrobe doors slam closed on your hand the moment you touch anything inside, and if you step on the wrong spot on the staircase, it collapses, and you plummet down to God-knows-where like a shot cuckoo.'' He kicked his foot down into his bootheel and stood up. ''Bloody hilarious. I damned near lost a leg.''

When he lifted his head, Julia was gazing at him with a peculiar expression. ''I didn't know,'' she said. ''I . . . left before he built this house.''

''Ah. Turned you out, did he? What a shame. It must be lonely for you these days, Julia. Trying to think up ingenious viciousness all on your own. What a jolly pair of hellhounds the two of you made.''

She smiled, an odd, twisted little curl of her lips, and came across the floor to stand in front of him. She rested her hands on his shoulders, her blue eyes roaming over his open collar and up to his jaw and face.

''When last I saw you,'' she murmured, ''you were sixteen and had pimples.''

''And you were a beautiful whoring bitch, just as you are now,'' he said politely. ''I was madly jealous of the old man.''

She acted as if he had not spoken, leaning away and measuring the breadth of his shoulders with her glance. ''You've certainly grown out well.''

''Thank you.''

''And a hero. A Knight of the Bath.''

He inclined his head modestly.

She slid her fingers up into his hair. ''I wouldn't have thought it.''

''Oh, I imagine I can be quite a knight in the bath.'' He flicked her cheek. ''Would you like to go another tilt?''

Her slight smile flattened. Her bosom rose and fell in a deep sigh. Sheridan grinned and pushed her back.

''Too damned cold for a bath,'' he said. ''I'm all grown up now, you see. I don't need you to pat me on the head and tell me I'm a good boy—which I ain't, I can assure you.'' He reached past her for a hairbrush from the dressing table. When he'd dragged the brush through the thick tousle of his dark hair, he eyed her again where she stood planted in front of him. "Still here? What *do* you want from me, my dear?"

She was silent.

Sheridan moved past her to pick up his coat. "Not money, I hope. I'm perfectly flat. You should have inquired as to financial particulars before you jumped beneath the bedclothes so eagerly." He slung the coat over his shoulder and gave her a lopsided smile. "Call it a charity job. Or a patriotic gesture. In lieu of singing 'Rule Britannia' on behalf of the homecoming hero."

"Sheridan," she said quietly, "I have something to tell you."

Her tone brought him up short in the doorway. He looked over his shoulder.

"I can save you a trip to the solicitor," she said. "I know the terms of your father's will."

He leaned against the doorframe. "Ah. Yes. I had my suspicions. It all goes to you, does it?" When she made no answer, he rubbed his chin. "Well, you certainly did more work for it than I."

"You never came to see him," she said softly, her face growing wistful. "Not once, after you were grown."

It was one of her best tricks, that look. As a boy, he had been gulled by it times without number. He stared at her face, that lovely affectionate lie, and felt something dangerous spring awake in the depths of his brain, as if a sleeping wolf opened golden eyes in the dark.

He made an effort to give her his sweetest smile. "I disliked him excessively. And there was the small matter of various admirals, you see, who kept suggesting that I postpone my social engagements until I was no longer needed to blow up hapless foreigners in the interest of His Majesty's peace of mind."

"You might have left the service anytime these twenty years."

The wolf lay there, watching from the shadow. He imagined a wall, built a cage brick by brick to keep that other self at bay. With his fists safely trapped in his pockets, he said, "And done what, my love?"

She clasped her hands and looked down with a little shrug. "Gone into politics, perhaps. Certainly with your reputation you could have—"

"Starved to death quite nicely, I'm sure. You seem strangely naive for a woman your age, Julia. Medals are helpful, no doubt, but it takes hard cash to buy a seat in Parliament. And no"—he pushed himself away from the door abruptly—"my father would not have paid for it, I assure you."

"You don't know that."

"I know it," he said deliberately. "Do you think I'm still a ten-year-old fool, dear?"

Her smooth brow creased in a little frown. "What will you do now?"

Sheridan cast his coat over a chair. He walked to a small table and picked up the dusty decanter that sat atop smooth mahogany, blew on the crystal stopper and opened it, sniffing the contents. "Do you suppose this is actually brandy, or some droll imitation that will cause me to fall down in amusing convulsions?"

"I worry for your future," Julia said.

He ignored that and set the decanter down again. "Best to let Mustafa try it. Nothing will kill him. I've attempted it myself several times, but no luck."

"Sheridan," she said, "what will you do now?"

"Now that I have no prospects whatsoever, you mean." He turned to the window, where the last ghoulish gray of daylight still flowed into the candlelit room. He put his hands on the sill. "I've been thinking about that. Cataloging my assets. I have my medals—I imagine those will bring a farthing for the lot, at the very least. My epaulettes might be worth fifteen guineas if I cleaned 'em up well enough. I've a presentation sword I can pawn." He leaned on one hand and massaged the back of his neck. "But perhaps I should keep hold of that. I'm a knight, after all. I might post a notice outside debtors' prison. 'Dragons slain. Princesses rescued. Naval battles and accidental harebrained heroics a speciality.'"

"You're in debt?"

"Oh, yes. Quite spectacularly." He laughed, looking back at her. "And the devil of it is, I didn't even have any fun getting dipped." He shrugged. "Can you imagine that just a few years ago I swallowed the bait again—that I was idiot enough to believe my father when he offered to loan me the money to invest in a stock he recommended? One of these damned railway notions, it was—with a locomotive engine, if you can credit that. It was certain—*certain,* mind you—to make so much blunt hauling coal, I could afford to leave the navy within the year."

She stood watching him, her fine lips pursed.

He shook his head and stared out the window. "I was ripe for the taking, I'll tell you. Been hanging off Burma in the monsoon for six months, waiting on those poor suckers of marines holding Rangoon. Foodstores all gone rotten in the heat—flies everywhere, mud stink and rain and nineteen out of twenty on board dying of dysentery or cholera or some goddamned disease that I don't even know the name of—and the putrid corpses showing up in the mud flats every time the tide went out. No land transport, the stinking Irrawaddy in flood; not allowed to go back, no way to go forward—and here's this letter, delivered specially by a crisp-looking fellow in a chartered yacht who had me on board to dinner. We had venison pie and lemon pudding and a roasted pheasant. And fresh rolls." He leaned his hands on the windowsill and lowered his head between his arms. "Do you know what fresh rolls taste like? They're soft. They're *soft.* I could have cried. And then he handed me that letter from my father, and explained all the documents, and I . . ."

Silence closed in on the room. All he could hear was the sound of his own breathing, and his heartbeat pounding in fury—at himself, who should have known better, at one insane moment of weakness that had taken all his hard-won savings and bought him disaster for life.

"Well," he said, pushing away from the sill, "you can guess the end of this story. The railway is of course a dead issue, the authorizing bill having been thrown out of Parliament. I believe it was determined that the line would disturb the afternoon naps of two spinster ladies in a cottage outside of Crewe. I own the whole of the shambles, since it appears there was a minor clause in the documents which guaranteed I would assume on my loan the shares of anyone who wished to sell. Oh, and yes—here's the best part. My esteemed father also thought it would be a humorous touch to barter my note to a moneylender in St. Mary Axe, who hasn't ceased dunning me since for his four hundred thousand pounds."

Julia gave a little gasp. "Four hundred . . ."

He smiled. "It really is a vastly amusing tale, don't you agree? But you take your inheritance, Julia, and don't mind me. I won't inconvenience you. My moneylender's still a bit reluctant to press a patriotic figure like myself, but I think I'd best be off directly." He swept up his coat and shrugged into it. "I'll just skulk back to India, steal myself a wooden bowl and sit on a street corner with the rest of the beggars, looking suitably wretched."

She stood still and erect, staring at him thoughtfully. Her figure seemed carved of black-and-white marble. Sheridan grew impatient. He was about to send her to the devil when she seemed to start out of her reverie. She frowned and asked sharply, "Is this the truth?"

"Do you think I dreamed it up?" he exclaimed. "If only! I ain't here to weep because the old bastard finally had the grace to cock up his toes, I'll tell you that. I knew he wouldn't leave me anything apurpose, but I hoped to hell he might have died without a will." He curled his lips and held out his arm in a stiff little bow toward her. "No such luck, apparently."

"No," she said. "No such luck."

"Well." Sheridan shrugged. "Nice of you to stop by for a sympathetic coze. Or was it in the way of an eviction call? I suppose the house is yours, too—although I warn you, it's a damned cold mausoleum full of vicious pranks." He swept a look around the room. "And ugly to boot."

Her fine bosom rose and fell in a sigh. She said slowly, "I imagine this bitterness was to be expected. I'd hoped we might deal together better."

"How kind of you. But I see no reason for us to deal at all, my dear. I do like a wench with experience and style, but not on these terms, thank you. I'll just be collecting my—"

"Sheridan," she said. "Stay a moment and listen. Your father did leave his fortune to you."

He halted in mid-stride. For a moment there was nothing but the jolt of surprise. He stared at her, realized he was gaping and closed his mouth. Then like a spring that burst into a fountain, the relief and elation exploded in him, crashing into his fingers and toes. He made a wordless exclamation. A thousand pictures whirled through his head; the things he could do; the life he could have: comfort at last, peace when he wanted it, hell-raising when he didn't, first-class travel to civilized places—and music . . . oh, God, the music. He could go to Vienna and hear it—Beethoven, Schubert, Mendelssohn . . . Lord, he could buy orchestras and composers and commission his own damned symphonies. And a French chef . . . all the soft white rolls a man could consume. He could sleep in soft white rolls. He could seduce women in soft white rolls. He gazed at Julia's bosom, overlaying that image with the floury sweet warmth of baking bread, and found himself chuckling giddily. He heard the crazy note that vibrated beneath the laughter and caught his breath. He managed to silence himself.

"Julia," he said. "Julia. You wouldn't lie to me, love? Not about this."

She shook her head. There was a peculiar tightness around her mouth, but he discounted that as jealousy. Why should she lie? He had a light-headed magnanimous impulse and blurted, "You can live here. Not *here*, that is—I'm going to demolish this granite horror. I'll build you a lodge off somewhere that you'll like, and you can live there the rest of your life, I promise you."

In the midst of that pledge he realized just what he was saying. The last thing he wanted was an aging whore anchored around his neck, particularly one who would happily slide a knife between his ribs the moment she saw some fun and profit in it. He knew well what Julia was, beneath that veneer of motherly sympathy.

But what of it? Promises were as free as air. And she still had a few good romps left in her, that was certain. He grinned and held out his hand. "We owe you that much, the old man and I."

She did not take his hand. She simply stood watching him. A trickle of premonition seeped in his belly.

"Deal?" he asked, still offering his hand.

She smiled, that dry curl of her lips. The trickle became a flood. Sheridan dropped his hand, suddenly smelling one of his father's jokes so strongly he could have choked on the stench.

"What is it?" he said suspiciously.

She wet her lips, a cat licking cream.

Between one instant and the next he lost himself. The wolf sprang alive, snarling for blood; the battle-fury rushed through his brain like a high wind. "Damn you—*where's the catch?*" he roared.

She took a step backward, her thick lashes going wide. She seemed to shrink a little, flinching away from him as her glance went warily and instinctively to his fists. Sheridan knew that gesture; had seen it a thousand times in whorehouses and back alleys and on waterfronts all over the world. She thought he was going to hit her.

As if a monstrous wave had washed him and passed on, the madness evaporated. He stared at her, breathing hard, feeling queerly fragile. For one horrible instant he thought he was going to break into tears.

He grabbed the decanter and aimed it at her head, giving her plenty of time to duck. It hurled past and shattered all over the damask wallpaper behind her with a satisfying crash.

She stood straight, only trembling a little. "Are you finished?" she asked when he made no other move.

He walked around her, keeping his face impassive to hide his shaken wits. He made a slow, considering circle. When he was satisfied that he was in full control of himself again, he came to a stop behind her and waited, watching her spine grow tense. Then he lifted an inkpot and dropped it on the bare floor.

She jumped like a cat at the sound.

"Perhaps I'm finished," he said softly. "Perhaps I'm not."

She took a deep breath and turned sharply to face him. "Have your fun," she hissed. "*Hero.* Maul me if you will. Kill me. And see what it gets you."

Idiotic baggage. She was damned ready with stupid invitations. He watched her narrowly, sniffing at the trap.

"What's the catch?" he said. "Do I have to marry you?"

She laughed at that, archly. "Would you?"

He looked at her, at the way she stood straight in spite of her wariness, and recognized from long experience the posture of someone who was certain they held all the cards. "I can think of worse fates," he said with a little shrug, and then added a nice touch by reaching out and stroking his finger down the line of her cheek. "Far worse," he said softly.

Her eyelashes lowered. She went still for a moment. He deepened his caress, taking her chin and pulling her toward him for a kiss, thinking sourly that it was about what he might have expected, that the old man would dangle all that money and then shackle him to a worn-out whore. Capital joke.

Except that Julia was not precisely worn out yet. She pressed up against him, writhing gently beneath his hands. When he finally had to come up for air, she leaned back in his arms, her eyes half closed. "Damn you," she whispered. "Damn you for a beautiful lying bastard."

He couldn't see damning himself for that, since it was clearly an advantage with the likes of Julia Plumb. If he wouldn't hit her, it was just as well the evil hussy lusted after him. So he gave her a squeeze and tried to kiss her again.

She pulled away, though, and stood breathing unsteadily. "Enough of that," she said, with a little proud toss of her head. "I want to talk."

But she had a look in her eyes that suggested if he chose

to override her, he needn't expect to meet serious resistance. To put her in mind of who'd come spooning around whom in the first place, he cut her dead; let her stand there ogling him, with her lips parted and her breasts heaving, until he reckoned she must have realized how fatuous she looked. Then he said in lazy mockery, "Oh, God, Juli—don't. How can I stand it when you tease me like that?"

Her mouth snapped shut. Color surged into her face. "I wasn't—" she said, and then, "You beast. I don't have to take this from you."

He watched her face, the little quivers of emotion and stress that flitted across it. "Why not?" he asked softly. "What do I owe you, Julia?"

It took her a moment to get her old dry curling smile back. "You don't *owe* me anything. But you'll give me some respect, ducky, I swear an' you will—you'll come when I call an' go when I tell you, and you'll smile about it, you will."

He took note of the way the Cockney crept in: she was rattled, all right—but not as rattled as he. That belligerent self-assurance gave him the willies. It belonged on bucko first mates and sargeants of marines, not aging East End jades. He frowned down at her, and for an instant she looked just slightly intimidated, but the arrogance surged back and she turned away with a proud sweep.

"The money is in trust," she said calmly. "You are the only beneficiary. Your father's solicitor is the only trustee." She lifted her head and looked over her shoulder at him. "You touch nothing yourself. The trustee dispenses all funds at his discretion. He has but one obligation, and one only—"

His jaw stiffened. She held the moment as if she were a painted tart in a Covent Garden melodrama.

"—to act solely and unquestioningly under the direction—under the 'whim,' as the will stated it—of a single person."

Sheridan took a step forward. He stopped. She smiled up at him in dry triumph.

"Myself."

* * *

"It is the grandest thing," squeaked Mrs. What's-'Er-Name, clasping plump hands and gazing at Sheridan like a cow in milk. "Everyone will be green, Mrs. Plumb, they absolutely will. It's just the peak of good fortune that I thought to call this morning."

Right-ho, Sheridan thought. *The peak.*

She picked up her cup and took an excited slurp of tea. Sheridan wished heartily for a brandy. He looked around Julia's tastefully furnished drawing room in despair, finding nothing more promising than a delicate little sewing caddy opened to reveal the glint of scissors and a pile of gaily colored floss.

"You must tell me everything, Captain Drake—but no, I should call you *sir,* I'm sure—Sir Drake—but that's not right, is it? Why, you see what bumpkins we are hereabouts—I haven't the least notion how you should properly be addressed!"

" 'Sheridan' will do, ma'am," he said. He didn't wish her to exert herself. Might fall dead of an overtaxed brain.

"And how wonderfully condescending! But I mustn't be so familiar. *Sir* Sheridan it is, of course. Start at the beginning, Sir Sheridan. *How* did you come to save the fleet?"

It'd be steep work with this female, clearly. "Please, ma'am," he said with a remote smile. "I didn't actually save the fleet."

Mrs. Whoever gave a little squealing sigh. "So modest! Oh, but you saved the admiral, and I'm sure anyone would agree it is the same thing. What is that old saying? 'For want of a shoe, a horse was lost; for want of a horse—'et cetera. I'm not perfectly certain of the sequence, but it leads right up to commanders and kings and countries, you know, and if you saved your admiral that is quite splendidly identical to saving England herself. Rushing beneath a falling mast to drag him to safety—did you ever *think*, Mrs. Plumb! Right here in your drawing room!"

Sheridan considered explaining that he'd been out of his wits at the time; that he'd meant to push the old imbecile in the other direction and make him into mutton hash. But Mrs. Mental Acuity's intellect was obviously in no case to survive a concerted attack of rational thought, so he refrained.

Julia looked on with a cool smile while her caller purred and cooed and fluttered. Sheridan stirred sugar into his tea and sank deeper into quiet desperation. Outside the comfortable house by the river it was sleeting rain, which was evidently the new national climate voted in by Parliament, inasmuch as it hadn't let up for a minute since he'd set foot in England. The ice crystals stung the windows and slid down the panes, creating little prison bars of light and shadow.

He caught Julia's eye once. She must have read something of the rebellion that was growing at the back of his throat, for she began efficiently to dispatch Mrs. God-Knew-Who back out into the rain. When the door had closed on the lady's laced-up rump, Sheridan sprang out of his chair and began to pace.

Julia walked back across the room and sat down next to the tea tray. "There," she said, "she is gone, is she not? Silly bitch. Sit down, now—I won't let anyone else come in and torment you, I promise."

He stopped and looked toward her. With bleak relish, he envisioned her stripped and tied to the shrouds, where she could find out the real meaning of that word, the same way he had.

His mouth tightened. He stared at her a moment and wondered, not for the first time, if she had known of his father's greatest joke—if she had been aware when the old man had called him down from school at the age of ten and told him his childhood dreams were coming true: he was going to Vienna to study his music with the masters—here was the ship, here was the name of the captain who would take him, here were his new clothes and his own trunk and some jolly good fellows who'd look out for him on the trip . . .

"Sheridan," she said. "Sit down."

It was intolerable. Now he must have Julia to pacify him and Julia to pet him and Julia to tell him what to do with every moment of his life.

"Sheridan," she said again.

He thought of debtors' prison. And India.

He sat down.

"Her Highness will return from her walk quite soon, I'm sure," Julia said, taking up the embroidery from the sewing box.

Sheridan balled one white-gloved fist inside the other and rested his elbows on his knees. Then he cradled his head in his hands, staring at his boots. "Haven't you got a bottle stashed somewhere about the place?" he asked peevishly.

"Nerves?" She looked up from her needle. "And I thought you were such a lady-killer."

"Excellent notion. God knows I'd be pleased to kill you, but then you ain't a lady."

"I can't think what is keeping the princess. I asked her to stay home this morning, but Her Highness must have her constitutional, even in this weather. I'm afraid she will freeze if she walks all the way to Upwell."

"Her Confounded Highness can walk all the way to Peking, for my money," he snapped, "and I hope she does."

Julia slid a bit of embroidery floss through her teeth to make a knot. "I must say, you're acting very badly about this. It seems to me you would view it as a golden opportunity."

Sheridan took a hold on his temper. He stood up again. "I'm here to rescue the princess from her dragon, am I not?" he asked sweetly. He waved his hand. "We knights simply dote on this kind of work. And what do I get for it?"

"The princess." She said it so matter-of-factly that for an instant he didn't see the slight dry smile directed down at her stitching.

"Oh, it's riotously funny, ain't it?" He narrowed his eyes at her. "You've got me in a cleft stick, no doubt about it. Promise to make a payment on that debt, let me do your dirty work and then go back on the bargain—there's a clever scheme, eh? It ought to work for another week or so, until the constable comes after me."

"Obviously I won't let the constable come after you."

She set the embroidery down in her lap and looked at him. "When you accomplish what I've asked, of course the debt will be paid." She smiled her faint smile and went back to her work. "Naturally we cannot have a Prince of Oriens dragged off by the constable, however little difference it might make if he dragged off Sheridan Drake."

Sheridan took her point on that, infernal piece of impertinence though it was. What she wanted him to do didn't gall him half so much as being blackmailed into doing it. All for patriotic purposes, of course. It occurred to him that he'd been blackmailed for patriotic purposes with depressing regularity in his life. Shot, starved, drowned and damned near strangled, too. If someone had asked him a month ago if he'd like to marry a princess, have all his debts paid and live like royalty for the rest of his life, he'd gladly have kissed a frog and begged for the honor of its webbed foot just on the off chance.

He turned his back on Julia and looked through the rippled glass into the empty street below. It was stupid to fight it, really. Julia had the right idea, living high and respectable off the Foreign Office—although how the deuce they'd come to the conclusion she was fit to be seen in polite society, much less qualified to chaperon a princess, he couldn't imagine. His father must have gotten her the position; it sounded like one of his pranks.

Well, if that was the kind of loose company royalty was keeping these days, Sheridan reckoned he was just the ticket.

There was apparently a shortage of available royal blood, but the prepared announcement Julia had shown him made much of his knighthood and his medals and his left-handed descent from Sir Francis—the bastard line of an English hero apparently being preferable to a strain of legitimate nobodies. More to the point, they'd even contrived to find a drop of blue blood in his pedigree—a great-uncle on his mother's side purported to have been the archduke of some piffling Prussian kingdom with a name long enough to stretch from one national border to the other. Sheridan wasn't inquiring too closely on that point;

if the Foreign Office was down to scraping the bottom of the barrel as far as princes went, it wasn't his concern.

At the sound of the front door opening below, Julia put her embroidery aside and rose. Sheridan gathered himself up to charm his princess.

"I'll send her in directly," Julia said, looking over her shoulder with her hand on the knob. "Remember your situation, Sheridan. Don't fail me."

That was a prompt he didn't need. Four hundred thousand pounds wasn't something he was likely to forget—much as he'd like to, since it played hell with his beauty rest.

Four

The second time in her life that Olympia looked up and saw Captain Sir Sheridan Drake was as disconcerting as the first.

He stood by the fireplace, smiling a little, a dark glittering figure in blue and white, golden epaulettes and medals, the broad star and red ribbon of his knighthood fixed bandolier-fashion across one shoulder. As she halted just inside the door, he made a court bow—deep, sternly formal. The fringes of his epaulettes slid and sparkled and light gleamed on the gold tassel that hung from the hilt of his dress sword.

Olympia heard the door close behind her. It dawned upon her that Julia had left them alone. Silence smothered everything except the hum of the coal fire and the faint, bitter crackle of sleet at the window. She found herself staring at his gloves, pale against the midnight blue. He came forward, one hand resting on his sword hilt as he reached out with the other.

He lifted her fingers to his lips, not quite touching, and then gently lowered her hand and let it go.

It seemed so preposterously formal after their first meeting a week before that she ducked her head and burst out, "Oh, please—I'm not a princess!" She clenched her hands at her own foolishness. "I mean, I *am*, but I'm not at all good at it, and I dislike it extremely, and I wish you would not think you must be—like this!" She waved her hand in a nervous circle toward him. Then she bit her lip and gathered herself and sank into a deep curtsy. ''It is I who should honor you,'' she said in a whisper.

There was another moment of profound silence while she bowed before him on trembling knees. Then in a soft, amused voice, he said, ''Here, now—we can't have this.'' He caught her arms and raised her. ''If we're both going to grovel, let's call it even and save our backs.''

She lifted her face under the firm pressure of his gloved fist beneath her chin.

''Silly princess,'' he murmured. ''Haven't they taught you how to play the game?''

Olympia had no answer for that. She gazed at him, at his smoky eyes and the curve of his mouth, the tiny pale scar that cut the outer edge of one dark eyebrow. He was smiling, a half-kind, half-teasing smile. She felt the pitch and dip of her heart as it tumbled helplessly in her breast.

''You obviously need better instruction,'' he informed her gravely. ''You're not nearly majestic enough. I've been to see the King, you know. You should hold your chin like so—'' He adjusted her head in a regal pose. ''And look down your nose at me like so—and say, 'Good work, old chap; honor of England and all that.' Then you bash me on the shoulder with a sword—while I hope to God you're sober enough not to slit my throat—hand over my ribbon and call for another round of rum punch to go with that syllabub and meringue. Easy enough, hey?'' He tilted his head and regarded her. ''But I'm afraid you'll have to put on about ten stone to get the proper effect.''

She stood there uncertainly, not knowing why he'd come. He was dressed so splendidly . . . and Julia had left them; she hadn't even introduced them, and she wasn't supposed to know they'd met. Olympia was terrified that something had gone wrong; afraid that he was going to rescind his offer to help, and shamefully hopeful that he would.

''Nonsense,'' she said, taking refuge in stalwart sensibility. ''You're exaggerating.''

He just smiled at her: this stranger—this figure of blue and steel and gold, his decorations shimmering faintly in the shadows. He seemed different in full-dress uniform;

more awesome and remote. Olympia made an effort to drag her scattered thoughts together, to put aside the uncertainty, along with the willful tug of other emotions that rose in her throat when she looked at him.

"You want to know why I've come," he said.

She glanced toward the door and back. In a low voice, she asked, "Has something untoward happened?"

"Depends on how you look at it, I suppose. Sit down, Princess." He touched her arm lightly, guiding her to a chair near the fire.

Olympia sat down and looked up at him with anxious eyes. He pushed his sword back and lowered himself in front of her, resting his arm across one knee and dangling his white-gloved hand casually. His eyes were on a level with hers, gray and steady; his mouth just faintly quizzical.

"It seems someone else has moved to solve your problem for us," he said without preamble. "The fellows at Whitehall have come up with a plan to block your uncle's designs on you."

She felt her flushed skin grow cold beneath the long sleeves of her woolen walking dress.

"I've had a message from Lord Palmerston," he went on. "Perhaps you've heard of him—he's one of those War Office beauties who make themselves experts on every bloody thing alive—including Orienian politics and exiled princesses. He's not at all keen on your uncle. He thinks you ought to marry someone else instantly, to forestall the other possibility."

"Marry," she repeated numbly. Her skin grew hot again with embarrassment.

"The idea never crossed your mind?"

"No. I mean, yes, of course it has, but I've always thought I . . ." She trailed off. "I assumed my grandfather would make an alliance. Who on earth does Lord Palmerston suggest I marry?"

He smiled a little and raised his eyebrows, saying nothing.

She frowned at him. "Unless he's aware of some eligible prince, I can't think how he expects me to marry 'instantly.' Besides, there is the revolution to consider. I can't marry; I must go to Oriens. I think our own plan has much more to recommend it." She lowered her voice. "Have you sold the diamond yet?"

He looked down at his gloved fingers. "I'm working on it."

"Good," she said eagerly. "And you're arranging for everything else? When should I come to King's Lynn?"

"Do you know," he said, "for a radical, you're rather a snob."

"A snob!"

He looked up. "You seem to feel the only men you could marry must be royalty."

"Well," Olympia said, "I am a princess."

He held her puzzled gaze for a moment, then rose and turned away. Light slid down the curved sheath of his sword as he moved across the room. He hefted a crystal paperweight from the writing platform of a glass-fronted secretary, turned the colored sphere over in his palm and put it down again. "Perhaps there's nothing more to say, then."

Olympia clasped her hands. She stared at the footstool in front of her, her thoughts occupied by her impending escape, as they had been for two weeks. She had a thousand questions for him and was afraid to ask even one. She hoped he hadn't delayed their plans because of this unlikely notion of marr—

Realization struck her. With a tiny gasp, she looked up at him.

He stood in profile, facing the secretary. At the sound, he slanted a half glance in her direction and then looked back at the books behind the glass doors.

"Not you!" she exclaimed. "He never meant I should marry you!"

His mouth flattened in a parody of a smile. He locked his gloved hands behind his back. "Obviously not, since the idea is so repugnant to you."

"No! It isn't—I mean, it's not possible; it's absurd. You must see . . . not that I wouldn't; of course, I'd be—" She pressed her palms together and held them to her lips to stop the flow of nonsense.

"I'm a commoner," he acknowledged quietly.

"You're a hero!"

"Well, I quite apologize for it." His voice took on a brisk note. "I really hadn't thought you'd lodge an objection on that basis."

She turned her face away, staring into the fire. "You can't wish to marry me."

A profound silence settled over them, over the room and the fire and the trickle of sleet at the window. Olympia lost all those small familiar sounds beneath the hum of blood and heartbeat in her ears. Then he moved; the floor creaked as he came toward her and lowered himself at her knee. He reached up and took her face between his hands, looking into her eyes.

"I can think of a thousand reasons you would not want to marry me," he said softly. "For myself not to wish it—I cannot think of one."

"They're forcing you to do this," she whispered. "I'm sure they must be."

He brushed his thumbs across her cheeks, white leather soft and warm against her skin. "No," he said. "I'm not such a special fellow, you know. I'm a convenience—a suitable body in the right place at the right time." He let go of her and stood up, turning aside to the window, to the sleet and the slow-moving river. "If you won't settle on me, I don't doubt they've got a list of other approved candidates for your consideration."

Olympia simply could not think of anything to say. She had spent the past fortnight working herself up to clear one looming series of fences and throw herself into the murky and terrifying landscape of the future beyond. Now it was as if, while she raced toward them with all her courage in hand, the barriers ahead and the mount beneath her had evaporated into thin air, sending her tumbling down some endless drop to nowhere. Her mind could not comprehend the change.

"Shall I list the cold-blooded advantages?" he asked. "It blocks your uncle's attempt to wed you, of course. It strengthens the ties between your country and mine. I'm not a prince by any standard, but apparently I enjoy some current popularity in Oriens; they all seem to think I'm a hell of a fellow for fighting Turks. I'm told it would be . . . acceptable . . . to your grandfather. It eliminates the need for you to go on a wild chase to see the pope, and it means Oriens can be spared your revolution. A constitutional state can be set up through legal means, which is exactly what our friend Lord Palmerston is hoping for."

She gripped her hands in her lap and nodded. It was easy enough to see all that. If she reduced it to the moves of a chess game, there was no doubt the plan had a better chance of winning than her own. It was sensible; it was safe; it had her grandfather's blessing and the backing of the British government.

And she wanted it. God help her, she could hardly think for wanting it. She could not look at him, for fear she would burst into foolish tears. To marry Captain Sheridan Drake: to be his wife, to give him her heart and her life, to find the most cherished hidden dream of her existence made suddenly real . . .

"Why?" she said to her white fingers. "When you agreed to help me before, it was amazement enough to me. But *this* . . ." She drew in a breath. "Why would you sacrifice yourself, throw away your whole life, for another's country?"

"Need you ask? Wealth, position, power . . ." He paused. "All the usual reasons for marrying a princess."

"You're making game of me."

He was silent a moment. Then he said, "Have it as you will. It must be because I'm a hero and a true friend of liberty."

She looked up at him then. The silvery aura from the window fell across his face, lighting a translucent, pale fire in his gray eyes. She could identify no telltale trace of humor or mockery in his features. There was simply his austere male beauty, that sullen perfection marred only by the little scar across his left eyebrow, which showed more clearly in the thin winter light.

"Now you make game of yourself instead," she said. "And you have not answered my question."

"I have." His mouth curved upward at the corners. "I've given you two perfectly good answers."

"I don't understand you." She shifted impatiently in her chair. "I've told you I often find jests to be obscure, haven't I? Please be serious."

He inclined his head. "Excuse me, Your Highness. I shall attempt to govern my unseemly frivolity."

"Thank you." She watched him for a moment. When his face remained perfectly grave, she said, "Please . . . I don't wish to be pompous. I only want to understand. It's very difficult for me to believe, you see, that you're not being forced into this." She bit her lip. "And I would hate that above anything."

"I have told you I'm not."

"But—"

"Do you accuse me of lying?"

Olympia drew back a little at the sharp demand. Then she sighed. "Yes. I think it's very possible you might lie. In this case. To spare my feelings."

He looked at her steadily.

She added, "You know there will be no wealth or power or anything of the sort for me after the dissolution of the monarchy, so that cannot be your reason. Even if I would think such a thing of you." She glanced down at her hands. "And I realize that my person is not very—attractive. I'm quite too plump, and my mouth is too small, and my eyebrows are too heavy, although I suppose that defect might be remedied by artificial means. But it seems . . ." Her voice wavered a little. ". . . excessive—even in the cause of freedom—to ask you to spend your life with me, only for the purpose of influencing the course of the next year in a place that can have no meaning to you."

"I like your eyebrows. They have character."

She put her hand to her face. "Pardon me, but I . . . it's very difficult to bear being made into a jest. In this."

"A jest! Of all the—" He lifted his eyes toward the ceiling and shook his head. "I'm afraid it'll seriously hamper my courting if you can't tell a jest from a compliment."

"Well," she said on a desperate note, "I can't, you know! I've never understood the things other people find humorous. And saying my eyebrows have character doesn't seem very complimentary. It doesn't even make sense. How can eyebrows have character? So I must assume it was said in jest. If you had told me you thought *I* had character, or that my eyebrows were . . . pretty, then I should understand it to be a compliment."

A silence followed her outburst. She stared down at her tightly clasped hands, then suddenly stood up and moved away, the brisk rustle of her skirts the only sound in the quiet. When she came to the tea table, she stopped, her back to the room, her hands still clinging together. She bowed her head, feeling miserably foolish to be speaking of such silly things when it was the fate of her nation at issue.

The floorboards creaked. She felt him come close behind her: a warmth, a presence that made her stiffen with awareness.

"You have remarkable character, Princess. Your eyebrows are lovely. Your chin is adorable and your eyes are gorgeous. Your figure is . . . utterly splendid. Just about too splendid, if I may be forgiven for saying so. It's been damned hard to remember I'm a gentleman." He put both hands on her shoulders and turned her around. "For God's sake, do you really think I'm here on some crack-brained philosophical principle?"

Olympia moistened her lips. His hands on her shoulders kept her pressed back against the table; his body planted solidly in front of her prevented any move in that direction.

It was all rubbish, of course, everything he said: kindly meant and terrifyingly sweet to hear. Olympia feared for how vulnerable she was to such nonsense, how often she'd tried to excise aristocratic vanities such as a concern for personal appearance from her soul. She was glad she wasn't beautiful; she was proud that her governess cared more for Olympia's wardrobe than she did herself. But sometimes, when she looked in the mirror at her round cheeks, her heavy brows and small mouth and ridiculously large eyes, all monstrously out of classical proportion, she longed with a shameful fierceness to have Julia's slender neck and perfect face.

In the silence that roared in her ears he moved closer. He put his hands on her imperfect throat and lifted her imperfect chin and bent his head to her flawed and trembling lips.

He kissed her.

And she fell in love. Helplessly; hopelessly—a consummate disaster. She felt it happen while his mouth came against hers and his gloved fingers pressed into the tender skin behind her earlobes. It was something physical, a tangible wound, a terrible rent in the fabric of her life, as if her whole self had been torn from her body and replaced by something else entirely. Something that belonged not to her but to him.

To her horror, that new, helpless, slavish self answered the kiss. She parted her lips beneath the pressure of his. Her fingers gave up their vehement hold on each other; they slid apart and flattened against his chest, opening and closing like a cat's paws. A little aching sound came from her throat.

His hold slackened for an instant. Only an instant, and before Olympia could break away, his hands slid forward and locked together behind her nape. The warm rush of his breath touched her skin: uneven and quick as he kissed her eyes and forehead and the corners of her lips.

"Princess," he whispered. "My silly princess . . ."

She cast down her lashes. It was impossible to look at him—unbearable. A whimper of miserable joy hung in the back of her throat. Kindness; she knew it was all meant for kindness and to spare her feelings. It was not his fault. How could he know? How could he see that it would cut her to the heart to be held this way? The nights she'd dreamed of it . . . before she'd ever seen him she'd dreamed of it, and then after . . . oh, after—when the boy-hero fiction had become a real man . . .

She pushed away and took a step past him. But he turned

with her, caught her as she moved. His arm trapped her back against his chest. He bowed his face to the curve of her throat. She felt his mouth against the soft skin just below her ear.

He did not kiss her. He held her. She stood still, trembling in that firm and quiet possession.

For an agonized moment she let herself think of it—that she might marry him for the sake of her country. The politics of it had a real and awful logic; it made too much sense from too many sides—from every side but his.

A formal ceremony, a blessing from the British government, a letter to Oriens, and her uncle's plan was shattered. She'd never seen Prince Claude Nicolas. Whenever she imagined him, she never pictured a face, only a cold and aggressive presence, a killing pride. She was in exile because of Claude Nicolas.

Sir Sheridan's arm tightened at her waist. "Princess," he murmured. "Let me protect you."

She stiffened. Gripping his braided sleeve, she pulled forcibly away. She walked quickly to the other side of the room and stood looking out the window, rubbing her hands up and down her sleeves.

She said, "Prince Claude Nicolas . . . my uncle . . . is a murderer. He killed my parents. Did Lord Palmerston tell you that?" She heard her voice shaking and bowed her head, trying to keep her agitation in check. "Do you know that it's you who would be in the gravest danger the moment that you married me?"

A long silence followed her words.

He said, "Do you think I'm afraid?"

"No!" She whirled around. "It's I who am afraid—I'm the lowest, the meanest, the worst of cowards! I spend my days wishing I were anyone—a milkmaid!—instead of who I am. I cannot marry you, or anyone else, simply for my own protection," she exclaimed. "It would be craven! It would be selfish to shirk my duty to my people and to liberty. It would be despicable. I won't put you in such danger in order to flee from my own responsibilities."

He gazed at her while she turned white with mortification at her vehemence. Then he smiled faintly and shook his head. "You relieve my mind. I was beginning to fear I'd offered myself to a woman of no sense whatsoever."

"You're jesting again," she moaned. "How can you? You offer me protection—Sir Sheridan, you don't know how easy it would be for me to accept it! But how long would you be allowed to stand in my uncle's way? He is a monster, I tell you. It would be nothing to him to have you killed in your bed, and then what would I do? How would I bear it?"

"I'd find it something of a tragedy myself, I assure you." He bowed. "But I see that my anxiety for your answer has made me unforgivably importunate. You need an interval of reflection on the proposal. With your permission, Your Highness, I think it's time I took my leave."

Just as the butler was about to hand Sheridan his plumed hat and cloak in the entryway, a set of long fingernails dug into his upper arm. Julia pulled him into the dining room. She shut the door behind them.

"Well?"

He tossed his hat on the sideboard and glared at her. "Why didn't you bloody well happen to mention the chit's uncle is a murderer?"

"Keep your voice down! Will she have you?"

"Have *me!*" he hissed. "I'm not available anymore, madam. Do you think I'm going to sign my own death warrant?"

"Nonsense. Claude Nicolas would not touch you. When you marry her, you'll have the full protection of His Majesty's government."

"Oh, that eases my mind! I give myself a full extra week with my throat intact." There was a decanter of port on the sideboard. He splashed a substantial ration into a wineglass and downed the whole thing in one swallow.

"The princess needs your help."

He punished another glass of port in short order. "So blackmail some other poor sod."

"There's no time. You're perfect. And," she added with a significant curl of her lips, "I've no need to find anyone else."

"D'you think I'm crazy?" he snarled. "Four hundred thousand is a tidy sum, but it won't matter to a dead man. This Claude Nicolas is clearly the kind of cold-blooded brute who knows how to run a country. If he's got a notion to do it, then by God I ain't the chap to get in his way."

Julia tilted her chin. She narrowed her glorious eyes at him, giving her face a subtle cast of viciousness. "I knew you hadn't changed. All this talk of heroics—it's nothing but gammon," she said softly. Walking to the window, she stroked her finger down the green silk shutters of the snob-screen that shielded the room from the street outside. "You were a slinking little coward in your father's day, and you're a poltroon still."

"And pish to you!" he snapped, slamming the drained glass back on its silver tray. He picked up his hat. "Good day, Mrs. Plumb. I've certainly enjoyed renewing our acquaintance, but I'm afraid I've urgent business elsewhere."

He didn't wait for the butler, but swung out the front door and threw it shut behind him, still yanking his cloak around his shoulders when he reached the bottom step. He had no need to call for his horse from the stables. He was too broke to buy a horse; he'd walked the four muddy miles to Wisbeach, and now he had to walk back again.

The wrought-iron gate clanged shut behind him. He stalked through the street beside the slow-moving river, scowling at the prickle of cold sleet on his hot cheeks. He was furious with himself for letting Julia's sophomoric spite needle him. Oh, he was a poltroon, right enough; he never fought if he could gracefully run; but it stuck in his throat to hear it from the lips of an insolent jade who'd probably never stirred out of her boudoir if it looked like rain.

He'd noticed, in the course of his life, that it was the dregs of humankind who were the most eager to judge everyone else and be pleased to find them wanting. Why he cared what Julia thought, why he'd ever given a moment's contemplation to his father's opinion even as a ten-year-old boy, Sheridan could not fathom. But the sordid truth was that he had, and he did—and if he hated himself for one single, fatal flaw in his character, it was that.

The freezing air had chilled the heat out of his skin long before he reached the Rose and Crown. Sheridan commandeered a booth in the darkest corner by rousting out an apple-cheeked schoolmaster and advising him to go cane a few of his pupils, who no doubt deserved it. The teacher at first seemed reluctant to gather up his books and remove himself, but educated puffings were no match for a naval officer in full-dress uniform and a foul mood, complete with sword and savage frown. Sheridan sat in the murk and nursed a pint, brooding over his situation and gloomily pondering the fastest way out of town, while the locals whispered about him and cast dubious looks toward his corner.

He'd have to run for it, of course, Not that it would trouble him much—he had no love for that stone monstrosity his father had built, or for the flat, marshy countryside he'd seen only through a sleeting rain—but he wouldn't get far on the change in his pocket.

He briefly considered proceeding with the sale of Her Revolutionary Highness's diamond, which was presently burning a golden hole in the lining of his coat where he'd split it open and sewn the gem inside. It took only an instant for him to discard that idea. Bamboozling the princess was one thing, plain theft was another, and far too risky a proceeding for his peace-loving soul. He'd long since abandoned the idea of selling it anyway, having reckoned that fencing somebody's crown jewels in an isolated rural town was a pretty glaringly stupid idea, for all it had seemed rather charming under the queer influence of a certain pair of hopeful green eyes.

A transient wish crossed his mind: that he could have stayed around and introduced her to the innocent pleasures of . . .

But the devil with innocent pleasures. He dropped his head back against the wooden settle, closing his eyes. His feelings about Princess Field Mouse were as guilty as sin. He wasted a few moments in imagining a warm bed and his head pillowed on her delightfully plump breasts.

His lust for her was the most peculiar emotion, unlike anything a female had ever before inspired in him: a sort of passion for peace, a ferocious itch to have her and the bizarre impression that he'd somehow gain serenity from the act, that he could lose himself in her as if she were some primal element: a pathless forest or an endless plain instead of a chubby girl. He opened his eyes and stared at a low black timber in the ceiling above him, then blew a long breath of self-disgust from his lower lip and downed a pull of ale.

He turned his mind to considering whether Julia was right and he'd be in no real danger from this Claude Nicolas if he happened to wed the man's niece. There was nothing but the girl's word that her uncle was a murderer—obviously he'd not been hung, or whatever they did to execute malefactors in a place like Oriens—and the princess was clearly inclined to some rather romantic notions, not the least of which was her unquestioning faith in Sheridan himself. But he'd learned to trust his own spine when it gave that telltale prickle, and what he knew of Prince Claude Nicolas made it fairly sizzle with wary suspicion.

On the other hand, there was the message from the War Office, delivered in person by an officer on Palmerston's staff, polite enough but damned grave and insistent that Sir Sheridan Drake would be doing his country yet another powerful service by shackling himself to a stray princess. The letter was full of backhanded implications that Sheridan had sold out awkwardly early in his career. "There comes a time when a man feels he must lay down his sword and rest on his well-earned honors, and yet it is still given him to strive to serve his country along the peaceful byways of law and diplomacy . . ." among other drivel, which mainly convinced Sheridan that the War Office thought he was a congenital idiot.

Beneath the sap, though, lay an undertone of steel, quickly confirmed when Julia had followed up the message with her financial threats. Sheridan suspected this fellow Palmerston was about on a par with wicked old Prince Claude as far as political ruthlessness went.

It looked like a damned foul wind on a lee shore—

between moneylenders and Claude Nicolas and His Majesty's government, with no immediate wherewithal for escape and a princess who didn't seem overly enthusiastic about marrying him anyway. He felt vaguely sorry for his little Highness, who knew what it was like to be bullied by greater powers. She, at least, had expressed some concern for his life span, which was more than anyone else had done.

Absently he fingered the hard shape of the diamond concealed in the seam of his coat. He stared moodily at the open door to the corridor, where a pair of solemn, bearded Jews filed past in traditional long-skirted black coats. One after the other, they glanced into the taproom under the wide brims of their low-crowned hats and passed on.

Sheridan finally abandoned his gloomy musing and set himself to being convivial. It wasn't hard. The local patrons had long since reckoned who he was, and in short order he was answering avid questions about his career, earning a free dinner of excellent mutton chops and a basket of scraps for Mustafa. By the time dusk fell, he was riding home in a gig that belonged to the schoolmaster Sheridan had thrown out of his seat—sharing the young man's drunken renditions of sailors' ditties and handing out sage advice on how to seduce women in foreign ports. He got down from the gig at the steps of Hatherleigh Hall and shook the other man's hand. When the gig had rattled cheerfully off into the twilight, he turned and looked up at the black, somber bulk of his father's house, where no light shone in welcome and no hand threw open the entry to receive him.

The front door shut behind him with a wail like a lost soul. He groped his way into the little study near the entryway and built up the fire.

Mustafa wasn't in evidence, probably curled up already in the only harmless bed upstairs, appropriating all the blankets. By the coal grate's feeble red glow, Sheridan checked the potted fuchsia on the windowsill for the stubborn signs of renewed life. They were still there, two bright green sprouts amid the withered blooms. He warmed the kettle for a while, tested the temperature and then carefully added a measure of water to the plant.

He thought of lying down on the divan to sleep. But he might have one of his dreams; one of the really bad ones. He sometimes did when he got rattled and moody. Staying awake all night was preferable to that particular curse.

He lit a candle and sat down at the desk. After rummaging in the drawers for paper and ink, he rested his chin on his fist and thought a few moments.

His mouth curved in a twisted smile. Taking up the pen, he sharpened the goose quill and began to write.

Five

To The Right Honorable Viscount Palmerston, Secretary at War

My Lord Secretary,

I scribble this in haste, praying it will reach you. In a few moments Her Highness and I embark from King's Lynn. The plan you suggested was rejected by the princess, and it is by God's grace alone that I intercepted her wild attempt to slip away and make a solitary journey to Rome to plead her cause with the pope. She is remarkably intrepid. (In point of fact, I suspect she'd give a reasonable account of herself in the 11th Light Dragoons.) However, I would certainly have returned her instantly to the care of her guardians, but *others* were apparently aware of her plans. An attempt was made on her person. Whether it was meant to be an abduction or worse, I am not certain, but I managed to bear her to temporary safety.

I devoutly hope you will approve my actions. I deem it imperative to remove her instantly from this area to a place of greater security, though I dare not communicate the location in this vulnerable dispatch. Given the unavoidable circumstances of our situation in traveling together, I shall of course insist upon implementing your original plan. Be assured that her person and her honor will be guarded with my life. I await anxiously the moment you can remove the danger which threatens her. Until then, I will contact you as I can.

Yr servant,
Sheridan Drake

Princess,

Since leaving you, I have come to realize that you were entirely correct. The plan Palmerston offered is insufficient to your purposes and could only delay the day of reckoning in Oriens. Therefore I propose that we proceed forthwith in our original design.

Tomorrow morning take your walk as early as will seem reasonable to your household. Go directly to your usual meeting place. Stovall will know where to convey you from there.

Bring no baggage, except as we agreed, nothing to arouse early suspicion. It is imperative that we gain a full day's start. The only thing you must do is compose a letter to be sent ahead of us to the pope. In it, describe *everything* you have told me. It is crucial that you be as complete and persuasive as possible—we may be delayed somehow, and your letter must reach Rome before a decision is made on the matter of your marriage. *Do not post the letter yourself.* I will take it in hand the instant I meet you and dispatch it through appropriate means.

If we wish to win through, you must follow my directions to the inch from here on. And dress warmly, mouse.

Yr servant and friend,
S. Drake

P.S. Destroy this letter instantly.

To His Serene Highness the Prince Claude Nicolas of Oriens

Sir,

Being, as I am convinced, most solicitous of the welfare of your family, and holding in particular affection Her Highness the Princess Olympia, you will, I humbly beg, excuse my impertinence in addressing you. I write in strictest confidence on a matter of utmost urgency.

Enclosed you will find a letter from the princess's hand, fortunately intercepted before it could reach its destination. As you will see, she is quite untutored in matters of policy and displays a regrettable impulsiveness, which she will undoubtedly curb as she matures. Until that time, it is clearly in the interest of all concerned to keep her under close supervision and delay her assumption of the throne.

As a sincere friend of your country, I have taken it upon myself to remove Her Highness to a safe location during this period of instability in the political situation. Be assured that I will impress upon her the strict necessity of inaction. In spite of her youthful impetuosity, she is a very good girl, and I am sure she can be convinced to listen to the wise counsel of her uncle in the future.

I am sure you will wish your niece to live in comfort appropriate to her station. A general letter of credit would be sufficient for this purpose, made out in the name of Mustafa Effendi Murad and conveyed to Belgrade to be deposited in the care of the Turkish garrison.

You must not allow the location to cause you any undue concern that the princess herself will be allowed to cross the frontier to Belgrade and enter Plague territory; most assuredly neither of us will come near the city at all.

A Supporter

Olympia left the fens at first light, along with the wheeling curtains of water birds that rose from the shining water around. As the punt moved in silence beneath those great, reverberating masses of sound and life, the moving flocks were silhouetted against a brilliant dawn, almost blocking out the sun itself as they spiraled and spread and intertwined, heading toward the open sea.

Her breath sparkled in the morning transparency of a hard frost. She huddled in the boat, dressed in a set of heavy trousers and a thick blue jersey that Fish had given her years before. With wool wrappings around her palms for warmth, the trousers stuffed into a pair of thigh boots and an oversized sou'wester whose brim flopped down over her shoulders to hide her hair, Fish pronounced her "a proper fen tiger, then."

At that moment, she would have been happy to be a wildfowler, in fact, and spend the rest of her life in the immense bleak beauty of the washes rather than leave the only place she'd ever known for a notorious and uncertain future. She loved the fens. Fish had taught her that, schooled her to watch the birds and know their flight patterns. She could clean the punt gun and load it, and knew how to lie flat on her stomach in the bottom of the punt and move it along with the stalking sticks until the ducks were within range of the gun. She knew how to set a trap for eels and net plovers, wading far out in the flooded washes to retrieve the birds and slogging back again.

Julia was beautiful and sophisticated and charming. She was well read and well traveled; she'd seen London and Paris and Rome. Fish Stovall could not read or write, and he'd never been beyond the edge of the fens at Lynn. He lived alone in the middle of a wash, in a house that flooded every third winter.

Julia was Olympia's governess, but Fish was her family.

He said nothing beyond necessary instructions about the punt and the sluices for all the long trip down the canals to Lynn. The canal gave way to the straight, wide channel of the River Ouse, and Fish had to row as the water deepened. The punt glided past gangs of flat-bottomed coal lighters towed by patient horses on the bank. When Olympia saw the steeples and towers of Lynn in the distance, she bit her lip.

"Where are you to leave me?" she asked, breaking the silence at last.

"Greenland public house."

He said no more. Olympia worked her cold fingers, watching the river widen and the traffic grow heavy. Fish's punt began to seem very small amid the boats and busy lighters and the heavy smell of the sea. When she saw the tall masts of the collier brigs and commercial shipping, she pressed her hands tightly together.

"He won't be here," she said with conviction. "How will I find him?"

"If he ain't here, I'll take you home."

She turned and looked at Fish, at his wind-roughened cheeks and graying beard in the shadow of his hat brim. He squinted at her and nodded once, then stood up and began poling them into one of the canal streets of the city. Olympia jumped out onto the quay and helped secure the punt alongside the customhouse.

No one took any note of them: a nondescript fenman with three sacks of plovers slung over his shoulder, and a short, stout young lad, muffled to his ears by a moth-eaten scarf, carrying the excess.

Fish sold the plovers to a butcher in King Street. They walked together to the whalers' public house, The Greenland Fishery. Olympia's feet slowed as her heartbeat increased. She kept her face down. If she hadn't been following at Fish's heels, forced to keep up in order not to lose him, her pace would have dwindled to a complete halt.

At the door of The Greenland, she looked up for a moment at the ancient half-timbered inn with its red tile roof and tipsy lean. This side of the door, she was still uncommitted; she could still tug at Fish's sleeve and nod back toward the river, and know that he would turn around without a word and take her back. On the other side . . .

She looked at Fish. He only looked back at her, awaiting her decision. She wondered if he felt the same grief at parting, if his heart lay like hers, lonely and aching already for the hours spent in silent companionship out on the empty washes.

His dark gaze moved over her face in the keen, subtle way it moved across the marsh. He dug in his pocket and pulled out a small canvas bag. "There," he said. "That's yours, boy."

Olympia's fingers closed over the hard little rectangle of Fish's well-used harmonica. She opened her mouth to protest. Then she clutched it harder, unwilling to surrender one last tie with her friend. Tears threatened sharply. She wrinkled her nose, and remembered to wipe at it with her sleeve like a peasant boy.

She gave Fish one quick nod, hoping he saw all she could not say. He pushed open the old plank door.

Inside, he sat down in a chair near the fire. Olympia started to sit down next to him, but he jerked his head. "Over there, boy."

It startled her at first, the gruff note in his voice. But it dawned on her that in her part as a boy, she was due no special attention. It was Fish's courtesy to the house to relegate her to the coldest, least desirable seat. She sat down where he indicated, at the end of a table that suffered a draft from the door.

She'd never been in a public house before—most certainly not in one like this, filled with seamen and greasy smoke, the dim light tinged with green by the leaded glass window at her back. The air was thick with wet wool and fish and sweat and odors she could not even identify.

As often as she dared, she lifted her head from contemplating the table and snatched looks around at the booths and tables. She could not imagine Sir Sheridan in a place like this. The last time she'd seen him, he would have graced a palace. With a rise of panic, she wondered if Fish could have got the instructions wrong.

Fish drank his ale, tilting back his chair and staring into the fire. He offered nothing to Olympia, ignoring her and everyone else. She rubbed her fingers together in her lap, miserably watching him finish off his fourth pitcher. She dared not speak. She could only turn slightly every time the door opened and watch the feet of anyone who came in.

Fish was on his seventh mug when heavy boots sounded on the stairs from the private rooms. Olympia glanced up and looked away from the two strange men who descended into the taproom, heading for the door. The leader had already shoved open the wooden portal when the second one stopped next to her. She froze, staring at the oaken table.

"This your boy?" It was a grating, unfamiliar voice.

After a pause, Fish said, "Aye."

The sound of boots came closer. The slice of afternoon light disappeared as the other man let the door fall closed and leaned against the frame.

"He lookin' for work?"

There was another long pause, and then to Olympia's horror, Fish said, "Might be."

She glanced up at Fish and swiftly down again, her face growing fiery.

"Stand up, boy," the stranger said.

She threw Fish another agonized glance. He only nodded, emotionless. Olympia felt dizzy with fright. She pushed back the bench and stood up.

Though she kept her face down, she heard the other man leave his post by the door and move closer. His loose sweater and dark coat filled up her limited field of vision. He put his fist under her chin and lifted it. Olympia stubbornly kept her eyelashes lowered, trying to breathe slowly enough to prevent herself from fainting. The hum of conversation in the room dimmed as the patrons seemed to find a moment of casual amusement in the situation.

In a disinterested tone, the man who was touching her said, "Pretty."

Her eyes flashed open at the voice. She stared up, suddenly looking long enough to see through the dark stubble and grime to the gray eyes and familiar tiny scar above his left eyebrow. A wash of relief swept her, so profound that it threatened to collapse her knees. She stood trembling under his touch.

"How much?" Sir Sheridan asked, still in that detached and considering voice.

From the corner of her eye, she saw Fish shrug. He didn't answer.

"He'd go for a cabin boy. Light duty." As Sir Sheridan

skimmed his fingers over Olympia's cheek, he smiled. "Very light duty," he added softly.

Hoarse chuckles erupted from a nearby table. "Mark 'im up dearly, Papa," someone said. "He's solid gold."

"Four pound." the man said who'd spoken to her first.

The offer was met with jeers from the table of onlookers.

Fish turned red. "I reckon that ain't enough," he mumbled.

"Six."

"The boy's mum won't like it. She be fond of him." Fish shuffled his feet. "What'll I say to 'er, then?"

"Tell her he's shipped aboard Yarborough's *Falcon* out of London. Twenty-two guns, bound for China." Sir Sheridan grinned. "Tell her he'll bring her back a nice silk shawl."

Fish frowned amid the guffaws. "You the captain, then?"

Sir Sheridan smiled and shook his head, as if that naive assumption amused him. "Mate."

"This *Falcon* make any money?" Fish's voice was sharp. "What's the cargo?"

"Opium. Very profitable, I assure you. And every chance of advancement for your boy if he can conduct himself."

"Not that he looks it," the first man said. "See that skin? Soft as a gel's, and he's fat as a bleedin' porpoise, too."

"Aye," Sir Sheridan said, in a much more appreciative tone. "I see it."

Everyone in the place roared. The first man curled his lip in contempt as he looked at Sir Sheridan. "Christ—don't you want a bit more spirit in a boy? He ain't never been out o' his mama's kitchen if he could help it."

Sir Sheridan just tilted Olympia's head one way and another, observing her with a fond smile.

"Well," the other man said with disgust, "for what *you* be needin', he might do. Ten pound for him, the little bugger. And that's all."

Olympia couldn't see Fish's face. The room grew quiet, waiting.

Finally, in a barely audible voice, Fish said, "Done."

The crowd in the tavern broke out in a babble of conversation, jeers at Fish for selling too cheap, congratulations to the new boy for getting a soft berth, and an undertone of something else, a strange sort of laughter directed at Sir Sheridan. Fish gave her name as Tom, and made his mark on some papers.

Before she even had a chance to say goodbye, the first man grabbed her by the shoulders and hauled her into the street. She almost cried out, trying to break away and turn back. It seemed all too real, this callous transaction. But Sir Sheridan came through the door after them. She bit her lip on the protest.

He stood in the street and paid the man who'd bought her—twenty pounds for the papers Fish had signed for ten. As Sir Sheridan tucked the documents into his sweater, he put his arm around Olympia's shoulders and caressed her cheek.

"Fat as a porpoise, are you, sweeting? Let's hope we can keep you so."

The other man gave her an ironic look. "I always tell 'em: 'Obey your mate's orders, and you'll come off right enough.' " He didn't quite smile; the expression was uglier than that. "So—do whatever he bids ye. Ever'thin', mark. You aim to please; don't you fight him in nothing. Or he'll make sure you're the sorrier for it."

"Come, now," Sir Sheridan said softly. "You frighten the boy. Go on back to your hole, my friend, and lay up for the next customer." He propelled Olympia around as he turned away, keeping her pressed close against his body. Under his breath he added, "Pestilent bastard."

They walked in the direction of the river. After a few yards, he stopped and bought a bag of sweetmeats from a street vendor, never letting go of her shoulders. He leaned against the corner of a shop window and bent over, offering Olympia the treat. "You're doing fine," he murmured, glancing sideways back toward the public house as he rested his hand against the curve of her neck. "We're going to board a ship; just keep on as you are—yes . . . silly child, that's all right; cry if you want to, it's quite in character."

"Fish," she said with a little gesture. "I wanted to say goodbye."

"Here." He pressed a sweetmeat into her hand. "Eat that."

"I don't want it. Can't we go back for just a—"

His fingers tightened on her shoulder. She winced and tried to pull away from the painful grip. "That's not possible. Eat the damned sweet." The vicious low tone was at startling variance with the affectionate way he smiled down at her. "That filthy crimp's still standing there watching us. Do you want him to get another close look at you? If he didn't manage to guess the truth, then he just might overcome his Christian disgust of fellows like me and steal you back to sell to the highest bidder."

"Steal me!"

"Aye. And if you think I enjoy passing myself off as a sodomite, I don't. It doubled your price, for one thing."

Olympia's eyes widened.

"Eat," he said. "I want to get out of here."

She put the candy in her mouth.

"Good." He smiled and patted her cheek. "Don't say anything, to me or anyone else." He stood looking down at her for a moment, holding both her shoulders. Then he bent and planted a kiss full on her mouth. Olympia pulled back in shock, but he held her fast. His mouth opened a little over hers, the dark stubble of his beard scratching her chin. His fingers tightened on her shoulders.

Oh, God, she thought, between terror and bliss.

He straightened. "There," he murmured ruefully. "That ought to ruin my reputation for good with the ladies in these parts."

Their cabin aboard the *John Campbell* was smaller than anything Sheridan had occupied for years. As a senior post captain, he'd had at least a few feet of open space, if not much in the way of luxuries to fill it. He kept his head down, avoiding the deck beams in the narrow companionway passage, and opened the cabin door to allow the princess to enter.

He didn't duck through after her. It wasn't possible, unless she climbed up into the single berth to give him room. He waited outside, holding back a smile at her expression of dismay.

She turned around once in the tiny space, a forlorn figure in the drooping hat and ragged jersey. "It's very small."

"It has a porthole," he said optimistically. "Think of the view."

She eyed the grimy, tarnish-green opening in the hull without enthusiasm. "Is your cabin close by?"

He broke the news to her smartly. Stepping forward, he grasped her at the waist and with a suppressed grunt lifted her onto the cot. She was a nice, tempting weight, all muffled in wool. He thought of exploring the shapeless mass to find the figure beneath it, but he didn't. Standing nose to nose with her in the narrow space, he had only to reach behind him to close the door. "My cabin's here."

"Here! It can't be here."

"Why not?"

She looked at him as if he were ready for Bedlam. "I can't stay in here with you," she said in a scandalized voice. "There's nowhere for you to sleep but—" She stopped, and dropped her face from view.

To the top of her hat, he said, "It's only for a night, until we reach Ramsgate. I'm afraid a princess who's slipped her cable must take what comes along."

She clenched her hands, kneading her fingers. "Oh, if only I could have said goodbye to Fish!"

Her voice was quivering. He knew of two ways to deal with weeping women, of which Her Highness was bound to become a prime specimen at any moment. It was too damned cramped to have a proper go at loving her, so in preparation for leaving he took a step backward and ran into the door.

"Did you write the letter?" he asked.

She nodded and snuffled, reaching beneath her jersey and pulling out a packet. The feminine curves of her figure suddenly took shape as the woolen garment sank back into place. She held out the bulky package without looking up.

Sheridan broke it open. She hadn't sealed it any too securely—it was a wonder she hadn't been leaving a trail of rubies and emeralds and gold from here to Wisbeach. He had the urge to shake her till her teeth rattled.

Discarding the idea as undiplomatic at this early stage in their acquaintance, he pulled the letter free. He laid the packet back in her lap, as if he had no more than passing interest in the tangle of pearl earrings, sapphire tiaras, diamond-studded chokers and jeweled rings that lay winking at him from their bed of paper and burlap.

"We sail with the tide," he said. "Before midnight. I'll have to dispatch this letter immediately."

She nodded, hidden by the hat.

"Don't leave the cabin," he ordered.

She hesitated, and then nodded again.

He narrowed his eyes, considering that moment of hesitation. "I know what you're thinking," he said. "You don't go looking for Fish. You don't go on deck. You don't open the door." He took hold of her chin and jerked it up. "Not even if the damned ship's sinking. Do you mark me?"

She looked satisfyingly startled. He pressed his fingers into her cheeks, drawing a little whimper and a quick nod.

"All right," he said. "See that you behave, or I'll burn your royal backside for you."

She cast down her eyes. "I only wanted to say goodbye."

"Well," he said, "feel free. Get up right now and walk back to The Greenland and say it. He's probably still there, hanging around and crying in his beer over going along with your harebrained schemes." He glared into her wide green eyes. "And then come on back, Your Noble Highness. Because you'll find you won't have to share this cabin after all."

Her lip trembled. She stared at him, all misery and sparkle, her dirty, round face still marked by the red imprint of his fingers. He had a moment of queer and terrible weakness, an urge to draw her into his arms and hold her tight against him.

"Christ!" he said, drawing back abruptly. He put his shoulder to the door. "Do what you please, ma'am."

He shut the door behind him with an ill-tempered thump. When he reached the posting station onshore, he was still in a foul mood. Instead of entering, he banged into the tavern next door and slumped in a seat, thinking of what he would do if he went back and found her gone.

The possibility heightened the peculiar hollow feeling in him. He realized that he'd stormed out so fast he'd left the jewels with her—reason enough to feel sick and empty, he thought furiously. And he dared not even post the letters, not while she might turn up tomorrow morning safe in her bedroom at home. That sad old fool Fish Stovall would take her back in a minute—he probably *was* waiting, hoping she'd change her mind, the sentimental dotard. He'd been superb at his task, following Sheridan's instructions to the letter, but there'd been a damned odd note in his voice at the climax of their little scene in the public house.

So let her go, he thought sullenly. If she was too homesick to leave the bleeding county, she'd be nothing but trouble every step of the way. He should have known she'd go into a funk on him. Wanted to say goodbye, for God's sake. Wretched female; he couldn't bear that kind of maudlin nonsense. And from a princess who intended to start a civil war in her own country, forsooth.

He examined the seal on her letter to the pope. The light steam from a mulled ale was enough to slip it open intact. A quick perusal assured him of the emotional contents, quite specific and satisfactory in their description of Prince Claude Nicolas as a villain of satanic proportions. He resealed it and leaned on the table, considering his own letters, still concealed inside his coat, one to Palmerston and one to the evil Prince Claude. He chewed on his knuckle until it bled.

A pox on her for fouling his plans already. The missives were calculated risks: Sheridan had written them to keep all his options open as long as possible—an old habit and a tactic that had served him well over the years. He'd developed stalling into a fine art during the length of his career.

But there was no point in committing himself until his princess had made up her muddled little mind. He kept the letters in his coat and got roundly drunk, having nothing else to do but spend the last of the money he'd gained by selling the gold chain off her diamond necklace. The rest had gone to pay for passage as far as Ramsgate and to buy the princess from the crimp—a necessary subterfuge to defeat Julia's initial pursuit. The diamond itself was in Mustafa's care, heading toward their rendezvous at Ramsgate by whatever convoluted oriental means of progress Mustafa could contrive.

The thought failed to lift Sheridan's spirits. It was growing dark. He found himself reluctant to return to the ship, and put it off until he realized foggily that he was running out of tide and money. If she went home and he missed his paid passage to Ramsgate, he was well and truly stranded.

The streets were empty as he made his way toward the quay, his pace only a little unsteady. The watch aboard *John Campbell* was preparing to warp the ship down the river on the turning tide. He clambered aboard, feeling drunkenly at home, hearing the soft voices and the creak of rigging in the night, clear and carrying on the water.

He stood by the rail, looking back along the river to the town. The reflections swayed and wavered on the surface. He rubbed his cold cheeks, taking a sobering draft of winter air. Below him, the peace was broken by the muffled notes of a mouth organ, clearly in the hands of a rank amateur of no talent whatsoever. The sour sound died away, and then took up again, mangling a tune that Sheridan finally decided was meant to be "My Lady Greensleeves."

He went below and paused outside his cabin. From behind the door came the pathetically halting bleat of the mouth organ. It didn't deserve to be called music.

He opened the door.

The sound stopped. He waited in the entry a moment to let his eyes adjust to the dark.

"I didn't think you were coming back," she whispered.

Sheridan leaned against the bulkhead. He couldn't see her, only a deeper blackness in the direction of the bunk. "You'll have to get up," he said.

He heard her move. She worked herself off the cot and into the little standing space. Sheridan shoved past her, squeezing onto the bunk. On his knees, he felt along the bulkhead at the foot of the cot until he found the familiar net of a hammock and secured both ends in the darkness above her berth.

He edged himself into the hammock carefully—no easy task in that small space, with the netting slung as it was so close to the deck above. He settled in. The hammock gave under his weight until he had four inches of clearance above his head. He made a mental note to remember that in the morning and pulled a blanket around him.

"All right. You can lie down again." he told her.

At the exploratory touch of her hand, he started, sending the hammock swinging in the confined space. She felt along his arm, outlining the shape and curve of the net. "Oh," she said. "A hammock."

"Hmm."

"Will you be quite comfortable?"

"Oh, quite," he said with heavy irony.

He heard her move into the berth below him. She bumped him and apologized at least seven times. Finally, she settled down. The creak of the deck and the gurgle of water filled the silence. Sheridan crossed his arms and swung gently.

In the berth below, Olympia lay with her shoulders propped against the hard bulkhead. She chewed her finger and stared into the shapeless dark above her. "Sir Sheridan?"

He grunted.

"I didn't go back to see Fish, you know."

He made another uninterested sound.

She fumbled in the dark at her blankets. "Fish gave me his harmonica. Do you mind if I play it for a little while?"

"Oh, God."

"Just for a few minutes. I'm trying to learn how. Do you mind?"

He moved above her, making the bulkhead creak. "My ears are plugged. Yowl away."

She propped herself up on her elbows and blew into the instrument. The notes came out quivering and flat, nothing like the sweet, mournful songs that Fish had played to her on rainy days before his fire. But it made her feel closer to him. She tried to find the first note of her favorite melody, attempting to keep the sound soft, working up and down the scale, never hitting anything that sounded remotely right, or even pleasant. She shifted in frustration and tried again, finally locating an off-key set of positions that made a sad parody of Fish's flowing notes. She worked on those, over and over, trying to perfect them.

"Give me the damned thing," Sir Sheridan said. His arm brushed her roughly as he groped downward in the dark.

Olympia withheld the instrument. "Never mind. I won't play anymore."

"Give it to me," he said.

It was a tone she was learning to recognize. Reluctantly, she allowed him to lift the harmonica out of her hand.

He made several sharp, huffing noises, as if he were forcing air through cupped fingers. Out of the blackness above her came a slow rill of notes—up the scale, down again. Olympia stiffened, about to tell him to leave Fish's gift alone and give it back.

Until he began to play.

The soft, sweet melody of "Greensleeves" started simply. It seemed to curl around the cabin and then fill it, embellished by runs and cascades that surpassed anything Fish had ever coaxed from the tiny instrument. Olympia listened in wonder, staring up through the darkness. The music seemed unreal, so unexpected was it in its mastery of the familiar tune, so sure and certain in its variations, like an easy conversation between intimate friends.

He came to an end of "Greensleeves" and began another melody, one she'd never heard before. It had a rhythm that made her want to pat the blanket in time, and hum along with the gliding wail of the notes. He played on without pausing, old tunes sometimes, but oftener there were unfamiliar ones, strange in composition, atonal but lovely, pouring out a plaintive beauty into the winter night.

The haunting songs seemed to come out of nowhere. She could not see him, yet she knew he was there—the hero who'd saved his admiral and his ship, the captain who'd kissed her and caressed her throat with white gloves, the man who'd found music where she'd made nothing but donkey's braying. And it was his own kind of music—uncanny in its combinations and rhythms, compelling and hard to predict.

As she listened to him, she knew that magic was beyond her. She could never learn to play like this. She could not draw such strange, fluid splendor from a piece of metal and reed. Not with years of trying. And what was more, she didn't want to.

She wanted only to listen to him play.

She wanted to listen forever.

Six

They left Ramsgate on the Post Office packet bound for Madeira and Gibraltar. After a fortnight in his company, Olympia stood in awe of the convoluted turn of Captain Sir Sheridan's mind—she could scarcely recognize herself in the chubby adolescent boy she played, far less believe anyone else would, or could possibly trace them through the series of false names and shabby lodgings on the Ramsgate strand.

But they had finally emerged from this threadbare chrysalis as an affluent, widely traveled gentleman and his invalid sister, bound for a sojourn in more salubrious climes. Representing one of those oddities picked up in the rambles of the true world traveler, Mustafa had rejoined them from out of nowhere, to go along as valet, cook, servant and all-around slave, leaving nothing for the maid Sir Sheridan had hired to do but dress Olympia. Which was just as well, she thought, because the girl was a singularly inferior lady's maid, having a marked tendency to sleep through the night and day both.

Olympia had no intention of complaining about such a trivial detail, however. She sat on deck, in a chair wedged snugly between a mast and a coil of rope, her only company an elderly consumptive lady in the next chair. Sir Sheridan had hung about asking solicitous questions while Mustafa tucked a blanket around her, and then they'd both disappeared with frustrating alacrity—as they'd done yesterday and the day before—to attend to obscure male business of their own.

Olympia sat gazing out at the sea, excited and restless and disappointed in the smooth course of events. Of all the things she had expected from her great adventure, boredom was not one of them. She'd spent most of the last two weeks staring at the various tattered curtains and chipped washbasins and grimy windows in one cheap set of rooms after another, not allowed to go out in public, not allowed to speak to anyone and not seeing much at all of her gallant protector, who'd spent the days outfitting and the nights elsewhere.

When she'd ventured to ask where, he'd said she had no business poking her nose into that kind of thing.

Olympia imagined secret meetings with agents of clandestine organizations: darkened rooms and passwords, letters signed with the aliases of high-placed, important men; and felt a thrill of admiration in spite of her annoyance.

The elderly lady's son came up and woke her in time to take her below for her afternoon nap, but no one came for Olympia. So she sat, supposedly not healthy enough to move about the ship on her own.

A sailor approached with a bucket of tar. He nodded at her shyly, his sandy pigtail blowing in the breeze, and knelt nearby, daubing at the cracks around the mast. He yawned as he worked, and yawned again.

"You must be sleepy," Olympia said, to start a conversation.

He twisted around, looking as shocked as if one of the stanchions had spoken. "Mum?"

"I said, you must be quite sleepy. You've yawned three times in the last few moments."

"Aye, mum." He shrugged. "That's just the way of it aboard this 'ere brig. We only gets four hours o' sleep afore they calls the watch again."

"Four hours?" Her eyes widened. "Why?"

"Cap'n's orders, mum. And excuse me, mum, but we ain't to converse wi' no one while we're on watch, neither—'specially the passengers."

"Whyever not?" she asked indignantly.

He shook his head. "Dunno, mum." He gave the stern a significant glance. "Cap'n said so."

Olympia was silent. The crewman went back to work. She chewed her lower lip thoughtfully. As the sailor moved nearer to reach a spot behind her, she whispered, "Is he very cruel?"

The man paused. He glanced around and then went back to work. With his head down, he said in a low voice, "Bad enough. Work all day Sundays and not a kind word spoken. Grub ain't fit for dogs, neither. Salt beef's rotten."

"Rotten! But surely—have you spoken to him about it?"

He cast her a quick look. "Common sailor don't speak to the cap'n, mum. That ain't the way't is. He gives orders an' we jump to. We daren't make no complaints, mum."

"But that makes you no better than slaves! Have you no rights?"

He didn't answer. Olympia took a gulp of air, feeling her blood quicken.

"Sir," she whispered, "I think—I believe I might be able to give you some help."

He slid her a sidelong look of surprise.

She went on stoutly. "I'm well versed in the matter. I know precisely how to go about obtaining relief and fair treatment for you." It was perfectly true; she had memorized all the pamphlets and treatises on the proper methods of instigating reform, but his expression changed to such incredulous skepticism that she was stung into adding, "You may think I'm only a female, but I assure you—" She stopped short of proclaiming her identity. He stared at her. Frustrated, she said, "You may well believe me. I tell you this in complete confidence, but I'm traveling incognito with"—she bit her lip—"with my brother. You may not recognize him, and you must not repeat this, but he is Captain Sir Sheridan Drake, and as friends of democracy, we're on our way to . . . to a place where revolution is imminent."

The sailor's mouth had dropped. "Gor!" he breathed. "Aboard this here tub? Cap'n Drake? The real bloke?"

She nodded. "A truly enlightened man. But you must not tell anyone, or let on that you know."

He licked his lips and shook his head.

She smiled. "So you see, I can help you, if you're willing to work with me. Are you?"

He wiped his mouth. At his tanned throat, she saw his Adam's apple bob convulsively. "Gor!" he repeated. "Aye! Aye, mum, I'm wi' you."

Olympia bit back the rise of elation. It was exactly as she'd known it would be—just a breath of the sweet wind of freedom was enough to make a poor downtrodden wretch sit up straighter. The sailor's face had a light of awe and joy in it. It warmed her heart to bursting to know that she was the source of it.

She would not fail him. Her destiny called.

"I knew it." The door slammed. Sir Sheridan braced his shoulders back against the wood, his face set in dark flame. "I should have tied you to the damned bed."

Olympia closed her mouth and let her hand slide from her throat with an exhalation of relief. "You startled me." She looked down at the portable desk in her lap. "I'm afraid I've smudged the Declaration of Grievances. But I'm glad you've come. Do you have any idea what the sailors on this ship are expected to eat? The poorest, most pathetic portions! The beef is actually rotten, I swear to you. And the biscuit! It's full of *maggots.*" She shuddered. "I broke one open and saw them myself. Not fit for animals! And the captain orders the crew on deck every four hours around the clock, trying to get two days' work out of one! It's beyond imagination. Oh—and I wished to ask: do you think two pounds of plum duff a day is adequate to a sailor's health?"

"Gagged you. Tied you in a sack and drowned you. Give me that." He seized the paper from her hand, glanced at it, snarled in disgust and crushed it between his palms. He threw it down. The ball of parchment rolled across the deck to her feet and back again under the sway of the ship.

"Have I done something wrong?" she asked anxiously.

He stared at her with a nightmare gleam in his gray eyes. The ship rose on a wave, a collection of sound and sensation that was familiar now after ten days at sea out of Ramsgate: the wailing creak of wood on wood, the pause at the crest, the wallowing slide into the trough on a long, low-pitched groan.

Olympia moistened her lips. "I've done something wrong, haven't I?"

"You're my invalid sister," he snapped. "We're on our way to Italy for your health."

She nodded quickly.

"Then why," he asked with soft menace, "do I find that the crew believes there's going to be an insurrection on behalf of the Rights of Man on this ship?" His eyes narrowed. "And why do they think . . . that . . . *I'm* . . . going . . . to . . . lead it?"

Olympia sat back, pressing her spine against the curve of the hull. "No, no, I never precisely told them—"

"And why," he interrupted savagely, "did a crewman pull his knife on the first mate when he didn't get an extra ration of rum?"

"Oh, yes—but you mustn't misunderstand that, you see. These poor men are practically starving on their paltry provisions. And he never meant to use it. It was simply to make a point about—"

"A *point*, for God's sake! It was a knife, ma'am—a lethal weapon drawn on an officer!" He pushed away from the door. "That bastard had better thank his God-given stars I'm not in command."

"And what should I think you'd have done?" she cried in perplexity. "Had the poor man shot?"

"I'd have made him wish he'd been shot." Sir Sheridan braced his hands on the edge of the berth and leaned toward her. "Listen here, Your Bloody Highness—d'you think the crew on this ship's got it hard? D'you think they've got grievances? They don't. Maggots are nothing—I've eaten more than my damned share of maggots and weevils and worse, and I'll tell you about grievance. Grievance is a man who's made to work when his mouth's so swollen with scurvy that he can't breathe for the blood. Grievance is an officer who flogs a midshipman to death for forgetting to set one flag on a signal. Grievance is a paranoic madman of a captain who orders unbroken silence in quarters and then withholds water rations from two hundred sailors for breaking it.'' His lip curled. ''Do you know why? Because he heard an officer humming—after a month of keeping his damned stinking silence. Humming!'' He pushed his face close to hers. ''I know what grievance is. You aren't talking redress. You're talking mutiny.''

She managed to hold her eyes level with his. ''I don't understand. I thought you would wish to help me.''

''I don't help idiots.''

The contempt in his voice stung like a backhanded slap. She made a sound of distress, a wordless whimper: all that would come out past the jam of furious confusion in her throat.

''Why should I?'' he demanded above the creak of the ship. ''If I wanted to be shot at sunrise, I'd commit some crime a sight more amusing than mutinous conspiracy with a noble-minded moron.''

She opened her mouth, breathing hard and heatedly as she cast about for an appropriate answer. He was too close to her; his aggressive stance made the berth a prison; each roll of the ship brought his face almost nose to nose with hers. With her wits in a turmoil, she cried, ''But it's for the cause!''

''Jesus.'' He pulled back. ''You'll ruin my dinner.''

''At least you have a dinner to ruin!''

''Well, I haven't always, so I like to enjoy it when it's on the table.'' He caught at an overhead beam to balance himself against an unexpected bucketing of the ship. ''You muddle-brained mooncalf—what the hell do you know about going hungry? You've never missed a meal in your life, from the looks of you.''

She pressed her hands over her mouth. She would not cry. A brave person would not cry, or turn away from the truth, no matter how ruthlessly it wounded.

''Get up,'' he said. ''I'll be damned if I'll let you sit down here making lists of grievances while I hang for it. If anybody has to pay for this, you can jolly well volunteer.''

Olympia obeyed woodenly, propelled by the snap of command in his voice. She tried to walk with her chin up, but the motion of the ship and his grip on her arms made her clumsy. She tripped on the companionway stairs. He caught her around the waist and lifted her bodily on deck.

As she blinked in the warm Atlantic sunlight he took her arm, providing a steady support against the constant wave motion, and strolled in the direction of the quarter-deck. Olympia became aware of men drifting toward them. She slanted a look sideways, but Sir Sheridan's hand tightened on her arm. A few more steps and there was a murmur of voices, more crewmen, a scuffing of feet on the white-sanded wood.

A sailor nodded at her: the pigtailed crewman who'd been helping her draw up the Grievances, but word seemed somehow to have spread much farther than that. One by one they looked up, every man on deck; dropped their tasks and fell in with the growing number. Up on the quarterdeck, near the great wheel, she saw an officer lean over and touch the captain's shoulder.

He swung around, a lean giant with big, awkward hands. For a moment he stared at the gathering men. "What the devil's the meaning of this?"

The grip on Olympia's arm vanished. She looked aside and found herself alone in the crowd of sailors. Sir Sheridan was gone; there was only the press of muttering men, carrying her with them toward the quarterdeck stairs.

Panic clutched her. She tried to stop and turn, to find him amid the huddle, but lost her balance in the movement and stumbled with the ceaseless heave of the deck. She fell against the shoulder of the crewman next to her, who grinned and set her upright, his marlinspike pressing into her arm as he steadied her. Around and behind, in the hands of the crowd, sharp metal gleamed and flashed in the sun.

"Stop," the captain demanded. "Stand by."

The sailors ignored him, shuffling forward with Olympia in their midst until she was standing at the foot of the steps. There, as if by unspoken agreement, they paused. All human sounds ceased, leaving only the rush of the water and wind, the creak of rigging and the snap of the flag at the stern. The captain eyed them. With an impassive face, he pulled a pistol from beneath his coat.

Terror pulsed through her. Her eyes were on a perfect level with the firearm as he stood with it loosely in his hand, pointed down toward the deck. She could see nothing but that gun, feel nothing but the bodies at her back and the wooden plank of the bottom step pressed across her ankles. The sound of her blood roared in her ears.

"Ma'am," the captain said to her, in a voice that seemed to come from very far away, "I can't credit this. You and your brother should be ashamed."

Olympia swallowed and looked up. The captain's expression was still unmoved, but she saw his fingers rub restlessly on the butt of the gun. When she had envisioned this moment, somehow she had always seen Sir Sheridan at her side. It was his voice she'd imagined, declaring the sailors' grievances in a steady and stirring tone that no reasonable person could ignore. Trying to summon words out of her own throat, she found that she was in dizzy danger of turning faint. The gallant image of Sir Sheridan standing forth for the cause of justice and human rights evaporated into a picture of herself—in a crumpled, cowardly heap at the captain's feet.

"What do you want?" The captain glared down, shifting his gaze to a man next to her. "Speak up or be sorry."

A hostile murmur rose behind her.

"Drake," the seaman said. There was alcohol on his breath. "We wants a decent man for a cap'n. We wants Drake."

Olympia turned on him in astonishment. "No!" She caught his arm, leaning heavily as the ship rolled. "That isn't what you want!"

He shook her off, amid a shuffle and rumble of agitation from the rest. "Aye, 'tis." He raised his voice. "Cap'n Drake—we all know 'im, by God, and what he done! We know he'll treat us fair! All the rum we wants—that's what he give the men sailin' under *him.*"

"No. No, you've misunderstood," she cried above the tumult of agreement. "Not rum! You wish to present your grievances—better food rations, and reasonable hours, and—"

"Drake!" The chant rose to drown her words. Spikes and belaying pins waved in rhythm above the crowd. *"Drake . . . Drake . . . Drake . . ."*

She whirled around. The captain and the other two officers lined the quarterdeck, all armed with pistols leveled into the crowd. The captain rubbed his sleeve across his mouth, glancing at Olympia and away and back again. The chanting grew louder and faster. She stumbled at the push from behind as the sailors began to thrust past her to reach the steps.

The captain aimed. For an instant she was looking into the black muzzle of a pistol. It wavered downward; the captain backed up with an alarmed curse, pointed it again toward Olympia and the surge at the stairs. She stared at it and thought, *He won't . . .* and then she staggered to her knees under the push from behind. A loud crack hit her ears just as something struck her shoulder. A ragged volley of gunfire followed.

He shot me, she thought in bewilderment, kneeling with her hands braced on the stairs. For a stunned instant, the crowd went still. Olympia raised her head, her shoulder throbbing in pain. She looked at the captain, standing with his pistol aimed at the sky, and then stared down at her shoulder.

There wasn't a bit of blood. She slowly realized she was unhurt, that the blow to her shoulder must have been nothing but a passing glance from a belaying pin.

In the frozen tableau, dizziness rolled in her head. She sank down onto the steps. Her vision wavered. The sounds of shuffling came to her through a haze. With an effort of will, she swallowed terrified nausea and lifted her face.

She found Sir Sheridan at last, leaning against a shroud with his arms crossed, watching them all with that faint derisive smile, like a fallen angel looking on at a meeting of pious saints.

Relief poured through her. He was there; he would stop it. Sir Sheridan would fix it all.

But he made no gallant speech or appeal to reason. Into

the expectant pause, he said, "Leaving aside the irregularity of this proceeding, I presume you drunken hayseeds realize I've no interest whatsoever in commanding you?" His lip curled. "I'd sooner take a half-dozen vicars in a river dhow."

The sailors hesitated in confusion.

"We'd get there faster," he added dryly.

"He don't mean that," someone yelled.

"Don't I?" Sheridan swept the gathered crew with a jaundiced eye. "If I didn't want to reach Rome before I'm ninety, I'd hang you all on the spot. And that French bucket to starboard's been overtaking us for half the noon watch."

Olympia dropped her gaze. It suddenly appeared silly; Sir Sheridan made it seem so, standing there with a lifetime of battle and hardship behind him, altogether unimpressed by their demands. A resentful muttering began in the back of the crowd. A few sailors glanced over toward the French ship off to starboard.

Sir Sheridan began to whistle the "Marseillaise."

His cool disdain reached even the captain, who perversely came to the defense of his crew. "They did well enough," he snapped, "until you fed them these radical notions and turned them from their duty."

"Really?" Sir Sheridan shook his head sadly. "Fifty guineas says the French brig overtakes us by eight bells."

"A hundred!" the captain roared.

Sir Sheridan squinted toward the other ship. His mouth curled. "How could I pass up a wager like that?"

Some sailor made a rude gesture at him, setting off catcalls and whistles. He ignored the jeers and glanced complacently up at the sails, then off again toward the French brig. The captain barked out orders. The crew set to work with a vengeance, leaving Olympia sitting alone on the steps as if there had never been a gun brandished or a grievance mentioned.

Sir Sheridan won his bet, but not for lack of willing and cooperative effort on behalf of the crew and captain. As the two contenders thrashed along, word of a race spread among the passengers. Soon wet and cheering spectators crowded the bow, all hanging onto the rail against the spray washing over the deck and the steep heel of the ship. Even the taciturn pair of dark-eyed Jewish jewelers came up to watch, looking more miserable than interested, crushing their wide hats down over their heads and clinging to the capstan for dear life while the black skirts of their coats flapped around them. By late afternoon, however, when the ship's bell struck eight times, the shouts and whistles had turned to glum silence long since.

Sir Sheridan led Olympia into the evening gloom below. In her cabin, he lit the lamp for her. In the instant of rising glow, between shadow and illumination, she happened to glance nervously toward him. For a fragile moment, as he looked down into the glass bowl to adjust the flame, she saw weariness instead of the anger she'd expected; strain in the slight tremor he blinked from the corner of his eye.

Without thinking, she reached toward him. Before her hand touched his sleeve he met her look with a dark smile, the illusion of fatigue vanished. "Well," he said briskly, "did you enjoy your mutiny, ma'am? Shall we put on another one soon?"

Olympia drew back, embarrassed. She sat down on the berth and stared at her hands. "I made a muddle of it."

"A muddle? Not at all. You were nearly shot, I was almost lynched and now we're to be put off the ship at Madeira. I think I'd call it a damned disaster." He lifted the lamp sharply. "But then, watching a lady get her head blown off always does make a fellow feel low."

Olympia drew in a shaky breath. "I don't believe the captain would have fired at me," she said in a small voice.

"Of course not. Which is why I made sure you were up for a target instead of me."

Her lips parted. She frowned. "Did you expect the captain to draw his pistol?"

He set the lamp in its brass holder. In the cramped quarters, each roll of the ship sent shadows reeling across his face. "There were weapons raised, my dear. I didn't think he was going to sing lullabies."

"And you left me there on purpose?"

"Somebody had to draw the poison. Better you than me."

"But I'm—" She broke off, turning red.

"A princess?" he suggested. "A lady? A mere dabbler in anarchy? Messy business, these rebellions. Naturally you would expect to leave the sordid details to the menfolk."

She bit her lip. "It isn't that. I thought they would listen to you more readily."

"No," he said gently. "I would simply have been shot more readily. I've been shot before, madam, and I found it a most unpleasant business. So I put you up front. The whole damned thing was your fault in the first place. The captain is a gentleman; I thought it doubtful he'd fire on a female, and a passenger to boot." He paused and then grinned, watching her through lowered lashes. "Fairly doubtful, anyway."

Olympia lifted her chin. "I'm prepared to face violence in the cause of freedom."

"Defied that fellow to his teeth, didn't you? Solid as rock."

"I am," she cried. "I have to be!"

He laughed, a white flash of mockery in the swaying shadows.

"All right!" She drew a choking breath. "You may make a joke of me if you please! I'm not like you; I'm not brave. But I'm trying to learn. You may think I can't, because I'm not a man, because I've no experience of battles and guns—you may think I ought to stay in my sheltered place and sew the lace on your shirt points, but I assure you that I haven't been brought up to that! I know my duty. I wish I *had* been born a man like you, who's never known petty fears, but God didn't see fit to give me that advantage, and so I must educate myself in courage by practice. I failed today; I stayed silent when I should have spoken. I shouldn't have been intimidated by a mere pistol. But next time—"

"Next time!" Sheridan said faintly. He leaned his shoulders against the door and put his hand over his face. "You're insane."

"I'm only inexperienced," she said stubbornly. "You could teach me, if you would."

He grimaced. "For the love of God—teach you what?"

"How to be brave." She looked up at him with that hero worship shining in her eyes. "I saw it, the way you turned those men from what they meant to do. You didn't flinch for an instant. That's what I want to be like. The way you are."

Sheridan glared at her. The silly dumpling—why did she insist on mooning at him as if he were God Almighty? "You don't know anything about the way I am."

She only kept her earnest gaze upon him, her lips parted a little, her great, green, solemn eyes full of foolish adoration. He felt an odd rush, a surge of protectiveness and resentment: the disgusting twist his normal desires seemed to have taken with this ridiculous chit. He wished he could tumble her and have done with it—and dispense with this hero farce at the same time.

No, she certainly didn't know anything about the way he was, or the dangerous state he was in—between anger and terror and lust, what with her preposterous rebellion and that bug bear excuse for a captain waving his pistol around, making Sheridan's heart alternately pound and petrify as the gun muzzle pointed toward her and wavered away. It would have been a vast inconvenience to have to explain to Palmerston and Claude Nicolas that she'd been executed for inciting a mutiny.

He wasn't too fond of the idea himself. After three weeks of travel and covert observation, he knew every curve and swell of her delicious body, the plump shape of her cheek and the delicate contour of her earlobe. He had to stay well away from her if he wanted to avoid torturing himself, and he'd done so—religiously. To make it worse, he'd quickly discovered that the maid he'd hired to accompany her, especially chosen for casual character and the come-along look in her eye, was nothing but cotton stuffing and skinny limbs under her long sleeves and corset. Sheridan hated scrawny women. He supposed he'd make do, but in ten days he hadn't gotten around to it, in spite of her willingness.

Sheridan was tired of playing hero. It was a dashed dull game.

"Princess," he said, going soft and noble, "courage can't be taught. You know that."

She lowered her eyes. "I thought—I hoped there might be a method. A catechism, perhaps, to repeat when one is feeling . . . daunted."

He couldn't help a brief laugh at that. "Such as—'Hell's bells, my back's against the wall'?" He shifted, pushing away from the door and sitting down beside her on the berth. "That's generally what I find myself repeating."

She sighed. "You're teasing me. But of course you've never been daunted by anything."

He slipped his hand around hers and turned her palm upward, tracing the pads of her fingers with his thumb. She stared down at their hands. Sheridan caressed the tender skin on the inside of her wrist. She blinked up at him, biting her lower lip.

"Princess," he murmured, looking into her eyes as he brought her hand to his mouth.

It was so, so easy. He could see her melting; feel it in her trembling fingers. She looked at his face, all misty admiration as if he were a visitation from heaven. "Sir Sheridan, I—" She ran her tongue over her lip, a tender pink tip, an unconscious teasing. He gripped her hand harder. "Sir Sheridan, I want to tell you—today, what you did; I thought you were . . . magnificent. You were—"

He stopped the sentence with his thumb pressed gently against her lips. The warm touch slid sideways across her mouth. "Don't ruin it," he murmured. "Shut up."

"But I think you're the bravest, most valiant—"

"Shut up," he said, and kissed her.

He wasn't gentle. He'd intended to be, to jolly her along until she opened to him freely, but she made him angry; she made him want to crush her close until she recognized *him,* until she understood she wasn't kissing some bloody white-knight fantasy man.

He slid his hands beneath her arms and made a low sound of appreciation, pressing his lips harder into hers as he realized what he was touching: no stiff whalebone corset, but female flesh beneath the fabric, real and soft, full of generous curves and dimples. He ran his fingers upward, exploring her body as his tongue explored her mouth, so intent and excited that he hardly noticed her stiffening. He spread his palm across her torso, leaning against her. pushing her down onto the berth.

Olympia sank beneath him, shocked by his weight and strength, and the way he used them—no gallant tenderness, no delicate appeal, but a masculine body, solid and heavy and suddenly real in a way he had not been real before. She made a faint sound, striving with the unfamiliar sensation of a man's mouth wide open and tasting deeply of hers, with his dominating weight, pressing her breasts, driving the air from her lungs and spreading something warm and aching through her limbs.

She gasped for air, meeting his tongue. His hand tightened on her waist. It slid upward and opened intimately, embracing the full shape of her breast. His thumb closed against his finger, teasing her nipple through the soft sarcenet fabric.

Sharp sensation shot through her. Olympia writhed and broke away from his kiss, panting. She wanted to pull away from his hand, but he held her, sliding his thumb in a slow, coaxing rotation. Her body shuddered and her throat closed on soft sounds of agitation at the queer, piercing ecstasy of it.

Sheridan felt her reaction. He smiled wickedly and kissed her again, hard, tasting sweet excitement as his fingers drew little twitches and a deep arching of her form, innocence catalyzed into untutored lust. His reason was dissolving: he wanted to take her completely. Right here. Right now. She was driving him crazy, close and yet forbidden. He wanted the storm and he wanted the peace that came after.

She was so much smaller than he, in spite of her bountiful figure; and so soft, so soft, like a baby bird or a newborn lamb, when life in general was so deucedly full of hard edges. He left off kissing her and buried his face in the warm curve of her neck, holding her tightly in his arms.

She pushed at him feebly. "Sir Sheridan. Please don't!"

He ignored that; women were always saying nonsensical things while they clung to a man's neck. She wasn't exactly clinging, she was putting up a halfhearted struggle, but he trapped her hands and touched his tongue to her earlobe, tasting the light mingle of salt spray and lemon-scented soap. He'd bought that for her, provisioned her liberally in Ramsgate with all the things he thought females liked and a number he was fond of himself, such as the lemony soap and white satin gloves and boots to match, with delicate little toes and a row of pearl buttons down the side—completely useless aboard ship, but when he'd stood in the shop, thinking about unbuttoning them to reveal her tender ankles, his throat had gone dry at the image. So he'd laid out ten guineas for the set. She was a princess, after all.

"Please," she gasped into his ear. "Please, you can't mean to do this!"

He tilted her chin up, his own hand in sun-darkened contrast to her delicate skin. "I mean it." He could shape her fragile bones; his hand was large enough that he could spread his fingers and touch both corners of her jaw at the same time. He kissed the pink-and-cream plumpness along the edge of his open palm. "I mean it, Princess."

"Oh . . . no . . ." Her body was trembling, moving under his with an enticing confusion of invitation and denial.

He brushed her lips with his and smiled at her, finding her virginal foolishness to be fiercely seductive. He wasn't much of a hand at virgins—had never had one, in fact; had always claimed they were overrated and too damned expensive—but the feel of her, the flutter of her breath on his cheek, the fresh cushion of her skin beneath his lips . . . he felt his wits slipping, a distant sense of dismay; Palmerston and Claude Nicolas and dying young be damned. He wanted her. Before she could speak, he outlined her mouth with tiny kisses, blowing delicately between each one. "Silly . . . soft . . . beautiful . . . princess . . ."

"Don't!" A new and desperate note came into her voice. "It is unkind, and I know you can't mean to be cruel."

He nibbled her lower lip lightly between his teeth. She began to struggle like an imprisoned rabbit, pushing at him with her hands and knees. But he had all the advantage, and he used it. It was no trouble to catch both her hands in one of his and pin her lightly beneath him. He slid his free hand down her side and discovered that she'd succeeded in working her dress up high on her thigh. When he touched bare skin, he lost all track of the diplomatic importance of preserving the royal purity.

She was squeaking protest while he shaped the round curve of her thigh. He kissed her again, to keep her mouth busy, and moved his hand up until his fingers found her lovely plump belly. Excitement surged through him; he spread his hand over the luscious swell.

"You're beautiful, Princess." Against her lips, he heard his own voice, husky and intense. He frightened himself with how much he meant it. "So goddamned bloody beautiful."

"No!" She twisted wildly, breaking his hold. Her elbow caught him a violent club on the temple as she flung herself away. He grunted, seeing stars for an instant before he blinked and focused.

When he could look again, he found she'd curled herself into the corner of the berth, pulled down her dress and burst into tears. "How could you?" she cried. "How could you? I know I made you angry, but it's beneath you to mock me so!"

He nursed his bruised face and stared at her.

"I know I'm not beautiful! Why must you make a joke of it?"

"A joke!" He rolled back onto his elbow. He touched the corner of his eye gingerly and winced at the sting, directing a dark stare at the far wall. "A joke," he muttered.

She sniffed and gave a little sob. "I suppose you meant nothing by it. I just never thought that *you* would—I mean, you are so good and kind and honorable; you've gone to so much trouble on my behalf, and after what you did today—you saved all of us from bloodshed, I know it. I see now that I botched everything." Her shoulders drooped abruptly. She looked down at her knees. "But I think if I must be punished somehow, I would rather be whipped than ridiculed—like this!"

He glanced toward her sharply and sat up. "That," he said, "is the most precious pack of rubbish I've been privileged to hear in a lifetime." He caught her by the arms and hauled her upright in the berth. "Listen," he snapped, holding her still. "Stop sniveling and listen. Hear that?"

She took a shuddering breath. Over the sounds of the ship and the water came the faint pitch of a human voice, a yelp and a cry, just discernible, then an instant of silence and another distant shriek.

"Hear it?" he demanded. "If it's whipping you want, madam, toddle on deck. You can get yourself seized up and flogged along with the rest of 'em."

Her eyes grew wide. "Dear God," she whispered.

He released her and sat back, crossing his arms and propping one boot on the mahogany trimwork. "Go on! The captain won't really touch you; he's too much of an old woman for that. But you'll want to nurse their bleeding backs and weep on their noble necks, I imagine."

She clasped her hands until her fingers turned white, staring toward the door. From his position slightly behind her, Sheridan could just see her chin trembling dangerously. Her bent head revealed the nape of her neck beneath the heavy twine of rusty-gold hair.

"Don't have the stomach for it?" he asked. "And I thought you were all eagerness for violence in the name of the cause!"

She reached up and wiped at the stream of silent tears that dripped from her chin. After a moment, she put her fist to her mouth and shook her head.

Sheridan snorted. "I see. Only for 'next time,' hmm?"

She rocked from side to side, a pudgy little huddle of misery. He watched her, meditating on what a naive, foolish, high-minded piece of humbug she was, just the sort of crusading missionary he could well do without. It was her kind that started wars, with their preaching and prodding and stupid philosophizing, until his kind ended up staring down the sights of a loaded cannon.

Clearly, it wasn't going to work. Traveling with her was about as safe as chaperoning a powder keg through a house fire. Really, he thought bitterly, he ought to slip her overboard when nobody was looking; it would be doing Oriens and the rest of the world a favor.

For a long minute he gazed at her. Then, for no reason he could identify, he reached out and touched her hair. She flinched, turning those wide, wretched eyes on him. Sheridan looked into the swimming forest depths: the shadow-green intensified by tears, the lashes spiky and clinging together.

He heaved a sigh and pulled her down against him, letting her bury her face in his neck and weep for lost and silly dreams. He supposed he must have had some dreams himself once—even if he couldn't remember now what the devil they ever were.

Seven

Their first evening on Madeira, Olympia could not sleep. She'd tried, but her natural inclinations hardly fitted the role of invalid sister who went to bed before dark. She pulled the filmy lace of her dressing gown around her and stepped onto the terrace outside her island bedroom.

Red reflections of late afternoon dyed the sea and the whitewashed houses, set the town of Funchal glowing against the steep plunge of the island. The air felt like silk on her skin. Below her, the leafy tips of orange trees and banana plants rustled, and from very near came the soft ripple of notes on a Spanish guitar.

The English wine merchant had insisted on offering them his home as soon as he learned Sir Sheridan and his sister were pausing in Madeira. Traveling incognito—at least for the Hero of Navarino—was over. As soon as the mail packet docked, it seemed the whole town knew that Captain Sir Sheridan Drake was among them. Olympia's cheeks ached from smiling and accepting well-wishes.

Mr. Stothard's hospitality was enthusiastic. Dinner had turned into a party in Sir Sheridan's honor, as everyone of any stature in the English community on the island came to be introduced to one of their country's gallant champions. She could still hear the murmur of lingering guests in the garden below, though no one was visible from her lofty point of view.

Along the terrace, other doors stood open to admit the

breeze. She realized as she listened that the sound of the guitar emanated from one of them instead of from the garden. A single door down from her own . . . the room where Sir Sheridan's baggage had been placed.

She slipped closer on silent feet, crossed her arms to hold her dressing gown tighter and peered suspiciously around the doorframe.

It wasn't the dawdling servant she'd expected. It was Sir Sheridan himself—sitting propped up on the bed, his feet and chest bare, his dark head bent over the instrument as he picked out a cascade of notes.

Olympia pulled back hastily. She'd thought he was still down in the garden with the others. Her heart thumped with a wildness out of all proportion to the mild surprise. For a moment she leaned against the whitewashed wall, cooling her skin against the stone. Then she moistened her lips and peeked again, watching him through the crack between the frame and the open door.

Sunset radiance flooded the room. It caught his face in strong profile, shadow and ruddy light, his eyes a clear gray beneath black lashes. He left off playing and shifted his shoulders into a more comfortable position. Before Olympia could pull back, he looked up and saw her.

He smiled—a sideways smile, a glance like a secret shared between them, brief and heartrending. It sparked a pleasure so swift and fierce that she felt bruised inside instead of glad.

Instantly, those moments with him in her cabin rose up to make her cheeks flame.

She'd tried not to dwell on the extraordinary memory. If she allowed herself to think of it, she could still hear him whisper she was beautiful, still feel his open palm sliding up her leg, still experience the ragged breath and mortifying surge of pleasure when he touched her naked skin.

The thought of it made her want to sink through the pavement. What if he'd guessed? What if he'd realized that her reaction had been a flood of dark hunger so intense that it still haunted her every time she looked at him?

She hung back, wondering if she could just slip out of sight without saying anything.

"Polishing up on your skulking?" he asked. "I daresay that'll come in handy for the next political intrigue, but I wonder if I ought to tell you that you're about as invisible as a camel in a chicken coop?"

She held the dressing gown around her as closely as possible and stepped into full view. "Excuse me. I heard the music, and I thought perhaps someone was in your room. Someone who shouldn't be here."

"Musical thieves." Making no move to rise, he lifted the instrument and stood it against the wall. "Dastardly fellows," he added dryly. "I'd advise you to avoid violoncellists in particular; they'd as soon rob you as play a fugue." He sat up on the edge of the bed and regarded her with leisurely intensity—a faint insolent smile on his lips as he took in her dressing gown and loosened hair.

Olympia hugged herself. "Well," she said, "I shall bid you good night, then."

But she didn't move. Somehow her feet seemed rooted to the floor.

He stood up. "Good night," he said evenly.

She kept staring at his chest, at the way the sunset drew a line down the center, outlining muscle and easy strength.

"Princess," he murmured, with a strange note of emphasis in his voice. "Good night."

She drew her gaze up, to his shoulders, his jaw, his smoky eyes.

"Do you really think I'm beautiful?" she blurted, and then put her hand over her mouth in horror.

"I think," he said softly, "that if you don't take your transparent gown and your green eyes and your suggestively loose hair and get out of here, we'll both regret it."

She curled her fingers and pressed them against her mouth. "Perhaps—would you mind—" She dropped her hand and hugged herself. "I can't sleep. Might I stay a while?"

He closed his eyes with a sigh. "Lord deliver me. We wouldn't want anything to be easy, would we?" His hands opened and closed, as if they needed to crush something.

"Olympia, assume that I am giving you this advice in a friendly, avuncular tone. *Get yourself the hell away from me.*"

He stood for a long moment with his eyes closed and his jaw set.

"Are you gone yet?" he asked.

"No."

"Naturally." He exhaled with resignation. "However, I am going to ignore the fact. I am going to lie facedown on my bed. I am going to go to sleep, because I happen to like living, and I'm afraid there are a few influential people who would be interested in my painful demise if I gave you what you're so prettily asking for."

Without looking at her, he turned his back and threw himself full-length on the bed, drawing the pillow over his head.

Olympia took a step toward him and stopped. He was right, of course. She shouldn't be here. It was insane. She had no idea what she was doing or what she expected of him. But the tight trembling inside her would not relax, the memory of his hands on her skin would not recede. She looked at the long line of his body, from his bare feet and strong ankles to the shape of his legs, his hips and his broad back.

Her gaze paused. She frowned. The angled light caught something she had not seen in the gloom of Hatherleigh Hall—a very faint tracery of pale scars across his shoulders and back.

She moved closer. With one finger, she touched him. His skin was warm and smooth. She followed the line of a vertical slash across his shoulder blade and down the taut muscle over his ribs.

He shuddered. "God," he said into the crook of his arm. "Must you do this?"

"You've been flogged," she whispered. "Someone's whipped you."

His torso moved beneath her palm as he heaved a sharp sigh. "My memory is perfectly clear. You needn't think you must provide me with a concise history of my life."

"Who flogged you?" she demanded furiously. "Why?"

He knocked the pillow aside, rolled over onto one elbow and scowled at her. "Why? Because I was a dumb bastard once upon a time. World's full of fools. I'm looking at one now."

She pressed her lips together and stayed where she was. But her cheeks burned.

His gaze lingered on her face and traveled downward. He dropped his head back on the pillow, his hand over his eyes. "Let me put it this way." He looked at her under his palm. "I had a moment of madness the other night, but you're poison, my dear. Purest poison. Go away."

She stepped back as if he'd struck her. "I'm sorry. Of course. How stupid of me!"

Of course. Of course she was poison. She'd never thought she was beautiful.

"Good night," she said quickly, walking out onto the terrace, blinking hard against the sunlight. She paused at her own door, leaning against the smooth blue-painted wood, tugging the gown around her. She could feel the plump shape of her body beneath the lace. How Mrs. Plumb's exquisite lips would have curved in that pitying smile if she'd witnessed the humiliation of this moment! How she would have shaken her head, and said Olympia had brought it on herself, always dreaming of things that could not be.

She sank down on the cool tile at the foot of her bed. She bowed her head and clasped her fingers, said her daily prayer in a mumbled rush and then knelt there, her face hidden in her arms, wishing she could grow fainter and fainter until she disappeared entirely into the soft evening air.

If only it had not been Sir Sheridan. If only, when she'd chosen to mortify herself, she'd done it before anyone but him.

Poison.

And to think he'd cared for the cause of freedom so much that he'd even offered to marry her, had gallantly pretended that he had some admiration for her so as not to wound her feelings.

But she'd forfeited even chivalrous politeness now. She'd

made a disaster of things. He was angry at her, and spoke the truth. She was a miserable failure, a pathetic parody of what she'd hoped to be, unable to accomplish even the first step toward a worthy goal without making a complete bungle of it. *Poison, poison, purest poison.*

She lifted her head miserably. Outlined in a rosy glow, her shadow lay in a long ripple across the simple bed and up the whitewashed wall.

Another—taller, broader—lay superimposed upon it.

She looked over her shoulder, bit her lip and scrambled to her feet.

"Don't mind me," Sir Sheridan said. He leaned against the doorframe. "And as long as you're praying, put in a word on my behalf, will you? Sheridan Drake—Knight of the Bath, thirty-first on the captains' list, disobliging bastard and general all-around heartless dog. You may have to jostle the Old Man's memory pretty hard."

She stood staring at him through a blur.

"Don't cry," he said.

She bent her head, ashamed of the weakness, unable to stop.

He came forward, silent on bare feet. "Damn it." He pulled her into his arms, against his chest, his fingers closing with casual cruelty in her hair. "Must you turn me into a mindless clown?"

Her scalp burned under the grip that tilted her face up to his. His kiss hurt; she could taste the anger in it, but the hot need welled up the instant he touched her. He drew one hand down through her hair, pausing in the small of her back, spreading his palm until his fingertips curved around her waist. He held her that way, the peaks of her breasts pressed into his bare chest through silk and crushed lace, their shape swollen and spread against him. It made no difference what she was, or who, or why he came—it all whirled away and left only awareness: his body a bruising pressure against hers, his hand locked in her hair and the taste of him consuming her.

Sheridan explored her, softness everywhere, her breasts and velvet skin surrendering and shaping to his mouth and fingers. It was that lush promise, that sweet unconscious yielding, that drove him past the last scrap of sanity and lit the short fuse to annihilation. He was past fighting himself or her. It was all madness, all weakness and stupidity—it would get him killed, and he didn't care.

Olympia spread her hands across his bare skin. His back was taut, hard and smooth, no physical trace of the faint scars across the broad muscled expanse beneath her fingers. But she remembered. The heat and desperate longing to cherish and hold him spread to her body—she burned where she touched him; she burned all through, a hot ache that coursed from the fierce possession of her mouth down to her breasts and belly and legs—a pleasure that bloomed between her thighs and made her move and press and mold to him as if she could make him part of herself.

"Enough . . ." he mumbled, a harsh breath against her lips. "That's enough. God, this is suicide; it's got to stop."

But he held her still; he didn't stop. He kissed her throat, pushing back her hair, coiling it around his fist. She opened her mouth and allowed her own tongue to taste the hot, bare skin at the curve of his shoulder.

She felt him groan. His powerful muscles moved, salty skin sliding past her tongue as he pushed her back on the bed. He hung above her on braced arms, cursing softly even as he grasped her shoulders and bent to kiss the base of her throat, to nurse and nuzzle while his body forced hers down into the unyielding bed.

She felt his hands at her waist, pulling the dressing gown upward, tugging the fabric with rough and frantic moves. Soft air caressed her bared calves, her thighs and then her hips. He spread his palm across the round curve of her belly and made a sound of excitement, a rough note deep in his chest. His forearm drove her shoulder back against the coarse weave of the sheets as he bowed to reach her breast.

He kissed it through the silk, his tongue finding the tip, drawing it against his teeth until she arched and whimpered with the searing swell of pleasure.

Sheridan lost himself in her body, tasting the delicious heat, sliding his hand into the silky crevice between her legs. He wanted her passionate, he wanted her arching that voluptuous figure upward, begging for what he burned to give. He caressed the plump downy mound at the apex of her thigh and slipped two fingers into her alluring feminine recess, his tongue and lips closing on the peak of her breast.

She was moist and hot, insanely inviting. He drowned in her, in the virginal tightness of her, in the way she closed her legs convulsively on his invading hand. His fingers slid, pushing, exploring deeper and deeper until she began to gasp and tremble beneath him.

He tugged at her nipple, curling his fist in the satin cascade of her hair to hold her head down as she tried to lift it with a moan. His fingers met the unbroken barrier inside her. Heat flashed through him, the fierce desire to ram and force, to crush her, spread her, take her delicious softness in absolute possession.

He started to withdraw, to reach for his breeches and free the aching pressure there, but her body followed the move. Her hips curved upward. She tossed her head, pushing into his hand while her fingers raked his back. With the awkward desperation of inexperience she clutched at him, holding his head to her breast. She arched with a strangled moan—that long, lovely strain of female ecstasy—and then her body was shuddering against him in a way that made him want to explode with response.

But he didn't. From somewhere amid her collapse into panting oblivion he found a vestige of reality. He shoved her away from him, sitting up supported on a shaking arm.

He looked around.

The door to the terrace was wide open, the last of sunset still poured through, the sound of polite conversation still drifted up from the garden below.

"God Almighty," he said, and thrust himself off the bed. His body throbbed with frustrated violence; he didn't dare look at her—he knew what he would see revealed in naked and tempting disarray. Fatal—fatal to see her, fatal to stay here—he had to get hold of himself. He put a shaky hand over his eyes and muttered, "You bloody born fool, you braying ass—got your dashed brains between your legs . . . Lord—what am I doing?"

"Sir Sheridan?" Her voice was a breathless whisper behind him.

He braced against the door without turning. "Go to bed," he snapped. "Don't follow me, or I'll kill you."

Striding out onto the empty terrace, he swung into his own room, pulled the door closed and shot the bolt. He grabbed the bellpull, yanked it twice, and then again for good measure. Then he paced, prowling the sparsely furnished room, picking up an empty vase, putting it down again, dousing his face in lukewarm water from the basin, kicking the Portuguese rug back into place—moving, and moving again.

He could not do it. There was no conceivable way he could continue. Damn her and her bloody tears, her face; curse her bloody charming plump buttocks that made him get up from a safe bed and go trailing after her like some puling adolescent half-wit. He rested his elbows against the wall and locked his hands behind his head, staring at the ceiling while his body raged.

Mustafa answered his ring, sleepy and grumbling.

"I want the maid," Sheridan said shortly. "Lily. Lavinia. What the devil's her name?"

"Mary." Mustafa yawned and bowed. "It is done, my pasha." He shuffled away.

Sheridan sat down on the bed. He shifted, tugging at his breeches, a futile effort to ease the stiff discomfort inside them. He thought of Olympia, wondered if she'd gotten into bed, had a flashing picture of her lying there with her legs spread invitingly and her gown around her waist. He dropped his forehead into his hands and groaned.

There was a quiet knock at the door from the inside corridor. The maid he'd hired for Olympia slipped into his room. Sheridan looked up hopefully. She was skinny, but he was desperate. He stood up and gripped her arm.

She came willingly, no blasted tears, no naively trembling lips, no figure whatsoever—all bones, and a strong sample of Madeira's famous wine on her breath. Sheridan turned his face and put his hands on her shoulders, feeling the sharp jut of her collarbone beneath his fingers.

He couldn't help it; he thought of Olympia's smooth

white bosom, her beautiful round breasts. As the maid melted against him, he took a step back, glancing down at her face. Her eyes were closed and her mouth slack, and he had a terrible vision of a crow: black hair and thin gaping beak.

After that it was hopeless. He tried. He grasped her breast and her buttock, what there was of them, but all he felt was revolted and hot and ready to kill something with his bare hands. He pushed her off and said, "Never mind."

She stumbled back. For an instant she stared at him blankly. Then chagrin and surly resentment sharpened her thin face even further. "Never mind? I've had a hard day's work; I leave me dinner to come up here at your beck and call, and it's 'never mind,' is it?"

"Yes." He sat down in the single chair and gave her a cold stare. "Tell Mustafa you're to have something for your trouble."

"You're a bleedin' queer bastard, ain't you? I been lookin' forward to it, being bulled by a great handsome jack like you; I been waiting a bleedin' fortnight for you to get the itch, and now here you are lookin' like you got a bleedin' bread loaf in your pants, telling me never mi—"

She broke off, scampering back as he threw himself out of the chair and made a nasty swipe at her. He missed her by a mile, but his fist connected with the empty vase on the bedstand and exploded it where it sat with a smash of splintering glass.

The maid ducked and fled.

Sheridan threw himself facedown on the bed. He had to get away; his carefully planned options were disintegrating in his hands. If he played along with Palmerston and married his princess, he was a marked man. If he delivered her as a royal bride to Claude Nicolas—deflowered, possibly even pregnant, by a common sea captain—he could count his days on one finger. And if he stayed to shepherd her along, stayed to see that delectable body every day, stayed to feel her light touch on his arm as he escorted her to a chair—and worst, worst of all: stayed to endure the knowledge of what she became in his arms—if he stayed and could not have her, he'd go utterly mad.

He had to get shut of her. Somehow.

Olympia had a difficult time keeping her mind on her purpose. Indeed, she had to admit guiltily that in the past two weeks on Madeira she'd almost forgotten it, going about in this daydream that seemed to have more in common with reckless intoxication than happiness. When Mr. Stothard came out into the garden to inform her that Sir Sheridan had finally returned with their palanquin and wished to leave for their dinner engagement immediately, she rose from her reverie with pink cheeks and a shamed start.

She'd been thinking of him and that amazing thing he'd done to her . . . that intimate touch that had ended in a physical explosion like nothing she'd imagined in her life.

Thank God, he had not touched her like that again. She didn't know what she would have done if he had. But his subsequent conduct—his unerring solicitude, his special thoughtfulness, the covert smiles when no one else was watching: improbably, everything indicated that he'd formed an honorable lover's attachment to her. Those other feelings . . . they were *her* flaw, and not a very pretty one, considering that instead of treasuring the polite public proofs of his admiration and regard, in the depth of the night she relived those passionate moments in her bed over and over, imagining his hand on her body, the drift of his dark lashes downward over her skin.

While she'd been idly dreaming of such disgraceful pleasures, Sir Sheridan had been busy all afternoon with business, with *her* business, taking her jewels to the proper people to have them appraised and to determine what should be sold to finance the remainder of their journey.

He was late returning. Normally that would have made little difference in the informal Madeiran society. But tonight was different. Tonight the two of them were invited to dine out aboard H.M.S. *Terrier*, at anchor in Funchal's harbor, as special guests of Captain Francis Fitzhugh.

Her heart quickened when she saw Sir Sheridan out in

the tiny street, waiting with his foot propped up on one of the wooden runners of the palanquin while their host fussed about settling her with a shawl. Sir Sheridan shook hands and swung up onto the seat beside her. The Portuguese attendants adjusted the rope brake and gave the palanquin a shove. The sled runners began their strange grating passage downward on the cobblestoned street that was too steep and narrow for any carriage to negotiate.

"Here—" Sir Sheridan reached beneath his coat and after a moment's search brought out one of her jewels, a sapphire pendant tinged with a rare heliotrope color and surrounded by diamonds. "This will flatter that gown, don't you think?"

Olympia, who had never cared a thing for what jewel would flatter what, found herself blushing with pleasure and self-consciousness as he fastened the clasp around her neck. He touched the stone, his fingers brushing the skin just above her neckline as he turned the pendant and laid it flat.

"Thank you," she said, and bent her head to cover the blaze of her feelings.

For her to be in love, body and soul, with Sheridan Drake was the most natural thing possible. *Not* to be in love with him would have been absurd. But she'd always assumed her devotion would be unrequited, a silent adoration from afar, as befitted a hero and a pudgy, plain girl with unkempt eyebrows.

But for him to want her, to be attracted to her, to actually return her love . . .

She didn't believe it. At first she really had thought it a form of mockery, those moments when he'd kissed her and called her beautiful—for no reason, for no logical motive she could fathom, except that he meant it. He'd said he meant it. He wouldn't lie. He'd held her while she cried, and no one had ever done that before.

It was unthinkable. It was a dream.

Sir Sheridan Drake—gallant, courageous and admired, impossibly handsome and fascinating; the greatest naval hero of his generation—Sheridan Drake was in love with Olympia.

With *her.*

It was no wonder she felt intoxicated. She almost felt frightened.

In the last of daylight, their odd conveyance passed beneath the exotic shadows of tall blooming cacti and palms. As the street widened out near the base of the mountain, Sir Sheridan said something in Portuguese and the palanquin halted. He put his hand on her arm. "Shall we walk from here?"

Olympia's heart froze somewhere between delight and terror. They'd had moments alone, temporary instants of privacy in the past two weeks, but never long enough for more than a word or a brief touch—nothing outwardly different from normal sibling affection. It was only in carefully timed whispers and significant glances that he said more.

He was looking at her now. She swallowed and ducked her head and nodded.

He helped her out, dismissed the attendants and took her arm, guiding her toward the gentler slope of one of the side streets while the palanquin was already moving down past them with its peculiar grate of wood on stone.

"If something should happen to me," he said without preamble, "I want you to go directly to Captain Fitzhugh and put yourself under his protection. He will conduct—"

"Happen to you!" she exclaimed, stopping in the street. "What do you mean?"

"He will conduct you to the British consul and represent your situation," he continued calmly. "You must tell him the truth first, of course. Be certain to make it clear that Lord Palmerston himself is concerned that you're properly safeguarded."

Olympia gaped at him in consternation. "But what could happen to you? We shan't even be here in a few days' time! Nothing will happen. Whatever makes you speak that way?"

He looked past her, out over the harbor, where *Terrier*'s decks glittered in welcome, her lanterns shimmering red and green and white on the quiet water and lighting the dour outline of the only other large ship in port—a convict transport on its way to Australia. There was a boat approaching the dock, no doubt to greet them at the quay and take them aboard *Terrier.* Olympia had been pleased and proud at the attention Captain Fitzhugh had shown to Sir Sheridan while the survey ship paused at Madeira: calling on him at their host's home four separate times and now preparing this special dinner on board in his honor.

Sir Sheridan looked back down at her. "Young Fitzhugh's a bit headstrong, but I reckon he'll be steady enough in a pinch," he said obliquely. "You'd be perfectly safe if you wished to take ship with him, but unfortunately he's bound for Patagonia and the Tierra del Fuego."

"Nonsense." There was a shrill note in her voice. "It isn't a very good joke to play upon me, saying such things." She started to walk ahead.

He caught her arm and turned her to face him. Warm light from a distant doorway cast a faint illumination on his features. His face was serious, his beautiful mouth set in moody shadow. "It's not a joke, my princess," he murmured. "There's danger here—for me only. Not for you."

"No." She drew in a breath. "No. If there's some kind of danger, we share it. You won't send me away for my safety and face it alone. I won't go."

He touched her cheek. "Listen to me. I'm afraid the world doesn't revolve around you alone, my dear. I have the utmost concern for your safety, which is why I speak of possibilities." He hesitated and then smiled a little. "Rest assured the only danger to you is the remote chance you might lose your stalwart champion. Let's have no romantic faradiddle about standing together in the face of peril. You do as I tell you. This is a small matter that is out of your scope."

"What is it?"

He shook his head and took her arm again. "Just remember Fitzhugh."

She planted her feet against him. "What is it?"

"Come along, my love. We shall not want to be late."

"Sheridan," she hissed. "Tell me. I have a right to know."

She could see the glint of silver as his eyes narrowed. "You make too much of it. I wished only to be certain you're prepared to act sensibly should the worst happen. I have no intention of allowing it to occur."

"But there *is* some danger."

"Life at best is always a hazard, madam."

"I wish you would not call me 'madam' in that odious way! Or play games with words. If you won't admit me as a companion in arms, then respect my own honor, at least! Am I to stand by while this unnamed threat strikes you down and then go merrily on my way, after you have done so much for me?" She stared up at him, gripping his arms. "Tell me what's wrong. I'll do nothing without your leave, I swear it. But I should know."

For a long moment he said nothing. The chilly night breeze ruffled his hair. Olympia felt her heart fill up with adoration and fear for him.

"*Sthaga*," he said simply, at last.

Eight

Her fingers tightened. "My God," she breathed. She looked compulsively over her shoulder into the waiting dark. "The Stranglers!"

"Not just here, actually."

There was an undertone of dryness in his voice. He gently pried her hands off his arms and turned her again to walk downhill. He seemed easy and unconcerned, but to Olympia, the night had suddenly taken on eyes.

"Are you certain? How do you know?" she whispered.

"I know," he said in a normal voice. "I told you about them, don't you recall?"

She recalled. How he had been leading a shore party to a fort somewhere in India, carrying gold for the paymaster, when he and the marines had been struck down in the jungle by cholera. How a young, wealthy Brahman boy and his servants had found Sheridan between delirium and unconsciousness, the sole survivor, and stayed to nurse him: forcing him to take water and salt, carrying him on the boy's own pony when Sheridan could not walk, showing him how they'd kept the government gold locked up safely when he was out of his wits and too weak to care. Feringheea was the boy's name. He'd been no older than fourteen, traveling to visit his uncle. Like many high-caste Indians, Sir Sheridan had said, young Feringheea spoke English perfectly, warning of bandits and urging Sheridan to stay with their well-armed party until they reached the English garrison at Calcutta.

Oh, yes, Olympia remembered. Sir Sheridan had a quiet, composed way of telling his stories that was chilling in its effectiveness. She could vividly imagine how Feringheea had helped Sheridan onto the pony and walked beside him all the way to each campsite, through the rotting, steaming jungle with parakeets and monkeys shrieking above; she could see him clinging weakly to the beast, feel how it must have felt when he passed out on the pony's neck and woke to find Feringheea holding onto him so that he would not fall. She could taste the charred flavor of the chapati the Hindus shared with him, smell the open fire, sense the way his strength grew as the days passed and he recovered.

At that point in the narrative, he'd drawn a yellow scarf from his pocket and begun to toy with it. Sipping occasionally at his wine, he'd seemed distantly thoughtful, almost bored, while his listeners—including Olympia seated next to him—had been leaning forward in their chairs, waiting for the shouts and howls of the murdering thugs who were sure to attack the little party in the jungle at any moment.

"But you don't wish to be wearied by this long tale," he'd said. "Let's talk of something else."

Everyone protested vigorously. He smiled and shrugged, drawing a Portuguese escudo from his pocket and examining the large coin absently, turning it over and over in his hand. The yellow scarf dripped like a banner from his fist. "Perhaps Mrs. Stothard would play the pianoforte instead," he suggested, rising. He leaned on the windowsill just behind Olympia, adjusting the shutters to let in more breeze.

"Absolutely not," their host's aunt said resolutely. "At dinner you promised me thugs in the drawing room, and I shall have them."

From the corner of her eye Olympia could just see him, still playing with the yellow silk. He dropped the escudo inside a knotted fold and tightened the scarf around it.

"Very well," he said. "Where was I?"

"About to be strangled," Mr. Stothard said cheerfully.

Sir Sheridan smiled. "Ah. The night of the thug attack,

then. We'd eaten; we were sitting around the fire while Feringheea played the sitar and sang. Have you heard the sitar? No? No one?'' He paused and then said quietly, ''I suppose I'm something of a musical enthusiast. I found it wonderful; indescribable, the harmonies they use, but I won't prose on about that. I was well enough to ask him to teach me something of the instrument. It's a pleasant memory, when I think of it—sitting on the strongbox with that great tall thing they play across my lap. There was a little owl chirping up above us . . . and one of Feringheea's servants standing by, on watch and armed to the teeth. We were feeling pretty safe. I confess I was just glad to be alive, grateful as a groveling peasant to that amazing boy.'' Sheridan shook his head. ''I'll never forget him; he was nobility personified, courteous and patient, leaning right over my shoulder so he could show me how to place my fingers on the strings. He'd just called for tobacco to share between us.'' He stopped and looked up. ''Mrs. Stothard, I should close this window. I'm afraid a bat has got in.''

Olympia followed everyone else's glance, looking up into the shadows above.

And suddenly she was strangling; a band of fire gripped her neck and stopped her air, a terrible clutching sensation swelled in her chest, demanding air that could not come.

She grabbed desperately at the silken noose that had flashed around her throat. Strong fingers caught her wrists and dragged them away. She writhed in instinctive convulsion for air, unable to break free, panicking as her vision clouded—but then abruptly the pressure loosened and she could breathe again.

Sir Sheridan chuckled behind her amid a shocked flurry of exclamations. ''Can't manage it myself. I'd need a *shumseea*—a hand-holder—to keep her trapped until she died. That's what the servants were for. He had two, not including his instructor who stood guard, because he was still young and I was to be his first murder for his goddess.'' The scarf slithered away from her neck, leaving her trembling. ''An object lesson,'' he said calmly. ''Never trust a Good Samaritan on the road in India.''

"Good God." Mrs. Stothard hurried to Olympia's side. "My dear Miss Drake, are you quite all right? Sir Sheridan, your poor sister is in no case for such—such— Oh, *dear!* I must say I believe that was a most dangerous and completely specious demonstration!"

"I understood that you wished for thugs in the drawing room," he said innocently.

Olympia laughed, still shaky, rubbing her throat and trying to brush Mrs. Stothard away. "Yes—I'm perfectly well—it was nothing. I was only startled. Please, don't scold him. I think it was a very good demonstration."

"Certainly graphic," their host said. "You don't mean to have us believe it was this Feringheea—this child who befriended and nursed you—who was a murderer?"

"*Sthaga.* It means deceiver." Sir Sheridan sat down again, giving Olympia a brotherly hand-squeeze. "Was I too much a villain, dear? You really are all right?"

"Perfectly," she repeated, even though her heart was still pounding in her ears. That instant of strangulation when she couldn't break free of his hands had been horribly frightening, but she wasn't about to admit it aloud. Besides, it had indeed given her a true idea of what Sir Sheridan must have experienced, alone and undefended in an Indian jungle instead of in a polite drawing room. "Did the helpers seize your hands like that?" she asked weakly. "How did you get away?"

He shrugged. "I'm a sadly suspicious brute, I'm afraid. The whole situation puzzled me." He wrapped the scarf around his fist. "I found out later that an initiate always chooses someone old or weak as his first victim. They aren't allowed to kill someone who is ill, so they had to wait until just the right moment, for an omen to show when I was well but still feeble. The little owl told them." His mouth curved slyly. "I suppose I had it fooled, too."

"You knew they were thugs?" Mr. Stothard demanded.

"No. It was—Lord, a decade ago, at least. The Company barely even knew the thug fraternity existed, and I'd never head of 'em. I just thought it was dashed queer, all that sympathy and friendship."

"But they saved your life, did they not? And cared for

you so well,'' Mrs. Stothard protested. ''You must be cynical indeed, to have mistrusted them after that.''

He looked at her for a moment. After a little silence, he said merely, ''We've lived in different worlds, ma'am.''

''So you fought them off, did you?'' their host said. ''Good show. Four at once?''

Sheridan spread his hands. ''Nothing so stirring as that, I fear. I'd not be here now but that all of a sudden they let go of me and jumped back like I'd burned 'em. We all stood there staring at each other while that little owl flew past, hooting softly.'' He cocked his head, looking down at the yellow silk. ''I had a lucky inspiration then. I don't know why, but I guessed their problem had something to do with the owl. I pointed up at it, and by God, if just at that moment it didn't land on a branch and stop its cry. The poor fellows were terrified.''

''Of an owl?'' one of the guests asked in bemusement.

''They had little reason to fear me. The *sthaga* don't fail once they close in for a kill. But they live in dread of their goddess's omens—and the *soft* cry of an owl is the darkest of all. Not that they're stupid. They don't let victims free to prattle; they can't afford it. They'd have talked themselves out of worrying about hell itself if I'd given 'em the time.'' He shrugged and smiled. ''So I said it meant I was to join their band.''

Yes . . . Olympia well remembered his account of the secret society of stranglers who murdered for Kali, the goddess of destruction. She'd listened in horror to all he'd learned of their ways in the year he'd spent with Feringheea, wandering lost in the vast Indian plains and jungles, driven by their omens from one place to another in search of victims to befriend and kill, forced to play a character in their deceptions—always a just-recovered Englishman accompanying the party for protection in order to encourage other travelers to trust them.

He'd had to pretend he was fully one of them, wishing to participate in all the rituals and training. But they were always suspicious. He was watched so closely he was unable to leave or betray the band, never knew when he lay down if he would be strangled in his sleep, until finally he escaped and managed to reach an English magistrate. When he'd testified against the gang, the magistrate and everyone else had called him overwrought from his illness and ordeals—no one would believe him, or admit that they did—and Feringheea and his followers had gone free to murder again.

And she remembered, too, the question neither she nor any of the other listeners had found the nerve to ask—whether he had passed his apprenticeship in that year and used the yellow *rumal* himself. Of course, she was sure he hadn't, so there was no need to ask. Or for him to tell . . . which he did not.

He merely drew a vivid picture of the thugs' superstition-ruled life and laws. They must never kill a woman; they must bury their victims with proper rituals and never allow a drop of blood to touch the ground. He translated the haunting words of the hymn to terrible blood-drinking Kali: "Because You love the Burning-Ground, I have made a burning-ground of my heart—that You, the Dark One, may haunt it in eternal dance . . ."

He explained some of the signals: *bajeed* meant all was well, and was the order to strangle, just as *tombako ka lo*, bring tobacco, was also a signal to murder as the befriended travelers sat singing around the fire. Sir Sheridan, with his placid account, had everyone starting at shadows before the evening was over.

Now, in the island night, Olympia was equally nervous. She had a difficult time keeping herself from pressing up against Sir Sheridan in a most craven fashion.

"Really," he said mildly, loosening her taut fingers on his arm again. "I'm sorry I even mentioned it. I had no idea you'd be overset. I told you that they swore to avenge themselves if I escaped and betrayed them, but it's been ten years, after all, and half a world away. I've heard that fellow Sleeman's nearly wiped them out in India anyway. I imagine the signs are a coincidence."

"Oh, yes," she said. "No doubt."

He looked down at her as they walked, smiling. "You aren't convinced. But think—how could they have found me?"

"They might have followed us from Wisbeach."

He chuckled. "How? On the same two ships? I think I would have noticed."

"You said that they're masters of disguise."

"They aren't that good. They never take off their turbans, for one thing. They might be inconspicuous in Bengal, but I'm afraid they'd have stood out a bit in a milliner's ship in Ramsgate."

It did begin to seem unlikely there were thugs about, what with ten years and turbans. Olympia relaxed her grip a little.

"Good girl," he said. "I shouldn't have brought up such nonsense. Here's our naval escort to greet us in style."

Sheridan sat at table in *Terrier*'s cabin, feeling rather like a piece of worn leather, poorly kept and getting stiff at the joints in comparison to these two fair flowers of youthful fanaticism.

Captain Fitzhugh was hardly older than Princess Olympia herself—not a complete fool but managing to conceal the fact, torn between the dignity of his first command and eagerness to impress Captain Sir Sheridan Drake and his sister. He talked too loud and gave his opinion on every possible subject. His only redeeming quality was a modicum of sense: his opinions weren't hopelessly stupid as long as he kept off religion, which he generally didn't. But even Sheridan would admit he was a good sailor and an exacting hydrographer, attributes to be earnestly respected in all circumstances. Well, in all circumstances except court-martial over running one of His Majesty's precious ships aground, in which case an inaccurate navigational chart was a convenient document to possess. Sheridan had always kept several on hand.

With Olympia, Fitzhugh was painfully polite. The color beneath his freckles heightened and he looked quickly away every time she caught his eye. He'd even ordered some poor naturalist away from his dinner in the wardroom to come up and wax poetic over the geological rarity of the heliotrope sapphire at her throat. Judging from the prevailing symptoms, Sheridan had an idea that Captain Fitzhugh actually cherished a notion of becoming his brother-in-law. It seemed deplorably apparent that the fellow had not truly called four separate times and invited Sheridan to dinner just to bask in the light of his charming company—even if he was a hero.

Young pup. Sheridan looked around the plush cabin, fitted out in accordance with Fitzhugh's wealthy background, and indulged in a bit of cordial scorn. He inspected the crystal goblet, hoping to find a chip in lieu of something really sordid, like weevils in the wine or a great-uncle hung for treason and sodomy. He wished he could inform the pink-cheeked, ink-stained upstart captain that there'd be no princess in *his* marriage bed, in spite of the fact that he'd read all those radical French rabble-rousers she was always prosing on about.

But of course she could get herself leg-shackled to Fitzhugh if she cared to. It would make no difference to Sheridan what the devil she did, thank the gods, once she was off his hands. He knew Fitzhugh's sort, the poor, dull dog, all sermons and chivalry and righteous beds of roses with the ladies. He'd never be bright enough to take improper advantage of her. Really, it was a wonder the human race managed to reproduce itself.

Sheridan watched the two of them talking shyly together in the lamplight, and felt old. His left knee ached. It seemed early days for rheumatism—he was only thirty-six, for God's sake. Then the thought occurred to him that he couldn't be thirty-six, that it was late January . . . the twentieth, the twenty-first? The twenty-first of January, 1828 . . . and a frowning calculation informed him that he wasn't thirty-six, or even thirty-seven. His birthday had been yesterday. He was thirty-eight.

Old.

"I'll never forget that," Fitzhugh was saying. He suddenly looked toward Sheridan with an expectant expression. "Nor you, sir, I daresay."

Sheridan put down his glass. "Quite a skirmish," he said vaguely, having no idea what Fitzhugh was talking about.

"It was in '22," Fitzhugh said to Princess Olympia. "I was a midshipman of the foretop."

Naturally Fitzhugh would remember his precise station. Sheridan had to count backward underneath his napkin to figure out which ship he'd been commanding.

"Dear old *Repulse,*" Fitzhugh said, supplying the answer with a faraway sigh. "How long ago it seems," he added, as if 1822 had taken place a few decades before the Deluge.

"Six years," Sheridan said peevishly. "And she leaked like the devil on the starboard side."

Fitzhugh turned to Olympia with a confiding air of amusement that made Sheridan want to growl. "Your brother, Miss Drake, never took command of a ship but that the whole of the navy started to call her the Glee Club. We had to sing madrigals and tie off our reef points at the same time."

Sheridan steepled his hands and looked through them at his young host. "Perhaps you should have requested a more dignified berth."

"Never," Fitzhugh declared with unexpected fierceness. "I was proud to serve aboard *Repulse.* I know why you insisted on it—if we knew our drill well enough to perform those horrendous tangled melodies at the same time, we knew it well enough to keep our heads in a crisis. We could outsail and outmaneuver anything afloat. Under your command, she was the most disciplined fighting ship I ever saw."

Not that you've seen such a bloody lot of 'em, Sheridan thought. *Laying it on a bit thick, old man.*

But the princess swallowed it whole, of course, gazing at Sheridan with an enraptured expression. With his calculated campaign of romance, he had her so infatuated with him that she'd probably eat grass if he informed her she was a sheep.

She'd choke on the diet soon enough, he reckoned. She'd marry Fitzhugh or be off home where she belonged with her little sheep's tail between her legs. The best thing for everyone, including himself. The best thing by far, and no reason to get so damned depressed about it, just because he'd gotten old without noticing and hadn't been able to work in a decent farewell tumble with her before he cut line.

He glanced at the chronometer mounted behind Fitzhugh's head and judged it time to take their leave. He said so, and then waited with concealed impatience through Princess Olympia's expression of thanks to their host. She was being overly profuse, he thought; Fitzhugh was young, but hardly all *that* handsome.

He wasn't even a knight.

The pipes shrilled a salute as they left the deck: a nice courtesy for a retired officer. Sheridan raised his hand and touched his hat, back in charity with Fitzhugh for the gesture. Onshore, he smiled down at his princess and suggested that they walk along the quay a bit before calling for the palanquin.

He felt a small twinge at her bashfully eager reaction to the proposal. She was such a willing dupe—the devil himself would feel an instant of remorse. It was a suitably dark night, he'd made certain of that when laying his plans. The quay was lit only by reflections off the water. The soft illumination made her look exceptionally pretty, with her shining eyes and tremulous smile still aglow in the aftermath of Fitzhugh's admiration. The damned fellow had practically drooled on her, always leaning over in that innocent-confiding way of his to look down her dress when he spoke to her. Maybe he wasn't such a slow-top as he let on. In the cool breeze her ripe, sturdy body was warm and provocative, close enough to brush Sheridan's coat front.

"Perhaps you should take off the sapphire and let me carry it," he suggested. "What a damper it would be for you to lose it out here in the dark."

"That would be vexing, wouldn't it?" She stood still while he unclasped the chain and slipped it beneath his coat. "You think of everything."

"Everything," he said, and hoped to hell he had.

He took her arm and began to walk, humming an old country air and thinking depraved thoughts as they strolled along the silent waterfront. Her fingers moved softly on his sleeve. By degrees, she pressed a little closer to him. Sheridan smiled. He allowed his arm to slip around her waist.

"I like to hear you sing," she said suddenly, keeping her face down.

His step broke for a half instant. He looked down at the top of her head in surprise. "Sing?"

"At night, when you leave your terrace door open."

He cleared his throat uneasily. He hadn't thought it was loud enough for her to hear. "I didn't mean to disturb anyone."

"It doesn't disturb me. I think it's lovely. I lie in bed and listen until I fall asleep."

That image conjured the most peculiar sensation of lust and self-consciousness in him. He nodded at a pair of passersby, the two Jewish men who'd boarded the ship with them at Ramsgate. In the moonless dark, their faces were nothing but dim, pale shapes beneath the broad hats.

" 'Greensleeves' is my favorite," she murmured.

They had reached the end of the quay. Sheridan stopped. No one in his entire life had ever told him that they cared to hear him sing.

She looked up into his face. "Will you sing it for me?"

He just stood there, feeling incredibly awkward, as if he'd just been caught cheating at a penny-point card game. As if part of his heart were on the pavement between their feet.

"Well," he mumbled.

She nestled her cheek into his shoulder, a shy, quick move. In her soft husky voice she began to sing—not entirely on key.

Sheridan closed his eyes. This would bring back his bad dreams, damn it; this kind of thing always did. Why did she have to do it? Curse her, curse her—the little rough quaver of notes, half muffled in his coat, wrenched at him in a way that was preposterous. She turned toward him, sliding her fingers through his.

He swallowed. Really, it was too much; her droning would curdle milk. She ought to be muzzled.

In a whisper he let his voice follow hers. Just to drown

her out. But the music caught him up as it always did; he found his own pitch amid her wanderings, and heard her leave off as he sang in quiet notes, with his arms around her, lost in the slow, gentle rhythm of the old, old song.

> "Alas, my love, you do me wrong
> To cast me off discourteously . . ."

He hummed another verse, swaying her softly with his forehead pressed to hers. Then he lifted her chin and kissed her, carrying the last hushed note deep in his throat. From the corner of his eye he could see dim figures drifting toward them.

He held her, once and hard, and let her go. He stepped back, creating a necessary distance.

Olympia gazed up at him. She could barely see his face, but it seemed to her he had a strange expression: ardent and chagrined at once—like a sulky, uncertain angel glowering faintly at her from the shadows, bestower of a forbidden miracle and wary of the response.

As she started to smile, the night burst into chaos.

Nine

The dark coalesced into something alive, moving fast and brutally. Olympia's scream choked to a squeak, killed by a gag rammed into her mouth as Sheridan's face vanished. She heard his startled grunt, but everything seemed to have gone murky in front of her, blocked by something blacker than the night itself. A merciless grip on her hands held her paralyzed, then just as suddenly let her go. She fell sideways under a hard push, hit the pavement and gasped for wind through the gag and the jolt of pain.

The sounds of scuffle filled the darkness. "Wait," Sheridan exclaimed amid the confusion. Something pale and narrow flashed, catching the dim light. "What the dev—"

His voice ceased in a gargle of sound.

Sthaga.

A shot of terror sent her upright, half strangled by the gag. She lunged toward the sound of Sheridan and the shapeless nightmare attackers, throwing all her weight into the assault. Her hands met rough wool and sent the body beneath it reeling. For an instant she saw Sheridan's face in the shadow, twisted with wild emotion. He whirled, his arm outstretched, his shoulder taking all of them down in a bruising tangle.

Olympia landed on one of the thugs. A gasp whooshed out of him and his black headgear rolled away to reveal a turban and a familiar bearded face. She sobbed for air through the gag, trying to grab at his slithering shape beneath her. But something lifted her bodily from behind, hauling her aside. Sheridan dropped her as if she were a puppy and threw himself after the assassin.

He missed. She heard him hit the pavement and swear at the darkness. "Bloody—bunglers!" He panted hoarsely. His boots scraped on the stone quay and his shape rose above her. "By God—those jokers were trying to *kill* me!"

Olympia squeaked behind her gag and managed to rise to her knees. She stumbled into him and leaned against his leg, wilting with shock and suffocation.

His hand went around her head. He hissed, and she felt him drop down beside her. "Bastards!" He tore at the gag. "Those stupid bastards! I didn't—I never meant—" He bit off the words and pulled the gag free. "Hell. Jesus Christ. Are you all right?"

She gulped in air. "It was the—Jewish men!" Her voice came out a pathetic little whistle. "Not Jewish—I mean—the disguise—on the ship—you know!"

His hands froze on her shoulders. He looked down at her, and back into the darkness where their attackers had fled. "Jewish?"

"No . . . no. Disguised . . . their—hats! They were—on the ship—and tonight . . . on the dock. They've been following you!"

He ran his hand through his hair. "On the ship? That's impossible."

"Their hats!" she insisted. "I fell on one, and his hat came—off." She drew a desperate breath. "He had on a turban!"

Sheridan looked at her sharply. In the very faint light, she could see his expression change as understanding dawned on him. "Oh, God," he groaned, and felt his throat. "Who'd have thought it?"

"You saw the—signs." She still didn't have her breath back. "We should have—taken them more—seriously. Come on, I think we should go instantly—"

A new voice, heavily accented, interrupted her. "Trouble, senhor?" There were footsteps coming toward them from the dark. "You need help?"

Sir Sheridan stiffened as if someone had struck him. For a long instant he stared in the direction of the sound.

"Senhor?" It was a second voice. "We see you and the senhora go this direction. It is not safe."

Olympia turned. The newcomers were close, but still almost lost in the darkness. She thought there were several, from the sound of their boots.

Sheridan brushed his palm across her hair. "Here's help," he said. "Just sit and rest, and I'll have them bring the palanquin."

He rose and moved away before she could protest, his dark outline blurring into the night with the others.

"Bajeed," one of the new strangers said in a conversational tone. *"Tombako ka lo."*

Olympia finally gave in to despair and grief at four a.m. and let them carry her home from the search.

Sheridan Sheridan Sheridan—

She closed her eyes on hysterical tears, leaning her face into her hand. She could not believe it. Not killed, not Sheridan, not strangled by those horrifying savages . . .

"My dear," Mrs. Stothard murmured, putting her arm around Olympia.

"Wait until dawn," Mr. Stothard said more heartily. "Don't underestimate your brother, Miss Drake. He's come out of worse scrapes than this."

But he knew. They all knew. They'd all heard the truth from Sheridan's own lips: the thugs killed and vanished with their victim, mangling and burying the body with ritual and guile.

Hope was vain. Waiting was futile. If Sheridan had escaped, he would be here with her now.

But he'd blended into the dark on the quay, and she'd heard the fatal command and a peculiar shuffle and then nothing. By the time she had scrambled to her feet and lurched in the direction of the noise, he was gone.

They were all gone, those faceless voices. Vanished into night and silence. The search by torchlight had found nothing but his hat.

"You must try to sleep." Mrs. Stothard's hand was

trembling as she drew Olympia toward her bedroom. "I've had Cook make a tisane."

In a bleak haze, Olympia drank the herbed tea and submitted to the maid who helped her undress. Then she sat on the bed and stared into the dark.

Sheridan, Sheridan . . .

It seemed so impossible, so sudden and unreal. One moment warm and close, his voice a welcome comfort in the darkness, and then . . .

Not there. Vanished. Gone.

Dead.

She remembered his description of what the thugs did to their strangled victims before burial, the gashes and disfigurement in the name of Kankali, the Man-Eater. Olympia's breathing grew quick and shallow and her head reeled.

Someone scratched at the door. It opened slowly and a voice whispered, "*Ismahiili*, ma'am. Excuse me. Excuse me."

She recognized Mustafa's high-pitched voice and took a deep breath, trying to clear her head. "Come in," she mumbled through the blur.

He slipped through, shielding his candle and bowing with every step. He sank to his knees, a huddle of white cotton galabiyya and red fez, and touched his forehead to the floor at her feet. "*Emiriyyiti*—my princess—" He lifted his head, his brown face tracked with glistening tears and misery. "It is true?"

She bit her lip. Her throat closed. She nodded and then squeezed her eyes shut, rocking from side to side.

Mustafa made a little whimper. He caught her ankles and pressed his face against her slippered feet. A groan of anguish burst from him, swelling into a wail that seemed to fill the room with grief. It echoed off the walls, died away and was taken up again, strangely beautiful and haunting in Mustafa's sweet soprano voice.

She listened. The lament was like wind from an empty desert, lonely and stark. Tears slid down and flooded her mouth. She felt as if the desert were inside her, dark and still and lifeless forever.

Mustafa's mournful voice cracked and faded away on a sob. She bent and touched his shoulder. He raised his face, leaning his cheek against her knee like a child begging for comfort. "*Emiriyyiti*, what will we do?"

"I don't know," she whispered.

"I was not there. Allah took him, and I was not there. O my master, forgive me, I was lazy and sleeping, I am a sloth and a dog, the son of swine, an eater of pork; *ya allaah*, I should have been there!"

She shook her head. "It wouldn't have made any difference. You couldn't have done anything."

"I should have been there! He saved my life and the life of the Great Sultan, and the Sultan gave me to him and told me to keep him safe and well. Twenty years I have followed him." His voice rose, quivering hysterically. "I am lost! I will kill myself."

"Mustafa! Don't be silly." She gave him a shake.

His small frame trembled. "You did not know him, O Beloved. He was a great man; the Sultan loved him like a brother. If we were in Stamboul, Mahmoud the Everlasting, the Sultan of All the World, would strangle us both for failing to keep him safe."

She took a shuddering breath, feeling empty and stupid with crying, too battered to really care what Mustafa said.

"Sheridan Pasha," Mustafa moaned, his face crumpled in grief. "My pasha! Oh, if you could have seen him when he was the Sultan's slave—when he was only a half-grown boy, wild as a Bedouin warrior and beautiful as a woman, and they beat him every day for impertinence."

Olympia finally focused on Mustafa's words. "A slave," she whispered dully. "He was slave to a sultan?"

The little servant jerked his head up, as if he had just recalled she was there. He looked frightened. "O Beloved, I am a liar! Never listen to me."

Olympia looked at him in bleak question.

He bowed his head. "But it does not matter now."

She stared unblinking down at the small Egyptian. "No," she said slowly, "not now."

They sat together, Mustafa weeping quietly against her knee. After a time, he said, "I cannot even bury him, my pasha.'' He straightened. ''We should speak of him, then. So that Allah may know he is not abandoned and forgotten.''

She closed her eyes. It was hard to bear, when all she wanted was to be alone, but she tried to remember that Mustafa had been with him far longer than she.

''He was a brave man, *Emiriyyiti,*'' Mustafa said in a hushed voice. ''You saw him die. Will you tell me how he met his end, so I will know? So that I may send to the Sultan a tale of my pasha's courage?''

''I don't know how he died,'' she said through her fingers. ''It was dark.''

''But he was like a lion?'' Mustafa said plaintively.

''Yes.'' She wiped at her tears with the back of her hand. ''I'm sure he was.''

''Like a lion. Like a fierce black djinn, he cut them down, but they were too many against one, cowardly dogs! His sword was quicksilver—two he killed, and then five, but more sprang up to overwhelm him—''

''He didn't have a sword.'' A surge of brooding anger flared within Olympia's grief. She twisted her nightgown in her fists. ''He wasn't even armed!''

''Animals. Barbarian filth! The Sultan of All the Earth will visit his revenge upon them; they cannot hide. Tell me what they looked like, *Emiriyyiti*, and I will set the Sultan's wrath on the foul pigs.''

''I don't know,'' she cried. ''I don't know!'' With her forehead bowed in her hand, she described what had happened, how the two in their Jewish disguise had struck first and run away, and then Sheridan had walked in trust to meet the others in the dark.

''He went to strangers?'' Mustafa looked uncertain. ''After he had been attacked?''

''Yes. He thought they were going to help us.''

''But he had no weapon, O Beloved.''

She shook her head.

Mustafa sat back on his heels. ''That was unwise.''

''It's my fault. I should have stopped him. I should have insisted we go back to safety as soon as he said he'd seen the signs of *sthaga.*''

The servant's eyes widened. He cocked his head like a small brown sparrow. "My princess, do you mean that Sheridan Pasha had warning of this?"

"He told me he'd seen signs. Just this evening. He wanted me to go to Captain Fitzhugh if something should—something should ha-ha-happen—" Her voice dissolved into a whimper. "What difference does it make? If only I could go back and change it!"

Mustafa hesitated, his smooth-shaven brow wrinkled beneath his fez. "*Shidi heelik, Emiriyyiti.* Be strong. Allah has willed." He stroked her hand and kissed it. "I myself will go to the Sultan. Sheridan Pasha will not be unrevenged, I swear it. O Beloved, do not weep so! We will go together. We will take the best of your jewels, the jewels of a princess, and make a gift to the Sultan, so he will know our pasha was the greatest pasha—"

"I can't even do that!" She pulled her hand away. "They're gone. He had them all with him."

"No, no, do not fear that. He gave them to me to keep safe."

"He had them this evening," she said dully. "He was going to find out which of them would buy us passage to Rome."

Mustafa shook his head decisively. "No; you are mistaken, *Emiriyyiti.* He said nothing of that to me, and only I know where they are hidden." He felt at his breast to where he always wore the golden crescent and star amid the voluminous white folds of cotton.

Olympia covered her eyes, desperate to be alone, fighting irrational annoyance and the urge to push him away. "Never mind! I assure you he had them. He gave me the heliotrope sapphire to wear. I even showed it to a naturalist aboard Captain Fitzhugh's ship."

Mustafa made a strange noise and looked down so sharply that his fez almost slid off, his mouth growing round as he gazed at the white front of his galabiyya. For a stunned moment he stared at Olympia and then scrambled to his feet, disappearing silently out the door.

Olympia felt instantly guilty for her sharp words. She gazed after him in misery. Just as she was about to follow and beg him to pardon her unkindness, he reappeared at the door.

He stood there an instant, his brown face flushed, his small body shaking so hard that his deep sleeves fluttered. The sound that came out of him was like the hissing of a mad cat.

"Christian pig!" he shrieked. "Jackal! Brother of vile and unspeakable things! *He is not dead!*" Mustafa tore his fingers down his face, leaving fiery marks. "Foul offspring of snakes and crocodiles!" He flung himself against the wall and pounded it; leapt up and down, stomping his bare feet in a furious dance. "He has left us! I throw his entrails to the dogs! I abandon him in the desert! I stab him and spit in his face!" His voice reached a shrill of passion as he clutched his head. "He has left! *He has left us!*"

Olympia had sprung to her feet. "He's not dead?"

Mustafa shrieked, "I'll kill him with my own hands!"

She grabbed for the gyrating figure. "Mustafa!" He slipped out of her grasp, but she managed to trap the loose sleeves of his galabiyya. "*Mustafa!*"

He was so light and small she could almost lift him off his feet, but the instant she had him bound, he turned and embraced her, sliding down her legs until he was kissing her slippers again. "Take me with you! I'll track him down for you. Like a cur. Like a traitor. I'll strangle him with his own sash! I'll bring his head and lay it before you, his skull stuffed with straw instead of brains!"

"How do you know?" she cried amid his piercing vows of violent slaughter. "How do you know he's alive?"

Mustafa beat his forehead on the floor. "It was a trick, a trick, a trick! O Beloved, forgive me; pardon me that I was too dull and stupid to see it. Foul dog, lying snake, he has taken the jewels and tried to fool us with a sham! This attack, these *sthaga*, it is all a trick, a wicked device to let him steal away! I know my pasha. Never—*never* would he disregard a warning on his life. Never would he go to strangers in the dark. And look, *Emiriyyiti.*" He slipped the fez off his shaved head. A lumpy leather bag fell from inside. He poured the contents into his trembling hand.

It was nothing but a tangled collection of cheap paste jewelry and pebbles.

"They were here this afternoon. And the *hilaal*, the precious *teskeri* of the Sultan—it was here—hidden safe around my neck as my pasha commanded, so that he does not suffer the dreams it brings him when someone sees him wear it!" He prostrated himself, scattering trash and rocks with a metallic tinkle. "But I fell aslee—" He interrupted his own words and said quickly, "Drugged, O Beloved! He gave me a sleeping draught in my coffee! I know it! Why else should I lie like one dead, like a lazy donkey sleeping in the day?"

Olympia stared at the scatter of tin and paste. She felt that the breath had been knocked from her lungs.

A trick.

She closed her eyes, trying to remember. A trick. The jewels. It had been so dark! What had he said—what had he looked like? Her heart wanted it to be true, to know that he was alive; her mind reeled at the crush of such a betrayal.

She put out her hand and felt blindly for the bed. The strength seemed to have left her knees. She sat down hard.

Bunglers, he had said. *Bloody bunglers.*

But the men in disguise—the two fake Jewish men with turbans under their flat-brimmed hats—they'd boarded the ship at Ramsgate . . .

They were trying to kill me! His astonished and bewildered voice rang in her head. He'd been surprised at it, even after all of his own spine-chilling stories about the *sthaga.*

And there had been two sets of attackers. One that spoke with Portuguese accents. And one that never spoke at all.

Oh, God, he'd groaned. *Who'd have thought it?*

She sat up. "They were real," she exclaimed. "Some of them were real. They had turbans."

"What if they were?" Mustafa cried. "You pushed them down and saved him"—he swiped up a handful of paste jewels—"and so! This is how he thanks you!"

She put her palm to her forehead, trying to think. "But—could he have left this with you on purpose? As a—a decoy—or something of that sort? To mislead anyone who might try to steal them."

"And not tell me of it? Why? Mark me, my princess! There is some ship which leaves this harbor before dawn; *wallahi-l'azeem,* he is on it."

"He wouldn't," she said plaintively. "He wouldn't."

Mustafa made a rude noise. He held up his hand, his fingers spread wide as he ticked them off. "He left me in Stamboul. He left me in Spain at Albuera. He traded me to the pirates, the Laffite Pashas in New Orleans. He sailed without me from Rangoon. He gave me to the First Admiral of the White after the battle at Acre, but the admiral gave me back. Five times has Sheridan Pasha tricked me. He would do it, O Beloved. You may believe it. He will have an explanation, that is sure; he will make you think that night is day . . . but look—" He shook the front of his galabiyya. "He has taken the *teskeri,* the Sultan's safe-conduct. It must have been him—why would any other thief take plain brass, as worthless as this paste to anyone who knows not what it means? Who but my pasha would lift it from my very neck? Who else knew it was there? No, this is no accident. He meant to leave, and the *teskeri* he would not go without."

"But—to steal my jewels. To become a common thief—"

Mustafa straightened indignantly. "I said nothing of that! He is no common thief."

"You're accusing him of it yourself!"

"Not some low, ignoble, common thief." Mustafa lifted his eyes to the ceiling and said reverently, "He is il-Abu Goush, my pasha, the Father of Lies, full of feints and subtle stratagems, crowned with cleverness and cunning." He looked back at Olympia. "It is we who are common, my princess. We are common fools. You should know better."

"How can you say—" She balled her fists. "I trusted him with my very life!"

"Aye. It is fortunate he only took your jewels. Now see where you have left us. In the soup."

"I can't credit it. I just can't credit it. Someone else must have stolen them."

"Of course not," Mustafa said scornfully. "Such a ruse as *this*—no one but Sheridan Pasha could design it. *Allaah akbar!* God is good. How fortunate for us that you saw through the trick before it is too late." He pressed his forehead to her ankles like an adoring dog. "What shall we do, my princess?"

"Well, I . . ." She bit her lip, feeling bewildered, numb to her soul. "I don't . . ."

"Perhaps you would wish to order your humble slave to the quays. For intelligence of this ship that the vile British devil thinks to slink away upon."

She bent her head. "I don't know. I can't believe it. I just can't . . . believe it . . ." Her voice trailed off in painful bafflement.

"I will go and carry out your praiseworthy plan, O Beloved. You are his equal in guile; you shine like the North Star in beauty."

Tears pressed at the back of her throat. "I'm a fat, stupid coward."

Mustafa cocked his head. "That which Allah creates is beautiful," he said. "You are a gazelle, my princess; your eyes are like the cool green waters of the oasis; your hair is like the morning sun; your hands and feet are as soft and gentle as the dawn wind. You are admirable in all ways, Beloved of my wicked pasha. I go now."

After the door had closed behind him, Olympia stared at the blank wall.

Go to Fitzhugh, he'd said, all brotherly concern. *If something should happen to me.*

How noble, she'd thought. How selfless, how gallant, how brave.

What a fool she must have looked. What an idiotic, mindless, calf-eyed little fool.

Her body was shaking. Never in her entire life had she felt like this. The numbness was beginning to wear off. Her mind began to function, to perceive the full extent of outrage and humiliation. She stood up, her toe encountering the dull tinkle of fake jewelry.

She reached down, swept up a bracelet of tin and paste, and bent and twisted it between her fingers until it was a shapeless, broken mass.

Who did he think he was? To beguile her, to lie to her, to steal from her and expect her to skulk away like a beaten cur in a gutter?

She would not.

She was a princess. Her ancestors had led Hannibal across the Alps; they had stood with Charlemagne when he was crowned Holy Roman Emperor; her family's blood ran in the veins of Austrian Hapsburgs and French kings and Italian popes.

Who was he? A common nobody. The descendant of some piddling baseborn English sea dog, and a bastard line at that.

Oh, yes. She would go to Captain Fitzhugh. She and Mustafa would track the vicious traitor down. They would find him.

And then . . .

Then she would do what the thugs had not. She would kill him with her own hands.

Ten

You are indeed an admirable woman, Miss Drake,'' Captain Fitzhugh said. ''You have an excellent grasp of international politics.''

''Thank you.'' Olympia refilled his cup with tea, not even splashing any under *Terrier*'s ceaseless motion. After three months aboard the survey ship as she made her way across the Atlantic and slowly down the South American coast, pausing frequently to update Captain Fitzhugh's charts, Olympia was an old hand. This daily time for tea and intelligent conversation with the young captain had become a routine, a small way of repaying him for his endless consideration. He seemed to enjoy it. Indeed, he sometimes appeared to go to amazing lengths to make certain he would not miss it.

''It seems a shame that a lady of your education and talents cannot exercise them in a civilized location,'' he said.

''Yes,'' she said faintly. ''Australia. I never thought . . .''

''Forgive me.'' He was quick to look chagrined. ''I didn't mean it quite that way. I'm sure Port Jackson must be quite genteel. And fascinating, too, for a person of your perceptive habits.''

''I'm sure it will be very interesting.'' Olympia kept her face down. She still could not believe she was doing this. She could not believe she was aboard the *Terrier*, bound for Cape Horn. It had been incredible enough to be on her way to Rome with Sir Sheridan, but *this*—sailing off toward the end of the earth on the word of a strange little man she barely knew, pretending to be a person who didn't exist, trusting herself to the kindness of a stranger who helped her because he thought she was the sister of a hero . . . a hero who was either a foul thief or dead.

Murdered and mutilated and buried in an unmarked grave.

Captain Fitzhugh said, "You must follow your brother's instructions, of course."

"Yes." She nodded into her cup. "There is nowhere else to go."

She looked up in time to catch the frown which he hastily smoothed from his face. "It is—unfortunate—that he made no arrangements for you to return to England."

"Si—" She remembered in time to drop the "sir." "Sheridan always said I should go to our cousin if something—untoward—happened."

"Yes. It just seems that . . . I mean, forgive me, but—*Australia* . . ."

She lowered her face again, afraid he would try to argue with her or ask her more questions to which she'd have to make up hurried answers. "I shall be quite all right."

There was a long silence. Captain Fitzhugh looked upset. It was fortunate, Olympia thought, that he didn't know her real destination might be far worse than Australia and some long-lost cousin. *Kutaradja, Acheen, Sumatra:* the names were like dreams. Like nightmares. She envisioned savage islands, hellish jungles, snakes and glaring cannibals.

But he would go there, Mustafa had said with absolute certainty. If Captain Sir Sheridan Drake—K.B., Royal Navy, pasha, former slave and erstwhile hero—had stolen a fortune in jewels, he would go to this barbaric island of Sumatra and live out his days like a rajah with some equally knavish acquaintance of his who'd already established a personal kingdom there.

It was Mustafa's idea that Sheridan had escaped Madeira aboard the convict ship that had been in harbor with *Terrier.* And indeed the ship had weighed anchor that dawn after his disappearance, bound for Botany Bay. Catch up with him in Australia, Mustafa had advised—the words of an expert on tracking Sheridan Drake. It made sense.

It made an awful sense.

She should have gone back to England.

Panic existed constantly in a ball in the pit of her stomach. It was only the disbelief, the dreamlike quality of everything, that kept the panic from blossoming into pure terror. She'd always been a coward. She knew it. She should have gone home; she could not do this; she'd never known how or what was required, not for anything. All her childish fantasies of saving her subjects from tyranny, all her dreams of a shining future had come to this—that she was going, without really knowing where or why, only moving, to escape the pain of betrayal.

She should have gone back. There were worse things than marriage to face.

But in a moment of rage and grief, she'd committed herself to this course. She'd put herself and her future in the hands of a bizarre tiny slave who was as fluent with lies as with compliments. Everything had gone too far too fast during those few days after Sir Sheridan had disappeared; she'd been too furious and ashamed and distraught to think straight. Mustafa made suggestions, and she accepted them. Mustafa propounded theories, and they sounded reasonable. Mustafa told her what to do, and she did it.

And here she was.

Mustafa had stolen one of her jewels for certain, stolen it when they were all supposed to be in his safekeeping, and brought it out with considerable pride to show her how he had outwitted his master in this one small matter. The chain of perfectly matched pearls was to pay, one by one, for their passage on this wild chase across the globe. Sometimes she half thought Mustafa had stolen the rest, too, and laid the blame at his master's feet.

But to believe that was to believe that Sheridan was dead.

Captain Fitzhugh would hear nothing of payment—not for the orphaned sister of a naval colleague. But she and

Mustafa could go no farther than South America with him. Mustafa said they would find another ship at Montevideo. He sounded certain. Olympia felt terrified.

"Miss Drake," Captain Fitzhugh said, "I should not . . . perhaps I . . ." He swallowed and turned red as she looked up at him. "I mean to say . . . we haven't known each other long, but I admire you immensely. I'm—pardon me, please, I don't wish to seem encroaching—but I'm afraid for you. I don't see how I can leave you at La Plata."

She bit her lip.

Don't leave me, her mind cried. "That seems to be the only course," her mouth said.

"But what if you can't find a ship? You may have to wait for weeks—months—for a decent passage, alone in that vermin-ridden place. If you or I knew someone in Buenos Aires; but you've no companion beyond your maid and that odd little fellow of your brother's—neither of whom inspires much confidence, if I may be perfectly blunt." He put down his cup with a clatter and started to pace. In the cabin where Sir Sheridan had had to bend his head to avoid the beams, Captain Fitzhugh could stand quite straight as he passed. "I've been thinking on this for weeks. We'll make Montevideo in another fortnight, but—Miss Drake—I just don't think I can bring myself to abandon you."

"What," she said in a voice that barely carried over the sweep and creak of the ship, "—what do you suggest?"

He turned suddenly, unexpectedly, and dropped down onto his knees before her chair. He took her hands. "Miss Drake." He swallowed, met her eyes, looked away and met them again. "Do me the honor . . ."

It was a shock. She had anticipated cautions, arguments—anything but this. She stared at him with her lips parting.

He grasped her hands harder, his palms moist and hot. "Do me the honor of becoming my wife, Miss Drake," he said steadily. His cheeks were burning. From the deck above came a faint shouting of orders, barely audible in the cabin. He blinked, his eyes shifting upward with an officer's instinct before he disregarded the disturbance and looked back at her. "You could stay aboard with me. You needn't go on to your cousin in Australia." He wet his lips and smiled bashfully. "It's not a lady's life, precisely, but you're an excellent sailor . . . I've been watching you. And as soon as we've finished this survey we'll be going back to England. Perhaps a year. Sixteen months at the most. You don't have to decide this moment; we're well out from—"

Someone knocked at the door. Captain Fitzhugh scrambled up just in time to avoid being caught on his knees by a second lieutenant who looked to be at least a decade older than he was.

"We've been hailed, sir," the lieutenant said. "Captain Webster, brig *Phaedra* out of Salem, bound for Sydney. He wishes to bespeak us, sir. Mr. Goodman asks if you care to come on deck."

Captain Fitzhugh's frown changed to consternation. His red flush went pale. "Sydney, you say?"

"Yes, sir. Ten weeks out of Salem, sir, bound for New South Wales."

Olympia met Captain Fitzhugh's dismayed gaze. He looked as if he would say something, or as if he thought she should say something. His left fist curled into a ball and he tapped it against his thigh in an agitated rhythm.

"Port Jackson, Miss Drake," he said suddenly. "That is the harbor at Sydney."

She felt as if all the breath for words had left her lungs. He stared at her. Olympia looked back helplessly. She had only to give some sign, she knew. A smile, a nod, and he would stay below and answer this new ship's overture with a polite rebuff, responding with flag signals only in the merest military courtesy, as he'd done several times before on this voyage.

But she had no sign to give. It was all too sudden; her life now seemed to go in fits and starts, weeks of boredom and then momentous decisions that had to be made in an instant, and she only knew what she didn't want, and nothing of what she wanted.

She was a coward, afraid to commit herself either way.

The moment seemed to stretch, a frozen tableau: the

lieutenant awaiting Captain Fitzhugh and Captain Fitzhugh awaiting her. Another shout drifted down from above, slightly louder through the open door.

"Well," Captain Fitzhugh said at last. He cleared his throat gruffly. "I'll come up, then."

He made a stiff bow in Olympia's direction and walked out the cabin door.

Olympia huddled in her cloak. Another deck, another sunrise at sea, this time with freezing wind on her cheek and the American Stars and Stripes instead of a familiar Union Jack snapping at the peak of the foremast. The *Phaedra* rolled remorselessly at her anchor, her upper rigging shivering and whining in the icy gale. The harsh profile of the island to windward, a barren and dismal gray lump on a barren and dismal gray sea, did nothing to protect the ship from the bitter and steady breeze.

Captain Webster stopped his slow pacing to bid her good morning. He was a garrulous and kindly old man who had already, in the week since she'd left *Terrier*, given Olympia the life histories of his singularly uninteresting son and daughter, and was well into the second rendition of his children's detailed résumés.

"A brief stop for water, Miss Drake," he said over the wind. He moved around so that he blocked the gale from her face. Olympia smiled gratefully. "It may take a day to replenish our casks, but I deem it a prudent measure before we attempt the Horn."

"Where are we?"

"The Falklands." He turned and pointed. "This here is New Island. That's Swan, and off beyond her—the big one you can just see all along the horizon—is English Maloon. Delightful place, ain't it?"

In all the world Olympia could not imagine a more terrible desolation than this. She'd grown up amid the bleak geography of the fens, but there at least had been life—vibrant life and color in the huge circling flocks of waterfowl. Here there was nothing but a single albatross, looking lonely and miserable as it floated up and down on the windswept surface of the swells with its head tucked under one folded wing.

"Do you think so?" she asked in surprise, and Captain Webster laughed.

She glanced at him, confused, and then realized he had been making a joke. She smiled belatedly, trying to be polite. "It is inhabited?"

"My Lord, no. Who'd care to live on godforsaken rocks like this, child? There's nothing here but tussock grass. Sealers and whalers come and go, but no one cares to stay long."

Olympia looked past him to the hill which rose away from the harbor, blanketed with a strange hummocky texture of drab olive green. Even the whitecaps were gray. The wind whipped them into long smears across the choppy sea. Her eyes stung and her ears burned with cold, and she couldn't even feel the tip of her nose. But it was a choice between the icy fresh air and the stifling bilge-stink below, so she stayed on deck in the leaden light, watching the crew lower a boat to land.

"Now, what the dickens is that?" Captain Webster exclaimed as he frowned toward the eastern horizon, where the sun was watered to a dull silver glow by the overcast sky.

Across the grim low hills of Swan Island the horizon showed a rising billow of white. It looked like a cloud to Olympia, but the captain stared at it with intensity. The mate moved up behind them, squinting toward the sight with equal concentration.

"What do you think?" Captain Webster asked abruptly.

"Smoke, sir," the mate said. "That's what I think."

"Sealers?"

The mate shrugged. "Maybe, sir." He paused, then added slowly, "Not many seals left here, I wouldn't think."

Captain Webster tugged at his beard. After a long moment, he said, "Call back the boat."

"Aye, sir."

The mate turned away, hailing some of the crew. Captain Webster remained frowning at the ascending white mass on the far horizon. "It's not on Swan, I don't believe," he murmured. "Farther away than that. The other side of Maloon, perhaps."

"Is it another ship?" Olympia asked.

"Hmm?" He turned around, lifting his bushy eyebrows as if he'd forgotten she was there. "Ah. Miss Drake. Wouldn't you wish to go down out of the wind?"

"No, thank you. The smoke—is there some danger?"

He chuckled, patting her shoulder. "We shall stay well clear. There's just a little worry of renegade Spaniards in these parts. But no doubt it's only some of my own stalwart Yankee sealers, camped apart and sending signals to one another. Prudence, prudence—that's my maxim, Miss Drake. We shall investigate with caution."

Olympia was forced to retreat to the cabin while the ship weighed anchor and made sail again. Mustafa sat in a shivering huddle of blankets, sipping coffee and mumbling something in his own language. The maid Sheridan had hired for her—years ago, it seemed now—lay snoring on a rumpled berth.

Olympia thought of the *Terrier*, and Captain Fitzhugh's neat cabin. She thought of the pretty terrace on Madeira that looked out over the gardens and the sea. She thought of her room in Wisbeach, and of Fish's cottage, cozy and clean. She tried to remember the princess who had set out on this insane journey, who had made each decision that had brought her to where she was, and could not. She didn't feel like a princess anymore, or a radical, or an advocate of the Rights of Man.

She just felt numb. And stupid.

So incredibly stupid.

She sat down with a sigh. Mustafa slid to the floor and pressed his forehead to her knees.

"We will find him, O Beloved. Have no fear."

Olympia did not answer. She didn't think they would find him. She didn't know what she would do if they did. Leaning her shoulder against the bulkhead, she closed her eyes, her head swaying with the motion of a ship going someplace . . . any place . . . she no longer cared where or why, or what would happen when she got there.

They were all day following the smoke. Olympia returned to the deck, watching the rocky coasts of several islands slip slowly by. The ship left one group behind and struck out across a great, gloomy bay, still chasing smoke from the dark shape on the far horizon.

"By my soul, I believe that's coming from the Anacans," Captain Webster said, lowering his eyeglass. "Who would camp on those rocks?"

The chief mate rubbed his lip. "Not Spaniards, sir, I wouldn't think. Not by choice. There's no anchorage, and too much reef. Nor it ain't likely to be sealers, neither. Place ain't big enough to be worth the effort."

Captain Webster took an agitated pace around the wheel. He came back to where Olympia and the mate were standing by the rail. "By golly, there's some poor soul wrecked in that awful place. You tell me there's not."

The mate looked troubled. "Maybe, sir."

"We'll have to find out."

"It might be a trick, sir. An ambush."

The captain raised his glass again, peering for a long time at the desolate little cluster of minor islands that hung off the larger coastline. "Can't see a thing," he said. "No sign of a vessel. Where would an ambush be?"

"I dunno, sir. I dunno."

"Well, I think we must go and see." Captain Webster closed his eyeglass with a snap. "If we won't take a bit of risk on behalf of our fellow mariners, we can't hardly call ourselves Christians—can we now, Miss Drake? But I think I'd like you to stay below with your servants, if you please."

Olympia obeyed. She sat dismally considering the possibility that her days would end at the hands of Spanish smugglers, which was not at all what she'd hoped for out of life. Just as the dusk was beginning to obscure the far corners of the cabin in murky blackness, Captain Webster's hoarse voice gave an ebullient roar of satisfaction as he thundered down the stairs.

"Great news, Miss Drake!" he cried. "We've come to the rescue of your countrymen!" He pulled her up from her seat with one white-haired, gnarled hand. "It's a wreck, all right—British frigate cast on the rocks. A good many survivors, from what I can see of 'em on the shore. Thirty at least. They're bringing the officers off now, and some fellows who look to be marines from their uniforms. You can come up, if you like."

Olympia and Mustafa hastened behind him on deck. *Phaedra*'s longboat was just arriving back from her mission of mercy onshore. While the carpenter rigged a ladder, Olympia and everyone else leaned over the rail, trying to see into the boat through the deep twilight. The men huddled there were only vague figures, but they halloed and waved with wild enthusiasm. Olympia found herself waving back, jumping up and down in excitement along with everyone else.

The first of them came scrambling on deck, a short, heavyset man in a tattered blue coat that was torn at the shoulder seams but still carried the tarnished epaulettes of a captain. He grinned and spat and pumped Captain Webster's hand while the crew crowded around.

The rest clambered aboard, ten newcomers in all: a bearded and scraggly band in spite of their scarlet uniforms. It was almost full dark by the time the last tall marine reached the top of the ladder and swung his boots nimbly over the rail. He leaned back over the water and gave a hand to a sailor from *Phaedra* who followed him. Then he straightened and looked up, the only clean-shaven one in the group.

Olympia blinked. She gripped Mustafa's arm. The tall marine returned the *Phaedra* crewman's friendly clout and swung around into the lantern light, grinning.

His elated gaze met Olympia's.

The grin froze and faded from his handsome face. They stared at one another with the tumult of greeting passing around them.

"Hell," said Sheridan Drake. "Bloody hell."

Eleven

Rage.

Olympia ached with it; she blazed and quaked with it. She felt as if she radiated it, as if everything she touched should burst into flame.

Until this moment, she had not thought he was alive.

Not really. Not in the face of all Mustafa's certainty. She'd listened, she'd acted, but in her heart she'd not believed. She'd been waiting for a miracle, unwilling to accept his death, unable to accept his betrayal. She'd moved in a blind, numbed, foolish fantasy, somehow believing that she could find him, and when she found him, he would be the man she'd always thought.

Now she stood staring at him—at his hell-angel face, the smoky eyes and beautiful sulky curve of his mouth shadowed in the swaying lamplight—and knew the truth.

The hero she'd loved with all her being had not died. He'd simply never existed. This person . . . this thief, this liar, this fraud—this was not Sir Sheridan Drake. Love shifted and shattered and exploded in fire, burned to ashes and rose again as something else.

Hate.

She squeezed her eyes closed. When she opened them he was still there, still watching her with that lazy lift to his brows, so familiar that she wanted to choke. He moved toward her, and she hated him so much that she could not make her limbs work to turn away or flee or even speak.

"Come to spread democracy among the benighted penguins, Princess?" he murmured.

"You *bastard,*" she spat, the foulest name she knew, and wished she knew one fouler.

He glanced away from her, toward Mustafa, who took it with a queer calm, this unexpected end to the hunt. Sheridan held out his hand toward his servant, palm upward. Mustafa shuffled his feet and bobbed twice, and then to Olympia's enraged astonishment slipped the string of pearls from the folds of his robe and blankets and put it in Sheridan's palm.

"Just a *moment!*" She sprang forward, grabbing at the necklace, but all she met was his empty hand. "Give it to me! What are you doing with that? They're mine!"

Sheridan frowned at her. "Hush," he said. "Let's not stir up a fuss, ma'am."

"I will! Where is it? Where are all the rest? I'll—"

"Shut up!" he hissed. "Everything's safe enough."

"Then give it back to me! Do you think I'll whisper on *your* account? To protect a sneaking thief!"

"For God's sake—"

"Captain!" she cried, frantic with fury and drawing every eye around them. "Captain Webster! I suggest you take custody of this man for stealing!"

Captain Webster turned from his conversation with the others who'd come aboard. "What's this?"

"He's taken my pearls." Olympia grabbed Sheridan's arm and in her passion actually managed to drag him a step toward the captain. "Right in front of my face—he's got them there in his pocket. And after stealing all my other jewels in Madeira!"

"Stealing your—" Captain Webster frowned, hooking his thumbs into his waistcoat. "My dear Miss Drake, are you serious?"

"Yes! He tricked me in Funchal and took every bit of jewelry I had. And he just now took my pearls right out of my—out of Mustafa's hand. Search his coat and you'll find them."

"Now, don't upset yourself, miss." The captain brushed back a thin strand of his windblown gray hair.

"This will be some misunderstanding. These poor fellows have been here a month and ran out of food several days ago. They may not make much sense, eh? What's your name, lad?"

Sheridan leaned on the rail. He crossed his arms and regarded Olympia with a dark smile and a hint of exasperation. "Drake. Sheridan Drake, sir. And I see that this female has been passing herself off as my sister again."

"Passing my—" Olympia started to exclaim, then shut her mouth.

"You know each other?" Captain Webster looked between them. His astonished expression darkened. "Now look here—what kind of gullery is this?"

"It isn't any kind of gullery," she cried. "It's plain theft. May I speak to you in private, Captain? I can explain everything."

Captain Webster hesitated, glancing around at the avid listeners, a mixture of bearded and clean-shaven faces in the windy night. "We don't really have time for this. I need to make some accommodation for these men. They must have something to eat; it's full dark and we'll have to land some sustenance for the rest of them that we've left on shore."

"Yes, of course—but he's a *thief!* I tell you, he stole my jewels—thousands of pounds' worth—and he just took my pearls! If he isn't locked up instantly, there's no thinking what he'll take."

"Pardon me, Miss—ah"—Webster cleared his throat uncomfortably—"Miss Drake. Those are strong words. I've no proof at all—"

"Search him! Look in his left pocket, and you'll find my pearls."

"Aye—" One of the shipwrecked men, the one in the ill-fitting captain's coat, suddenly shoved forward and jerked Captain Webster back against his chest. He pushed a pistol under his captive's chin. "Search 'im."

Phaedra's chief mate sprang with a shout, lunging toward his threatened commander, but two of the wrecked company brought him down. The trio thrashed together on the deck. An instant later one of the bearded attackers stood up, wiping a bloody knife on his red coat and grinning in the lamplight. *Phaedra*'s mate lay facedown and still.

The other gave the body a kick. It didn't move. Suddenly there was not a sound but the wind and the squeak of the lantern swinging from the rigging.

"Cal!" The man holding Captain Webster twitched his chin toward Sheridan. "Strip 'im. Find these here pearls. You, Bill—get in t' cabin. Find any officers and kill 'em quick. But ye don' go hurtin' no sailors. Leave well enough alone. We'll be needin' 'em."

Captain Webster said, "Now—think this over. You don't want to do this." His voice was steady, almost gentle, but his gnarled hands were shaking.

The shorter man shoved the pistol hard up against his jaw. "You be a dead old man, d'you come cross with me. Don't forget it."

Olympia cast Sheridan an appalled look. He stood still, only watching, saturnine and unsurprised. When the big man named Cal took hold of him, he submitted without resistance, meeting her eyes only once: a swift shaft of anger and contempt just before Cal gave him a vicious shove with both hands. Sheridan stumbled back up against the rigging and caught his balance, then straightened and obeyed the man's snarled order with a resigned expression, pulling off his coat and handing it over to be torn apart.

The pearls did not appear. Sheridan was relieved of his pistol, waistcoat and shirt next, and then his boots, leaving him barefoot and half naked on deck in the freezing wind.

Still no pearls.

"What's this here?" Cal clutched at the gleaming crescent that hung around Sheridan's neck.

"It's only brass," Sheridan said, resisting Cal's jerking pull on the chain.

Cal lifted the pendant and bit it, then scratched at the metal with his knife, squinting down at it in the lamplight. "Yeah." With a disgusted flick, he let the crescent fall back against Sheridan's chest. "Trumpery. Give over the pearls."

"There aren't any damned pearls." Sheridan spread his arms wide and turned around. "Do you see 'em on me?" He grimaced at the man who'd shredded his clothes. "Be sure and look in my bootheels."

Cal backhanded him across the face, sending him reeling a step.

"Jesus," Sheridan said, nursing his cheek. "I take your point."

He turned his head and said something in Arabic. Mustafa asked a question, and for a few moments they argued back and forth while the others glared in growing impatience. When Cal took a step toward him, Sheridan jerked his head and snarled an order to his servant. Mustafa shuffled forward, the string of pearls coiled in his open palm. Cal snatched them up, but a quick shout from the leader of the wrecked company brought him reluctantly around. He handed them to his chief, who shoved them in his inner pocket.

"Little bugger got t' rest, Drake?" the leader demanded. "Deliver 'em over."

"The rest are on the island."

"Where?"

"I'll have to show you."

"Who be this here stout femaline party, then?" The wrecked leader nodded toward Olympia.

Sheridan looked at her. There was a faint shivering tremor in his chest and arms. The icy wind tore at his dark hair. He blinked slowly and said, "My sister."

"No, she ain't. Some lowlife like you—servin' on a convict ship? You got no sister what owns a set o' matched pearls an' talks like that. Who she be?"

Cal made a threatening move. Olympia opened her mouth, but Sheridan's voice cut across hers. "My sister," he said sharply. "She got the pearls off her mistress in Funchal. We were to rendezvous at Port Jackson." His lips curled in a dry smile. "We have the occasional sibling difference of opinion, as you may have observed."

The leader stared at Olympia, never taking the gun

away from Captain Webster's chin. "A workin' gel, then," he exclaimed with a skeptical lift to his brows. "Doin' wot?"

"Lady's maid," Sheridan said.

"I'm thinkin' t' bitch can answer, ain't you?"

Sheridan dodged a cuff from Cal. "Certainly. You don't have to hit me, you know. I'm in an excessively cooperative mood."

"Who be your missus, gel?"

Olympia wet her lips, baffled and aghast and certain that something important was riding on her answer by the way they were all staring at her. Instinctively she wanted to disclaim this lunacy, to declare her innocence in the face of Captain Webster's shocked distress. She wanted to deny being a thief and the sister of a thief, and most fervently wanted to reject any connection with Sheridan Drake whatsoever.

But she recognized her mortal danger. She saw what she would be to them if they knew the truth: a prize of infinite value, a captive who might bring riches to desperate men. They were off the transport ship; their uniforms could be nothing but a thin disguise for convicts who'd escaped the wreck. She shook her head and tried to keep her hands from fluttering. "My mistress was—ah—Mrs. Stothard. But I took the pearls from one of her guests," she added, for an extra touch.

The man regarded her keenly. "I tell you what. You learn me somethin' a lady's maid 'ud know. You learn me"—he wrinkled his nose—"as how you take spots out o' silk."

"Why—" She took a breath, trying to remember what her maids had done. "What type of spots?"

"All kinds, me lyin' puss."

She took a guess, not daring to hesitate. "You soak them in milk, of course."

"Aye," Sheridan said disgustedly, and in that instant Olympia saw from her interrogator's expression that she couldn't have been more wrong. "No wonder you've been sacked from every position I've got you and ruined the half of my waistcoats. Forgive my sister, gentlemen, she's—''

"She ain't yer sister,'' the leader snarled. "And she ain't no lady's maid as sure as me name's Bob Buckhorse. Who is she?''

Sheridan rolled his eyes. "Who do you want her to be? A bleedin' princess?'' He clapped his arms in a glacial chill. "She's my sister. Have the pearls; I'll take you to the rest tomorrow, but give me my boots back and something to wear or you'll be interviewing penguins to find out where I buried it.''

"I'll be interviewin' you, and not takin' any sauce, by God,'' Buckhorse said. "Tie 'em up—all four.'' He gave Captain Webster a shove. "And put this old mutton chop where none of the crew gets at 'im.''

It was the first and last occasion, Sheridan thought, that he would attempt to be a felon. Being a natural-born bastard was quite stimulating enough. He didn't need this kind of excitement.

But he was well hoist with his own petard this time. On top of shipwreck in this godforsaken desolation, here was his princess popping out of nowhere, braying about her damned jewels in front of as desperate a gang of convicts as ever should have swung by the neck—the only other survivors from the government transport besides Sheridan himself and one poor ass of a marine colonel. The colonel, having made it through the shipwreck, had given it as his view that he was now in command and would make sure the criminals continued on to Botany Bay at the first convenient opportunity. The criminals thought this a sadly uncreative outlook, and promptly shot him for his lack of imagination.

Sheridan, seeing the high standards of conduct to be met, had immediately set about making himself indispensable. He'd rigged a cable and raft and begun salvaging the wreck for what he could recover of food and supplies. The convicts, however, had seemed to have other things on their minds, such as killing each other over the remaining rum. It was nothing but God-given luck that

Phaedra had found them before they'd resorted to stone spears and cannibalism after ten weeks in this place, and petty God-given revenge that their rescuer happened to have Her Royal Inconvenience aboard.

She was going to be even sorrier for it than he was, Sheridan feared. Right now, her eyes were so wide with fear and anger and confusion that he was terrified of what she might say or do. He stared at her, trying to catch her attention, trying to send a message with his eyes: *shut up, keep quiet, let me do the talking.*

Buckhorse, ever suspicious, checked the bonds himself after Sheridan had been tied. The convict leader followed Cal as he bound the others, strutting around in the late captain's dress uniform, poking and prodding. When Cal finished with Olympia, Buckhorse slid his hand behind her. She jumped, gasping indignantly at his hard pinch on her bottom.

"Put 'er in t' big cabin," he said. "Mine."

Sheridan was two paces toward Buckhorse with a furious denial on his lips before he realized what he was doing. He towered over the squat convict, but a pistol pointed at his belly brought him to an abrupt stop. Cal hit him anyway, a hard, unexpected clip to the back of his neck that sent him to his knees.

It left his head ringing, but he scrambled up before they got the bright idea to kick him to death, that being the kind of entertainment they seemed to favor.

"Never mind me," he muttered hastily. "I seem to have forgotten what I was going to say."

They took him below, dragging away the bodies of two other luckless officers—the second and third mates, most likely. The rest of *Phaedra*'s crew just looked on in dull horror, unarmed and deprived of their leaders with a murderous efficiency that was calculated to inspire respect in the most loyal of seamen.

Cal tied Sheridan into one of the dining chairs. From a corner of the main saloon a sobbing female scrambled quickly aside without looking at him. Sheridan recognized the skinny maid he'd hired for Olympia in Ramsgate. She and Olympia were hustled into the captain's cabin with

Mustafa. No one bothered to find Sheridan any clothes, so he sat there freezing while Buckhorse hunkered down in front of him.

"Now. Where's these here jewels hid?"

"On the island," Sheridan said. "I told you, I'll take you to them directly tomorrow."

"Say where they is, and I'll get 'em right now. You an' t' little bugger stink o' double cross, all that babble in some kinda heathen talk between ye up there. I can't hardly abide a man who's too damn smart fer 'is own good."

Sheridan gave him a level look. "No trick. I'll tell you where they are now, if you wish. But you can't find them in the dark. And you'd be a fool to try that surf before morning. The sailors won't take you."

"Huh." The convict glared at him. "Old muttonhead 'us goin' to send 'em back."

"He was going to land stores, not men—I'll wager you that. He'd rig some casks and float them in."

Buckhorse frowned thoughtfully. He motioned to one of his minions. "Go ask t' old codger. Don't tell 'im nothin'. Ask 'im wot he 'us goin' to do."

The man disappeared on deck. Sheridan looked toward the door of the main cabin, where Olympia was locked. He wondered if she was planning anything really stupid, like escaping through a porthole. She'd probably get stuck, half in and half out, and freeze her chubby, lovable little rear end off, which might be a far better fate than some others that appeared imminent.

"Who is she, Drake?"

He turned his head. "My sister, Buckhorse."

The convict stood up, his hands at his waist. His messenger returned, pounding down the steps and slipping off the bottom one as the ship rocked on a wave. "He's lookin' peaked, that old man. Shakin' all over. Bill said he thinks he might be goin' to have a seizure. But I got the word from 'im; I got it all. He says he'd been going to tie some boxes together and line 'em with canvas and put in food, and then float 'em on shore."

Buckhorse gave Sheridan a concentrated stare. "Now . . . 'ow come you know so much?"

"I've been at sea."

Buckhorse snorted. "Doin' what, then?"

Sheridan looked at Buckhorse coolly. "Commanding a British seventy-four, as a matter of fact."

Buckhorse twisted his lip in an ugly curl. "Right. An officer toff commandin' a ship o' ta line. An' you and your sister is a pair o' pickpockets." He nodded at Cal. The man moved a step closer. "Tell me the truth."

"Buckhorse!" The convict called Bill burst in, almost falling down the stairs in his agitation. "Buckhorse—that old man's gone and died on us!"

"The devil 'e has," Buckhorse roared. "I told ye—"

"I didn't touch 'im, I swear I didn't. Ain't a mark on 'im. He just choked up and rolled over, white as a sheet."

"Begad—you certain he's dead?"

"No question. Go look for yourself. And if he ain't dead as a hammer, he sure ain't in no shape to give no orders."

Buckhorse cursed violently. He paced around the cabin, hitting the bulkheads with his fist. Then he whirled and faced Sheridan. "You. Ye know as how t' sail this here ship?"

Sheridan looked at the convict's squat figure, bursting the seams of the blue coat. Slowly and clearly, he said, "Not if you lay hands on my sister."

There was a silence. Somewhere loose blocks thudded, a syncopated chorus in the wind.

"And why 'ud I want t' bad-tempered bint?" Buckhorse said at length. "T' other one'll do."

"Then let me loose," Sheridan said. "I need some clothes, man."

Buckhorse just called him a smart-ass and ordered Olympia and Mustafa out into the saloon. Olympia came first, face lowered and subdued, which Sheridan saw with vast relief. He began to think they might somehow scrape through this.

Buckhorse tramped into the cabin and shut the door to amuse himself with Olympia's maid. Sheridan sat in silence, judging it best not to speak, since his red-coated convict guard appeared to be a little cranky over his failure to concoct a suitable excuse to break Sheridan's ribs.

He passed the time by watching his princess. She looked up at him once: a glance like a poison dart, utter loathing in eyes so green they could annihilate a man—slaughter him down in that little place inside where he'd held aloof from everything else.

Make him strange to himself.

He had a grim suspicion that he'd missed her. That the jolt he'd felt when he looked up and saw her on that deck had not been entirely vexation. A vague unease filled him, unrelated to Buckhorse and his ugly crew.

He could tell she was near to paralysis with fear. He knew her that well; knew the way her plump shoulders hunched so that she looked like a sparrow fluffed out in the cold. He knew the way she kept her eyes down and shot frightened glances from beneath her furry lashes. He knew how she would have looked up at him, worship with endless confidence, when she'd thought he was really a hero.

Well, she understood him now. She didn't look at him like that anymore.

He wasn't given to regrets. In the past three months he hadn't thought about her. He was quite sure that he hadn't. His life had been perfectly under control, except for the frequency with which he woke up in a sweat with his night terrors, and that, at least, she could hardly be blamed for. He'd abandoned her because she was too damned much trouble, with her mutinies and her innocence and her deuced green eyes that made him do things that were stupid.

Now here he was trying to make deals with that murdering brute Buckhorse, when a man of any sense would have sold her at a profit. If she hadn't made such a fracas about her bloody jewels, Buckhorse and the rest might have gone ahead with their simple plan to play captain and marines and passengers, stayed low and quiet and peacefully slipped away at the first port.

Instead, what they had now was a crisis and desperate men.

Sheridan hated crises and desperate men. His face hurt. He wished he'd thrown her overboard in a sack when he'd had the chance.

From the closed door of the cabin came a series of thuds. Olympia's head snapped up; she looked in that direction in horror. The cabin door flew open and Buckhorse stalked out, fumbling at his pants.

Sheridan gripped his hands together behind his back. His guts tightened, his body reacting instinctively to the look the convict gave him.

"Lying bastard." Buckhorse grabbed Sheridan's shoulder and knotted his fist. He plowed it full force into Sheridan's belly.

The world splintered into blackness and one white-hot focus of agony. His lungs froze; his heart exploded; the chair hit the wall and something came out of the dark like an anvil and smashed his ear, pain on top of pain, layers of it, so that he could not breathe or think or see.

The hurt gripped him, tore and twisted him, and then slowly, slowly, began to let go. At first it was distant sounds that tried to organize themselves into syllables, then shape and color and the ability to pull air into his punished lungs.

"Who is she, Drake?"

He sat blinking at the blur in his eyes, taking a long time to find some sense in the words. His body throbbed.

"My sister," he said hoarsely.

Buckhorse's face came clear through the mist. "That's all right, guv'nor. Be an ass."

Sheridan moved his eyes, finding a new face—Olympia's skinny maid staring down at him with trepidation. Buckhorse stood with one hand still pushing Sheridan's shoulder back into the wall, tilting the chair, the other hand loosely fisted. Sheridan gazed for a moment at that ready fist. A sense of doom moved through him.

Buckhorse leaned down close. "This here gel o' hers says she thinks yer lyin'. Says you two don't act like no brother an' sister what she ever saw."

"Well," Sheridan said, wishing he were someone else, "she's wrong."

Buckhorse ducked, putting the full driving power into his blow. It sent Sheridan forward, doubled, his shattered senses closing to bright, burning darkness and his muscles contracting. He heard himself and some other, higher sound of distress as he spun down the bruising well. The muddy blur of his perception shook and began to stabilize, and then pain exploded in his ear, knocking him sideways, his tied hands clutching for support that wasn't there until a third smash sent him back upright like a puppet jerked on broken strings.

His confused brain tried to find the murky well and sink, but the blessed darkness slipped and wavered and slid away. He opened his eyes. Buckhorse was in front of him, swelling and fading like a nightmare. He stared at the image, not having the ability to move his head.

"Oh, don't!" a feminine voice was pleading. "Don't hit him anymore."

Sheridan wet his lips. His tongue stung where he'd bitten it. Blood tainted his mouth. He felt vaguely aggrieved, some distant part of his brain having recognized that it wasn't Olympia who'd spoken up for him.

So I'll tell. Worth thousands. Claude Nicolas. Prince of . . . He closed his eyes, trying to remember.

"I won't hit him," Buckhorse said. "Not if 'e's smart enough t' talk. Who is she?"

"Sister," Sheridan said thickly. "My sister."

He was already tensing his aching body when the pain smashed into him. He hung forward in the chair, trying to find himself amid the black agony. There were noises in his ears—the sound of his own throat, struggling for air. His heart pounded, clouding his brain and his vision with waves of dark and light.

This time. This time I'll tell.

Buckhorse shook the chair. "She ain't yer sister. We all know't, by damn. So who is she?"

Sheridan opened his mouth. For a moment his tongue would not form words. He parted his lips and panted.

"Sister," he whispered.

From the corner of his eye he saw Buckhorse draw back his arm. Sheridan flinched helplessly. *Don't. I'll tell you. I'll tell.*

"You'll kill him, Buckhorse," someone said from a great distance. "Then how do we get out of here?"

The blow Sheridan had braced for did not come.

After a moment, which he spent staring at the decking above, his head braced back against the bulkhead and his chest heaving, he heard Buckhorse say, "Don't matter. I'll think o' somethin'."

"The hell you will." The other voice—Cal's, perhaps; Sheridan could not tell and couldn't look—sounded impatient. "You won't get it out of him like that nohow. He'll go out 'fore he'll say, if he hadn't yet."

"Wot d'ye want, anyhow? Beat it out o' *her?*"

Sheridan swallowed around the lump of nausea in his throat and lifted his head.

"Not if she's worth something to somebody. I know somethin' better. Takes a towel and some water. Works like a charm, nor it won't kill him, neither."

Buckhorse shoved off from Sheridan's chair, sending his head banging into the wall before his feet came to the floor. He sat there with the world spiraling around him.

"Have a go, then." Buckhorse clapped Cal on the back.

Sheridan released a whisper of relief and misery. He sat with his head bowed and his body burning. People moved and spoke around him, but he paid no attention, concentrating on each aching breath.

Cal grinned at him. "I ain't going to hurt you," he said.

Oh, God. Sheridan's heart quickened. He closed his eyes in panic.

"Bring that here," Cal said at the sound of bootheels on the companionway stairs. "Yeah, it'll do. Here—set 'er down and take that pitcher, then."

Sheridan sat still, waiting with growing horror while Cal deliberately dawdled, making commonplace comments about the bruises Sheridan was likely to have from Buckhorse's beating. "Now, then," Cal said gently. "Who's this little lady, Mr. Drake?"

Sheridan stared at him, at the towel and the bucket and

the pitcher. Cal's friendly manner made his spine crawl with ice.

"Just don't want to talk about it, we don't?" Cal shook his head. "That's a shame. That's a bloody bad shame." He stood above Sheridan and laid the towel flat over his face. Water swished and splashed and then came pouring slowly down over the cloth.

At first it was only cold. It even felt good for a moment against Sheridan's battered face.

Then he tried to take a breath.

The wet cloth sucked against his mouth and nose, an instantly discomfiting sensation as it interfered with his breathing. He opened his lips to draw more air and the water came down again, flooding his mouth. He swallowed, closing his lips, trying to breathe through his nose. But his chair tilted back, someone grasped his hair and more water slid across his face and eyes and plastered the towel to his skin. He sucked for air and got a surge of water.

He began to strangle, gagging on his own efforts to save himself. His body jerked, fighting for what it needed, arching up in an uncontrollable spasm against the hand that twisted in his hair and held him down, drowning.

I'll tell you! I'll tell. I'll tell.

The words were only a sound, a gurgle in his throat, but suddenly the chair tilted down and the towel slithered from his face and he was bending over and coughing in between great draughts of air and life.

"She ain't worth it, is she?" Cal asked softly. "Blow me—ain't nobody worth it."

Sheridan couldn't lift his head, but he looked under his dripping lashes toward the corner of the saloon where Olympia sat. She was staring at him, her plump chin tucked under and her eyes like something caught in a trap at night—a blank rigid blaze of animal fear.

He made a soft *whuff* of dismay. She was gone. Broken already. There was no chance she would make the decision for herself and spare him this.

So I'll tell 'em.

"Who is she, guv?" Cal whispered.
Now. Now I'll tell him.
The pitcher swished and burbled, filling again.
God have mercy. I'll tell you, I'll tell, I'll tell . . .

Twelve

Olympia jerked when the cabin door slammed. She was afraid of Buckhorse. She was afraid of all of them, and her mind would not function beyond it. She'd watched while Buckhorse used his thick, compact frame as a dead weight with power enough to fling Sheridan against the wall. She'd watched Cal cover Sheridan's face, pull back his head and pour water down on him; watched Sheridan choke and gag and struggle and collapse. But it was as if there were a wall of glass between her and the scene.

The sound of Buckhorse returning brought her out of the stupefied haze and resurrected the sharp edge of immediate terror. She felt herself curling, pressing back against the wall behind her, but Buckhorse merely glanced at her and then at Cal. His quick survey stopped at Sheridan, who was slumped forward against the rope that bound him to his chair. Water dripped from his hair down his slack body.

"I thought y' wasn't going t' kill 'im," Buckhorse snapped.

"He ain't dead," Cal said.

"Nor 'e ain't breathin', neither."

Cal hooked the chair with his foot, sending it toppling. Sheridan hit the floor with a thudding clatter. His body spasmed in a fit of coughing.

"Didn't say nothin' worth knowing, hey?" Buckhorse

grinned, sweeping up the soggy towel and wringing it with his blunt fingers.

Cal shrugged. "I drowned him five times. All but did it for real this last one. He ain't got nothin' to tell, or he'da spilled it by now."

Both of them looked at Olympia. Her vision grew dim with fright.

"Get up," Buckhorse said.

She obeyed, standing on shaky legs.

"Untie 'er and put 'em both in that room." Buckhorse waved his hand. "I want 'im on his feet and right in 'is head by daybreak. That'll be your little job, you see, *sister.*"

They put her in the murdered chief mate's cabin. In a shaft of light from the main saloon, she sat on the berth and rubbed her swollen wrists, watching through the door as Cal cut the rope that held Sheridan to the fallen chair. He began to cough again as he was freed, rolling onto his elbow, his head hanging. It took three of them, cursing and grunting, to force him to his feet. He stood, swayed, and then Cal hauled him bodily into the cabin, let him fall next to Olympia on the berth and slammed the door.

Darkness enclosed them. She couldn't see Sheridan, only hear and feel him: his labored breathing, a muffled, gurgling cough, and the wet press of his body seeping moisture through her cloak and into her dress.

She moved away, reaching for the flint and lighting the oil lamp by feel. The white glow flickered and expanded to light the room.

Sheridan lay curled up on his side. As she looked, his body tightened and shook. He opened his eyes and reached out; his fingers splayed and then clutched on nothing. He turned his face down and vomited into the blanket, expelling a rush of water.

He was still for a moment, panting. Then he pushed up onto one trembling arm. "Princess," he said, his voice all wrong, hoarse and squeaky.

She stood staring at him, at his black hair plastered to his face, at his arm and shoulder quivering under his own weight.

"You deserve it," she hissed. "You deserve it, do you hear me?"

He lifted his wet lashes and took a long, hollow breath. His head dropped forward, a shift of precarious balance that nearly toppled him onto his face before he caught himself. "Bad," he murmured in that grating whisper.

"Loathsome," she said with feeling. "Foul, rotten, detestable cheat. Thief. Traitor. Swine!"

He shook his head with a rusty sound that could have been a chuckle or a wheeze, but ended up a chain of violent coughing. He reached out and gripped her arm, his fingers closing painfully on her sleeve as he used her to lever himself up to a sitting position.

"Warned you," he rasped.

"Let go of me!" She jerked her arm away.

"Princess." He rested his face in his hands for a moment, spreading his fingers through his wet black hair. He cleared his throat. "Princess. I didn't . . . tell them."

"Bastard," she said.

He lifted his head. There was such distressed confusion in his face that for an instant she felt a flicker of shame. "I didn't tell them," he croaked. "I could have. And they wouldn't . . . they wouldn't have—" He lost his voice in a choking cough and gestured toward the door.

She narrowed her eyes. "I despise you."

He looked confounded, blinking up at her with water still shining on his brows and lashes. "You don't understand. You don't . . . know—"

"I understand." She pushed his hand away. "You think because you didn't play me foul again, I should feel awful for what they did. I should feel sorry for you. But I don't. I detest you and what you are, *Sir* Sheridan. I wish I'd been the one to beat you myself."

He sat looking at her. The bewilderment faded slowly; his thick lashes lowered and his mouth went sulky. "Well, so do I," he muttered. "Given the choice."

"Stand up, if you please." Frightened exhaustion made her voice sharp. "You've ruined the blanket."

He flashed her a look, petulant and dangerous—like Lucifer brooding on some secret fantasy of rebellion. But he did as she ordered, pushing himself off the berth with that soft rusty sound that seemed to come out of him involuntarily. He bent across the bed and gathered the wet blanket in a ball, hanging over it supported on both arms for a moment until a paroxysm of coughing passed. He was shivering as he tossed the woolen spread in the corner. Reaching past Olympia, he pulled open the locker and probed in it.

"No more blan . . . kets," he said, with a catch and a quick breath. "Would it displease Your Bloody Highness if I borrowed this fellow's . . . clothes?" He coughed, once and hard, and then leaned on the locker. "Or am I to be exe . . . cuted by frostbite for my crimes?"

"I don't care."

He shook his head. "You'd better . . . c-care. If I'm sick or dead at daybreak, our friend Buckhorse'll take it out of you, sis . . . ter dear."

Olympia bit her lip, recalled forcibly to the fact that he appeared to be her sole protection, in spite of what he'd done in Madeira. She glared at him. "You probably can't sail this ship anyway. You probably aren't even Sir Sheridan Drake at all. I don't doubt you murdered the real Sir Sheridan and took his place before he ever got to Norfolk."

He rested his head and shoulders against the locker. A drop of water fell from his hair onto his bare collarbone, and he shuddered. "I suppose you can take a . . . chance on that if you . . . like."

His voice sounded queer. Suddenly he spread his hand on his belly where Buckhorse had punched him. The golden crescent-and-star twisted, falling over his fingers. As Olympia watched, his face went pale and stark and his knees began to buckle. He slid slowly down the locker, each breath a deep vibration of distress.

Olympia felt her own insides squeeze in spontaneous empathy. She wasn't used to being hard; she'd have felt sorry for a snake that looked so wretched.

Which was exactly what he was. A snake.

"Here." She took off her cloak and threw it around his shoulders where he huddled on the deck. He wrapped his fist in the cloth, gripping it until his fingers turned white. He sat still, not even breathing, his head bowed into his knees and his neck corded with strain.

After a long minute, he tilted his head back against the locker and began to breathe again in deep, relieved gasps. "God," he mumbled, "I wish that would stop."

Olympia frowned at him. "What's wrong?" she demanded.

He gave a weak shrug. "Nothing fatal, I'm . . . s-sure you'll be sorry to hear. A residual . . . twinge, courtesy of Mr. Buckhorse." He lifted his thick lashes wearily. "Not so bad now, but quite an experience when somebody's pouring water down your . . . nose."

She pressed her lips together. "Can you get up?"

"Of course."

She waited. He made no move to change position.

She bent over impatiently. "I thought you said you could."

"Tomorrow. Next week. Don't—" He curved away from her hand. "Don't touch my . . . face, thank you."

Olympia drew back, frowning at him. The only signs of his battering were a smear of blood on the back of his hand where he'd wiped it across his mouth, and a faint darkening at the corner of his left eye. "You don't look very badly hurt to me."

"Someday," he said in his hoarse, mild voice, "I'll bash your head in to broaden your education."

She glared at him. "You've already broadened my education quite sufficiently, I assure you. Get up. You're going to be ready to sail this ship for those men tomorrow."

He looked up at her, his gray eyes darkened to infinite frosty shadow in the lamplight. "Decided to . . . throw in your lot with a different . . . devil, Princess?"

She came near to saying that anything would be preferable to him, but the thought of Buckhorse and Cal and their convict gang made her pause. "I'm not throwing in my lot with anyone," she snapped. "You and your treachery have taught me that much, you may be sure."

"Lesson One," he said, grasping the locker door and hauling himself to his feet. With a wince, he ran his fingertips gingerly down the side of his face and gave her a painful smile. "The hardest one to learn."

She looked at him leaning unsteadily beside her as if he were the village drunk. She thought of a hero in a glittering captain's uniform, with a gold star and white gloves and shimmering epaulettes. Tears rose in her eyes, sudden and devastating. She turned away, tucking blindly at the bedding. "Yes," she whispered. "Hard to learn."

When she finally turned again, having blinked back the telltale weakness, he was still standing against the locker. His eyes were closed. He looked, she thought, strangely melancholy, where a man of any sensibility at all would have looked guilty or desperate or angry or afraid. The cloak hung from his shoulders, half falling, but he seemed not to care.

"Lie down," she said.

He opened his eyes. For a moment she thought he was going to say something, but then he obeyed her, moving onto the bunk as carefully as an old man. Olympia caught up the cloak and leaned over to lay it across him. He grasped her arm.

"You, too, Princess."

"What?" She tried to draw back.

"You can't stand . . . up all night."

"There's a chair. I'll sleep in it. I'm not the one who has to have his wits about him at daybreak."

He held her. "To keep me from taking a chill, then." He looked at her with an intensity she could not interpret. "We don't want to disappoint your . . . friend Buckhorse."

Olympia pulled away. She turned down the lamp and felt for the chair. It was hard and very cold.

"Princess," he said, a soft plea out of the dark.

She sighed and sat down on the edge of the berth. His hand found her, shaping her arm and pulling her steadily down. The berth was chilly and damp. She deliberately faced away from him as she lay down, holding herself to the far edge, as distant as possible from his body.

He gave a muffled cough and cleared his throat. With

slow, shaky moves, he spread the cloak over her. Olympia felt the tears rise again, stinging her nose and eyelids.

He rested his hand against her hair.

"Princess," he said, "I meant for you to go home."

She made no answer. The warm moisture slid down her face and plopped onto the damp bed.

"So . . ." the rusty voice whispered behind her. "Why the hell didn't you go?"

Morning was gruesome. Sheridan awoke sharply from a dream of battle, of turning over a mangled body and finding a woman's face, her bloodied hand reaching for his throat—but as his bayonet plunged in defense, the face turned into his own face and he couldn't stop the weapon; it tore into his belly, shooting pain that jerked him into panting consciousness.

He lay still for a moment, holding his stomach, trying to find reality. As the muscle spasm passed, Her Royal Highness rolled over in Her Royal Sleep and bludgeoned him again in the stomach with Her Royal Elbow. It took him another full minute to get his breath back.

He worked his battered body out of the bunk, climbing over her by agonizing increments. He was ravenously hungry, but that was an ancient and familiar discomfort. Dressing in the late first officer's clothes was far worse torture. Sheridan's torso looked as if an elephant had been waltzing on his ribs.

He tried some experimental stretches. There was a fierce catch in his left side when he moved in one direction. His tongue was swollen and aching where he'd bitten it the night before.

He sighed, wincing even at that small motion, and lifted his arm with a violent grimace to drag the brass *teskeri* over his head. He pulled on a shirt and a pair of dry trousers by tiny progressions and stowed the Sultan's crescent-shaped brand in a safe pocket, concealing it with a familiar sense of release. He peered in the mirror. His face looked strange, almost frightening, faintly blue over both temples and down the side of his jaw, the rest darkened by beard shadow. The lightest touch made him cringe. He looked at the shaving equipment organized neatly below the mirror, almost turned away and then glanced toward the berth.

His princess lay curled, buried up to her nose, her hair a bright flood of sunlight in the chilly dawn. He looked back in the mirror at his spooky appearance, all black and pale and haggard. He decided to shave.

By halfway through the procedure, he had serious doubts about his sanity. It hurt like the devil, and the water was freezing. Viewing himself from both sides, he couldn't see that he looked any better. Possibly worse. But he finished, cursing under his breath, and managed to ease into the mate's peacoat. It was too tight across the shoulders, but he couldn't move without gasping anyway, so it suited his situation.

He slowly and systematically looted through the locker and cabin, filling his pockets with any small item he could carry: flint, needles, loose change, soap, traveling chess set, two tallow candles—anything that would fit. He had a bad feeling about his future, which always brought out the guttersnipe in him.

In the midst of his quiet plunder, he reached across Olympia's sleeping form to lift a magnifying glass from a hook on the bulkhead. One lock of shining hair spilled over the side of the berth. He paused, looking down at her, and ran his fingers carefully over the strands.

So soft. He wondered what had happened to the little satin boots with pearl buttons that he'd bought.

Thrown overboard, more than likely. She seemed just a bit aggravated with him.

Lesson One, Princess. The hardest one to learn.

He turned away. With his eyes closed, he leaned against the locker and listened to the ship, putting together the sounds and motions that had been drifting at the edge of his awareness all night. The brig had a sharp chop to her while lying at anchor, which might be her natural action or might be several other things, all of them worrisome. He tried the door handle. It was open.

So much for imprisonment. Sheridan peeked out and found Cal snoring in the dawn shadows at his feet. Stepping gently over the prone body, Sheridan located his knife where it had been thrown aside the night before, wrapped it in a rag, stuck it through his belt beneath his coat and headed up the companionway ladder.

There was no watch, as he'd reckoned there wouldn't be. He stepped on deck, the wind catching his hair with gale force. The tide was up. He saw instantly that they were in trouble; the ship had broken her sheer and drifted over the chain cable, now riding the anchor on far too short a scope. Every wave brought up her bow, jerking the chain taut against the hawsehole and bitts with a sinister smash.

"Buck—" Sheridan bellowed down into the cabin, then clutched at his ribs, instantly chastened. "—horse," he finished in a far less enthusiastic tone, adding, "I'm turning out all hands!"

He left it at that. They could come if they pleased; he'd warned them, at least, so maybe they wouldn't shoot him where he stood as soon as they got on deck.

Holding his belly, he limped toward the forecastle, stepping over the stiff body of the chief mate still lying in an ugly black stain of frozen blood. Sheridan took an extra moment to bend painfully and seize the late hero's woolen cap. He crammed it over his ears.

In the forecastle, he managed to rouse some of the crew, who appeared to have found their way into the liquor stores—the besetting weakness of sailors in every crisis. He'd warned Buckhorse, but Buckhorse wasn't the listening kind. Before Sheridan had them organized, the convict leader and Cal came pelting up the companionway.

"Stand!" Buckhorse aimed his pistol. "You! Stop 'er right there!"

"The tide's in," Sheridan said, with as much calm as he could muster when faced with a loaded gun. "She's riding far too short. We'll drag or break loose if we don't do something about it."

Buckhorse pointed his weapon at the nearest seaman. "What's 'e mean, then, hey? That true?"

The youngster looked anxious. "I dunno, sir."

"What d'ye mean, y' don' know? You a navvy 'r not?"

Buckhorse fired the pistol at the youth's feet. The deck splintered and the crewman leapt aside with a screech.

"I don't know!" he cried. "I don't! This is my first time out."

"Well, I guess that makes you pretty damned useless, don' it? You'd best make certain I don' take ye in dislike." Buckhorse waved the pistol at the others. "What about it? This bastard right? He's a liar, mind ye; a rum 'un and a liar, and that's a fact. What d'ye think?"

A big African crossed his arms, shifting from one foot to the other. "He lyin' agin, then, sir. Captain Webster, he were a thorough-goin' seaman. He never did do nothin' wrong like dat."

"Look at the chain, for Christ's sake," Sheridan said. "The tide's come up."

Buckhorse pointed his gun at another man. "What's yer guess, then? You reckon this 'ere gennelman toff's plannin' mischief an' trying t' hoodwink honest folks?"

An excited discussion erupted among the sailors. Sheridan waited, feeling the ship haul and tug at her short cable. Something gripped his arm. He looked down to find Olympia blinking in the wind.

"What's wrong?" she hissed.

"Democracy at work," he said sourly. "We're voting on whether or not to break off our anchor and drift onto those rocks."

She turned an appalled glance in the direction he indicated. Downwind of them, the surf smashed in white explosions against the barren shore. She stared back up at him. "Is that a joke?"

He ignored her, watching the argument keenly. A few spoke up in favor of Sheridan's assessment, but no one held onto that opinion for long in the face of Buckhorse's reloaded pistol. In a few moments, it was unanimous: Sheridan was wrong.

"Goddamned terrific," he said under his breath.

"What's 'at, Drake?" Buckhorse demanded. "You got a word for the rest of us t' hear?"

Sheridan smiled gloomily. "Just voicing a small personal aversion to shipwreck twice in one voyage. Since we all seem entitled to an opinion."

"O-pinion, says 'e. I ain't all that worrit 'bout yer o-pinion. Makes me suspicious, then, that ye got a maggot fer messin' wiv this 'ere ship so prompt-like an' all." He waved the gun. "T' rest o' ye—get that boat back in t' water. Mr. Gennelman Drake's got somethin' important to show us that I reckon 'e ain't all that anxious t' show."

It took three times as long to lower the pinnace as it should have. Sheridan sat down on a hatch cover and kept his mouth shut concerning the various blunders, partly out of bad temper but mostly out of self-preservation. When the boat was riding empty and reckless on the heavy sea, pounding into the hull with every wave, Buckhorse stepped back and gestured toward the ladder.

"You first, Drake. Then yer sister."

Sheridan glanced at him in consternation. Bringing Olympia along, and all the reasons for it, was an ominous sign indeed. But Cal shoved him in the back, sending a shaft of pain through Sheridan's ribs. He nodded and went while Buckhorse was busy arming Cal and himself with ammunition and three extra pistols apiece—enough firepower to kill a round dozen of inconvenient comrades.

Climbing down the Jacob's ladder and into the wildly sawing boat was no casual effort. With spray splattering his face and green water washing past, Sheridan gauged his moment and leapt, landing with a jolt that paralyzed him for an instant of sharp misery before he caught his balance against the gunwale and glanced up.

Olympia was leaning over the rail, looking terrified. Cal and Buckhorse didn't appear much happier about the prospect of going over the side on a hemp ladder into a boat that was swaying outward a full man's height with every rise and fall. But Buckhorse was prodding at Olympia. With one petrified glance at him, she gathered her cloak around her and scrambled out over the rail as Sheridan had done, clinging to the comforting web of shrouds that descended from the mast above. His heart rose in his throat as he saw her tilt backward when the ship rolled. Buckhorse was covering his own apprehension by yelling at her, reaching as if to push her hands off the safety of the shrouds.

"Avaaast there!" Sheridan's roar of command could have carried from stern to bow of a triple-decked ship of the line. It sent Buckhorse flinching back. *"Don't you touch her!"* Sheridan's ribs protested with piercing agony as he bellowed, but he had no time to think of that. He began working to ship the rudder, lashing it to one side. "You frigging bastard," he muttered. "You bloody damn bastard." He looked up and cupped his hand around his mouth. *"Olympia! Listen to me! Listen!"*

She gave no sign in reply, only clung there riding the slick platform of the shroud channel, with her cloak whipping in the wind.

"Nod!" He kept his voice strong and steady, absolutely confident—the only way to deal with white-faced midshipmen and panicked princesses. "Nod your head twice."

She made two quick jerks, her hair straggling in spray-darkened strands around her.

"What d'ye think—"

"Silence!" The command cut across Buckhorse's objection, as cocksure as if there'd been a bos'n with a rattan cane standing behind the convict to back it up with painful clarity. "Olympia," Sheridan barked. He was working frantically to lengthen the painter and hoist the lugsail. "When I say *step,*" he shouted over the flapping of the sail, "you take one. Down. Not one instant before or one second late. Understand?"

She didn't move.

"Understand, mister?" he roared.

She made a quick nod.

"Step!"

She put one foot gingerly on the first rung. Sheridan threw himself into the stern sheets, pulling the tiller free with one hand and handling the line from the madly cracking sail with the other. The boat fell back, canvas filling.

"Step!"

She obeyed him. Sheridan gauged the pinnace's roll, which was considerably stabilized by the sail.

"Step!"

She did it, low enough now that foam splashed her feet when the ship wallowed down in a wave. He sent the helm hard over, took a fast turn to lash it and stood up as the pinnace's stern worked in toward the hull.

A wave lifted the boat. *"Step!"* Sheridan reached for her. *"Now! All the way!"* His shoulder seams ripped as he flung his arm around her. He stumbled back, hauling her with him, a killing crack in the ribs as they collapsed together on the thwart. "Good girl!" he shouted, and buried his face in her neck. "You did it, you did it—you're a hell of a princess." He kept the last words between his teeth, with her wet hair whipping in his face, her body shaking and trembling in his lap. He gave her an instant's elated squeeze and pushed her off.

Buckhorse had gotten himself over the rail and halfway down the oscillating ladder. Sheridan looked up and felt a sudden devil take hold of his soul.

With a vicious grin, he freed the tiller and deliberately sent the boat swaying out away from the ladder. Buckhorse was fumbling at the next rung, looking over his shoulder. He yelled angrily and Cal pointed a pistol at them over the rail.

Sheridan reconsidered, having done it out of nothing but sheer malice and the tumult of the moment—but in the instant the pinnace began to swing inward, a bloodcurdling report cracked through the air as anchor cable three inches thick fractured under intolerable strain. The ship lurched. The ladder snapped sideways. Buckhorse grappled wildly, lost his footing and hung screeching and twisting from the rope.

"Cast off!" Sheridan shouted. He sprang past Olympia and threw off the painter. The pinnace slewed, fell away from the massive hull that bore down on them, then steadied and plunged ahead under his hand while *Phaedra* slid rapidly astern. Sheridan looked back to see Buckhorse still twisting frantically, with Cal hauling at the ladder and the rest of the crew scattering to man the yards as the ship drifted backward with the sundered end of her anchor chain dangling a foot out of the hawsehole.

There was one faint pop above the wind and waves: a pistol report, but the bullet never came near them.

"I knew it!" Sheridan howled. "God, I knew she'd break loose. Serves 'em right." He pulled a bucket from beneath his feet, where three inches of frigid water sloshed briskly as they rode the waves, and tossed the thing toward Olympia. "Here's to anarchy, Princess. Bail!"

Thirteen

"Where are we going?" Olympia cried. "Aren't we going back?"

"To those hellhounds?" Sheridan leaned out over the side of the boat, weighting it down against the wind. "Get up on this side. Bail, damn it."

She splashed water overboard with the bucket. Her fingers were numb already, her arms shaking with fear and cold. It was one more terror on top of all the others, to be suddenly down at the level of the waves where the crests rose like living things and broke at a height with her head, splattering her cloak with foam.

"Are we going to land?" she called desperately. "What are you *doing?*"

He glanced back at *Phaedra.* The wind plastered his hair against his woolen cap. When he turned forward again he seemed to Olympia like some made sea devil, laughing amid this chaos, his eyes the color of the sliding shadow in each wave trough. "God knows," he yelled. "But at least we won't be shot in cold blood by the likes of Mr. Buckhorse."

Olympia bailed, looking over her shoulder at the ship's tall form. Only her tall masts were clearly visible now from the boat's perspective down among the tossing waves. Some of the sails had broken free, pale blossoms against the gray sky. "But *Phaedra!* Will she go on the rocks?"

"How should I know? They're probably still voting on it."

Olympia pressed her lips together. The spray-laden wind stung her cheeks. Between buckets, she kept straining to look over her shoulder. More sail came free, clothing *Phaedra*'s masts. "What if she does? What about Mustafa?"

He only tilted back his head to check the sail, wiping water from his face with one arm without answering.

"Are you just going to abandon him?" she cried.

"Certainly. But I daresay it won't work."

"We have to go back! We can fight Buckhorse."

"Are you crazy?" He ducked spray from a wave. It splattered onto his trousers and boots. "Just who do you propose to fight him?"

Olympia glared at him. "Not *you*, of course—you cowardly blackguard!"

"Right-ho. If I could get a good, clear shot at his back, I might have a go, but there's not much chance of that."

"You can't leave Mustafa," she wailed.

"I won't go back!" he shouted. "They were going to kill us, blast you! We'll drown anyway if you don't move that bucket with some sign of enthusiasm."

"He's your friend! Your comrade! If you were any kind of a man—" Olympia broke off and bailed water madly. "What if the ship wrecks?"

"Well, I can't help the damned ship—" He broke off, doubled over in a cough and then caught his breath. "Greedy . . . bastards. They wrote their own death warrant on that. Just couldn't spare half an hour to clear the cable before they got to their bleeding jewels."

"*My* jewels! And it wasn't Mustafa's fault. Or my maid's."

"Did you hear what I said?" he yelled. "They—" He lost his voice in another choking cough, gripped the tiller with both hands and added hoarsely, "They were going to kill us! I got a chance and I took it." He gulped a shuddering breath. "I'm not going back and risk my neck on some bleeding-heart . . . charity mission for that lot. Mustafa didn't have to come after me, and he knows it. Neither did you, or that skinny little . . . baggage who tried to tell Buckhorse you weren't my sister." His face looked demoniac. "That bitch can drown and be damned to 'er."

"You . . . are . . . despicable." She tossed water with savage fervor. "Despicable!"

"Fine. And you're alive. Stick with me, and maybe you'll stay that way."

"Coward! Craven swine! I wish I'd never laid eyes on you." She dropped the bucket and wrung her freezing fingers together. "I wish—" A sudden harsh sob shook her. She turned away from him, facing the wind. "Oh, God."

"Ditto," he snapped. "Bail."

In spite of his declaration, Sheridan kept the pinnace within sight of *Phaedra.* Not because he gave a damn about anybody else's neck, of course, but because he'd told his princess the ugly truth: he really didn't know what he was going to do.

Landing on the island was out of the question. There were still a dozen desperate convicts ashore, and if they saw *Phaedra* go down, they'd be in a killing mood. If the ship managed to escape, Buckhorse—or Cal, if Buckhorse had by some divine providence lost his hold on the ladder and fallen in—would be all over that rock looking for the jewels. And for Sheridan.

He was utterly certain that they'd planned a mass execution. He'd seen the extra pistols Cal and Buckhorse had stuffed in their pants. Not that Sheridan could blame them; it made perfect sense from a blackguard's point of view. They could get rid of all witnesses and claim they'd never found any jewels when they got aboard again. Just good business. Why split the loot any further than it had to go?

That was the one redeeming thing about brutes like Buckhorse. They were so wonderfully predictable.

The weather was thickening, gray showers moving across the tossing desolation, pelting sleet against his face—a new misery added to his list of woes. He snarled a directive at Olympia and came about, using *Phaedra*'s sails as a heading. The merchant ship was backed under her fore course and falling off the wind. They'd either found a real sailor somewhere or gotten luck they didn't deserve. As he watched, *Phaedra* braced up sharp and began slowly to move, under control and off the rocks.

He chewed his frozen lip. It was too numb to hurt, but he drew blood. He could taste it.

For a long minute he stared with narrowed eyes—not at *Phaedra,* but at the figure huddled with him in the boat. She was still bailing. Between buckets, she put her fingers to her mouth, sucking to warm them.

Not exactly the companion he would have chosen for this—but he had run out of choices.

"Look lively," he said. "We have an appointment on the other side of town."

Bracing his leg on the rudder, he gritted his teeth against the host of reawakened cramps and bruises and hauled on the mainsheet. The pinnace bounced and took a cold drenching, nosing up close to the wind, turning away from *Phaedra* toward thirty miles of riptide, open sea and forbidding weather; heading—Sheridan very sincerely hoped—for the invisible shore of English Maloon.

After hours, Olympia's jaw no longer hurt from clenching it against the cold. She simply couldn't feel it at all.

It was snowing now, the flakes blurring her vision as they clung to her eyelashes. Her feet had gone to aching numbness long ago, her shoes and stockings were soaked in the frigid water that sloshed in the bottom of the boat.

But she kept bailing. It seemed the only thing to do. Her fingers were so stiff she could hardly hold the bucket, but always there were the waves, breaking again and again into the boat. She'd come to think of them as personal enemies, as malevolent sly beasts, that waited until she had nearly cleared the bilge and then rushed to swamp it again in a freezing torrent of white and green.

What Sheridan was doing, where he was going—the question had faded to dim insignificance in the face of her ongoing battle with the waves. The threat of Buckhorse seemed distant and trivial, the hope of warmth and comfort so far away that she could not imagine what either felt like anymore.

She'd asked Sheridan once, hours ago, how he could tell his heading, and he'd answered that he couldn't.

But she kept bailing. When her mind would have given up, her body kept on.

"*There,*" he said suddenly, the first word he'd spoken for endless lifetimes, and then shook with a fit of coughing. The pinnace took a wave as he lost control of the tiller for an instant.

Olympia cried out, but he caught the handle back. The boat steadied. She bailed, anxious to rid them of the watery weight that made the pinnace wallow sluggishly. Behind her, Sheridan made a sound like a dying groan, but when she looked around in dread, he was only fighting to unlash one of the oars and keep hold of the tiller at the same time.

"I'll do it," Olympia said.

He gave her a glance, then dropped back with a grunt and a nod. "Breakers to windward. Free a pair, but hang onto 'em until I can—"

"I know how to handle an oar," she snapped. "Do you want them shipped?"

He looked at her, a speculative stare against the wind. It was like being gauged by an iceberg.

"All right," he said at last. "Ship the oars, Your Highness."

Olympia worked her numbed hands, turning to squint across the sea as they rose on a wave. She saw the line of breakers, dim white below a faint dark smudge in the teeth of the wind. The idea of rowing for that made her heart sink.

"Current's in our favor," Sheridan said from behind her, as if he read her thoughts.

She began to work at the lashings. It was one thing to row a small punt on the wind-rippled surface of the fens and canals of Norfolk—she was an expert at that—but another entirely to handle the long oars of a seagoing ship's boat amid the tossing waves. There were ten sets lashed along the bottom of the pinnace, indication enough of how many men it usually took to handle the boat.

She faced the stern and slotted the oars into the center

locks. The handles lurched and fought her, cutting into the waves and out again.

"Get down," he ordered. "I'm going to take in sail. Try to keep us steady on."

As soon as he let go of the tiller, everything seemed to become mayhem; the boat spun in the grip of the sea, dropping into a trough broadside to an oncoming swell. Olympia dug in frantically with the starboard oar, backing foam and water with the other. The pinnace swung, riding up stern-first over the wave.

Sheridan was working just as furiously to contain the sail and lash it down; he dragged the trailing canvas aboard with a sheet of freezing water, stumbling hard against Olympia's shoulder. She said something, only realizing after he'd given her a startled glance and pushed away that it had been a word worthy of the most foul-mouthed sea dog. Sheridan made the last rope fast and went down on his knees on the seat in front of her.

"I'll take 'em. Keep me on my heading."

His hands covered hers on the oars, twice as large and twice as cold. The grip hurt. Olympia slid her fingers from underneath. He took a long pull on both oars, his mouth pressing into a grimace as he put his weight into it.

"Damn," he muttered, and then flashed her a pained grin. "As we better-mannered sailors say."

Olympia rubbed her aching hands together and ignored him.

Just outside the roaring lines of surf, Sheridan lay on the oars, taking great heaving breaths and staring through the vapor. The huge incoming swell rode them up and down.

"God." He stared at the surf. "I don't know if we can do this."

Olympia was too numb to react to the comment. She sat by the tiller, shivering.

"Can you steer?" he asked.

She nodded.

"All right. We're going to wait for a big one. When the stern lifts, I'll try to get her on it. You keep us out to the wave; don't let us broach—you know, get sideways to it—

or we're dead. Straight in. When we hit the beach, I'll try to drag her up with the wave."

Olympia looked at him apprehensively, recalling the grunts and grimaces of pain. "Can you do that?"

"Are you volunteering?"

"I only thought—you might be too badly hurt."

"I am. That's what I get for being a hero on your behalf."

He was so calm, even smiling a little, as if it were a joke. Beneath the woolen cap, his dark brows were stark against his face. She wondered if he was afraid.

Olympia was. *I can't, I can't, I can't,* her mind ranted as the swell lifted them and dropped.

Sheridan began pulling strongly, leaving her no time to think of more than keeping the boat stern-in toward the wave that rushed them forward. He bent into the oars with concentrated power and drew a succession of deep, urgent sweeps.

The stern mounted on a monstrous swell. The thunder of foam filled her ears. She fought with the tiller. Sheridan yelled and gave one last desperate pull as the wave picked them up. He broke the oars free, sending them outward in two pale flashes that hit the water, curved upward and disappeared into the roaring crest. The boat swept down the face of the wave like a flying horse, the swell growing larger and larger as it drove them ahead with spray sheering out from the bow in two great arcs of silver.

An underwater shape swept by just inches from the boat; she recognized it as a rock after it was gone, looked ahead, saw another, and then that was past, too, and the beach was in front of her as the wave behind curled over and thundered down, shooting them up on the sand amid a freezing confusion of breaker and spray.

Before she could move, Sheridan was waist-deep in water, hauling the boat on the boiling destruction of the wave. He stumbled and went down in the surf to his chin. The boat thumped on solid ground, tilting wildly as water poured in on her with a shock of murdering cold. Sheridan was on his knees, the bow rope over his shoulder, the torn seams of his sodden coat gaping white as he strained against the combined forces of boat and ebbing water.

By the time she splashed out, he'd dragged the pinnace just barely above the controlling tow of the water. He stood at the bow, panting and coughing hugely, squinting past her at the sprawling threat of the next wave.

Olympia leaned on the boat, trembling. Her stomach reeled with hunger and stress. She swallowed nausea and looked around.

It was almost night; all she could see of the beach was a pale stretch studded by dark flat rock in either direction and a steep bank a good distance ahead. Snow was beginning to fall again.

"Now what?" she said.

He took a deep, rasping breath and made a shaky caricature of a bow. "If madam will point out her bandbox and trunk . . . ?"

She crossed her arms. A shudder ran through her. "What are you talking about?" Her voice held a mournful, desperate note. "We're stuck here, aren't we? Wet to the skin. Freezing. As good as dead, with no fire or food or shelter."

He made a face. "It would be my luck, wouldn't it? To be stranded on a desert island with a person of gloomy intensity."

"It's getting dark."

"I see that."

"It's going to get colder. We'll have frostbite before morning if we don't do something."

He regarded her with resignation. "It must be the revolutionary temperament. All that brooding about injustice."

She leaned against the boat, fighting tears. "All I'm brooding about now," she whispered, "is staying alive."

"There." He smiled—a faint, grim curve. His eyes caught the lingering gray light, "That's more the thing. You *are* alive, after all—you can tell by how wretched you feel. Don't be in such a damned hurry to kill yourself off." He touched her under the chin, his finger cold and clumsy. "You know—you're a jolly good helmsman, Your Highness."

Olympia pulled away, too tired and miserable to be actively hateful toward the enemy, but still refusing to look into his face.

He caught her left arm. "You've cut yourself."

Olympia looked down at her hand. There was a bright smear across her palm, staining her cuff. She spread her fingers and saw the cut, a deep gash between her thumb and forefinger.

"I can't feel it." She bit her lip. Foolish tears welled. "I'm so cold I c-can't even f-feel it."

"Fine. Then it won't hurt to have it cleaned."

He pulled her firmly toward the water and made her hold out her hand while he poured freezing seawater over it from the bucket. Then he took off his coat, wincing, and unbuttoned his shirt.

Olympia sucked in her breath at the sight of his chest as he stripped off his shirt. "Dear God. You're black-and-blue."

"Disgusting, ain't it? I suppose it comes of being the sort of person in whom distressed princesses confide their secrets."

She didn't care for the twinge of feeling that touched her. "It comes," she said meanly, "of being a monstrous, contemptible thief."

"Here." He ripped at his shirtsleeve, tearing it loose at the seam. "Being utterly devoid of all human decency, I'll selfishly bandage you with a piece of my own scant attire so that you may keep yours. I wouldn't want you to live through the night, would I?" He wrapped her palm and tied off the bandage, none too gently.

Olympia watched him rebutton the mutilated shirt and shrug into his wet coat. *Thank you* stuck in her throat. If not for him, she wouldn't be here. She would be warm and well fed in . . .

Wisbeach? Oriens? Rome?

She didn't know. She didn't care. Anything was better than this misery.

"I'm hungry," she said.

"So am I." He looked around at the empty beach. "Any ideas?"

"No."

"Well, then, I expect we'll just have to lie down and die. Perhaps you'll go first, and I can dine on leg of princess."

In the gathering darkness, his features were harshly etched: that strange inhuman beauty of his, compelling even here. Especially here, where it echoed the stark grandeur of the beach and the sea. He seemed a part of the surroundings. The cold was her adversary, the falling night was her terror, but he seemed to integrate with it like a lonely spirit blended with the gray mist of evening.

He held out the bucket. "Find us some fresh water before dark. I'll do what I can for shelter."

Olympia turned away, blinking against the snow. It was falling thickly now, dusting the ground. She trudged along between the island and the sea, looking aside to find a way up the bank. Her skirt had begun to freeze; it dragged and crackled around her legs. Her clothes were soaked through, even under the cloak. The wind seemed to cut right through them to her skin.

With each step it became harder and harder for her to move her cold limbs. She stumbled on a piece of wood, climbed painfully to her feet and staggered on. When finally she reached a low point in the bank, she stood staring at it through the dimness, trying to remember what she was to do. A fit of violent shivering rattled her body until she could hardly stand.

After a long time, she attempted to grab a dark tussock of overhanging grass at the top. Her fingers would not open. She pulled back and looked down at them, shaking all over. The snow seemed to fly into her eyes on purpose. She reached up to wipe it away and ran her fist into her nose. She could not feel them, her fingers or her nose or her ears, not even when she touched them together. That seemed to have some frightening significance, but her mind was becoming too sluggish to focus on it.

The wind howled past her. She could hear the sea, a dim and constant roar that seemed to recede and come closer. On hands and knees, she scrambled and heaved and clambered up onto the bank, her frozen clothing rubbing raw places on her skin. At the top, she was surrounded by the dark bulk of the huge tussocks. The night had come down, but the dust of snow and clouds seemed to glow with their own light. She shoved between the mounds of grass.

With a crunching sound, she found herself sitting down, the breath knocked out of her by the fall. An instant later her right hand began to burn and ache. She looked down and found it buried beneath an inch of broken ice and freezing water. She whimpered and drew the wet hand into her lap, bending over.

She ought to get up. But her body had lost the ability, and her mind could not summon the will. Her head ached. Tears spilled over and froze on her cheeks and lashes. She listened to the wind cry mournfully above her.

She was sleepy. Her lids drooped and her lashes tangled. Cold. It was so cold. Sheridan would be angry; he would be expecting her back with water, but she couldn't make it. They were going to die here anyway. Sleep seemed the best thing. She would sleep, and then maybe it would seem warmer.

For a while. Just for a little while.

Even with the footprints to follow in the light powder of snow, he almost stumbled past her, thinking she was just another mound of grass in the gloom.

He fell on his knees beside the huddle of frozen cloak. Ice broke under him as he grabbed her. "Princess." His voice cracked with sudden fear. "Christ—wake up—" His fingers dug into her shoulders. He shook her frantically. "Open your eyes—oh, Jesus, *wake up.*"

She stirred with a little moan. "Sleep . . ." she whimpered.

Sheridan felt something terrible release within his chest at the sound of life. "Bird-witted female," he muttered, closing his eyes for an instant. "Oh, God. Oh, God."

He tilted her head back and shook her again. Without waiting for a response, he got an arm around her and dragged her back into the shelter of two huge tussocks. Her cloak and skirt rattled stiffly. Sheridan stood up, cast about and began tearing at the dead-grass base of a nearby tussock. The long leaves came free, along with handfuls of a dry, lightweight kind of turf from the center. The whole tussock was taller than his head; he peeled it down and then attacked another, piling the straw and crumbled sod into a deep bed under the windbreak.

He stripped her of the frozen clothes. She whimpered and muttered feebly while he worked at her buttons. "So cold . . ." she whispered. "Going . . . to die . . ."

"Stuff," he said, panting with exertion.

"Can't . . . I can't . . . do . . ." Her head drooped as he yanked her bodice open. "Die here . . . die . . ."

"You ain't going to die, my dear." He pulled the dress off, revealing a plump, limp figure in white pantaloons. "Though I suppose it's just your style—something melodramatic and martyred. Too bad there ain't a tyranny worth defying in three thousand miles. Sit up."

He dragged her into the dry bedding, piling more dead grass on top, weighting it down with the frozen cloak. Then he burrowed into the lumpy nest beside her, contorting himself to strip off his own clothes and her damp pantaloons with difficulty. He pulled her cold nakedness against him, grunting at a hard shape that wedged beneath his bruised torso. As tussock dust and grass settled around them, he sneezed.

He pressed his body against her buttocks, breathing heat on the nape of her neck. Trying to get closer, he thrust his leg up between hers and wrapped one arm around her waist, sliding the other under her head. He bent over her, rubbing his palm across her belly, blowing his own warmth in deep breaths against her throat, her cheek and her temple.

He hugged her to his chest, feeling her grow warmer already. He spread his palm around something soft and full and interesting, and buried his face in the curve of her neck. Through the salt and cold she smelled unmistakably female, and his body, battered and exhausted as it was, had an instant answer for that. He pressed himself into the round shape of her naked bottom where it curved suggestively against him, feeling an age-old heat source begin to burn.

He hardly knew whether to laugh or cry. He was clearly a hard-core case of skirt-smitten, if he could think lustful thoughts under these circumstances. But he did, taking full advantage of the situation to apply himself with more masculine hunger than high-minded altruism to the task of rubbing and warming and breathing on her soft white skin.

He lifted one cold hand and kissed her wrist, keeping his lips conscientiously pressed to her pulse until the chill changed to heat. He explored her breasts and caressed her belly, careful not to miss an inch of plump surface. He warmed the tender dimple above her fanny with a humanitarian application of his heated body, stopping there only because his bruises warned him against more vigorous activity with agonizing insistence.

He settled for the gallant course, sliding closer and contributing his best warming effort: pushing the most smoldering portion of his anatomy into the inviting crevice between her thighs, giving heat and taking it, breathing raggedly against her shoulder.

"Going to . . . die . . ." she mumbled.

"Yeah," he muttered, with a slow, exquisite pressure into the cushioned curves and valleys of her. "Die and go to heaven."

Fourteen

"How dare you!"

Sheridan jerked awake with a gasp and a groan. It was barely light. He held his ribs and bit his lip as she rolled and thumped against him in her frantic search to find her clothes.

The movement tore the grass nest apart, letting icy particles of snow sift through and sting his bare skin. He didn't answer; he was having a hard time catching his breath amid the pummeling from her hands and elbows. She found her cloak and sat up, dragging it around her with most of the tussock-cover. Frigid air flowed over Sheridan's body.

"Oh," she said, drooping her head into two fistfuls of cloak, "I feel dizzy."

"You need . . . water." Sheridan managed to get the words out amid a convulsive shudder. By pained degrees, he reached down into what was left of the dry nest and found his pants, still damp and stiff with salt, but warmed from the heat of their bodies.

His battered muscles protested every move. It was one continual panting, shivering grimace to sit up, locate his stockings, shake the grass out of them and pull on the trousers. Amid a host of pressing matters, modesty was not high on the list. He looked up in the course of the process to find Olympia staring down at his body.

He stared back, tying his flap. "Impressed?"

Her face was pale and uncertain. "It's just that . . . I've

never seen . . ." She closed her eyes. "Oh. My head's . . . spinning."

"Very gratifying. But maybe you'd better lie down." He bit down on his lip and carefully eased into his shirt.

She obeyed him, subsiding into the lumpy cushion of turf and pulling the cloak up to her nose. "I feel ill," she said plaintively.

Sheridan worked himself into his pea jacket. He didn't feel so wonderful himself. He'd last eaten thirty-six hours before and had his stomach bashed in in the meantime. His boots were frozen solid. He forced his feet into them and clenched his teeth against the aching cold, breathing puffs of vapor through his nose.

The weather was bitter; the low gray clouds sliding past, a few streaks of dawn pearl behind the silhouetted bulks of the tussocks. Grainy snow barely dusted the ground. Above the murmur of the wind and surf, a single sea gull circled. Sheridan crawled to his knees and levered himself painfully to his feet, dusting off the clinging white particles of icy snow. He grabbed the bucket and hobbled out onto the frozen pond where he'd found her. In the center of it, he used his heel to break through with a kick that sent excruciating pain up his whole body. He drank as many frigid handfuls as he could stand and then limped back with the bucket to the shapeless mass beneath the tussocks.

She fussed and whimpered and tried to tug at the cloak until he dropped down on his knees beside her. "Come along," he snapped. "D'you think I don't know what you look like in the buff? I spent the night pressed as close as I could get to the Royal Bo—"

"Never mind!" She fumbled with the cloak and got up onto one elbow. Her breath came in short, uneven gasps, mingling in little clouds with his.

Sheridan helped her, put his arm around her bare back and pulled her upright, wincing at the move. He rested the half-full bucket in her lap.

She stared into it numbly.

He shifted, giving her a gentle jog. "Drink."

She cupped her quaking hands and put them in the bucket, shivered and took them out, empty and dripping.

"*Drink,* for Christ's sake! I've got no patience with you."

She bit her lip. "Why bo-bother?" she whispered. "Look at this p-place. How are we going to live?"

Sheridan wanted to shake her. "Drink," he said again.

She was shivering uncontrollably. She began to cry, soft dry sobs of despair. "We d-don't have any sh-ship's stores. No f-fire. No shelter. No dry c-clothes. We can't live. What do you think we're going to d-do?"

He looked down at the top of her head. The dawn gleamed on her tousled, wind-matted hair and touched the bare skin below. Beneath his arm he could feel her trembling.

"I don't know," he said.

She took a shuddering breath. "Why didn't you just let B-Buckhorse shoot us and be d-done with it?"

He let go of her. "What bloody kind of a question is that? Because I want to stay alive, damn it all." He hauled the bucket aside, shoving himself to his feet. "I want to stay alive, and this is how I know to do it. One day at a time. One minute at a time, if that's the way it is."

He stalked painfully across the frozen clearing toward the beach. At the first tussock he had another thought. He stopped and went back.

"I'll take the bucket," he said, "since you've decided to end it all. Forgive me for not putting you out of your misery by shooting you on the spot, but someone stole my gun." He regarded her sourly. "You ought to be dead by midnight, at any rate. I'll come back tomorrow. I could use the cloak."

Olympia lay shivering, sick and angry with herself and with him and with the universe. Her head pounded with an ache like an iron bell compounded of hunger and cold and thirst. She wanted to die, but found she didn't even have the courage for that—not here, not this way. The prolonged misery of it was too much.

She clutched at her damp, cold clothes, trying to sit up.

Each time she lifted her head, dizzy nausea spun around her. She puffed and gasped and finally inched into her sodden dress. She couldn't manage the chemise and pantaloons, or the buttons, so her back was bare to the freezing wind. Lying on her side, hugging the cloak around her with shaking fingers, she stared dismally across the snow-dusted ground toward the pond. Grass stems near her eye formed black, fuzzy arcs across her vision. She could feel her heart laboring in her breast.

She waited, hoping he would come back. He did not. Finally, when the sun was a dim silver glow, hours up through the fleeing low clouds, anger and need overcame the sick muddle of distress and she worked herself onto her knees.

She could not stand. The nausea overwhelmed her. The pond seemed a hundred miles away, its fractured center already frozen over with a dark, thin film of ice. Olympia stared at it, crying.

On hands and knees, she began to crawl. Snow crunched under her palms, burning cold against the skin unprotected by Sheridan's bandage. When she reached the ice, it froze to her fingertips, pulling skin from her palm when she tried to move. For a long moment she simply sat swaying on her knees, clutching her hands beneath her arms and staring at the black-and-silver network of fractures. It looked like a shattered window into the infinite night sky. She struggled around until she could scoop up a frigid handful.

It stung her throat and made her teeth ache, and for a moment she feared her body would reject it. But a roll sideways and a brief rest seemed to control the sickness.

Living began to look possible.

Her head still pounded. In her other life—as she had come to think of England—that was a familiar sign of missing a meal. Out on the washes with Fish, she'd stayed until the task was done: till a decent count of plovers was netted, or a good catch of mallards and wigeons bagged. She'd often rowed back to his cottage in the late morning with her head splitting from a skipped breakfast. But here there were no handy tins of biscuits she'd brought from home, no steaming cups of tea, sweet with sugar and cream; no Fish to spit thick slices of bread on the firedog's prongs for toast and butter.

She bit her trembling lip. But the tears seemed finally to have left her. She was too hungry to cry, too weak and cold. With a careful struggle, she rose slowly to her knees and then lurched to her feet.

At the sudden movement, the nearest tussock exploded with motion. An owl took wing, spreading a flash of white underwing, before it landed again on another tussock and stared at her with flat yellow eyes.

Olympia wondered, for the first time in her life, what roasted owl tasted like.

Not that she had any chance of finding out, with no gun and no fire.

The wind stung her cheeks. She could hear the sea, a steady roar in the direction of Sheridan's footprints. All around the pond, grass tussocks much taller than her head rustled ceaselessly, like a crowd of whispering, waving sentinels. She walked unsteadily toward the path he'd followed, wincing with each step on her frozen feet. Just a few yards into the tussocks, she came in view of the shore.

Wind pounded her face. The pale sand, marked by low tide and dark rocks, spread away in both directions. A short distance down the beach, she saw the boat pulled up into the shelter of a notch in the clay bank. Covered with a camouflage of tussock on the ocean side, the green-painted pinnace was barely visible from where she stood.

The scene was deserted. Even Sheridan's footprints in the sand below the bank had been wiped out by the tide that had come and gone while she lay helpless.

Good, she thought defiantly. *I hope he drowns. I hope he breaks his leg and dies in agony. I hope I never see him again.*

She eyed the dismal coast and the island rising behind her to low hills. There was not a sign of life anywhere.

Wrapping the cloak around her, she scrambled down the bank to look for him.

It was late afternoon before Sheridan made it back to the pond. In one hand he had the bucket with his meager offerings: one crab, a dozen mussels, and as much green seaweed as he could fit in around them. Under the other arm he clutched three pieces of driftwood as if they were bars of solid gold. It had taken him all day to collect everything, working miles down the coast, climbing on the rocks, dodging waves and frigid spray. He'd nearly bought it once, when a stray breaker had taken him by surprise and knocked him off his perch and into a tidal pool, washing him brutally against the rocky walls. He'd barely saved the bucket, and lost the big cache of mussels he'd been collecting all morning.

He didn't try to replace them. He couldn't. He could feel himself near the edge of endurance, wet and cold and starving, so he just took as many as he could scrounge on the way back to the pond. He had to eat something soon, and Her Highness would undoubtedly be ready with the next royal complaint.

But she wasn't there.

He stood at the edge of the frozen puddle, shivering and frowning. After a moment, he set down the bucket and the wood and went back to the beach, trudging toward the boat. He called her name.

No answer.

A quick search around the pinnace showed small footprints of indeterminate age. They wandered off down the beach and into the tussocks. He was about to turn back, reckoning that if she was strong enough to get lost, she was in adequate shape to stay alive, when her plump figure tumbled out of the tussocks a few yards down the bank.

She caught her balance and pulled the cloak around her with one hand. "Where have you been?" she demanded.

Sheridan eyed the cloak enviously. It covered every inch of her, head to toe. He lowered his eyelashes and gave her a mocking bow. "Damned near killing myself trying to come by something for dinner, Your Highness."

"Well, you shouldn't have."

"Excuse me. I suppose we should have had a debate and a referendum on it first."

She huddled in the hooded cloak, her body hidden, her

bright hair a frame around her owlish face. A day and night without food didn't seem to have harmed her; she looked as chubby as ever. Chubbier, beneath the voluminous wool. Sheridan stood watching her, feeling his way around the notion that he was relieved and glad to see her. He concluded that any company must be better than none in desperate circumstances.

"Perhaps we should have," she agreed, looking at his empty hands. "Did you find nothing?"

The sharp surge of resentment almost made him turn away without answering. But he didn't, and that made him angry, too. "A crab. Some mussels. Three pieces of driftwood," he said sullenly.

"That's all?"

"Be damned to you," he snapped, swinging away.

"Wait."

He stopped and turned back with his mouth set in bitter temper.

She had a peculiar look on her face, a little upward quiver around her lips. Her eyes were very wide and green. "You brought wood. Is there any way to start a fire?"

"I've got a flint." He shrugged. "Don't look for a roaring blaze to keep you warm all night, not with three pieces of drift."

"Well," she said, with an odd shaky break in her voice. She shifted her arms beneath the cloak and spread it open. "I thought we might cook this."

Sheridan blinked. "My God," he said, his brows rising. "My God."

In trembling hands, amid barren sea and sky a thousand miles from the least sign of civilization, she held out a goose. A fat, dead goose, plucked and dressed and ready to roast.

"I snared it," she said as their fire popped and flickered in the shelter of the windbreak Sheridan had erected out of the sail and extra oars. "There's a little stream over there where the flock comes to drink. I made a noose out of the ribbons from my—" She reddened. "My—uh—"

"Chemise," he suggested cheerfully. "You needn't

mince words with me; I'm old enough to know all about those things. Corsets, petticoats, stays—the works. I bought 'em for you, you know.'' He plucked a gaping mussel shell from the fire and grinned, his face a hellish cast of blue bruises and beard shadow. ''Bally good thing I've got such vulgar taste in ladies' underpinnings, too.''

Olympia ducked her head. She busied herself with spitting the goose on a long splinter of shattered oar, regretting that she'd once complained of the excessive lace and ribbons to Mustafa, who had undoubtedly carried the tale to his master directly. ''I never said 'vulgar.' I thought the style unnecessarily extravagant.''

He scooped the mussel from its shell with one of her whalebone corset stays, dumped it with the rest into the bucket and regarded her beneath his lashes with a slow interest. ''I like extravagance. If you'd married me, I'd have dressed you to the teeth.''

She turned away and stared rigidly into the fire. ''Fortunately, I did not.''

''I don't know . . .'' He tossed a handful of rinsed seaweed in with the mussels. ''Shipwrecked alone on a desert island—even if we're rescued . . .'' He stirred the contents with her stay. ''I'm afraid you may be stuck with me now.''

She raised her eyes to his beautiful, battered face and said with clear deliberation, ''I'd become a streetwalker first.''

The whalebone utensil paused for a fraction of an instant. He looked at her sideways, his eyes light and gray like the misty clouds that swept overhead, his mouth expressionless.

''Would you prefer mussel, crab and seaweed stuffing or mussel, crab and seaweed soup?'' he asked mildly.

She turned back to the goose. ''Anything that's food.''

''Stuffing, then. We'll have had enough of seaweed soup before long, I suspect.'' He handed the bucket across to her.

Olympia peered into it dubiously. ''Are you certain this seaweed is safe to eat?''

''The Chinese dote on it. Sea lettuce. And this other—''

He poked in the bucket at some thick reddish leaves amid the translucent green ones. "It looks like dulse to me. They eat it dried in the Maritimes. Tastes beastly, but there it is. I tried to get us decent lodgings, but you would insist on a room with an ocean view."

Olympia looked up in puzzlement at the peculiar comment. He rolled his eyes and turned away from her.

When the sun began to set, the wind died, leaving a crisp, biting cold and the constant roar of the surf. The stuffed goose went on their makeshift spit, supported by lashed oars. As Olympia turned the bird and Sheridan tended the fire, she stared into the flame, watching the careful way he prodded and nursed it with pieces of tussock, trying to wring the last bit of heat from the driftwood. The glow reflected off the side of the overturned pinnace, lit his face and cast shadows on his thighs as he stood over the fire or knelt to add fuel. He looked dark and magnificent against the fading sky, like the Devil intently tinkering with his hellfires, the better to torture lost souls.

She turned the spit, over and over, her stomach anxious and her mouth watering. The smell of roasting meat amid the windblown desolation brought a weakness to her chest that went beyond hunger. A sheen of hot oil had formed on the browning goose skin, sliding downward into rivulets and drops as she turned the spit. He ran the whalebone stay over the goose, skimming the clear drippings, and held it out to her.

"Eat that. No use wasting it in the fire."

She bit her lip and took the glistening stay. Hot oil ran onto her finger. She licked it, and the first taste of nourishment, warm and delicious amid the nightmare of cold hunger, made the weakness in her chest tremble into a rush. She sat in a huddle by the fire, licking the whalebone corset stay, turning the spit and crying silent tears.

Sheridan squinted quizzically down at her across the flames.

"Excuse me," she said, taking a mortified swipe at her eyes.

"Never mind. Any person of sensibility would weep

over goose cracklings.'' He shrugged. ''I rather feel like it myself.''

''I don't know why. It's just that—this goose—'' She sniffed, and wiped her face again. ''I daresay you won't understand.''

He said nothing. She gazed at the roasting bird and then ventured to glance up at him. He was smiling gently at her.

''It's just that,'' she exclaimed in a wavering voice, ''—it's the first time I've ever done anything really . . . *vital!* I suppose you think I'm . . . si-si-silly.''

He knelt and retrieved the corset stay, settling down next to her cross-legged. Skimming it over the goose, he caught the fresh drippings, then closed his eyes, tilted his head back and sucked at the whalebone until it was clean. ''In terms of historical importance,'' he said, regarding the corset stay respectfully, ''I daresay this goose will rate somewhere between the Magna Carta and the Second Coming of Christ.''

Through the blur of tears, Olympia felt a tiny smile tug at her lips at the ridiculousness of that notion.

He glanced at her, his gray eyes resting for an instant on her mouth, and then returned to a solemn contemplation of the goose. ''We'll commit the details to memory, of course, so that when we're interviewed for the Encyclopaedia—three full pages of description, you know, to be inserted just before the Gutenberg Bible and right after the Glorious First of June—we'll be able to recall the decisive facts that led to this momentous goose. For instance—how long has it taken this goose to cook, would you say?''

She looked longingly at the bird. ''I would say about ten thousand years.''

He laughed, an abrupt hoot that startled her. But it seemed to relax something inside her, that sudden masculine music. She smiled shyly, acutely aware of his knee pressed against her thigh as he reached from his cross-legged position to skim the drippings again.

He handed her the corset stay and watched her as she licked it. ''No doubt it will be known to future generations as simply The Goose,'' he remarked, ''but I think the gravity of the occasion requires something more formal, don't you agree? I propose 'The Glorious Goose of Her Royal Highness Princess Olympia of Oriens, English Maloon and an Impressive Assortment of Other Godforsaken Places.' That way it will still fit into the G's, you see."

"Yes," she said, "but it seems a shame that Admiral Howe and the First of June should still come before."

"The Glorious Bloody Goose, then. You certainly shan't be cut out by some paltry admiral. He only sank five seventy-fours and two eighty-gun French battleships, by God."

Olympia found her smile expanding into a giggle.

"What hey—" he said, peering at her. "Are you laughing? There's a change." He put his arm around her shoulders and bent his forehead to hers. "How pretty you are!"

She stiffened, turning quickly away. But he didn't let go, and the night air was so cold, and the island so lonely, and the situation so desperate, that she sat still where she was and allowed him to touch her.

He didn't move away even when they took down the goose and used her pocket scissors and his knife to cut off portions of meat. Corset stays and fingers made spoons and forks. He sat next to her, his shoulder against hers, dividing the portions with exacting equivalence.

Olympia bit into the first piece of sandy, slightly charred goose and closed her eyes against the intensity of that lifesaving pleasure. It seemed unreal, so familiar and smoky and delicious was it—except for the gritty sand and strange, salty taste imparted by the seaweed. Olympia ate the rubbery green stuff along with her share of the mussels because she was starving, but the sensation of eating solidified ocean water was almost stronger than she could stomach.

When they had finished half the goose, Sheridan put his arm around her again, stopping her move as she reached for another piece.

"That's enough for tonight, my greedy mouse. Think of breakfast."

Olympia pulled back, embarrassed. "Yes, of course." She sat stiffly in the curve of his arm, not knowing where to look. "But you should have some more. I'm convinced that your larger frame requires much more nourishment than mine," she added conscientiously.

"I've lived off less. And you're not conditioned to it." He squeezed her shoulder. "I intend to keep you alive and in proper trim to do all the goose-getting around here."

She looked up into his eyes, struck by the painful desire to allow herself to sink back into the protection of his embrace. It seemed a powerful shelter against the weariness and fright that flooded in on her now that her hunger was diminished. He was so confident, so easy and assured, while the edge of panic pushed at Olympia every moment.

He smiled down at her. Olympia's scruples wavered. She let her rigid spine relax a little, resting tentatively against the curve of his shoulder and chest.

"I suppose," she said, "that you've been through much worse than this."

"Much," he said comfortably.

Compared to her cold cheeks and hands, he felt very warm where his body touched hers. She searched for something to take her mind off it. "What's the worst thing that ever happened to you?"

He gave her a dry look. "Now there's a charming topic of conversation."

"I imagine you've been through some terrible battles."

The rhythmic, solacing brush of his fingers on her arm stopped. He didn't answer.

She glanced sideways at him. He was staring off into the night. As she watched, a faint frown seemed to slide over his face like a shadow.

"I'm sorry," she said. "Never mind."

He shifted a little, loosening his hold on her. "It's a natural thing to wonder about."

And he left her at that. Wondering. After a few moments of silence, she said, "Did you never think of leaving the navy? After the great war was over, I mean."

"Madam, I've lived, breathed and dreamed of leaving the navy for thirty years."

"But you never did."

He made an abstract design in the sand with his knife blade and wiped it out again. "I came close."

"What happened?" She tilted her head.

"I tried being a destitute civilian once. I wasn't very good at it." His breath glowed in the firelight and mingled with hers for an instant before the rising breeze took it. He gazed down at the knife, making another little circle with the point. "Sometimes," he added softly, "I was afraid I might hurt somebody."

She frowned at him.

He looked up and met her eyes, staring at her for a moment, and then blinked. He shrugged and grinned. Before she could pull away, he dropped a light kiss on her forehead. "Show a little cheer, Princess. We ain't dead yet."

Looking down at her lap, she murmured, "Are you not worried?"

"Are you?"

She bit her lip. "I'm frightened to death."

He was silent for a moment. Then he said quietly, "Well, it don't do to say so, you know. Doesn't go down well with the adoring masses. People get the notion you're a poltroon."

She lifted her eyes. "You *are* afraid."

"Quaking in my boots. But after you've been quaking in 'em for thirty years, you get pretty good at hoaxing."

She stiffened a little, frowning.

"Did you think heroes were never afraid, Princess?" His mouth turned up in a mocking curl. "Do you suppose dragons look any smaller at close range? They don't. They look a deuce of a lot bigger." The firelight cast his face in glow and shadow, making his brows seem heathen slashes, his mouth grim and merciless. He could have been one of the dragons himself.

"But after all," she said, recalled to what he was, quivering between renewed anger and disappointment and cautious not to show either, "you've dispatched them. A great number." She paused and asked carefully, "Or has it all been a great hoax?"

He shrugged. "I suppose I'm a fairly downy bird when

it comes to hoaxing dragons. But when one of 'em ties you down and punches you in the stomach, not to mention beating you over the head and drowning you by degrees, it's high time to retire from the field with what grace you can muster.'' He looked at her, his dark lashes swept low over the silver firelight in his eyes. ''I'm sorry you were caught out in the middle, but it's no place for princesses, you know. Dragons have a particular taste for a sweet and helpless royal highness.''

''I thought that was what the hero was for,'' she said tartly. ''To rescue the princess.''

''Well, you're not eaten, are you? And we heroes weren't created just for the convenience of some feather-headed princess gone astray. We have lives of our own. Hopes, plans, railway stocks . . .'' He shook his head. ''But nobody ever thinks of that. It's just rescue the princess and live happily ever after. I've never heard precisely what we're supposed to do when the princess would prefer to start a revolution than marry the poor sod who risked his neck to rescue her. Or announces''—his smile held a bitter twist—''that she'd rather become a streetwalker.''

Olympia sat up away from him. ''Steal her jewels, perhaps,'' she said acidly.

To her astonishment and rage, he had the gall to catch her back. Olympia struggled, pushing at his hands, but in spite of her fight he held her up close to him, his arm around her chest. ''You'll have your damned jewels returned,'' he said into her hair.

''Release me!'' She went stiff and utterly still. ''I hate you.''

''I said you'll have them back! That'll have to be good enough, curse you.''

''Good enough!'' With a mighty effort she tore away and scrambled to her feet, turning on him savagely. ''You don't understand anything, do you? You don't have the first notion of right or wrong or loyalty or honor! Nothing would be good enough! I thought you were a hero, oh, yes. A *real* hero, worth respect, and admiration, and—and *love.*'' She gave the end of a burning log a hard kick, sending sparks spiraling off into the night. ''I loved you!

Can you comprehend that? I *loved* you, and you did that to me—betrayed me and robbed me and left me alone. Alone, when I'd given you all the trust and devotion I was capable of giving! When I'd read about you since I was fifteen, and pasted every report from the Naval Chronicle into my scrapbook; when I'd treasured every clipping about your medals and your ships and the things you've done—when I dreamed about meeting you every night of my life!'' She squeezed her eyes shut and clenched her hands, feeling the wild tears coming. ''I *loved* you.'' Her voice trembled into a squeak. ''I loved you . . . and you . . . betrayed me.''

The tears leaked from beneath her eyelids, hot tracks on her icy cheeks. In the windy silence, the fire popped. Her lip trembled. She put her fist to her mouth and turned away, unable to bear looking at him.

''You loved me, did you?'' His voice was quiet and cutting. ''You never knew me.''

''Obviously,'' she said.

After a moment, he said on a queer, soft note, ''You might have. I would have let you.''

She whirled around. ''Good God, why should I wish to? Who are *you?* A thief. A blackguard.''

He looked up at her, one arm braced around his knee. All the humor had left his face, leaving the bleak, battle-scarred remnants of perfection. ''I gave up on ethics before I was fourteen. I settled for plain survival. One day at a time, Princess—I told you, that's all I know how to do.''

She pulled the cloak around her. ''How can you live like that?'' Her voice was scathing. ''What's the point of it?''

He stared into the fire. His breath seemed uneven for a moment. Then he lifted his face to look at her with a faint, wry wistfulness. ''That maybe tomorrow will be an improvement?'' he suggested. ''That I might be around to see what color the sunrise will be? That I might have a midshipman called home before he's blown apart in battle, or hear a princess laugh? I don't know. What's the point?''

He looked down and began covering the rest of the

goose in seaweed, carefully collecting every bit of flesh and bone and adding it to the bucket.

"It seems to me," she said shakily, "that the point is to try to make the world a better place."

"How?" His voice was flat.

"You know how. You've done it—in spite of yourself, I suppose! By fighting injustice and tyranny."

"Yes, that's what the papers call it, don't they?" He bent over the fire, pushing sand onto the coals to preserve them. "Glorious stuff. For instance, take the time I attempted to recite a poem on the topic to an Algerian corsair. They took out my cabin and the whole of the second gun deck in one volley." He sat back on his heels, staring out into the night. "Not a bad shot for Berbers, actually. Odd how the enemy seems to cherish the backward notion that we're the tyrants. Makes 'em downright violent." He paused. His face grew very taut and strange. "Stupid of me to underestimate that. I lost a lot of men." He turned back and stared at her, his eyes like silver smoke. "I'm already pretty well damned to burn, you see. I've got more than stolen jewels on my soul."

She held his gaze for a long moment. The cold breeze lifted her hair and touched her neck the same way a queer, shuddery finger of emotion touched her heart. "You're trying to make me feel sorry for you," she snapped.

He laughed softly and stood up. "Maybe so." Firelight cast moving light on his hands and face, blending his dark hair and clothes into the night behind. "Why not?" he asked quietly. "It's lonely out here with the dragons."

Fifteen

She was in her bedroom, snuggled down to her nose in her own bed against the freezing air. Mr. Stubbins bent over her with his golden hair and his lesson frown. "You must drink," he said. "History teaches us that the will of the people overcomes tyranny. Drink."

She tried to move and couldn't. Her head felt like a leaden weight.

He wore a uniform, braids and epaulettes that gleamed against the dark. "I am willing to fight," he exclaimed. "I am willing to die. Don't be afraid."

With a steel flourish, he drew his sword. A sensation of horror gripped her. She turned in the dark and something was there—she heard its breath; she felt its hot touch; she tried to scramble up and run and found herself mired on the ground. It hunkered over her, pinning her down with warm weight, the soft underbelly pressing on her body.

Terrified, she arched her head back and saw the glittering blackness, the huge frame and graceful tail—a nightmare hiss and slash.

A dragon, *she thought. And then, with strange wonder:* How beautiful it is.

"For the People!" Mr. Stubbins shouted, lifting his sword.

No, *she tried to cry,* no, it's a dragon!

She could not form the words. The sword swung in a bright arc against the night and the dragon moved like a cat, a sudden shimmer of black and silver that flashed and struck in silence.

The uniformed figure lay still on the ground, leaking blood that dulled the polished braids and ruined the golden epaulettes.

"He's dead," the dragon said, holding her trapped when she would have run to the fallen form.

She stared at the limp and broken body while the blood spread and stained the deck. "You killed him!" she cried. "I loved you, and you killed him!"

The dragon's hold dug into her shoulders. "I'm not a dragon. I'm a man."

"I hate you. I hate you. I loathe you!"

His belly slid against hers; he buried his head in her naked shoulder—and suddenly he was kissing her skin, forcing weight on her, his body pressing warmth and lust into hers.

"I want to touch you," he whispered, his hand on her thigh.

"Oh, God." She trembled and arched. "You can't. You can't do this."

His palm slid upward, caressing her thighs, her inner skin. She moaned with the feel of it, the intimate heat moving toward a center of fire. They were both naked, his male shape pressed down on her, into her.

"No," she whimpered. But her hands molded the length of his back, the breadth of his shoulders—passed along the flame-touched curve of muscle and bone. "I hate you. I can't. Why are you doing this?"

He did not answer. His kiss scored the arch of her throat; his hand sought the heart of her tumult: a pressing, violent, sweet sensation.

"I hate you." She twisted and clutched and moaned in desperation. "Oh, I hate you!"

His body enveloped her, covered her in hot darkness and passion. She felt his touch on her lips and throat. She tried to see him and saw dragon eyes in the night, glittering silver.

"I'm a man," he whispered. "I'm a man."

"I won't," she cried. "I can't!"

And yet she reached for him, tried to pull his body close in shame and urgency.

"Oh, please," she said, "oh, please . . ."

He covered her, drowned her in black fire and glittering darkness. And she let him, weeping with humiliation; moving and pulsing with pleasure.

Olympia opened her eyes with a faint start. The ache of excitement still throbbed between her legs. She shifted underneath the sealskin and blinked past the dream to consciousness.

A foot away, Sheridan was still asleep. Cold sunlight filtered through the tussock roof of the stone hut, lighting an uneven streak on the sandy floor. From outside the door came the sound of rooks, arguing and fluttering, and beneath that the ever-present murmur of the surf.

She stared at Sheridan for a long time.

He was stretched out beneath her cloak, which he'd been using as a blanket since they'd found only enough fur skins to make a single bed in the ruined sealers' hut. He lay on his side, one arm curled up under his head and the other extended, as if he'd been reaching for her.

The streak of sunlight crossed his hand and bare forearm. His palm lay upturned and half open, the fingers curled gently in relaxation. She could see his pulse beating beneath the smooth skin of his inner wrist, and the almost healed blister he'd got from rowing the pinnace with wet oars.

Stripped of his halo of heroism, he was infamous. He was vile and tantalizing, with his soft mockery and his unfamiliar maleness. She squeezed her eyes shut and threw herself onto her stomach, burying her mortification in the soft fur.

For a week she'd dreamed it—or something close enough. She despised him, and he haunted her. He was a coward and a thief, yet she found nothing so fascinating as to watch him as he slept. It was bewildering and distressing and shameful. It was unbearable.

Slowly, so slowly, she slid her fingers across the sealskin. They came within a fraction of his. She stopped. She had only to open her hand to touch him. In the dream he had touched her, slid his palm across her skin, made the ache into sweet fire . . .

She opened her fingers and brushed his hand.

He didn't stir. Glancing up, she watched his breathing, deep and oblivious. He was tired; he'd spent yesterday rebuilding the last portion of the hut, hauling rocks from the hill behind the beach while Olympia cut tussock grass to thatch the roof. She'd missed her attempt at a goose. The flock was growing wary. By the time she'd given up, the tide was too high to reach the mussel beds, so all Sheridan had had to eat was the contents of two handfuls of tiny, spiraled periwinkle shells in a thin broth of seaweed and goose bones. There had been a half breast of the last goose left, but he'd stubbornly refused it.

She needed it more, he said.

She slipped her fingertips along the pads of his. His hand was so much larger than hers—brown and firm, where hers was pale and plump and chapped. She'd tried to help with the rocks, but he didn't like it. She was too slow, he said; she was in the way, and she'd only get hungrier and look at him with her big eyes and he'd end up giving her his portion again. Go stalk a goose. Or keep a lookout.

Sometimes it was hard to hate him.

She'd been content with stalking the geese, as long as she could catch them. But she hadn't taken one for two days now. And no ships came, not *Phaedra* or any other.

She smoothed her fingers over his sun-warmed palm. There was an ache in her, a restlessness, on the edge of something she wanted and could not have.

The hut was not as cold as it might have been before they'd learned to dig the peaty turf from beneath the tussocks to burn. Last night's fire was banked against the stone hearth. Her dress and chemise, dry at last, hung from a bleached whalebone rafter. Beneath the sealskin she was naked.

The cloak had fallen back from his shoulder, revealing the velvet swell of bare skin and muscle. A flash of the dream came back: a weight on her, a masculine shape between her hands. Her fingers curved, pressing into his.

She imagined smoothing her palm across his shoulder. Her heart beat faster. She could see the outline of his body beneath the cloak, the fluent shape of his torso and hip, powerful relaxed perfection, his leg drawn up a little in a sleeper's balance.

She wished she could slip the cloak back. The dream lingered, a remembrance of sensation. She stared at his hand, her fingers drifting, tracing the curve at the base of his thumb and moving up the open flex of his forefinger, feeling the smooth skin and roughened places. It seemed amazing to touch him, to be so close to a man—to *this* man, who set her insides in turmoil and harried her dreams in dragon-shape.

She raised her lashes and found him watching her.

She almost snatched her hand back—then didn't, on the hope that it might seem an accident of sleep—then nearly did, on the logic that she would if she'd just woken up and found it there—and then didn't, for no reason at all except that she was paralyzed.

He smiled at her: a strange, sleepy, heated smile, his eyes a tangled brush of dark lashes and pale smoke. Gently, his hand closed over her fingers. He caressed her palm with his thumb.

Olympia wet her lips. If he'd held her by force, if he'd spoken, she would have pulled away. But the silence made it seem unreal. She could see the tendon in his wrist flex as he stroked her.

He opened his hand and slid his fingers backward between hers, curling them over and down into his palm. So slowly that she never found the concentration to resist, he drew their locked hands toward him. He bent his head to the back of her palm and pressed a soft, caressing kiss to her skin.

"I'd like to," he murmured, his fingers tightening. "God, I'd like to." His lashes lowered as if he were tasting honey. "But better not, Princess. Not here."

Olympia jerked away, coming to her senses in a fluster.

He rolled onto his elbow at her side. His gray eyes were marked with laugh lines as he leaned on his hand and looked down at her. "As your chief minister of affairs, it's my unfortunate duty to report that I'm exerting myself manfully, but should I be awakened tomorrow with a back rub, I'm afraid it may go hard with you."

"What are you talking about?"

His face lost its humor. He watched her for a long moment, his gaze moving to her mouth and shoulders with raking leisure and then up again. "I think you know what I'm talking about," he said softly.

Olympia felt blood rush to her cheeks. She turned sharply away and stared at the tussock roof. "If you will kindly leave for a moment, I can get dressed."

His mouth curved up at one corner. He threw off the cloak and turned over, hiking himself up. Olympia pretended to stare at the roof, but she watched him from the corner of her eye. Though he was wearing pale trousers, he slept with them open. In the moment before he reached for his shirt on the hearth, Olympia bit her lip with a small sound of dismay. He tied the double trouser flap, containing the startling sight behind a bulge of fabric, and glanced questioningly at her.

Olympia knew what his body normally looked like. In spite of her sick weakness on that first morning here, the momentary view she'd had of him was quite vivid in her memory.

"Are you ill?" she asked sharply.

He seemed surprised, and then shook his head. "Devilish tired and hungry. Do I look ill?"

"That's not painful? That swelling?"

"Swe—" He stopped, blinked—and then a slow grin lit his face. "Ah. *That* swelling."

Olympia recognized his grin. She'd said something ridiculous; laid herself open to his subtle mockery. She stiffened beneath the seal fur and turned her face away. "Never mind! I'm sure I don't care if you swell up and turn purple all over."

"That only happens if I hold my breath. This is a different kind of malady, Princess Peahen."

"I see," she said with arctic majesty.

"Actually, it begins to appear that you don't. Would you like me to tell you about it?"

"No."

He said gently, "I think perhaps I ought. We might rub along better."

"I'm sure there's no need," she said, and then added rather wildly, "I know all about it."

He shook his head. Sunlight glanced off his black hair. "You don't know the first damned thing. Which I might have guessed, given the kind of well-informed opinions you hold about the rest of the world." He pulled on his coat, scooped up her dress and chemise and headed out the door. "Don't go far," he said blithely. "Professor Sherry commences his famous lecture on Modesty and Morality in the Modern Female in just a few moments."

"You don't have the morals of a cat!" she shouted after him, trapped naked beneath the fur while he had her dress. "Or the modesty either."

"You've got fifteen minutes," he called. "You'd better be back under that fur when I get back, or we'll have a demonstration instead of a lecture."

Olympia took him at his word, scrambling out from under the sealskin and performing her morning ablutions in frenzied haste. Long before he returned, she was huddled in place with the fur up to her chin, staring at the stone wall in miserable anger and uncertainty. Worse than the fury and bewilderment was the confused sense of excitement, all tangled up with the dream and his hands and the way she'd watched him sleep.

It was wrong. It was wicked, like he was—and it held the same impossible allure. She thought of what he'd done to her in Madeira, the way he'd made her feel with his hands and his kisses, and felt sick with agitation.

She heard the rooks squabble and scatter and went rigid in anticipation. When he came through the door, she was pretending to have gone back to sleep, but she knew perfectly well when he rekindled the fire, filling the hut with the tangy smell of peat smoke. Her pathetic effort at sleep dissolved as soon as he sat down so close to her that his leg pressed hard against her hip. Something rustled dryly. She opened her eyes.

To her astonishment, he was unwrapping a small packet of waxy paper.

She sat up, barely remembering to clutch the fur skin over her. "Whatever's that?"

"Breakfast."

"What is it? Where did you find it?"

He smiled, holding up three sticks of horehound candy, spiraled with pale green and white. "Our late friend the chief mate had a sweet tooth. I've been saving 'em for a special occasion."

Olympia's lips parted in awe. "Oh," she said faintly. "Oh, my. You don't know how I've been dreaming of comfits!"

"I daresay I had my suspicions." He pulled out his knife and sawed at one stick, dividing it with his careful and exacting fairness. "Here, my mouse." He laid the sweet in her upturned palm, pressed her fingers over it and kissed the top of her fist before she realized what he was about. She snatched her hand away.

He only laughed softly and stretched out beside her with a stick of horehound in his mouth. He'd shaved, which he did frequently, in spite of arguments over proper use of their single bar of soap. Olympia slid down into the protection of the fur, sucking her own portion of candy with nervous bliss.

He crunched down on his stick, making short work of what Olympia was savoring, and then watched her for a moment. "Do you know how to make a baby?" he asked.

Olympia almost swallowed her candy stick.

"Specifically, I mean," he added. "Not just get married, y' know, and then go look under a cabbage leaf."

She hesitated, crimson. He was propped up on his elbow, regarding her with casual attention. She shook her head slightly.

"Just as well," he said. "At least you're not suffering under some bizarre misconception about doorknobs or something. You wouldn't believe some of the weird ideas thirteen-year-old midshipmen can circulate as truth." He sucked at the tip of his second piece of candy, regarding her over his fist. "But I'm sure your notions on the subject are much more mature."

"I never thought about it," she said stiffly.

"Oh, really?" He lifted his eyebrows. "A virgin and a liar to boot."

"I haven't dwelt on it," she amended abruptly.

"Why did you touch me this morning?"

She turned her face away. "I didn't touch you. I despise you."

"Yes, we're all well aware of that. I'm a villain and a blackguard—every quaking little maiden's nightmare." He lowered his lashes, watching her with a moody smile and eyes like smoke. "But some get a taste for the devil, don't they?"

Olympia drew in a sharp breath. "This is nonsense! I want to get up."

"By all means," he said mildly.

She glared at him, still trapped underneath the fur by her nakedness. He showed no inclination to leave.

"Don't you want to know?" His question was soft and provocative. "Knowledge is power, Princess. Did your learned tutor never pass along that political lesson?"

Olympia glared at him.

He lifted one eyebrow in a subtle curve. "Wouldn't you like to torment me? You can, you know. You've got revenge right in your hand."

"Oh, I'm sure you intend to tell me exactly how I can torment you."

His lashes lowered on a silver gleam. "I might."

"Why?"

"It's a game, Princess. I can tell you how to play, but that doesn't mean you'll win."

Olympia gave an unladylike snort. "I'm sure if it were a game, you'd cheat."

He tilted his head. "Now, cheating is an interesting subject. For instance, is it actually cheating if one doesn't get caught?" He looked back at her. "But the rules are pretty flexible in this particular competition, so I encourage you to connive against me to your heart's content. If you think you can."

This challenge, delivered with a sly smile, made her sit up on her elbows, pulling the fur up under her chin. "I'm tired of your idea of riddles. If there's something I ought to know that you can tell me, do so directly."

He reached across her, spreading his fingers in the fur as he caught her arm, pulling her against him. Her face was on a level with his, her skin flushed. Her loosened hair spilled down over her shoulders and the soft bedding. For an instant he stared at her, so close she could feel his breath on her eyelashes. As her lips parted to speak, he lowered his head and kissed her.

Olympia made a sound in her throat: furious protest and unwilling excitement. His grip tightened on her arm. Heat and sweetness invaded her, the taste of sugar on his tongue, the scent of horehound candy and of him—honey and salt mingled, unexpected and fascinating.

The sound of the ocean seemed to rise to a roar in her ears. She was drowning in him, in the length of his body, in the heat of his mouth taking hers, when he suspended the kiss with an abrupt move. He left her breathing hard and raggedly. She stared up into eyes of cloudy silver beneath black lashes.

"Direct enough?" he murmured.

"Let go of me."

"When the lecture's over. We might require further demonstration on certain points." He bent to brush caressing kisses at the corners of her lips, his breath warm on her cheek. "Don't fight it so, my little mouse. I won't hurt you."

She closed her eyes with a faint trembling in her chin, a strange, painful pleasure spreading through her. "You will," she whispered. "Yes, you will."

His light caresses stopped. In the silence a rook cried above the sound of the surf. Olympia pressed her mouth closed against the quivering.

When she opened her eyes he was looking down at her. The teasing smile was gone, leaving the grave, beautiful curve of his mouth. He lowered his lashes, and the sulky expression stole in to shadow his features. He glanced away toward the fire. "If it's guilt and regret you want, you're looking at the wrong man."

"I don't want anything from you. Not anymore."

He turned back, his eyes smoldering. "That's a lie, Princess."

She felt herself redden beneath his hot look.

"Unlike you," he said, "I happen to have a jolly good notion of what you want. And it's fine with me, but for the fact that we're stranded on this damned desolate island for the foreseeable future, and I don't wish to have three of us to worry about instead of two."

"Three!"

"A baby," he said politely. "I don't want you pregnant. Not here."

Olympia's blush deepened into scarlet. "That couldn't happen," she exclaimed, covering her agitation and embarrassment with a scathing tone. "We aren't married."

"Well, what do you think, that they wave a magic wand at the ceremony and you start littering right there at the altar? That ain't the way it works, as I've been at pains to try to explain to you, if you'd come down off your high ropes and listen."

"How does it work?" she demanded in alarm, and then a dreadful thought occurred to her. She stared at him, horrified. "You *kissed* me." Then an even worse memory blazed, of scandalous intimacy in Madeira. "And . . . and touched—" She swallowed frantically. "Oh, God."

He threw back his head with a bark of laughter. "Aye, I did, didn't I?" He grinned wickedly. "Feeling a bit queer yet? Any sign of dizziness? Queasy in the morning?"

She sat up, pulling the fur around her. "The only thing that makes me queasy is you! Go on. Tell me everything, and if you lie to me, I swear I'll make you sorry."

"I'm terrified." He smiled at her, his glance lingering on her bare shoulders. "All right, then—listen up. Forget all that rubbish about wifely duty you've undoubtedly been stuffed with. It'll give you terminal respectability. Think of the way you felt when you were touching me this morning."

She wet her lips, evading his eyes.

"You don't have to be shy. It's only me, you know . . . despicable old Sheridan the Thieving Coward and Fraud. There's no one else to hear. And you don't care what I think, do you?"

"Not in the least."

"There." He smiled a little. "Now—how did you feel when you were touching my hand?"

Olympia shifted uncomfortably, holding tight to the fur.

"Restless?" he suggested gently. "Excited?"

She bit her lip.

"Where?" he asked.

She didn't answer. She couldn't. Watching him stretched out like an easy cat, with his gray eyes and tangled lashes and faint lazy smile, was bringing back the feeling in force.

"Here," he supplied for her, and spread his hand on his abdomen. Olympia stared at it, at his fingers as they slid downward toward the apex of his legs. "And here."

His palm rested over the place where she'd seen his body change. The thought made waves of heat and agitation wash over her. She thought of the dream, of Madeira: the sweet center of fire. Her own body began to feel queer and melting there in the same place where his hand lay.

"I feel that way, too," he said softly. "When I see you, or think about you in particular ways—sometimes if I think about what I can't see . . ." He half closed his eyes, dreamy and diabolic. "Your ankles . . . I think about how small they are, and how they're shaped . . . the way they curve down to your pretty white feet. I think about how soft they'd be if I could touch them . . . how they'd taste if I could kiss them, how warm and smooth and . . ." He lifted his hand. "See?"

Olympia blinked at the change in his anatomy, her face burning a furious red.

"I'm not ill, Princess. I'm just a man, and I want you."

"What do you want from me?" Her voice was a suspicious squeak.

"In spite of my brain's better judgment, my body wants to get a child in you." He shook his head at her shock. "It's nothing perverted, unless you've got a quarrel with the way God made us. All of us. This ain't just me and my rotten character, you understand. If you'd been stranded here with Fair-Haired Fitzhugh, he'd have felt the same way. Probably worse, since he's still young enough to get himself desperate thinking on the topic. Only he'd have lied about it, to you and to himself, being one of those manly and virtuous nincompoops that seem to abound in the world."

She closed her eyes, breathing rapidly. The mere thought of carrying Sheridan's child made her feel peculiar: not proper disgust at all, but mortification all mixed with excitement and agitation. The idea of him imagining her ankles sent liquid heat pulsing through the place he'd awoken.

"And you, too," he murmured. "What you're feeling—the reason you want to touch me—it's all part of the same thing. It's natural, and I'm not lying now, Princess. Don't ever let some holy fool tell you different, or make you feel ashamed. It's a joy, and God knows there's little enough of that in life sometimes."

It didn't exactly seem like a joy to Olympia. The way she felt seemed more like slow torture. "I want it to stop," she mumbled into the seal fur.

"Yes, it's certainly an inconvenience here. Short of building separate huts, or moving me into exile on another island—"

"No!" Olympia felt a surge of terror at the idea. "No, don't—leave. I—I think we do better together."

"Well, I'm in neither the mood nor the shape to build another hut, and I doubt it would help anyway. Once this sort of thing gets hold of your mind, it doesn't take much more than imagination and the occasional encounter to keep it hot as hellfire."

"Perhaps if we just put our thoughts to something else." She looked at him hopefully. "Would that help?"

He lifted smoky eyes and regarded her, his mouth a seductive curve. "Would it?"

Olympia stared at him, at his shoulders and hands, at his dark hair and Satan's brows and the strong line of his jaw and throat. She pressed her hands over her face. "Oh, why?" she moaned. "Why *you?* I hate you."

"Thank you. I'm flattered. I suppose I can assume it's my fashionable air and speaking eyes that are so irresistible."

"I *hate* you," she wailed, hugging her knees and burying her face in the fur to escape his knowing look and the truth—which was that she could not see him, or think of him, without watching the masculine power and grace of his movements or imagining the weight and feel of him against her. She'd been months with Captain Fitzhugh and never experienced the slightest desire to be nearer to him than a respectable teatime distance. With Sheridan, she burned with it—worse now than before. "Why did you have to bring this up?" she demanded miserably. "Why couldn't we have gone on as we were?"

He sat up, turning on her fiercely. "Oh, forgive me, Miss Innocence, but it wasn't me who started fondling you in your sleep! You've been making your naive sheep's eyes at me since the day we met, and I've about reached the end of my rope." He jerked his head. "You've had me living on top of this particular volcano long enough, damn you. You touch me like that again and I'll show you how to deal with the problem—and there won't be any babe, either, because I can manage that well enough, too."

Olympia held the fur over her mouth. She met his intense gaze, feeling her heart pound until her ears were full of the sound, until faintness hovered at the edge of her vision. Her body ached for him.

"Can you?" she whispered through the dimness.

His face changed. The violence faded away into a sudden, silent watchfulness. He looked into her eyes and said, "Yes."

She couldn't seem to get her breath. "Then . . ."

The word trailed off. The tussock grass above rustled, casting dancing dots of sunlight.

"What do you want?" he said very softly.

She closed her eyes. She could feel him next to her, even blind. Her hand slid from her knees. She looked down and spread her palm on the ground between them, a bare inch from his fist.

He was utterly still. "You give me the right to touch you."

It was a statement and a question. Olympia bit her lip. She thought of the dream, the dragon in the night, beautiful and terrible and strange. *I'm a man,* it said. *I want you.*

"Yes," she whispered, and reached for his hand. "Yes."

Sixteen

"Good God,'' Sheridan muttered, seized with a sudden doubt.

It had been a joke, this teasing: petty revenge for her cutting remarks and low opinion of him. The last thing he'd expected was acquiescence. Not in this.

From the start of their sojourn, he'd resigned himself to endless tantalizing torture because there was no other rational choice. And well he'd known that she was struggling with her own demons; he'd seen the way she looked at him in the firelight. But he'd kept the barriers in place, tolerating her hatred because it was the strongest.

Now, suddenly, it wasn't there.

He should have seen what he was meddling with. Damn his sense of mischief. One push, and the walls crumbled. She was looking at him in wary fascination, like a wild bird brought to hand. The sealskin flowed around her, revealing a glimpse of white shoulder here, a dimpled elbow there.

His chest felt tight. She was delicious, all tousled and plump. Her fingers rested over his hand. He closed his fist on nothing and turned his head.

Winter was closing in. He wasn't fooled by this one crystalline day. They'd be lucky to live through the season. He ought to get up now and go out and build himself his own shelter. He was crazy if he stayed with her; insane to think that once he touched her, he could remember caution.

But he was going to. He knew he was going to. Already he'd gone too far.

"Lie down," he mumbled without looking at her.

She obeyed him, silent and solemn. She was such a wide-eyed, serious mouse, taking everything that ever happened as if it were the God-given Judgment Day. He pushed his hand through his hair, rested on his palm and gazed down at her.

He found himself at a loss. He had no idea how to start—never mind the days of his corrupt youth, when he'd lectured ridiculous, randy middies on the facts of life and then, for a lark and an outrageous fee, conducted them in a giggling flock to some dockside brothel. He thought of the words he'd used then, the blunt warnings and casual jokes, the gaudy rooms and nonchalant bawds all painted and dressed and smelling of sweat beneath their perfume.

He could not use those words with her. But the thought of them made him draw a profound, shaky breath and close his eyes for mental balance.

He was going to regret this. It would kill him. To feel like this and not have her would be absolute annihilation.

"You want to touch me," he said into her palm. "And I want it." He kissed the curves between her fingers, one after another. "I want it." He looked into her eyes. "I'm going to show you where . . . and find the places that give you pleasure."

She wet her lips. Sheridan stared at the tip of her tongue and felt heat curl in his belly.

He hesitated and then said, "I might—it's possible I might—uh—forget myself. If I do something you don't like, you only have to say so, and I'll . . . stop." He drew a breath. "I'll stop."

A moment of silence passed. In a small, wistful voice, she said, "I think you could have been a nice hero."

"I doubt it." He sat up and shrugged off his coat, pulling the single-sleeved shirt over his head. The air in the hut was cool against his hot skin as he stretched out beside her. He pressed her palm against his chest, splaying his own hand over it. With his eyes on her face, he pulled her open hand down his bare torso in a slow, sensuous slide. "Being the villain is a deal more fun," he murmured. "Particularly for a man with a beautiful female in his clutches."

She moved restlessly beneath the fur. "I'm not beautiful."

He tightened his fingers over hers. "I'm sorry to say you've got no idea what you're talking about. Which comes as no surprise to me. You generally don't."

"I'm too plump," she said breathlessly, bracing against his slow pull downward.

He would not let her free. He rested on his elbow, exerting a steady force. Their hands reached the band of his trousers. Sheridan swallowed and closed his eyes. "There," he said, not breathing very evenly himself.

"Oh!" she said.

"That's all right. That's—all right. Don't . . . pull away."

"I'm hurting you."

"No." He shook his head. "Oh, no." Slowly, he moved his hand from hers and tugged at the trouser laces. As the fabric fell, he had to grab her wrist when she tried to snatch her hand away. With gentle stubbornness, he made her touch, holding her hand on him, wrapped in his own, while he brushed his cheek against her hair and bit his lower lip until he drew blood.

"You're shaking," she said timidly.

"An excess of enjoyment." His voice was strained. "It feels good. It feels so good."

"I'm embarrassed."

He brushed her pink cheek with his lips. "Why?"

"Because . . ." She made a sound of agitation. Her fingers tightened and relaxed in little convulsive movements that made the world go dim around him. "I don't think I . . ." She licked her lips and looked up with plaintive eyes. "I'm sure I shouldn't like to do this!"

"Do you like it?"

She didn't answer, but color burned in her cheeks. He opened his hand, and hers stayed. After a moment, she turned her head a little into the curve of his shoulder, hiding her face. Her fingers began a hesitant butterfly exploration, up and down, finding his shape and dimensions, while Sheridan crushed his mouth against her hair and pressed her head into his chest.

"Oh, God." The words exploded from him at last. "I think—that's—enough."

She pulled away instantly. Sheridan relaxed his convulsive hold.

"You see . . ." he said, making an attempt to steady his breathing, ". . . how you can . . . torment me."

Her eyes widened. She looked down at the place she'd been touching, her burnished lashes lying for a moment on her cheek. Then, with a slight tilt of her chin, she glanced up—a sidelong skim of his body and a speculative lift of her lashes. She stared at him like a cat watching a canary. Her hand slid back toward the place he'd shown her.

Sheridan groaned. "I've done it now, haven't I?" He caught her wrist and held it away. "Perhaps we'll go on to the next step."

She bit her lower lip. "I like this one."

"I can see that, you little tart. But I've been lying here letting you look at me, and touch me, while you're covered up to the chin. Now . . ." He lowered his head and nuzzled her temple. "I want to look at you."

He felt her stiffen.

"Will you let me?" he murmured.

She didn't answer.

He said nothing more, just kept caressing her hot skin, pressing light, whispery kisses over her forehead and temples. Sun through the roof burned a warm patch on his back and shoulder. He slid his fingers into her tangled hair, outlining the curve of her ear.

"All right," she whispered, so quickly and softly that he almost missed it.

Sheridan smiled into her hair. He pushed himself up onto one hand. She had her eyes squeezed shut, martyr-like, her body rigid. With a private grin, he sat up and straddled her on hands and knees. Still she wouldn't move.

"Open you eyes, Princess," he said softly. "Look at me."

Her lashes lifted, but she continued staring at the wall.

"Princess."

"I can't," she said tensely.

He waited a moment. Her lips worked; her eyes squeezed shut again.

"I can't! I just can't."

"Why not?"

"I'm too—fat!"

"You're enchanting," he said.

She shook her head vigorously. "You won't like me. My figure—I'm not at all pleasing."

"You're splendid," he said. She shook her head again and started to speak. "Yes," he interrupted, "you are. What makes you such a bloody expert on the female form, anyway? If this is any example of your judgment, then you'd better stick to radical revolutions, that's my advice."

"But—"

He took hold of the sealskin and sat back, pulling it with him in one smooth motion until he was kneeling upright across her, the satin warmth of the fur draped across her calves beneath him. He spread his hands on his taut trousers, his fingers pressing into his thighs as he gazed at her.

She was beautiful. He'd known she would be: blame that vicious old cat Julia for convincing her she was fat and unattractive. A hot, protective anger surged in him as he watched the way she bit her lips and shook with more than the cool air; the way she pressed her arms to her sides and balled her hands into tight little fists.

"Listen." His voice was hoarse. "Listen to me, Princess. There ain't a man alive who wouldn't sell his soul for a glimpse of you." He took a deep breath. "And I'm going to tell you exactly why, d'you see? I'm going to start at your hair, which I see all the time, and which always makes me think of sunrise—and of waking up naked in bed with you. Especially now, when it's all tumbled around your face like a halo." He closed his eyes briefly, feeling the fur and her shape beneath his legs, recalling a thousand erotic fantasies of this moment. "And then," he went on huskily, "I'm going to tell you how lovely and green your eyes are, and how your eyelashes are gold at the tips, and how your eyebrows are dark and sultry—and have character, too—which isn't an easy feat for eyebrows."

"You're making fun," she whispered, but her voice was hesitant.

"I'd think you'd know me by now," he said. "I'd think you'd guess. Sometimes it's not so easy to say something, so I tease a little."

She turned her head and stared at him. He smiled crookedly. The tip of her tongue touched her upper lip again, sparking a wave of heat that made his smile fade.

"You have an adorable chin," he said. "Perfect to kiss. And your shoulders are straight and wide, just right, not gaunt or bony at the collar like some underbred shopgirl's, but smooth and flat and white. So, so white . . ." He leaned forward on his hands over the tender pale crevice between her arm and the upward swell of her breast. "Like pearls. Like alabaster." He kissed the plump cleft, brushing his lips over skin as delicate as porcelain, but warm and yielding and soft, so seductively soft, with a sweet, salty female scent that he savored in deep breaths.

"Oh, my," she said faintly.

He sat back, letting his hand slide over her skin and shape the curve of her breast. "And here . . ." He had to swallow and close his eyes for an instant before he could go on. "This is beautiful. Perfect and round"—he cupped her other breast, gazing down, his mouth going dry—"with the most exquisite rosy nipples, oh, God, they're luscious—cream and pink and arousing. I've dreamed about them . . . about kissing them . . ."

She watched him, her eyes wide and dazzled, while the tip of her tongue played nervously over her upper lip. Sheridan returned her look with his eyelashes lowered, his body burning.

He drew his fingers beneath her breasts and down her torso. "An ideal waist." His hands slid and shaped her. "The finest proportions, with these magnificent curves above and below . . . the lovely way your hips swell, and this—'' He traced a path downward, his breath coming faster. ''This is my favorite, this charming satiny belly . . .'' His knees pressed against her hips. ''Exciting—oh, Lord, so pretty and plump, undulating down to such a beautiful rich crop of curls.'' He tangled his hand in them, looking down. ''Like sunlight. Like . . . silk.'' His voice cracked. ''Christ, I'll make myself insane.''

She was staring at him in wonder, as if he'd already lost his mind. ''Pretty?'' she whispered.

He moaned. ''Glorious.'' He spread his fingers across her and pulled them lower. ''Delicious. You're magnificent. And I was going to . . . go on . . .'' His blood was pounding. ''But I don't think I . . .''

The sentence trailed off into a wordless sound of fervor as he touched the tender curve of her upper thighs. Olympia sucked in her breath. She felt his weight, the pressure of his legs against her bare skin, hard and hot. He was looking down at her, his thumbs skimming that place he had touched before, creating a sensation that made her want to writhe and whimper.

She felt that her whole body must be fiery with shame and excitement. She wanted to close her eyes; she wanted to scramble away and hide, but she could not stop looking at him. He was breathing deeply, his lashes a dark sweep against his tanned face as he looked down at her body and watched what his hands were doing. The splendid curves of his chest and shoulders rose and fell in rhythm with the stroke of his thumbs through the curls that hid the source of sweet flame.

She pressed upward under his hands with a soft moan. He leaned forward, the opened trousers brushing her thighs and a new heat pressing where his fingers had been. His hands gripped her waist and his thighs tightened as his hips took up the rhythm his hands had begun. That mysterious silky hardness her fingers had explored touched her now with scorching intimacy. It pushed and slid against her as he moved. With every stroke that rubbed across the bright center of sensation, Olympia gave a faint, eager gasp. He stared down at her face, his lips parted in a harsh smile, his eyes gleaming with knowing mockery.

Blood rushed to her face. She tried to pull away.

He bent and trapped her between his hands. "Oh, no. Don't leave now," he murmured. "It won't prove a thing, except that you're a hypocrite. And there's really nowhere worth going, is there?"

She tried to get her breath. It was hard, with him above her, his gray eyes light, his legs spread, the trousers stretched across his thighs and revealing his rampant maleness as it touched her in an act of the most arrant sensuality. Without shame he moved, slowly arching his head back with a groan and a long, heavy push against the moist sweetness between her legs. It set sparks to the place he touched, sent fire through her spine and up to her breasts. Her thighs trembled and tried to open against the prison of his legs.

He rose suddenly, freeing her, kneeling between her legs to slide his hands beneath her knees as the fur fell away. His palms shaped the back of her thighs, lifting, skimming down to slip between her buttocks and the sealskin.

"Oh, Jesus . . . Princess . . ." He bent his head and kissed the inside of her raised knee, his hands pulling her toward him as he knelt with his folded legs spread wide beneath her hips.

Olympia felt the renewed contact of his body against the warmth that was opened wide to him. His hardness moved again across that point of hot pleasure, even closer now, more forcefully, slipping easily on the moistness that spread amid her downy curls. Her hands stretched and closed. She could not reach him; she could only moan and clutch at nothing with the agonizing stimulation of each slow stroke. It seemed their bodies were made for this, that his manhood caressed her exactly, slid and pleasured her until she would explode. His breath came harsh and fast. His shoulders and arms were trembling with strain: she felt it as she crushed her legs against him convulsively.

His head bowed. He groaned, leaning forward with a

sudden, hard push. Olympia sucked in her breath when the movement brought a change, a slip and a startling new sensation as his male hardness, instead of sliding across her, pressed into her—and unexpectedly her body yielded, accepting the unfamiliar invasion, stretching and filling with a queer mixture of discomfort and relish.

"What are you doing?" she gasped weakly.

He went still, his head down and his muscles shaking. "Making . . . a mistake." His voice was a muffled croak.

She could feel him, frozen and tense, except for a sudden throb and shudder of his body—one and then another, just inside her. It felt peculiar . . . but delicious. She moved her hips in a slow, delighted squirm.

"Don't!" He gripped her legs. "Oh, Jesus. Don't—do that."

All she could see of him was the disarray of his black hair and the powerful, taut line of his shoulders. His arms were clenched around her upraised knees, his fingers pressing into her skin.

"Oh, God," he whispered without moving. "Oh, God, oh, God . . ."

She stirred her hips again. She couldn't help it.

He made an anguished sound. With another shudder, he pushed forward slightly, a heavy fullness inside her. She squeezed her legs against him, tilting her pelvis upward. Sensation hovered: she wanted something; she wanted what he'd given her before, and it seemed that if she would just move in the proper way, she would have it.

On the stifled moan, he mumbled, "Christ have mercy. Don't move. Don't move."

She reached for his hands on her thighs, pulling his fingers open. She drew them down, pressing them over the place his thumbs had caressed, arching to meet the exquisite pleasure of the touch.

He lifted his head. His chest rose and fell in labored pants while his eyes held hers, hot and silver.

"Please," she whispered.

He gave her a look that burned her like dragon-fire. Then his dark lashes lowered and he began to move, pushing into her just a little, until the stretch almost became pain, then withdrawing again with a luscious slide of his thumbs against the moist and aching focus of sensation—thrusting again, and again, always only just to the point of hurting, until the faint pain began to seem like pleasure and the dragon's fire blazed through her body.

She moaned and twisted under his hands, trying to draw him closer, deeper. But he would not come. He turned his face away toward the wall, sliding his fingers across the melting center of ecstasy until she could no longer think of what to do but answer with an arch that brought the pain closer, mingling with elation. She could not breathe for the singing excitement, the queer flooding anxiousness. She was quivering, twitching; unable to stop the growing sounds of frenzy in her throat.

She gasped his name as he leaned over her with a move of his fingers that sent the universe whirling apart. Her body jerked ecstatically. In the moment of explosion he pulled back and dragged her into his arms, driving them both down full-length onto the furs.

He held her hard, one arm crushed around her buttocks, his stiff male shape pressed against her abdomen. His teeth scored her shoulder as he thrust his hips against her with a rough, frantic motion. A shudder racked him, a hard throb at her belly. "God!" His cry was hoarse and smothered in her hair and her throat. "Oh, God." He clutched her tighter and shuddered again, his whole body rigid, pressed against her as if he were dying.

His shoulders trembled. For a long moment he held her enveloped, moaning deep in his throat, her cheek pressed awkwardly against his heaving chest.

She pulled back her head, seeking air. Something warm and wet slid between their bodies. He sucked in a huge breath and relaxed his hold. A sound escaped him, a whimper like a child's.

Her limbs felt weak and watery. She slipped from his arms, panting, and looked up at him in amazement. With one finger, she touched the wetness on her body and then on his.

He caught her hand and rolled, resting half on top of her, his face buried in her hair. "Well," he muttered, "you're technically still a virgin, at any rate. And don't ever think, damn you," he added, breathing heat on her shoulder, "that I'm not a hero."

That afternoon she found the penguin he'd been hiding. She was collecting nettles to boil, as much because it was an excuse to stay away from him as because she thought they would make a decent soup. Lost in thoughts that brought color to her face and sinking agitation to her stomach, she had wandered out of the tussocks and so far up onto the hump of the island that she could see the rocky beach on the other side. The clouds moved, casting sullen shadows on the shore and burnishing the sea to the color of gleaming lead.

A gathering of rooks circled and swooped far down the windy slope. Beneath them she recognized Sheridan: a dark splotch inside a gray circle. She almost turned and ran like a scared rabbit before he could see her. But he had to be faced; she had nowhere to hide, and night would come soon enough, forcing them together in the little hut. She watched him from the hill, nervous at first, then with growing concern when he didn't move at all.

Carefully stashing her nettles in the windbreak of a lone tussock, she pulled her cloak around her and started quickly down the hill. She called to him twice, but the cold wind was against her, whisking her voice into nothing. Drawing closer, she slowed, realizing the gray ring was a rock wall. Sheridan squatted down in the middle of it, his back to her.

Olympia ducked a wheeling rook and stopped silently a few yards away, wrapping her cloak close in the tearing wind. He did not see her, absorbed in the task of prying limpets out of their conical shells. In front of him a plump, downy ball of silver feathers hopped crazily about, stretching up as tall as his knee on its short legs. Its beak gaped eagerly, dipping and rising as it uttered shrill cries. When Sheridan wasn't quick enough with a limpet, the baby penguin lowered its head and ran around in a drunken circle, waving one flipper and displaying a bandage on the other, composed of a piece of linen and one of Olympia's extra garters that had gone missing three days ago.

A rook made a dive for Sheridan's head. He swiped at it with his sharpened oar handle and a curse, throwing one arm out for balance as he ducked and stumbled. His handful of limpets scattered, the rooks swooped in and the inflated balloon of feathers hopped around his legs, nipping at his knees and complaining.

"Ugly brutes." Sheridan stood up, still facing away from her, kicking out at a pair of rooks that went after the waddling silver fuzzball. "Leave the poor chap alone, can't you?"

The rooks settled for fighting over the limpets, but the baby penguin continued to gaze up at Sheridan, waving its good wing with pathetic cries.

"Well," he said to it, "I'm bloody hungry, too, y'know."

The penguin shrilled and flapped. It looked like a furry, excited bladder, toddling up and down in frustration. Olympia put her hand over her mouth.

"All right." Sheridan shoved his oar at the quarreling rooks, scattering them for an instant. He grabbed for some stray limpet shells, sweeping them up and snatching back just in time to avoid the ravaging stroke of a rook's powerful beak. "Christ! If I lose a hand for this—" He muttered grimly to himself, prying a limpet out and bending to let the penguin gobble it off the tip of his knife. "Ah—keep your distance, you feathered football; I need that toe. Bugger you! You little—" He stepped back from an enthusiastic onslaught of silver fluff. "Bite my knee, and I'll muster you into the royal service. Then it's the stewpot and be damned. Her Highness ain't sentimental about making a fellow into cannon fodder for a righteous cause, I assure you." The penguin squeaked and flapped. Sheridan held out another limpet. "Not impressed, hmm? You should be. She's the terror of the upland geese. A desperate cutthroat. She'd have you plucked and roasted before you could say mackerel."

"I wouldn't," Olympia said indignantly.

Sheridan jerked upright. He turned. The rooks scattered, then fluttered in again and renewed their bickering over the limpets. The penguin shuffled between Sheridan's legs and sat down.

His face turned a deep red. "What are you doing here?"

Stifling a smile, she watched the penguin preen its silver fluff. "I saw you from the hill. I thought you might be hurt."

"I'm not."

"No." She tilted her head. "I see that."

He was positively crimson. Olympia observed him with interest. She'd never seen Sheridan Drake embarrassed.

"I found it," he said with a touch of belligerence. "The rest of the flock's all left. These damned rooks try to tear it apart whenever it comes out of that crevice in the rocks." He slashed at the big, gull-like birds with his oar. They dispersed for an instant, then fell to pecking and feuding again.

The penguin tilted back its head, looked up at him and uttered a long cooing shrill of admiration.

"A hero again," she said.

"I suppose I just can't help myself," he said tartly. "I do try to be a cad."

Olympia looked at his tall, windblown figure in the frayed peacoat. He stood with the oar planted as if it were a lance: a tattered knight with a huddle of silver feathers that nestled in absolute trust on the top of one boot.

"Sometimes," she said softly, "I don't think you try very hard."

Sheridan glanced down. The penguin shifted and settled, blinking round black eyes and then closing them with a sigh of contentment.

"Don't I?" he asked. "Then I'm sure I'll live to regret it." He stabbed at the rooks with a sour grunt. "I always do."

A week later Olympia sat back on her knees, panting, and watched Sheridan as he attacked the icy ground with a broken barrel hoop. They worked in the howling wind not far from the hut, Sheridan digging and Olympia pushing the loosened sand and rock up out of the trench with the tin pail.

The pit was to house their signal fire, which would not stay lit in the increasing winter gales. Sheridan straightened for a moment, wiping the sweat from his face with one arm. Olympia looked quickly away, hoping he hadn't caught her staring at his body. The way she felt was still too new, even after a week of his intimate touch; his lessons in the spark and fire between a man and a woman, in the pleasures her body was made for, were too amazing, too raw and throbbing—like a new wound that was passion instead of pain.

But he didn't even look at her. He was watching the crowd of rooks that sat staring from the sidelines, just out of rock-throwing range, their dark feathers ruffled by the freezing wind.

The arrival of a baby penguin in camp had brought no particular hardships beyond an excess of the big, quarrelsome birds and the neccessity to collect a few extra limpets every day. The rooks loitered around the hut, always alert to steal scraps, but the penguin seemed to draw them in more enthusiastically greedy numbers. A door of canvas kept them out of the hut itself, where the penguin was penned, but the rooks sensed possible prey.

"Bastards," Sheridan muttered, and flung a rock, dispersing the feathered band for an instant before he went back to digging. As he moved in the downstroke, his elbow caught for the fifth time on the handle of his knife, which protruded from its sheath on a sealskin strip hung around his neck and arm. He cursed and threw down the barrel hoop.

"This isn't going to work." He yanked the knife over his head and tossed it aside.

"I was afraid it wouldn't," Olympia said, retrieving the loop and sheath and laying them on a boulder. "I'll make it another way."

"Do that."

He went back to digging, having delivered this suggestion in biting tones. Olympia ducked her head to hide a smile. The design had been his suggestion, carried out with a sail needle and twine by Olympia after a spirited argument over the various merits of several other ideas she'd proposed to protect the single most vital item they possessed. Her pocket scissors were of use in some situations, but nothing would replace the strong, curved blade of Sheridan's big Malayan parang, which chopped driftwood and cut peat and whittled delicately through whalebone with equal facility.

She held her hair back against the wind and tilted her head, looking at the rhythmic rise and fall of his shoulders, thinking of the night before: his face in the firelight, his chest and arms, the way his muscles moved and his throat worked in ecstasy as he pleasured her and himself. The things he taught her brought heat to her cheeks; it was as if she became someone else when he touched her, someone without shame or inhibitions. It was impossible to be guilty and abashed with him; he simply said he had no patience with silly missishness and kissed her until she could not think.

He was rather good at that.

And he minced no words: her education had included some clear and very physical instruction on female matters. He explained the meaning of her monthly cycles, the token barrier that kept her a virgin; he gave her warnings, told her what was natural and what to do to any chap who had the insolence to suggest she participate in what wasn't; he lectured her on the signs of pregnancy and demonstrated—with masculine pleasure—several methods to protect her.

In a week, she'd become as worldly-wise as any professional streetwalker—as he'd informed her with a dry grin. When she'd frowned at that, his look changed to complete innocence and he added that he'd understood her to say streetwalking was her ambition in life.

She never knew what to make of him.

A sudden squawk and flutter made her glance aside. She squealed in dismay, scrambling up and lunging toward the pair of rooks fighting over the glittering handle of the parang.

Both birds retreated in haste, but amid the thrashing

takeoff, the sealskin loop tangled and caught in a claw. The bird rose, wings beating powerfully, carrying the knife just out of Olympia's frantic reach.

Sheridan bellowed. A rock went hurling over her head, but it missed as the thief tilted and rode the harsh wind upward, knife and sheath dangling. The bird circled, heading down the coast. Sheridan outdistanced Olympia instantly in the chase, leaving her to hike her skirts and run awkwardly after. Her heart rose when the rook landed, but it took off again as soon as Sheridan came close, the knife still twisting and bobbing in midair.

She fell farther behind, and finally came to a panting walk after losing sight of both Sheridan and the rook. She sat down, staring toward the steep headland that marked the end of their beach. A long time after she'd regained her breath, she finally saw him again—a silhouette at the top of the headland. She watched anxiously. When he leaned out over the edge of the steep cliff, looking down at the sea below, she bit her lip. Then he moved back, making a vicious heave toward the sky with his arm, and walked out of sight.

Olympia closed her eyes against the cold wind and wondered how they would survive without the knife. She could think of a hundred things that she'd taken for granted—cutting tussock grass, fashioning utensils, prying limpets from the rocks for the crucial nourishment that kept them alive when all their other luck was out. Even something as apparently inconsequential as Sheridan's stubborn insistence on shaving, which she'd begun to suspect was critical for him to maintain his steady morale—and therefore hers—depended on the razor-sharp blade of the parang.

She covered her eyes in despair. Such a small thing, such a silly thing: a villainous bird and a moment of inattention, and suddenly life became more precarious than ever.

Sheridan returned, striding with his jaw set. He didn't even stop when he saw her, but just snapped, "Come along. I need you," as he passed.

She jumped up and followed him. "Is it gone?"

"Likely."

His tone discouraged further questions. Olympia felt a flood of guilt. She should have been watching the knife. She should have put it safely inside the moment he took it off. It was her fault.

At the hut, he gathered all the rope they had from the rigging on the pinnace. She watched, a dismaying suspicion growing in her mind. It strengthened and flourished as she followed him back the way he'd come, all the way down the coast and up the rocky slope of the headland.

She was huffing by the time they reached the top, where the lumpy tussock grass gave way to a windswept table of black rock. Sheridan led the way to the edge and took her elbow. "Have a look."

She peered over the brink. Far below, amid huge fallen boulders, waves crashed in green-and-white glory. She squinted against the sharp wind, searching—and then saw it. A third of the way down the rugged face, the knife hung on a protruding rock, still sheathed, twisting and swaying in the air.

She pulled back, holding onto his arm with a tight grip.

"Now," he said over the sound of the surf, "we have to go get it."

She wet her lips. "On that rope?"

"Unless you've got wings." He shifted the coils off his shoulder. "I just hope to God there's enough."

She frowned at the flat surface they stood on. "There's nothing to tie it to."

He looked at her, his eyes steady, deep with gray shadows. "One of us anchors it. One of us goes down."

"But that won't do," she exclaimed. "I can't support your weight!"

He shrugged and smiled dryly. "On the other hand, I'm confident that I can handle yours."

"Oh, God," she said weakly.

He just stood looking at her, a faint lift to one dark eyebrow.

Olympia drew in a desperate breath. Hate rose suddenly and sharply; she wanted to curse him for his cowardice, but in the same moment reason intruded its cold facts. He was right. There was no choice. One of them had to go, and there was no hope that she could play the part of anchor with Sheridan on the other end.

She closed her eyes, breathing rapidly. "I can't do it," she said. "I can't do it. I know I can't."

He said nothing, no arguments, no advice or encouragement. When she opened her eyes, he was still watching her steadily.

"I'm afraid," she said in a trembling voice.

He waited.

"There must be some other—" She swallowed, hearing the pleading in her words. "I can't. Oh, God, I have to, don't I?"

His eyes were infinitely patient.

"I have to do it," she said. "We can't live without that knife."

"I won't let you fall," he said quietly.

"I have to do it." She couldn't quite conquer the quiver in her voice. "I will."

He took her face in his hands and kissed her hard. Olympia leaned against him, twisting her fingers in his shirt as if she were holding on for life itself already.

But she was the one who broke the kiss, working free of him with sudden resolution. If she was going down there, she wanted to do it and be done with it.

Sheridan seemed to understand, for he let her go immediately and hefted the rope. Carrying it to the edge, he lowered it over to measure the distance and nodded, hauling it back up.

"Come here," he said. "Take off your cloak. I'm going to tie this end to your waist, but that's only a safety measure. You won't have to hang on it." With brisk, efficient moves, he pulled the rope around her as she stood shivering in the wind. "You can trust my bowline knot, too," he said as he pulled it tight with a little jerk. "I've had a hellish lot of practice."

Olympia giggled nervously.

He gave her a little shake. "For God's sake, you think all the wrong things are funny. Someday I'll teach you a proper sense of humor."

She heard herself titter again, as if it were someone else making that ridiculous high-pitched noise.

"Breathe," he ordered, and Olympia realized with a start that she hadn't been. She took a deep gulp of air.

"Slow and even. That's better." He caught the rope near the other end and reached down. Olympia was too terrified to even question him when he drew up her skirt in a bundle and passed the line between her legs, around her hip, up between her breasts and over her shoulder, then down across her back, padding it with her cloak. "Now. Left hand here. Right hand here. Try it. Move away from me; let the rope slip around you as you go. See?"

She shivered, feeling goose bumps rise on her bared legs. "Are you just going to stand there and hold it?"

"No. I'll have it tied to me and braced around my back, like this."

"You shouldn't tie it. What if I fall? I'll pull you off."

"It'll save me throwing myself after you in remorse." He touched her icy cheek. "I said I wouldn't let you fall, mouse."

She looked up into his eyes, her fingers trapped together and twisting. She wanted to lean on him, to be gathered into his arms; she wanted warmth and safety and home.

But the wanting wasn't having. There was no one else to do for her what she refused to do herself, and no one else to believe in if she wouldn't believe in him.

She closed her eyes and opened them. "You won't let me fall," she said. "You won't let me fall."

"Not while I'm tied to the other end, by God."

The hysterical giggle bubbled up again. She swallowed it and moved toward the cliff edge.

The first horrifying moments, when she had to get over the brink, almost undid her. It was easy enough to let the rope slide around her on flat ground, but when she had to put her weight into it, it tightened around her painfully, tearing her palms as she held herself against the pull.

But just at the edge, a strange sense of detachment came over her. Though the icy wind scored her legs, her body seemed to lose its shaky weakness and grip and balance with a strength she hadn't known she possessed. She planted her feet and leaned backward, out over the water, finding security in thin air as the rope supported her.

She knew better than to look below. The last thing she saw before she inched down the rough black wall of the cliff itself was Sheridan's face, set in a grin that might have been a grimace as he braced against her burden. Then there was only black rock that passed in a long blur of cold and pain and effort.

Fifteen steps down, she reached the knife. She was afraid to let go and retrieve it, but her body seemed to have a more phlegmatic attitude, having gone to the trouble to make this trip. She opened her last two fingers and snatched at it. It swayed out of reach. She bit her lip and moaned angrily, grabbed again and caught it.

Frightened that she would drop it, she worked it under her fingers, one by one, until it hung around her arm. She called out to Sheridan to pull her up. Nothing happened. She hung there, and suddenly became aware of the pounding sound of the surf far beneath her. She called again, more sharply. Panic hovered behind the strange wall of indifference.

The rope tightened on her. She took a step just in time to take advantage of the upward pull, and then another. Her heart pounded, louder than the surf. The cold air tore at her throat. Two, three, four . . . she lost count, wanting to stop and rest, but she dared not fail to respond to the rhythm of the lifting pull. One more step, and one more, and one more, and abruptly she could see Sheridan over the top. He was really grimacing now, angled on his heels and sliding the rope around his braced back, hauling in time with her steps. She pushed her knee over the edge and fell forward, clinging to the knife as she scrambled onto the flat.

"I did it," she cried. "I did it!"

He dropped the loose rope and reached her, falling onto his knees and enveloping her in a choking embrace. He was heaving for breath.

"I did it," she mumbled against him.

"Did it . . ." he gasped, squeezing her. "And . . . jolly damned . . . splendid . . . it was."

He kissed her ear, and all she could hear was his heavy panting; all she could feel was his arm pressed hard across her back as he held her. She leaned into his shoulder and noticed it was trembling, just before the world went fuzzy and darkness came up to cradle her.

Seventeen

Wind screamed around the hut, the voice of winter in mid-July, hissing in the roof and sucking smoke up the chimney into the howling dark. Olympia stirred at the watery contents of the bucket—seaweed and mussels, seaweed and limpets, seaweed and clams—seaweed and goose when she could catch it, which wasn't often. The main flock had fled the winter weeks ago. She stared at the fire, worried and restless.

Napoleon rustled, preening, and then waddled sleepily across the hut to settle himself on his tummy next to her.

"Yes, I know," she crooned, for something to fill the windy silence. "Aren't you a handsome fellow?"

Napoleon gurgled in soft agreement. The penguin had molted at last, his soft silver down falling out in bedraggled patches, until a most elegant black suit with a white waistcoat had emerged, enhanced by a stylish topknot of long red-and-yellow feathers. He graciously divided his patronage between Olympia and Sheridan, accepting a limpet or a small fish from either with enthusiastic cries and dips and bobs of his ornamented head. When they left each day, he followed a few yards, crying, slogging along in his determined waddle with his flippers outspread for balance. Nothing deterred him; he climbed over rocks in his path instead of skirting them, hopping and skidding down the other side on his knobby pink feet. Then, as if suddenly resigned to abandonment, he would stop, turn around and sit down to await their return at the door of the hut, where he could dive beneath the canvas to escape the rapacious rooks.

She smiled at him, glad of the company as he settled against her skirt. The night was black and lonely, and worry was beginning to turn to fear.

Outside, there was a faint sound above the wind. Olympia lifted her head sharply. She closed her eyes with a sigh of relief and joyful anticipation when the noise resolved into the crunch of footsteps on snow-covered sand.

Leaping up, she jumped over Napoleon, who scrambled aside and nipped at her with an indignant squawk. She untied the canvas at the door, poking her head into the freezing gloom. "You're late! I was just about to go looking."

The dark bulk outside solidified into a tall form. Sheridan swung the bag of peat off his shoulder and dragged it through the door. "I spent the afternoon in one of those charming burn-pits. Lord, why'd they ever bother to invent pool halls when the world's got delightful places like that?"

"Dear God!" As he limped into the firelight, she saw that he was covered with mud, his coat wet and his face marked with dirty slashes. "Oh, dear God." She threw her arms around him and pressed her face against his damp chest, holding onto him as if he might vanish from her arms at any instant.

He rested his cheek on her hair. For a long moment he held her close.

"You aren't hurt?" Her voice was muffled in his coat.

"Twisted my ankle." He kissed the top of her head. "Not badly. I finally managed to dig myself a reasonable slope and crawl out of the beastly place."

Olympia thought of the pits, where old signal fires set by the sealers had taken hold in the peat bog and burned for months deep underground. A small hold hidden beneath a tussock could be the entrance to a muddy mantrap fifteen feet deep and thirty wide. "I should have gone looking," she exclaimed. "I should have gone."

"Not at all. I enjoy digging my way through mountains with a barrel hoop."

She hugged him hard. "I'm so sorry."

"I'm hoping you had a prior engagement with a goose." He touched her hair. "I reckoned you'd get around to me by tomorrow, but I didn't fancy spending the night ankle-deep in cold water." He gave her a squeeze. "I've got better plans for the evening."

She lifted her face. He smiled down at her, his eyes silver and glittering in the firelight, his face marked with black streaks like some demonic jester. He lowered his head, meeting her lips, his kiss hard and ruthless as his arms tightened around her. Olympia shared the taste of mud and sweat, and thought it as sweet as scones and butter.

She was sorry when he let her go and sniffed in the direction of the hearth. "Seaweed?" he asked glumly.

Olympia thought of a joke. *"Potage à la Maloon Anglais."*

He grimaced instead of laughing, which was typical of his reaction to her jokes. "Again? We had that last night." He limped past her and sat down in the sand by the fire. "I'm going to advertise for a new chef if you don't start showing some enterprise." He picked up his big clam shell, tilted the bucket and dipped out a steaming cupful. He drank it down without pausing for breath and wiped his mouth. Napoleon puffed out his feathers, shook himself and huddled in the far corner. Sheridan tossed a thatch of woven tussock grass over the penguin to block the firelight. Napoleon made a clicking coo, rustled once and was silent.

"There are ten crabs," she said.

"The deuce you say." His face brightened. "You're an angel."

She lifted her cloak from the sand, untying the ribbon that held the woolen bundle together. Sheridan took it, peering carefully inside the wriggling package at the crabs netted in a mesh of twisted tussock grass which she'd braided with sealskin strips around a frame of oar pieces.

"Blow me—look at that."

"I baited it with goose tripe," she said.

With gingerly moves, he tipped the net and shook a

hapless crab into the bucket, one, and then another, snatching his fingers away just in time to avoid the pincers of the third as it tumbled into the steaming water. When six were splashing amid the seaweed, he retied the bag and set it aside, always careful to save something for tomorrow.

"An angel," he said again.

Olympia clasped her hands behind her back, blushing faintly.

He looked at her sideways. "Come here, angel," he said softly.

She crossed the little hut and sat down beside him. He held her close, touching her chin with a grimy hand. "Don't ever come looking for me in the dark, my mouse. I'm a pretty tough bird. If I can't hold out for help till daylight, I wasn't going to make it anyway."

Olympia rested her head on his shoulder. The strength of her feelings was frightening; the idea of losing him unthinkable. In this place, her whole world came down to him. She might have survived by herself now, with the hut he had rebuilt and the food they had learned to find; physically she might have lived, but everything inside her would die.

It seemed strange that she'd ever thought him cowardly and wicked. Sometimes when he was away from the hut, cutting turf or digging far down the beach for clams, she remembered the jewels, but it almost seemed now as if that had happened to someone else, someone as distant from herself as the white-gloved figure in the gold-and-blue uniform was distant from the man who sat beside her in a torn and muddy coat, poking impatiently at the fire with one hand and holding her close with the other.

He gave her another squeeze and stood up, drinking deeply from the canvas water bag he'd sewn from a piece of sail. Peering with one eye into the tiny mirror balanced on a rocky shelf, he tried to rinse his face.

Olympia laughed when he turned around. "Now you're a proper blackamoor." She pulled a piece of linen petticoat from their careful stash of cloth and wet it, standing close to him to wipe the smears of mud from his cheek and jaw. While she raised herself on tiptoe to reach his forehead, he warmed the inside of her wrist with light kisses.

She allowed herself to lean against him. He bent his head as she worked, nuzzling her temple and then her cheek. She gave up on the washing, parting her lips in anticipation as his long eyelashes brushed downward and his arm slid around her waist.

It was gentle for a moment, the kiss: a slow, warm outline on her lips. Then his arm tightened and his mouth opened over hers, tasting deep, driving out the cold and the wind and the gray desolation, spinning everything down to one hot, delicious center. He held her close, strength and comfort, the steady fire that kept her alive and leapt into blazing flame when he touched her.

His hands slipped down, spreading beneath her, rocking her against him so that she could feel his body's excitement. She stirred her hips in provocative answer, knowing what he appreciated—knowing all kinds of things that he had taught her. They were alone: she could do anything, be anyone, please herself and him without shame. She found she was passionate and eager . . . and best of all, she found the restless, miserable emptiness that had haunted her life and driven her dreams of glory filled with something much simpler.

She was happy. Here in this barren place, hungry all the time, cold and damp most of it, where every day was an effort to survive until tomorrow—she was happy. She was glad to wake up under sealskin on the sand, when it meant waking up in his arms. She was anxious to look for food, when she knew he would smile and congratulate her and eat a few meager crabs as if they were manna. She felt lucky to sacrifice her petticoat in order to wipe mud from his face, when he would kiss her as she did it.

He made a sound of pleasure, took her cheeks between his hands and pressed his forehead to hers. "A difficult choice," he murmured. "Food or frolic."

"Both," she suggested.

"Certainly. One at a time, or together?"

She closed her hands over his and pulled them gently away. "You need to eat. You must be starving."

"I'm always starving." He tried to catch her back, but Olympia sidestepped. "Very well, Mama. Dinner first."

A meal of crab and mussels seasoned with seaweed left her full and contented, a feeling she knew would be all too emphemeral. After they'd finished, she built up the fire and stacked the peat he'd brought that day to dry. Sheridan lay back on the sealskins. He'd taken off his damp clothes and hung them near the fire, so he sat bare-chested, propped up on a fur-covered boulder, with the extra skin thrown across his legs.

He was exhausted: she could tell it, in spite of his earlier enthusiasm. As she finished cleaning up their few utensils, he sat drowsing in the firelight. By the time she had checked the signal fire outside, carried the bucket down to the windswept beach and brought back a pail of wet seaweed to keep the extra crabs alive, he was fast asleep.

She stood for a moment, watching him. His dark head tilted over one shoulder, shadowing the muscled curve of his arm. She gazed at the pulse in his throat and the little scar that cut his eyebrow—memento of a splintered gun casing in a French broadside at Trafalgar. They made him seem achingly vulnerable; so easily lost—an inch of space, a second of time—a fall down a deeper hole, and it might have been a broken neck instead of a sprained ankle. He knew that, and yet he went every day to search out the fuel they needed to keep the hut warm and the signal fire lit.

Often at night, he played on Fish's harmonica, teaching her songs and sighing over her struggles to carry a tune. Sometimes he even made up new ones, right at the moment, melodies and words about something that had happened that day, while Olympia sat before the fire and listened to him, rocking softly in time.

Tonight, she only wanted him to sleep. She tried to finish her work quietly, but the scrabble of unhappy crabs in the tin pail made him sit up with a soft snort. He leaned his head back, rubbing his eyes.

Olympia straightened from carefully arranging the net

over the pail to prevent escapees. Sheridan lifted his arm in invitation. "Princess. Come give me something to stay awake about."

She pulled off her wet boots and socks and set them to dry, snuggling her feet down into the fur beside him. He pulled her against his naked warmth, his fingers working on the buttons of her dress, his mouth exploring her ear.

Olympia smiled and touched his hand. "Rest tonight."

"I'm not tired," he whispered, kissing the side of her throat.

"Liar. You're too tired for this."

He slipped his fingers into the open back of her dress and ran his thumb down her spine. "I'd be dead before I was too tired for this."

She caught his other hand as he reached for her and rested back against his shoulder, gazing down the length of his fur-covered legs to the fire. "Think of something else. If you could be anywhere in the world," she said, "where would you like to be?"

"Vienna," he said without hesitation.

She turned her head in surprise. "Vienna?"

He nibbled her bare shoulder. "Austria. In the spring. And we'd be waltzing to Strauss at the Schönbrunn Palace, and you'd be wearing a scarlet gown cut down to here"—he lifted their entwined hands and touched her bosom—"with one of those floaty hems that just showed your slippers and a shocking peek of ankle whenever you turned." He closed his eyes, his breath warming her shoulder. "And it would be the last waltz, so that you'd be all flushed and out of breath and rosy and gorgeous, and I'd be ready to take you past the Royal Guards up a great, wide, curved staircase to a bedroom with a huge bed and gold velvet hangings where we could still hear the music. And I'd be making plans . . . I'd be thinking about how I'd scoop you up and cast you on the bed . . . and spread your arms out . . . and lean over you . . . and kiss your beautiful breasts, and your pretty feet, and your ankles, and your calves, and your lovely white thighs . . . and your delicious . . . pink . . . mmmmhhh." He nipped at her neck with a growl, his tongue making a hot circle on her skin. "And you wouldn't have on any underwear."

Olympia pressed her fingers over a smile. "Have you ever been to Vienna?"

He shook his head, his mouth against her hair.

"What an imagination you have got."

"What else do I have to think about out there, digging to goddamned China in a peat bog? Besides—I've been at sea for the best part of a quarter century. Imagination is my life." He was working her dress lower with little tugs. "Where would you like to be if you could be anywhere?"

She bit her lip, staring at her lap. After a moment, she shrugged.

"Where?" he persisted. "Rome? Paris? Some tropical paradise?"

"Actually . . . I rather like it here."

"Here! The devil. On this island?"

"Well—" She rubbed her hands together under the sealskin. "Yes."

"You cork-brain." He tilted her chin up and kissed her nose. "Why?"

She lowered her eyes. "Because you're here."

He'd been kissing the line of her jaw. At her soft explanation, he stopped. "Me."

She nodded.

"Me?"

She stared at her lap. "Yes."

"Villainous Sir Sherry—King of the Bastards?" he asked hoarsely. "You don't mean that."

She glanced toward him. He was looking down at her hands. His beautiful long lashes hid his eyes and there was a faintly bitter tilt to his mouth.

"Yes," she said. "I do."

He lifted his eyes. "I suppose I should laugh?" he asked with a one-sided smile. "Is this one of your dubious attempts at humor?"

She took his hand and drew it into her lap. One by one, she outlined his fingers. "I'm not joking. You make me happy. Can't you tell?"

He gave a little laugh, looking confounded and pleased.

"I don't know how on God's earth I'd make you happy in this dismal situation. Unless you're happy with drudgery all day and nothing but a skimpy supper and a paltry excuse for a tumble at night. Lord, you're still more or less a virgin, much to my credit. Who'd have thought I could be so noble?" His mouth flattened. "Really, I'm surprised I haven't killed myself."

She bent her head. "I like what we do."

"Why shouldn't you? I'm the one who has to keep my wits about me. And I've managed to do it in some exceedingly dire circumstances, too, let me tell you."

"Yes." She looked up into his eyes. "I know you have.

His lips twisted wryly. He looked away.

"I don't care about the rest, either," she said. "The way we have to live. Except that I shouldn't turn away a hot scone with butter now and again, and I wish you had more to eat." She leaned her head against his shoulder. "You work so hard."

"Princess," he muttered. "Oh, Princess." His hand found hers beneath the fur and tightened around it.

Olympia watched him slantwise, admiring the spare elegance of his cheekbone and the line of his jaw. There was still a faint smear of dirt across his temple, half hidden by his hair. She caressed his hand, and felt him flinch almost imperceptibly when she hit a new blister amid the old calluses.

"So if you could be anywhere in the world, this is it?" He looked at her sideways. "Because I'm here."

She nodded.

He slid down, turning onto his elbow. "Then do us both a favor and imagine me making you happy somewhere else."

Olympia smiled.

He played with her fingers, then shifted closer, resting his head in the crook of her arm. "Imagine us in a garden. Sitting on the grass in the sun."

"With lilacs," she suggested.

"Lilacs. Roses. Pink-and-white camellias that match your skin. What else?"

She closed her eyes, dreaming. 'Violets in the shade of

the trees. A statue of Aphrodite . . . with songbirds eating seed from the dip of her shoulder.''

''Imagine we have cakes to eat.''

''Strawberries and champagne.''

''Mmm. You're good at this. Champagne it is, and I'm sure I've plied you with too much and got you nicely tipsy and kissable, wicked bastard that I am.''

She stroked his cheek and bent to press her lips to the top of his head. ''Wicked.''

''Imagine your hair has come loose around your shoulders. God, it's so beautiful in the sun—with little rainbows of color in it. Imagine—'' He paused. A long moment went by, with the wind keening around the hut. Then, very softly, he said, ''Imagine that I've asked you to marry me.''

Olympia's hand went still. She looked down at him, but she could not see his face.

''Would that make you happy?'' he whispered.

She moistened her lips. Her heart thumped in her throat, blocking words.

''I love you, mouse,'' he said. He curled his fist in the fabric of her dress. ''I love you.''

Still she could not force her mouth to speak. She stared at his dark hair. It began to swim before her eyes, blending with the firelight and foolish tears.

How strange that it should happen this way—so far from the world she knew; so different from the dreams she'd dreamed.

When life was stripped of everything: when there were no politics, no princesses, no heroes, no glory . . . when nothing mattered but life itself, reality came down to this. There was food enough to survive today, and fuel enough to keep warm tonight, and something that had built between them in the long, brutal months of desolation—something more real than anything she'd ever hoped or imagined could exist.

As the silence lengthened, his body grew tense against hers. Finally, he took a deep breath and rolled away. ''Not in the mood for sentimental sap, I see.'' Locking his fists behind his head, he frowned into space. "Never mind it. Starvation makes me maudlin."

Olympia bit her lip. But she sat silent still, ashamed of herself for having claimed long ago that she loved him—for wasting the words when she'd been too stupid, too blind, too selfish and small to know what they really meant. She'd loved an illusion made of fantasy and glitter. Now she knew a man, and had no way to tell him what was in her heart.

As the canvas rattled at the door, she stared into the red glow of burning peat, thinking. About love, about how poor the words sounded and how much she'd have liked to give him if she had it. After a long time, she reached across to the small bag that held her scissors and needles and harmonica and precious little else, and found a sandy piece of horehound candy, broken at one end.

She looked at him. His eyes had drifted closed. His head rested at an awkward angle against the boulder, his face turned into one open palm.

"Sheridan," she murmured.

She had no answer beyond the deep, exhausted pull of each sleeping breath.

With a little smile, she tucked the candy into the curl of his fingers. "Imagine," she whispered, snuggling down into the sealskin next to him, "that I've said 'Yes.' "

When the moans woke her, there was just light enough left from the glowing coals to see. In her sleep, she'd turned partially against him with her elbow pressing his back. He'd changed position entirely—he faced away from her, his arm curled over his head, his body making little jerks punctuated by the terrible low sounds coming from deep in his throat.

"Sheridan." She shook his shoulder.

With an explosion of breath he rolled, coming up clutching the knife, his body taut and his eyes wild in the half-light. He sat sprawled on his knees, panting, staring into the hut in a quick, wary search, half hostile and half bewildered.

Olympia stayed still, looking past the gleaming blade to

his face. "You were having a bad dream," she said carefully.

He looked at her, and then at the knife in his hand. And then he just seemed to sag, his shoulders and his head, and he flung the weapon sideways away from him. He sat for a long moment with his fists pressed together beneath his mouth.

"I thought somebody had a bayonet in my back," he said, muffled.

"It was me." She bit her lip. "I'm sorry. You were dreaming, and I had my elbow pressed against you."

He took a deep breath and shoved his hand through his hair. There was a weakness at the corner of his mouth, a peculiar quiver. It hardened into a bitter grimace as he stared down at the sandy floor.

Olympia put out her hand and touched his knee. She moved her fingers in a soothing stroke.

"Damn it to hell. Why am I like this?" He tilted his head back with a fierce sound of anguish and stared at the shadowed roof. "Why now?"

She reached up and squeezed his hand as if he were a frightened child. "Everything's all right," she said. "Go back to sleep."

The hard set of his mouth seemed to crumple; he brought both hands up suddenly, covering his face.

"Everything's all right, Sheridan," she repeated. "I'm here. We're safe."

He shook his head silently, still hidden.

"Do you have nightmares often?" she asked gently.

"Leave off. Leave me bloody well alone." He got up, averting his face, retrieved the knife and placed it carefully on the stone shelf far out of his reach. Then he lay down, his expression a mask, turned away from her and pulled the sealskin over his head.

Olympia lay still, gazing at the shadowy hump of his shoulder. A lock of dark hair spilled out over the fur. She moved closer, slid her arm around him and curled against his back. She held him close, resting her cheek on his warm skin.

He made a miserable sound and tried to push her hand

away. "I'm not good enough," he muttered. "Friggin' maniac. Not good enough for you."

She only lifted her hand and stroked his forehead, nudging the thick hair tenderly back from his temple. He gave a long-suffering sigh and ignored her. But his body stayed tight and his breathing soft and alert, and she never knew if he let himself sleep at all.

Eighteen

On the twenty-second of October, by the charcoal marks on the hearthstone, Sheridan came back from his daily foraging hours early.

Olympia looked up from the bubbling pail, where she was making soap with seaweed ash and seal blubber. Spring wind blew her hair in her face as she straightened up from the fire.

Napoleon flapped his wings and waddled happily toward Sheridan as he approached. The plump bird bowed and clapped his beak, bobbing and waving in his exuberant greeting ceremony. Sheridan stood looking down at the ardent little figure.

"The penguins are back," he said.

He brushed past the enthusiastic welcome without offering the usual treat and walked into the hut. Napoleon marched anxiously in pursuit until he stumbled into a hole and fell on his face. He worked himself upright, looked around as if he were astonished to see there was a hole there, then turned, muddled, in several directions until he noticed a pile of pebbles he'd made in the past week. He picked up one pebble in his beak and carried it solemnly to Olympia's feet, dropping it next to several others he'd brought in the course of the day.

She bit her lip.

The penguins were back. Napoleon would have to return to the rookery, of course. He was well grown and perfectly healed; he splashed and swam in the tidal pools among the rocks with ecstatic vigor, trekking back up to the hut like a stoic little soldier to settle down in his corner and wait for Sheridan to lay the grass-thatch over him. But he'd grown restless as spring approached, repeating his greeting ceremony again and again with relentless patience, moving pebbles from place to place and then standing sadly over the pile, his head cocked, first on one side and then on the other, as if puzzled as to why he'd put them there.

He wanted a mate, Sheridan said. His own kind.

Olympia looked at the canvas door of the hut. Sheridan hadn't come out. She lifted the pail off the fire and followed him, Napoleon at her heels.

Inside, Sheridan was leaning against the wall, staring at nothing. He turned as Olympia and the penguin entered, shoving his hands in his pockets and resting his shoulders against the rock. Napoleon, having been fed his fill of limpets by Olympia a half hour earlier, waddled over in his rolling gait and nestled between Sheridan's feet.

He pushed the penguin off. Napoleon tumbled, picked himself up and lifted his beak toward the roof, flapping into another shrill greeting. Then he bowed toward Sheridan and dipped his head zealously. When the ceremony was finished, the penguin regarded Sheridan expectantly.

"You're looking at the wrong chap," he said in a curt tone. "I'd think you'd have figured it out by now."

Napoleon waddled a few steps away, picked up a whalebone spoon and carried it back to drop at Sheridan's feet, wiggling his pointed tail.

"Stupid little bastard, ain't you?" Sheridan said. He tossed the spoon on a rock shelf and glanced at Olympia. "Give me your cloak. I'll wrap him in it and get rid of him."

Five months ago, Olympia would not have recognized what lay behind the callous words. She knew better now.

"May I come?" she asked.

He stood frowning down at Napoleon, his jaw set. "There's no reason."

"I'd like to."

"You're busy. I won't be back till sunset." He took the cloak and scooped Napoleon into its folds. The penguin wriggled and squawked once, then ceased to protest. Sheridan headed toward the door with the bundle under his arm.

"I'm going to miss him, too, you know," Olympia said softly.

He stopped and looked back. Napoleon made a smothered coo, barely audible above the ever-present sound of the surf.

"Hell," Sheridan said. He held out his hand to her. "Come along, then, if you must."

The instant their fingers touched, his hand enclosed hers, rough and firm, a welcome far warmer than his brusque invitation. Olympia let go a breath and met his eyes.

He pushed her ahead out the canvas door. "Just don't start sniveling on me, damn you. I can't stand that kind of rubbish."

She ducked her head, hiding her expression. "No," she said, feeling his hand pressed close at the small of her back. "I know you can't."

The penguin rookery lay on the windward side of the island, where the ocean broke with smashing white violence against the shelving rock. Outside the surf, strange ripples adorned the heaving sea—the plunging black bodies of the swimming penguins, diving together in flocks to avoid the sinister gaping mouths of the leopard seals that glided just beyond the rocks.

When an immense flock of penguins had collected in the sea, they all came together, a wave of splashing shapes that went pouring past their sleek enemies. Some always fell to the teeth of the leopard seals, but the agitated crowd swept past, protected by sheer numbers and confusion, to be hurled up in the surf toward the rock. They popped out of the sea like fat torpedoes, hurtling by the hundreds onto the flat shelf, stumbling and lurching away from the crashing waves on feet or flippers, often skidding along on both, using their bellies as sleds.

Once they reached shore, the hovering rooks were ready to attack any weak or injured strays, but most of the penguins made it up through the rocks and into the gully that led to the rookery. It was serious business, a life-or-death trek, but they were so comical and earnest as they waddled and hopped and trudged along with their flippers out for balance that it was impossible not to smile. A thousand little Napoleons—ten thousand—were on their way home, to set up a nest of pebbles among the albatross and the early arrivals and start a family.

Napoleon himself had begun to squirm as soon as they came within earshot of the raucous throng. Sheridan held the bundle tighter. They stopped at the top of the slope, watching the black-and-white bodies slog their awkward, patient way up to the rookery.

"There aren't too many yet," he said. "In the fall, they were stowed in here like smoked kippers."

The penguins ignored them. It was possible to walk right among them, attracting only a moderate curiosity and a halfhearted peck or two when Olympia or Sheridan stepped too close to a ring of nest pebbles. She wrinkled her nose at the pungent smell.

Sheridan went to an open area and bent down, unwrapping Napoleon from his woolen prison. The penguin flapped wildly and raced toward the nearest occupied nest without a backward look.

Where a human passing seemed to cause little comment, Napoleon's approach precipitated a riot. The closest penguins met him with chatters of rage and battering flippers, knocking him off his unsteady feet. He scrambled up, retreating, only to run into an attack from behind. He tussled, nipping back, and dashed in another direction. There, too, the residents objected to the trespasser with shrilling beaks and blows, until poor Napoleon was running a gauntlet of assault.

Olympia started forward to rescue him, but Sheridan caught her arm.

"They'll kill him!" she protested.

"There's nothing we can do about it."

She frowned anxiously at the commotion. The only way she could tell Napoleon from the others now was that he was the one every other penguin attacked. He lurched from one assailant to the next, crying and flapping, beset on all sides as he zigzagged his way down the slope.

"Oh, what have we done?" she moaned. "Do they hate him because of us?"

Sheridan was silent, watching. After a moment, he said, "Look there."

Napoleon's miserable progress had taken him off to the side of the nest area, where a huddle of penguins sat looking world-weary and blasé, staring around leisurely instead of collecting pebbles and squabbling over nest space like the rest. Bursting out of the nest area, chased by a penguin that nearly took the feathers out of his tail, Napoleon fled toward the silent group. Olympia tensed, waiting for this new company to turn on him. There was a brief skirmish when he cannoned into the nearest, driven by the attacker on his rear. Penguins toppled and scattered in a mass of flailing flippers. The aggressor marched back to its nest, preening itself irritably. The group of bystanders re-formed quietly, and Olympia suddenly realized that Napoleon had vanished from recognition, camouflaged among a host of identical bodies.

Sheridan chuckled. "Accepted into the Bored Young Bachelors' Club."

"Or made one of the permanent outcasts."

He put his arm around her. "I doubt that. He's a stout little blighter. When he sees his girl, he'll go after her." He looked down at Olympia with a faint smile. "I brought him up, y'know."

"Should that reassure me? No doubt he'll fall in with low company."

He turned around and grabbed her by the waist. Squeezing her until she squealed, he bent to her ear with a hard nip and a kiss. "We can only hope," he said, "that you impressed your serious and high-minded nature upon him before we learned what a splendid aptitude for sin you've got."

"Not here!" She was breathless, trying to wriggle away from him as he tugged at her buttons.

"Where?" He kissed her neck. "Where?"

"Well, I—"

"On top of the hill." He swept her up in his arms and began to walk.

"Wait!" Olympia clutched at his neck. "I'm too heavy. You'll hurt yourself!"

He laughed. "After carrying endless loads of rock and wet peat? Don't be a gudgeon. Besides—" His mouth tightened. "You don't weigh the half of what you did five months ago."

"I don't?" she asked hopefully.

"No. And the instant we get back to civilization, I'm going to put you on a strict course of comfits and rich puddings, I assure you." He reached the windy rise and let her slide down to her feet, shaping her hips with his hands.

"I did think my dress was somewhat looser." She looked down at herself with satisfaction.

He groaned, cupping her breasts. "You have no notion of proper female proportions. You're wasting away."

"I'd hardly call it that."

"I can barely tell you're here." He pulled her into his arms. "I have to—"

"*Sheridan.*" She froze in his embrace and then jerked away, staring beyond his shoulder at the sea. "*Look!*"

"Thank God!" Captain Fitzhugh kept repeating. "Thank God, thank God!" He gripped Olympia's shoulders the instant she stepped onto *Terrier*'s white-sanded deck, pulled her toward him and then recollected himself just in time. He let go of her and stood awkwardly, clenching his fists, before he stuck out his hand to Sheridan. "I never thought to see you alive again, sir! It's a God-given miracle. A God-given miracle."

Sheridan shook hands. He looked beyond a line of lieutenants standing in stiff, navy blue attention to where Mustafa huddled in a blanket, and commented dryly, "With some help from other sources, I think."

The little Egyptian bowed. *"Máshallaah!"*

"I won't argue with that," Sheridan said.

"Yes, he's a brilliant little chap, your man. Got away when *Phaedra* tried to slink into Buenos Aires, and came straight to me. Devilish lucky we were in port. No one else would have believed him." Captain Fitzhugh was still gazing at Olympia. "I could hardly credit the tale myself. But we dealt with that murdering rabble that took *Phaedra*, you may be sure, Miss Drake. They never reached the dock. The Yankee consulate was prepared to dawdle about due process and extradition, but fortunately we found an American naval frigate with a captain who wasn't too squeamish to hang 'em as soon as he heard about Webster. But come—" He took her arm with an anxious move. "We can talk of all that later. You'll want clean clothes and food. I've got your trunks off *Phaedra*, Miss Drake, and your cabin prepared, and the chef has orders to put steak-and-kidney pie on the table as soon as he may. That was your favorite dish, was it not? We loaded bullocks and a good deal of flour in Argentina."

"Rolls," Sheridan said dreamily. "Fresh rolls."

Fitzhugh paused and grinned. "Lieutenant!" he said to a man nearby. "Inform the steward. Fresh rolls."

Olympia and Sheridan exchanged a look of mutual feeling over the prospect, as brief and intimate as a touch. Then Captain Fitzhugh's arrangements separated them, Olympia to the spacious, spotless cabin she'd occupied before and Sheridan to wherever Fitzhugh chose to put him.

She sat down in a chair for the first time in months, gazing around her. The familiarity of her surroundings was haunting, almost uncomfortable. The cannon that shared the cabin lay like a polished beast crouched and waiting at its closed port: silent, but poised to roar should the order come to clear the decks. The mahogany lockers shone with rubbed varnish, the brass fittings gleamed and the blanket on the berth was tucked with military tightness.

She thought of her sealskin bed, warm with a lover's heat. A sudden and unexpected ache rose in her throat.

The knock at the door distracted her, bringing Mustafa with a slipper tub—something she hadn't seen since she'd left Wisbeach—and pails of steaming water, a tin of crisp sugar biscuits and a freshly pressed dress, smelling of lavender from her trunk. He bowed and kissed her feet when she tried to thank him for bringing rescue, then hurried away, muttering profuse apologies, to serve his pasha.

Olympia sank into the tub eagerly. After washing away months of accumulated salt, she struggled to dry and dress her hair, consuming the entire tin of biscuits in the course of things.

It was strange and difficult dressing herself. The cashmere stockings felt wonderfully soft, the linen chemise confining, the layers of petticoats ridiculous, and she left off the corset altogether. The traveling gown of emerald-green kerseymere was now too large, but its short pelisse belted with a ribbon of daffodil yellow seemed to hide the worst of the defect. Checking herself in the locker's looking glass, Olympia was surprised at how well she appeared, barring her wind-pinkened skin.

She bit her lip, suddenly shy at the idea of Sheridan seeing her like this—dressed again, really dressed, with feminine color and fashion in clothes that he had chosen, a lock of her hair pulled loose from its ribbon to curl coyly at her cheek. She sat down to button the pearls on the white kid boots Mustafa had brought.

Sheridan was already waiting in the state cabin, dressed in someone else's dove-gray coat. He stood near the great bank of windowlights that spread across the stern. Silver plate and crystal glittered on the white dining cloth like a half-forgotten dream of civilization, but he was staring out at the island. From *Terrier*'s position at anchor, their thatched stone hut was just visible, a forlorn and tiny pile of rocks on a lonely beach.

Olympia slipped her arm through his. He looked at her,

his slow glance taking in the green kerseymere and daffodil ribbons. With a shy upward glance, she waited for the smile that had warmed her through a winter of desolation.

It did not come.

As he regarded her coolly he seemed like a stranger, his black hair trimmed more neatly than she'd ever managed to cut it with her pocket scissors by the light of a smoky peat fire. In place of the mud-stained shirt, a crisp gray stock at his throat and a fall of ruffled linen below made him look elegant and distant and utterly different from the man she'd lived with in intimate isolation.

A faint fear welled up in her, consternation at the sudden distance that seemed to open between them, as if different clothes had made them different people. A world that had been simple suddenly shifted and wavered, tilting out of balance.

He looked back toward the island. "Tell me," he said. "Precisely what is this Fitzhugh fellow to you?"

She turned her head in confusion. "What do you mean?"

"Let's not be coy." With an impatient gesture, he moved a step away, turning toward her, his back to the windows. "We're not languishing alone in paradise anymore. I need to know how the wind blows."

She bit her lip. Before she could speak, the door behind them opened and the steward stepped through, carrying a laden tray and followed by some of the ranking lieutenants. Captain Fitzhugh entered, ushering her to a seat next to his at the head of the table. Amid the greetings and handshakes, the first officer invited Sheridan to take the opposite chair.

"You look wonderfully well, Miss Drake," Captain Fitzhugh said. "Not at all as if you'd been facing hardship and death but a few hours since."

"Thank you." She wished to be polite, but felt an unreasonable stab of annoyance at this innocent hyperbole. "But I assure you that to say we were facing death a few hours since is to exaggerate the matter."

He gave her a speaking look. "You are a heroine in my eyes. You must know that."

She shifted in her chair, uncomfortable under his admiring gaze. Across the table, Sheridan sat silent, an ironic set to his mouth. She was grateful when the steward placed a platter before her and lifted the silver cover to reveal a steaming pie with a golden crust. "That smells wonderful," she exclaimed, glad to change the subject.

Captain Fitzhugh served her personally, heaping her plate with meat pie and vegetables and a pair of rolls with hot, soft white centers dripping Irish butter.

He lifted his glass. "Gentlemen, to the safe deliverance of our dear, valiant Miss Drake and her gallant brother!"

Murmurs of assent and the clink of Fitzhugh's fine crystal echoed around the table.

Olympia cast down her eyes. She wished he would not make such a fuss. Every man at the table was looking at her except Sheridan, who was staring at his wineglass as he turned the stem slowly between his fingers.

"Let me assure you that we'll return you to civilization as soon as practicable," Fitzhugh announced, "but I hope you won't find our company too distressing for the nonce. I'm afraid I've orders to make for the Arabian Sea directly. We're to subdue the slavers there—something I'm certain that Sir Sheridan will be glad to hear!"

"Oh, infinitely," Sheridan said. He took a deep swallow of wine.

"Perhaps we can count on you for tactical advice. Considering your personal experience."

"All the advice you like." Sheridan's voice was amiable. He helped himself to the carrots the steward offered. "For what it's worth."

Fitzhugh nodded, his boyish face shining with freckles and enthusiasm. "It will be quite an advantage. Not only having fought these pirates, but having been a victim of the trade as a slave yourself, you—"

The clatter of silver stopped his words. Sheridan stared at him with an expression Olympia had never seen before. "That's a damned lie," he whispered.

Fitzhugh turned scarlet. He met Sheridan's eyes, and all the pleasantries of the moment vanished. Dead silence reigned. They were killing words, what Sheridan had said, a public accusation that held no option but to back down or face destruction.

Captain Fitzhugh cleared his throat. "My profoundest apologies, sir. I'm in the wrong, of course. Unpardonable mistake. Didn't mean—that is—not lying, certainly not by intention—I do hope you understand!"

Olympia thrust her napkin on the table. "It's my fault," she said quickly. "I mistook something Mustafa told me and have given Captain Fitzhugh a wrong impression."

Sheridan looked toward her. For a haunting instant, he appeared completely unnerved, strain visible in the rigid way he turned his head, the way he lost a beat in his answer and made a natural response seem awkward. "Quite wrong," he said.

Olympia smiled brightly at Captain Fitzhugh, desperate to retrieve the situation and cover Sheridan's strange reaction—as telltale and glaring as a printed announcement. She had no notion why the subject should affect him so, but moved instinctively to divert attention and protect him. "I'm so sorry. My imagination sometimes runs away with me! I fear you mustn't give me complete credence when I relate my brother's adventures—I'm so proud of him. I'm bound to mix things up and make him much larger than life."

"Most understandable," Captain Fitzhugh said. "But I humbly beg your pardon, sir, for such a ridiculous blunder."

"Never mind." Sheridan picked up his fork, laid it down and made a careless gesture—not quite easily normal, but almost. "Much ado and all that. Forgotten already." He grasped his wineglass and took a long swallow. "I'd believe anything a pretty girl told me, too."

A movement of relaxation rustled like wind around the table. Fitzhugh's shoulders dropped visibly. He smiled fondly at Olympia. "Yes, indeed—a man must take care, or he'll be making a regular cake of himself."

Sheridan's mouth twisted. He took another sip of wine.

"Captain Sir Sheridan," Fitzhugh went on in a forcibly enthusiastic voice, stopping Sheridan just as he was lifting a buttered roll for his first bite. "You must tell us from the beginning—how you come to be alive and hearty when we thought you laid in an unmarked grave. Now there's an adventure well worthy of the telling, I don't doubt!"

Sheridan put the roll down. He seemed to have recovered his full composure. Olympia could see a trace of resigned wistfulness in the way he looked at the waiting food on his plate "Not unless you take a special interest in blind stupidity, it isn't."

Her fingers tightened on her fork. In the tumult of their rescue, she hadn't even thought of this. For the first time in weeks, she remembered her jewels and the real story of how she'd arrived where she was. Of course Captain Fitzhugh would expect an explanation—the last time he'd seen her, she'd been mourning the death of her "brother" and heading for Australia. Now here was her brother alive, six thousand miles away from where he'd disappeared. The whole matter must appear extraordinary.

". . . the same old sorry tale," Sheridan was saying. "I wasn't on my guard, and I paid for it."

"But these thugs," Fitzhugh said. "How did you escape the heathen devils?"

"Thugs?" Sheridan looked puzzled.

"The thugs who attacked you on the dock in Funchal, man!" Fitzhugh laughed. "You won't claim you've forgotten them!"

Sheridan took a bite of steak, frowning. Then his face cleared. He glanced at Olympia with a wry smile. "My dear sister! What a romantic you are, to be sure. I'm afraid Miss Drake's imagination has run away with all of you. The last thug I ever encountered was haunting the road to Jabalpur."

"They were *sthaga,*" she protested automatically.

"I wish I could say so. It might make me look less of a confounded fool."

"What happened, then?" Fitzhugh asked. "We've gone on thinking you were attacked and murdered by these Indian savages for revenge." He popped a bite into his mouth and gestured with his knife and fork. "On account of your betraying their foul fraternity and trying to bring them to justice, you know."

Sheridan rubbed the bridge of his nose with his forefinger, looking embarrassed. "Yes—well . . . that was a deuced long time ago, after all. I'm afraid it was nothing so dramatic this time. I was just decked and robbed by some ruffians set loose from the convict ship, if you want the sad truth."

"They were thugs," Olympia insisted. "They used those words you told me."

He looked at her quizzically. "Did they?"

"Yes! *Bajeed*, and *timbalo.*"

"Tombako," he corrected. *"Tombako ka lo."* He tilted his head with a faint smile and winked at Captain Fitzhugh. "I'd just been filling her head with tales of my epic past not long before it happened, you see."

Fitzhugh's ruddy face grew even brighter pink beneath his freckles. He broke into an indulgent grin. "Indeed. I quite understand." With an affectionate glance at Olympia, he leaned over and added softly, "A natural misconstruction of events, I'm sure. No doubt you mistook their Portuguese."

"I did not," she exclaimed. "And what about the turbans?"

Sheridan smiled, breaking open a second roll. "Did they wear turbans? I didn't see that."

"I *told* you!" She was growing agitated, disturbed by the way he was distorting things.

"Yes, I remember you saying so. But it was dashed dark, my dear. You'll forgive me if I can't support the assertion with my own observation."

"Well, they had turbans, you may be sure! Under their hats."

He buttered the roll. "No doubt you're right, of course."

Olympia looked around the table at the patronizing

smiles, set her jaw and applied herself to her meat pie without another word.

"You believe the attack originated with the transport brig, then?" Captain Fitzhugh said, after a pause.

"If waking up on a convict ship with empty pockets and ankle chains is any evidence. Particularly when the agent insists that I'm down on the lists as a condemned felon named Tom Nicol."

"But why?" Fitzhugh demanded. "There was no ransom asked."

Sheridan put down his fork. "No need for that. Not when God's original fool announces to a company of genteel strangers that he's going to be carrying his sister's jewels for appraisal on a specific date, at a particular time and place. Not when that company happens to include an enterprising gentleman down on his luck and working as a government agent on a convict transport."

Olympia's head came up. "Lieutenant . . . St . . . St . . ." She frowned. "It began with an S."

"Stacy." Sheridan stabbed at a boiled carrot with his fork. "A thoroughgoing rogue. Not to speak ill of the dead."

Oh, he's dead, is he? Olympia thought. *How convenient.* She gave Sheridan a tart smile. "It was rather careless of you, wasn't it? To let the horrid fellow steal every jewel I owned. I'll never replace Auntie Matilda's emerald tiara."

He looked up at her, his hand arrested in the motion of helping himself to another portion of pie. "Replace it? What do you mean?"

"My jewels," she said sweetly. "I'll certainly miss them. I think I could bear it better, if only I hadn't lost every single one."

He slowly laid down his silverware, leaned forward and said in a low voice, "Tell me you're joking."

Olympia met his eyes. They were intense and utterly serious, without a trace of humor or secret rapport. With a jolt of confusion, she suddenly distrusted her interpretation of all that had gone before. "Well, I—"

"Where are they?" he asked sharply. "Did you check? They aren't with your belongings off *Phaedra?*"

She opened her mouth in helpless consternation. "No," she said. "Of course not. They never were. *You* had them when you were attacked in Madeira!"

He closed his eyes and sat back in his chair. "God! You mean you haven't had them since Madeira?"

She stared at him. She didn't understand. He wasn't lying—she would swear on her life that he wasn't. "No," she said slowly. "I thought you—"

The sentence hung unfinished.

"I didn't have them." He spread his hand across his eyes. "I decided to take the heliotrope only, because I wasn't going to have time to change before we left for dinner and the whole packet was too bulky to carry under evening wear."

"Yes," Captain Fitzhugh said unnecessarily. "Miss Drake showed it to us, you recall."

"I left the rest where they were." Sheridan lifted his fingers, staring at her. "And now you say they're gone?"

She nodded.

"Damn." He stood up and kicked back his chair. "Pardon me, but—" He slammed his fist on the chair rail. "Damn!"

"Most disconcerting," Captain Fitzhugh murmured uncomfortably. "Perhaps there's some mistake."

"When did you discover them missing?" Sheridan demanded.

Olympia moistened her lips. "Just after the—the attack. Mustafa looked for them, and there was nothing in the packet but paste."

He set his jaw. Then slowly one dark eyebrow rose. His hand tightened on the chair rail. "Oh, was there indeed?" He stood back. "Forgive me, gentlemen—my profoundest apologies. I shall be back in a moment."

He thrust away from the chair and strode out the door. A discomfited silence descended on the table. Olympia stared at her plate, suddenly unable to eat a bite. Beneath her confusion an awful suspicion was growing, the dreadful possibility that she had chosen the wrong interpretation of events since that horrible night—that, led by Mustafa, she'd tried and convicted an innocent man in her mind, and then been glad to see him suffer. It was so long ago, that night on the dock; it had been dark and frightening. She might have been mistaken. It was possible.

It was one thing to have forgiven Sheridan—it was another entirely to imagine she had wronged him all along.

It was so hard now to think of him as a thief and a liar after all they had survived together, and harder still to work her way through the evidence. He'd told the convicts he'd hidden the jewels, yes—but he'd been fighting for their lives. He'd also told them there weren't any jewels at all. He changed stories like a lizard shed skin, but he'd saved them from desperate danger. He'd done the right thing each step along the way, even to stranding them on a barren island—as proved by the fact that she was now safe and unharmed aboard H.M.S. *Terrier* with warm clothes and food to eat, instead of beaten and misused and murdered at the hands of Buckhorse and Cal.

The saloon door opened. Sheridan entered, with Mustafa behind. The little servant was abasing himself at every step. He shuffled around to Olympia and knelt at her side.

"*Emiriyyiti!*" He beat his forehead on her chair. "I am beneath forgiveness. I am a dog, a filthy jackal! I have told you untruths, my princess—foul lies against my pasha! I have your jewels; I have had them from the first—never were they stolen at all. And the rest, all the rest—stories and lies and twistings. It is I who have been a slave, in wretched bondage until my great and wonderful and generous pasha, may Allah bless him with strong sons and beautiful daughters, rescued me and bade me follow him if I would!" Great tears welled up and fell from his dark eyes. He clutched her hand and kissed it. "*Emiriyyiti*, I meant only good; I only wished to find him—I cannot bear to be sent away from my master! I will die! I beg you to intercede, to ask—"

"Enough," Sheridan snapped. He jerked his head, and Mustafa, with one last wet kiss on the back of her palm, scurried backward out the door, bowing as he went.

Captain Fitzhugh pursed his lips. "Strange little chap."

"Confounded thieving nuisance, plague take him." Sheridan glanced at Olympia. "Your jewels are safe in your cabin. He's had them all along. Pardon the interruption."

He picked up his silverware and resumed eating.

Nineteen

Sheridan lay resting on his berth with a sherry in his hand, trying to assimilate the novel sensation of being clean and well fed and to think of a brotherly excuse to spend the night in Olympia's cabin. Or for her to spend the night in his. Flare-up of an old wound, perhaps, which could only be nursed by his dearest sister, who would know just how to bring his fever down.

He grinned to himself, contemplating the emotions of the twenty-two officers and two hundred crewmen of *Terrier.*

Dream on, me hearties, he thought, without a shred of remorse.

But he felt strangely vulnerable, separated from her. The familiar surroundings of a navy frigate seemed disorienting, oddly threatening—as if the peace he'd found with her on the island could be pulled away from him somehow, like a blanket from a sleeping child. He wished he could have her here with him. Just to hold onto her. Just to lie beside her and watch her and be able to touch her whenever he wanted.

She'd stuck by him at the dinner table. He wanted to kiss her for that: for not throwing wrenches in his story, for rescuing him from his foolishness. He felt a deep sinking nausea when he thought of how absurd he must have appeared to her. He hated being called a slave, he loathed it, but he'd acted bloody berserk there at the table in front of them all.

At the pit of his stomach, there was a renewed tension—an old, old anxiety: he was back in the world; things were the way they'd always been . . . and he didn't like it. He didn't like himself. He was going to have bad dreams again.

He reckoned he'd better post Mustafa as a chaperon for her. No telling when young Fitzhugh might lose his head. The ship wasn't long out of Buenos Aires, so pressure was light yet, but a few months on and things would look entirely different. These noble, true-hearted bastards couldn't be trusted. They went along all sincere and righteous and bottled up, and then broke down into raving lecherous lunatics when you least expected it.

As Sheridan lay frowning and thoughtful, Mustafa sat sulking on the floor, muttering to himself. When his mumbles reached a discernible level, Sheridan gave him one silent look.

Mustafa hunched his shoulders, dropped his face into his hands and began to pour out apologies in Arabic. "Forgive me, O my master! I have done my pitiful best; I have regained the jewels of our princess from where you hid them in your infinite wisdom on the island; I have followed your prudent and cunning orders; I have preserved the treasure at terrible risk to my very life!" He raised his eyes and spread his arms. "I have brought this ship, this mighty vessel of your Sultan King George, across the broad waters of the earth to your aid; I have watched over your beloved in the day and in the night; I have confounded your enemies—"

"You'd have done better to keep your miserable mouth shut," Sheridan snapped in English.

Mustafa prostrated himself. "O my pasha, whose honors are endless, who rules the great oceans, whose countenance shines with the compassion and mercy of the blessed—"

"Quite. Perhaps I'll only cut your tongue out, instead of flaying you alive."

"I did not mean to do it!" Mustafa squealed, still in his own language. "It was in the darkest moment of grief and despair, when I thought you were lost to me!"

Sheridan sat up and leaned over. He grabbed Mustafa's arm and hissed in Arabic, "O son of swine, may Allaah curse your sorry carcass; may you die alone and godless and forsaken; may your body be left to flies and black rot if ever you call me a slave again."

A soft knock came at the door. Sheridan let go. He gave Mustafa one last look that made him cringe down to the floor and cover his face.

"*Yállah!* Hurry up! See to the door." Sheridan reached for the spirit decanter.

Mustafa scrambled up and obeyed. Sheridan rose, startled to find Captain Fitzhugh waiting in the corridor.

"Forgive me for disturbing you," the younger man said. "I hoped I might have a private word. I thought of waiting, but it's rather—" He paused, taking a breath. "Are you occupied presently?"

"At your service." Sheridan set down his glass and started toward the door, ducking to avoid a deck beam.

"No, no—you're comfortable here. No need to go elsewhere. I'll stand."

Sheridan glanced at him in mild surprise. It wasn't exactly common naval practice for the captain to do anyone the honor of calling in person, or to conduct business outside the spacious confines of his cabin and the poop deck. Sheridan's quarters, two decks down and crammed next to the surgery, where the sixth lieutenant he'd displaced was sharing with the chaplain, made a strange choice for an interview with the commanding officer.

Mustafa took his chance to escape and slipped out behind Fitzhugh. The door shut. Sheridan stood back to allow Fitzhugh room, grasping the decanter. "Will you take some of your own excellent sherry?" he asked politely.

"Yes, I—that does sound—salutary!" Fitzhugh's face was pink as he shifted, edging himself into a stable position in the tiny space.

Sheridan poured him a glass and leaned against the berth, trying to create some room without actually sitting down, which seemed a little too casual a move with a fellow officer and the man who'd rescued them—even if he was a damned apple-cheeked infant.

After a moment of quick calculation for the day of the week, Sheridan lifted his drink in the navy's traditional Thursday toast. "Bloody war and quick promotion." Then, not seeing how he could be asked to do anything inconvenient or unhealthy—not in the near future, at least—he added, "Look here, I hope you know there aren't words enough to thank you for what you've done for us. Any way I can oblige you, you've got my best at your service."

Fitzhugh waved his hand and shook his head. "It's nothing. Nothing. How could I have done otherwise, knowing Miss Drake was . . . and you, of course . . . countrymen in need, and all that." He bit his lip, turning redder. "Well, it was only a trifling digression to stop here. Practically on the way."

"Thank you for it. I hope we won't be a burden to you, toting us half across the globe."

"Nonsense. Retired officer, and with your record of service! It's perfectly in order. I counted you both into the provisions in Buenos Aires."

"Foresight," Sheridan said warmly.

Fitzhugh let out a long breath. "I'm just glad there was need of it. When your man—what the devil's his name? Mistafa?—after he came to me, I don't mind saying I was in a rare taking over his story. When I contemplate what might have happened . . ." His hand tightened around the handle of the locker. "I saw that those villains got their just punishment, anyway. It was a pleasure, I'll tell you, to watch them squirm at the end of a noose." He smiled grimly. "It was a damned good show, too. That Yankee captain had a fine trick with a rope—fixed it so that they'd not break their necks when they dropped. There was a pair of them didn't stop twitching for half an hour." He shook his head with relish. "But they deserved to suffer. Fiends! Dear God, that Miss Drake should be in such peril! I was praying. I could think of nothing else. I haven't slept for dread."

Sheridan looked down at his drink, tracing his finger around the rim.

"I'm sure she told you," Fitzhugh said shyly, "she was with us for most of her voyage."

"I'm in your debt."

"No. It was a pleasure. Her company was—a joy to me." He blinked at Sheridan earnestly and then dropped his eyes. "I admire your sister greatly, Captain Sir Sheridan. Very greatly."

Sheridan regarded his sherry, slowly swirling the golden liquid around the sides of the glass. He let the silence lengthen.

Fitzhugh moistened his lips. Sheridan thought he would stumble and stutter, but the young captain pulled himself up and leveled his gaze. "I request your permission to pay her my addresses, sir. I think you will find my family is a worthy one—we're the Surrey Fitzhughs; my elder brother holds the barony of Barsham, and my mother was a Bentinck. I've an independence of eighteen thousand per annum. My brother manages that for me, since I've been occupied with my career." Biting his lower lip, he waved his hand and then cleared his throat. "You may imagine that there is a reasonable accumulation of capital with which to set up house. I've had little use for it till now."

Sheridan thought of the crystal and silver and the white linen tablecloth, the good sherry and the damask curtains that adorned the captain's stateroom. "Haven't you?" he asked mildly.

Fitzhugh looked anxious. "Perhaps you don't think my income adequate to support her as she deserves. There's my officer's pay, too, and always hope of prize money, of course—though I should be dishonest to say I depend upon it, what with the present peace. But I—" He drew a breath. "I believe I could make her happy, sir. She has . . . given me reason to hope."

"Has she!" Sheridan smiled. His teeth grated together. "She had not mentioned it to me."

That set him back, the condescending brat. Sheridan watched expressionlessly as the young officer's face blazed red. A mere eighteen thousand a year . . . how could the man live? Poor chap, he probably couldn't even buy London Bridge if he wanted it.

The captain took a quick gulp of his drink. "I suppose—she could not have thought she would see me again."

Sheridan controlled his urge to deliver another snide setdown. The fair flower of the Sussex Fitzhughs could go hang, damn his eyes—but there was no percentage saying so yet.

No, there was nothing for it but to play the game. And Olympia would have to play it, too. If she told the lovestruck puppy to take the damper he deserved at this early date, things could get deucedly uncomfortable before they reached port.

"I'd like to speak to her about it. You understand." Sheridan put a hand on Fitzhugh's shoulder and squeezed—playing the stalwart elder brother. "But you're a good man, Fitzhugh. A good man."

Then he raised his glass in a silent toast and drank, watching Fitzhugh over the rim as the younger man's freckled face broke into a tremulous grin.

A good man. Just don't get your hopes up, you virtuous little sap.

Olympia peeped around the door in answer to Sheridan's knock, the lamplight behind her shining in a glow around her loosened hair and silhouetting her body through the flannel night rail. Sheridan took one appalled glance at her, cast swift looks up and down the corridor and pushed her back, stepping inside. He locked the door hastily.

"Jesus, what are you doing, answering the door looking like this? Do you know how many men are aboard this ship? By God, you're not even buttoned!"

She pulled the slipping gown up onto her shoulder. "The buttons are in the back. I can't reach them." She caught his hand in both of hers. "Sheridan, I'm go glad you've come. I wanted to say I was sorry." She kissed the back of his palm and cradled it against her cheek. "I've been so wrong—I've been such a fool! How could you let me do it?"

His mouth had been open to continue the lecture. He closed it.

She moved into his arms, pressing her cheek to his shoulder. "Forgive me." Her hold tightened around him, her breasts soft and provocative against his chest. "I don't know how that miserable little man ever made me believe you could be a thief! Sheridan . . . can you forgive me? I should have known you didn't do it. I should have known long ago."

He put his hand on her hip, feeling the tantalizing curve of bare skin beneath the flannel. With his lips pressed to her hair, he stood there calculating wildly, trying to decide how to handle this development. He'd never expected *her* to fall for that shaky tale he'd concocted—he'd been relieved just to have her go along with it in front of the others.

She wriggled her hip beneath his hand, pressing closer. He breathed in the fresh scent of her clean hair. Really, truth was such an abominably awkward inconvenience. There was no telling how she'd react if he blurted out a confession now in answer to her optimistic misapprehension. It seemed she'd finally forgiven him on the island, but they'd never actually talked about it. And things were different now. They were no longer alone and dependent on one another, and there was that nodcock Fitzhugh, too, the devil take him. If she wished, she'd have someone else to turn to for aid and comfort and . . .

A fierce wave of jealousy rose in him. The image of Fitzhugh touching her—God, the man wanted to marry her, to have the right to tumble her anytime he pleased, and he wouldn't have to drive himself to desperation forestalling the natural consequences, either.

It didn't bear thinking about. Sheridan buried his mouth against her hair and said, "Of course I forgive you."

She gave a little sigh and relaxed against him. Then, just as he was lowering his head to nibble insinuatingly at her ear, she pulled away. "You won't punish Mustafa? I think—I believe he really did mean well, odd as it seems."

"It'd be a miracle in our time if he did." Sheridan caught her back. Pushing his fingers into her loosened hair, he kissed the tender skin beneath her earlobe. "I know how to deal with Mustafa," he murmured. "But give me a respite from the gruesome thought, if you please. He's already been weeping all over my borrowed boots."

She bent her head with a tiny smile, resting her forehead against him and toying with the buttons on his waistcoat.

Sheridan's breathing quickened. His hands slipped down; he grasped the gown in his fists, gathering it upward. While she stood in the lamplight, he sank slowly to his knees, pulling her toward him to kiss the valley between her breasts through the soft fabric.

Olympia clasped his head with a soft moan of welcome and relief. She moved insinuatingly beneath his hands. It felt so good, so familiar and wonderful to have him come to her like this—in intimacy and passion. It made the world seem right again, washing away her uneasiness at those earlier moments of constraint. He sat back on his heels and shaped her legs downward, slid his fingers beneath the hem and touched her slippered feet. His face was on a level with the warm cleft between her thighs as he circled her ankles with his hands.

She responded with a surge of excitement, leaning back against the smooth bulkhead. He pushed the gown upward, a slow slide, kissing the inner skin of her thighs as the soft fabric revealed it.

"Flowers," he murmured huskily; "you smell like flowers."

She gave a faint, shaky laugh. "That must be a change."

"Sweet princess." He brushed his face against her, buried it in the contours of her body with a deep inhalation. "You always smell like heaven to me."

She drew in a sharp breath as his tongue searched and found the source that sent cascades of sensation flooding through her. She arched her head back, pressing it against the hard wall of mahogany.

"Sheridan," she gasped, curling her fingers in his thick hair.

He made a wordless sound in answer and slid his hands upward on her naked skin, cupping her buttocks, pulling her harder against his mouth. The teasing, arousing rhythm of his tongue made her writhe with exquisite torment. She bit her lip, trying to stifle the sounds that hung in her throat, trying to keep the breathless cries to moans, here where she might be heard.

He brought her to the edge of explosion, caressed and kissed her until her trembling fingers pulled at his hair. She found his shoulders and tugged upward, breathing in short fervent sighs, pleading for more.

He rose, lifting the gown over her head and pushing her back against the wooden wall in one swift motion. His kiss raked her mouth, tasting of her own excitement. He shaped her breasts, lifting, so that her nipples rubbed against the fabric of his dove-gray coat. The sensation of roughness against the tender, swollen nubs made her close her eyes and open her lips, but he subdued her cry of pleasure with his mouth, plunging his tongue deep as he pressed his arousal against her.

She rotated her hips, answering the hard, masculine message. Her fingers searched eagerly between them, touched and pressed and outlined the shape of him while he groaned against her mouth. She could feel the deep vibration in his chest against her breasts. She teased at the buttons on his breeches, releasing them one by one, slowly—so slowly that he finally pushed her hand away and reached for the last one himself.

"Damned civilization," he muttered. "Who thought up all these clothes?"

Olympia swayed and tilted her head back in his arms. She was smiling, stimulated by the new sensation of being naked against his full dress. "I like them, " she whispered huskily. "I think you look handsome . . . and elegant . . . and . . . so . . . so . . . tantalizing . . ."

His long eyelashes lowered on a gleam. "Do you, now?" He kissed her chin, tasting it with his tongue. His shaft throbbed against her, heat against heat. "I won't bother to take 'em off, then."

"Good," she murmured. "Good."

His low laugh blended with a kiss at the curve of her throat, his teeth closing lightly on her skin. He lifted her to him, pressing her back against the wall. Olympia knew what he intended. She arched in his embrace, slipping her legs open and closing them again on hot stiff maleness and sensation.

His luxurious sound of pleasure seemed to soak into her soul, igniting a tumult of desire. He didn't enter her, but began to move, cupping her buttocks, sliding between her thighs on skin moistened by anticipation, stimulating showers of wild sparks that fountained upward through her whole body. She clutched at him, breathing faster. His face was bent to her shoulder, his mouth open against her skin, the touch of him all heat and fire as he pushed her to the cool varnished wood.

She flexed into the thrusts that slid between her thighs, her urgency exploding. Her back curved, her neck arched, trembling against the desire to open her legs and be penetrated. This was what he had taught her—for her own protection, to prevent the disaster of conception on the island—but each time it became harder and harder for her to remember reason with his body moving on hers, his hands pulling her hungrily against him with every stroke.

In a haze of passion, she relaxed the tight clasp of her thighs and tilted her hips, bringing his next thrust with sweet, blunt pressure against her waiting entrance.

"Sheridan," she whimpered. "Sheridan, please—take me." She swallowed a gasp. "I want all of you."

His fingers pressed into her buttocks. "Princess—" His voice was a rasp, muffled in her hair.

"I want you inside me—I don't care . . . I don't care what happens." She tried to turn her head, brushing her lips to his hair and neck. The salty male taste of sweat burned on her tongue. "Please." She squeezed her thighs, arching against him. "It doesn't matter; what difference will it make? We can marry. Now. Tomorrow. We can tell them all the truth. Oh, God . . . please . . ."

"Don't!" The word came between harsh pants. "I can't think now; don't ask me to think."

She raised one knee, sliding it up the long muscular tightness of his thigh beneath the doeskin breeches. The move placed her so that his coming thrust would fill her.

With a little moan of pleasure, she pushed forward—asking—inviting . . . demanding that he impale her.

His hands froze. "No." He made a vehement groan as he stopped the drive of his hips. For a long moment he held her suspended, pressed against the wall, while he drew in short, sharp breaths and his shoulders trembled. He shook his head fiercely.

She stirred in his hold, creating a voluptuous pressure on the swollen intrusion, the part of him that said "Yes" instead. She wriggled, trying to draw him further, reveling in the feel of him, full and hard. He could bring her to final ecstasy in his own way, she knew that, but she wanted more. She wanted them joined, she wanted to have him deep within her, the ultimate invasion that would make her wholly and only his.

"Please," she whispered, drawing her fingers down the hot, damp skin behind his ear. "Sheridan, please . . ."

He moved suddenly, violently, not pushing into her but propelling her away from him into the wall. "Curse you!" He slammed his open palms against the wood on either side of her head. "What are you trying to do to me? It's too risky—you know why—God Almighty, do you think I don't *want* . . ." He closed his eyes and tilted his head back. The pulse in his throat beat hard and fast. "No." He swallowed. "No."

She kissed his forearm where it was braced beside her. "Please," she whispered again, touching him, using her fingers to coax and caress in ways that she knew would take him to the edge of endurance. As he shuddered, straining, she slid her hands around his hips to pull him back and murmured, "It would feel so good . . . you know how good."

"Be damned to you," he snarled, and shoved away from her.

Olympia's arms fell to her sides, empty. She stared at his taut back as he turned away. He buttoned himself, then stood with his white-knuckled hand on the brass door-knob, facing the blank wood. His shoulders rose and fell with deep, labored breaths.

Without turning, he said, "I have to talk with you. Would

it please Your Royal Highness to put on your bloody dressing gown?''

''Sheridan—''

''Put it on.''

She grabbed the rumpled flannel from the floor and dragged it over her head. ''There. Satisfied? Shall I wrap myself up in the blanket as well?''

''It damned well wouldn't hurt.''

Olympia plumped herself onto the berth. She drew the blanket around her, not because of him, but because the cabin that had seemed so hot a moment ago now held a chill. ''There,'' she said stiffly. ''You can turn around. I'm not going to accost you.''

He pushed away from the door and sat down on her trunk. He didn't look at her; he seemed to find the deck more interesting. His breeches still showed the heavy burden of arousal, and Olympia gazed at them wistfully.

''I'm sorry,'' she said in a softer tone. ''Don't be upset with me.''

He propped his elbow on the bulkhead and shoved his hand into his hair, frowning into space. ''I don't want to hurt you,'' he said in a hard voice. ''I don't want you in trouble. But God—it's difficult enough—do you have to make it unbearable? I'm no saint, Olympia.'' He took a deep breath. ''God knows I'm not.''

A surge of guilt and love washed over her as she watched his tense profile. ''Who wants a saint?'' she asked softly. ''I think I prefer my angels fallen.''

He smiled sourly and gave her a sideways glance. ''I never got high enough to fall. Virtue ain't my style. And it's not yours, either—that's coming clear enough.''

She pressed her lips together, feeling her cheeks grow pink. ''Well,'' she said defensively, ''if we were married, it would be all right. It would even be virtuous. 'Whoso findeth a wife, findeth a good thing.' Proverbs 18:22.''

''Jesus—you ought to be struck by lightning, quoting the Bible to me after the kind of thing you were saying not five minutes past.''

Her eyes widened. ''You're a prude!''

''I'm not a prude. I'm trying to keep my head. We *aren't*

married. For God's sake, everyone on this ship thinks we're brother and sister!'' He rubbed his temple. ''Let me tell you, it makes my blood run cold to imagine the consequences if you were to start increasing now.''

''We could tell them the truth. It would be such a relief! And then the chaplain could marry us.''

''You're not thinking,'' he said.

''There's no way my uncle could reach us now. Me *or* you. What do we have to fear? Everything's different from when we left England.'' She gazed at him earnestly, trying to put all of her feelings into her eyes. ''Everything.''

He held the look for a long moment, his expression strange and uninterpretable. He looked away from her. ''Yeah. Everything.''

She frowned, watching him. His strong fingers toyed with the latch of the trunk between his knees, marking an uneasy rhythm. He stared down at his hands, his face hidden.

For the first time, a worm of real fear coiled inside her. ''You asked me to marry you,'' she said. ''On the island, you asked me. Did you not mean it?''

The latch made a metallic clunk. ''I meant it,'' he said to the floor.

She drew a breath and waited.

The latch clunked again. He added caustically, ''I don't recall that you ever answered me.''

Olympia wanted to put her arms around him and hug him to her breast, but instead she only said, ''You fell asleep.''

He sat back, leaning his head against the wall, his eyes closed. ''I think I've been asleep for the past five months.'' He shook his head. ''Dreaming.''

''Dreaming?'' she whispered.

''Impossibilities.''

Her throat would barely sound words. ''You don't want to marry me now?''

''Looked at in the cold light of reason, it seems to me to be a stupid and dangerous idea. I can't think where I came by it.''

The shock numbed her. She sat with her eyes closed, trying to breathe.

"Use your head," he said harshly. "We're both at the mercy of Fitzhugh. You tell him the truth, and what's he going to do? Our precious young captain's the hanging sort—you heard what he made certain they did with Buckhorse and his gang."

"They were murderers. They deserved it."

"Aye, those brutes deserved it, God knows, but the man's got a righteous gleam of retribution in his eye. I know his kind. I've lived with 'em all my life. He can't get any normal satisfaction because of his damned tight morals, but he'll be delighted to take his thrills out of somebody's hide if he thinks he's got justice on his side." Sheridan stood up, prowling the tiny cabin. "And on top of that, the little bastard fancies he's in love with you. He's beside himself with lily-white passion. Just how do you think he's going to take to the idea that I'm not your brother, but a conniving blackguard who's kidnapped his adored object and been living in carnal intimacy with her for months?"

"He's not like that. And you haven't kidnapped me."

"How's he to know?" Sheridan shook his dark head. "We've lied, my dear. We've lied well and thoroughly. If we change the story now, we've got no credibility left at all. What's more fantastic—the truth or the tale as it stands? He's not going to believe you're a princess, and he sure ain't going to swallow the idea that I've been chaperoning you on the way to the revolution." His fine mouth curled. "Fitzhugh may be a self-righteous choirboy, but he's not as stupid as you'd think to look at him. It's only his rosy view of *you* that's made him miss the inconsistencies so far. Even Buckhorse could see we were lying till our tongues turned blue."

"And he believed us in the end."

"No, he didn't." Sheridan turned on her with a savage scowl, bracing his hand on the brass trimwork near her ear. "He just finally figured he wasn't going to beat it out of me. Besides, he had another use for me alive. Fitzhugh doesn't. I'm nothing to him, once I'm not the hero of his damned midshipman's fantasies." He thrust himself away. "And Fitzhugh's king aboard this ship, madam. He's God. If he gets some notion in a jealous fit, nobody here is going to say him nay. You can kill a man with a cat-o'-nine, Princess." His voice took on a mocking note. "Accidentally, of course. 'So sorry, the poor bastard looked tougher than that—who'd've thought he couldn't take two hundred lashes? Unfortunate business, but he was a pretty rum case, after all. Been pulling the wool over all our eyes for years.' "

She frowned, watching him pace the confinement as if it were a cage. "I don't believe Captain Fitzhugh's at all the kind of person you think. And I know him much better than you do. I've never once seen him lose his temper. He's always been good and kind and considerate."

Sheridan looked swiftly at her. His gray eyes glittered. "Marry *him*, then," he said angrily, "if he's such a damned paragon. Because I'm spiteful and selfish and I've got the devil's own temper, which I make sure to lose twice a day." He turned away, stuffing his hands into his pockets. "He's already applied to me for permission. I only hope he doesn't fall into an ecstatic swoon at my feet when I give him the glad news."

Huddled in the blanket, she stared at him in miserable disbelief. "Why are you saying these things? What's happened?"

"Reality." He shot her a sidelong glance, one eyebrow raised in derision. "Not one of your favorite subjects, I know."

She hugged her knees. Watching him, she remembered his face in the firelight, patient and sympathetic as he whittled a comb from whalebone to replace the one she'd broken in a fit of pique at the impossible snarls in her hair. She remembered his gentle hands, working through the mass of tangles himself after she'd wept with impatience because she could not. She saw him now, with that sarcastic twist to his mouth, and thought that reality was more tangled and frustrating than any mop of windblown curls.

"All right," she said at last. "We'll just go on as we are."

She thought he would say something cutting; she was braced for it. But her agreement met silence. He leaned against the wall, his profile reflected in the polished wood.

She looked down, picking at the blanket. "It was only an idea, anyway."

He straightened. He came to her and took her by the shoulders. His fingers slipped up the sides of her throat; he cupped her chin between his hands and held her, looking down into her eyes.

His own were smoke, intense and impenetrable, like a wildfire smoldering.

"Trust me," he said.

She stared up at him. "How could I not?" Her voice had a husky break in it. "I love you."

Something queer passed in his face, an instant and then gone, and she could not tell if it was shock or fear or exultation or a fusion of all of them.

He bent and touched his forehead to hers with a silent, negative shake of his head.

"I do," she repeated.

"Foolish princess; I've just informed you that I'd rather shab off than risk my precious hide to marry you. What do you want to love a scaly chap like me for?"

She arched her eyebrows. "Fishing for compliments?"

"God help me—I ain't that optimistic. Just checking, in case you might have turned up sensible on me. Pleased to see you're as half-witted as ever." He drew back, shook his head again and went to the door. He paused with it open and gave her a wry smile. "I won't be slow to take advantage of it, you have my word."

"*Emiriyyiti!*" Mustafa scratched on her door a few minutes later.

She opened it and found him in red fez and white galabiyya, standing with a roll of blankets in his thin brown arms.

"O my princess, where would you have me to sleep? Sheridan Pasha has said it may be outside your door or inside, as you prefer."

Olympia protested, but the manservant, with orders

from his pasha, only informed her that he thought it best that he lie down just inside her cabin door.

"Inside? That would be exceedingly improper."

"Of course you are right, my princess, in your infinite beauty of mind and form. My own comfort is less than nothing, and I shall be privileged to sleep in the corridor. I welcome the cold drafts and the kicks of these English sailors and their heavy feet, O Beloved; I would suffer a thousand bruises and broken fingers if you would only look kindly on me, a—"

"Oh, very well." She grabbed his elbow and pulled him inside. "But I don't know what everyone will think!"

Mustafa bowed deeply, gesturing as if to lift her hem and kiss it. "They will know that your charity extends to the ends of the earth, that the poor multitude kneels down in thanks at your mercy, and that I, made weaponless and fit to serve in the Great Sultan's hareem, will protect your honor with my life."

"Nonsense. Really, Mustafa, you say the most outrageous things. I ought to scold you to an inch for telling me lies about Sir Sheridan. And stealing my jewels, too—when we both were beside ourselves thinking he'd been killed. That was taking most venal advantage." She frowned at him and sighed. "But I suppose you hardly know better, do you? You have no more moral sense than a monkey."

His brown eyes widened. "*Emiriyyiti,*" he said in a grieved tone. "I obey my pasha's orders. I have told you no lies except at his bidding, may Allah bless him."

"No lies?" She made a huff of exasperation. "How you can be so brazen, I don't know." With a resigned shake of her head, she regarded him. "I suppose it's no use being vexed. You hardly comprehend if you're lying or not, I don't expect. But you should understand that taking my jewels and placing the blame on your master was very, very wrong."

Mustafa looked horrified. "No, no! Forgive me, but it is you who misunderstand, my princess. I did not steal your jewels, *Emiriyyiti*. I would not dare! Sheridan Pasha took them, but now we say that it was I, so that this silly camel of a captain will not be so foolish as to detain my pasha as if he were a common criminal.'' The gold tassel on his fez bobbed anxiously. ''You must say so, too. He has so ordered, has he not?''

''Certainly not. Mustafa, you mustn't be afraid of me and lie on that account. I especially asked Sir Sheridan not to punish you over this, but do please stop making up stories!'' She opened her arms. ''When I think of all that nonsense you told me about how he had been a slave of some sultan—it really is too much.''

He looked at her, his head tilted to one side as if she were a fascinating puzzle. Then he blinked, and said without expression, ''Thank you, *Emiriyyiti*, thank you for your kindness in speaking on my humble behalf.''

With another deep bow, he shuffled backward and began to spread his blankets on the floor. As he bent over, the lamplight caught the glint of the crescent and star that swung free of the folds of his garment.

Olympia frowned. She sat down on her bed. Something uncomfortable tickled in the back of her mind, not quite clear enough to be a thought. ''Mustafa—what is it on that chain you're wearing?'' she asked.

Mustafa went stiff. He turned back to her and bobbed briefly. ''It is called a *teskeri hilaal*, my princess.''

''Oh.'' She watched him arrange a pillow. ''Forgive me. I don't mean to pry, but—'' She bit her lip. ''Forgive me, but it doesn't mean your master's not a Christian or anything, does it?''

For a long time Mustafa made no answer, smoothing and tucking at his bedding. Finally he looked up at her. In a dignified, faintly accusing tone, he said, ''Perhaps you will say it is another story.''

She tucked in her chin and tried to appear stern. ''Will it be?''

He hesitated. Then a considering look came into his alien eyes. ''No, *Emiriyyiti*. I understand that I am not to tell you lies again.''

She nodded encouragement. ''Good.''

''I tell you the truth, sworn upon my mother's milk. The *teskeri* is—'' He frowned, searching for words. ''It is a talisman. A badge of the Great Sultan's favor. It is my task to see that my Sheridan Pasha wears it so that he is honored and protected from lesser men's slights. I am very zealous for my master, you know that, *Emiriyyiti*. I try to be strict with him and persuade him to wear it. When I shave him, I always place it on his neck. Sometimes he allows it to stay there. For a day, perhaps. Or a week. He wore it for a whole month, once, when we had just left the navy. But mostly"—he shrugged—"mostly a devil is in his head and he cannot bear to touch it or see it or have others know it belongs to him, and so I keep it safe." He lifted the gleaming crescent over his head and handed it to her. "Can you see the writing? It says that the man possessing this *hilaal* is a beloved and trusted sla—" He stopped suddenly, and with a lift of his eyes toward heaven, muttered something in his own language. Then he added fervently, "Forgive me, my princess, I was about to tell a lie, but I will not. What it truly says is that this man of the *hilaal*—and it describes him, so that no one else may have the advantage of it—is beloved of Allah, who is the One God, and of Sultan Mahmoud, who is His Shadow on Earth, and that any who dares harm the least hair of this man's head will be tracked down to the ends of the earth and destroyed by Their terrible might."

She turned the crescent over in her hands, squinting at the delicate tracery of Arabic lettering and design that flowed across the metal, interrupted only by one deep, thin scratch zigzagging over the face.

She smoothed her fingertip over the piece, feeling the ragged indentation that marred it. A vision came to her—of the deck of *Phaedra* in the torchlight, and the convict Cal showing his strong teeth as he bit down on the crescent around Sheridan's neck and then scraped his knife tip across the metal.

She pressed her lips together in thought. Mustafa knelt at her feet, looking up at her, his eyes dark and perceptive.

"He had it with him," she said slowly. "He was wearing it when we found him."

Mustafa bent his head. All she could see of the little

man was the cylindrical top of his fez. ''But, *Emiriyyiti*—you understand—I have told no story.''

She tilted her head, looking down at him with a frown.

Mustafa spoke into his lap, his head still bowed. ''I have not lied and said that he took the *teskeri hilaal* when your jewels disappeared. No, I have not—because if I had, then you might be encouraged to believe that he wasn't robbed as he claims, but intended to take the jewels and leave us, and only such a purpose would induce him to touch a thing he hates. You might even think that he planned it all, stealing your treasure and buying passage on the convict transport. I would not say those things, my princess. I have promised not to tell you stories.''

Olympia put her hand to her mouth, chewing her knuckle.

''No stories, O most respected princess,'' Mustafa went on. ''I will not say that he hid your jewels on the island where he was wrecked and then told me—in sign and my own tongue—right in front of everyone, how to find them.''

''How to find them?'' she murmured dubiously.

Mustafa sat up, throwing his hands wide. ''That is a story that would make my pasha seem great and clever and brave, would it not? To pretend that he made it seem we were arguing over the pearls while he was giving me instructions in the very faces of our enemies—but I will not recount it, for I would be lying.''

He pressed his forehead to the deck, a white huddle in the lamplight, and grasped her ankles. Olympia pulled away, tucking her legs under her on the berth. ''Please,'' she said. ''I wish you wouldn't do that.''

Mustafa drew back. ''Forgive me, my princess,'' he said humbly. ''I am not fit to touch the smallest fringe of your garment. I would not build up my useless self by lies and tell you that it was I who recovered your jewels from their hiding place after you escaped the ship *Phaedra* with my pasha.''

She curled her legs tighter and crossed her arms, hugging herself, staring down at him.

''I am a dog and the son of a dog. But I tell no more

lies. I do not say that when the convict devils went to the island to look for the jewels, they began to kill each other and ordered me to bury the dead.'' He bowed deeply. ''You must know, *Emiriyyiti*, that I am stupid and slow, and it would be false if I tried to make you believe that I took the chance when they were not watching to retrieve the treasure in secret.''

She felt her breath begin to come with effort. She bit her lip, holding back the reaction to his words.

''And of course,'' he added meekly, ''I never hid the jewels and kept them safe until *Phaedra* reached Buenos Aires, and my Sheridan Pasha was never the lover of your Mrs. Julia Plumb. Never did he receive her on the very day you came to him for help; never did he ask for your hand in marriage, because for her own designs she forced it upon him and made it the only way he could reach his father's fortune—I would not expect you to believe that. All lies, *Emiriyyiti.*'' He rocked his small body up and down in prostration. ''It is all lies, and I will not tell them.''

Olympia swallowed. She closed her eyes, leaning back with her hands over her face.

All lies. All, all lies.

She had no right to be furious at Sheridan. To feel a fool, yes—to grit her teeth and push at her pillow and toss in her bed in the black night, staring into darkness and reviling herself as a naive little nodcock—oh, yes, she had every right to do that.

But at first, anger had flooded out every other emotion: the passionate wrath born anew, fresh rage at the way he'd betrayed her, robbed her, stripped her of all her dreams and deserted her. How could he? *How could he?* She hated him!

How easy it was, that anger. How simple, how pure and self-righteous . . . how much less painful than the aching hurt that sat like a stone beneath it, immovable, gradually rising to the surface as the torrent of fury flooded past and subsided.

She lay awake, listening to Mustafa's high-pitched snores.

Dreaming, Sheridan had said, and he'd been right. She thought she'd forgiven him for deserting her, but she'd only managed to forget. The real world had receded. Now it was back, and she'd found she was a coward again. She'd believe anything to avoid looking truth in the face. How quick she'd been to swallow that poppycock story he'd made up to cover himself, jumping at the hope he was innocent against all rational evidence.

And of course he had not contradicted her. Why should he? He knew what a fool she was, so he'd merely taken advantage of her foolishness, the same way he'd supported her on the island—because he wanted to stay alive and had needed her: the skills she had, the food she gathered, the companionship she provided. He'd been kind to her because she'd been more useful to him as a friend—as a lover—than an enemy.

Just as she was more useful to him now as a sister than a wife.

It was simple. That was the kind of man he was. A realist. A scoundrel. A liar. A shabby knight with a baby penguin asleep on his boot.

Julia . . . Julia . . . Julia . . . he'd had Julia as a lover.

Julia! Gorgeous, graceful, self-possessed Julia. How he must have laughed at Olympia's untutored fumbling!

Oh, she *had* been a fool, a lovesick fool, and she still was. To think that somehow he had changed and she could trust him now.

She could never trust him, or believe anything he said.

The realization brought no anger with it. Instead of bitterness, she felt only a dull despair: grief for the dream that could not survive reality, and the pain of seeing clearly when she wished she could be blind. As well stand naked in the winter and curse the wind as rage at Sheridan for lying to someone who wanted with her soul to believe in him.

She couldn't even hate herself for being twice a dupe. He was so very good at it. Even now, she knew that if she gave him a chance, he could convince her again, make her believe he loved her as he'd never loved before.

Loved her. A chubby, plain mooncalf like her. She was a mooncalf indeed if she could believe that. Simple common sense ought to have told her that she shared nothing with a man like Sheridan Drake. She'd nothing to offer, not beauty or wit or experience. She was stubborn and childish—even she could see that for herself. One of the solemn, virtuous buffoons of the world, one of the upright idiots who made an easy target for his ruthless humor.

Trust me.

The devil would say that, in just that compelling way. While behind those silver eyes, that flawless act, he'd be laughing at the way she still clung to her ideals in spite of everything—she *would* do some good, somewhere, if she could manage it—while he held to nothing: not friendship, not truth, not even simple decency. He was worse even than Mustafa, who only took the orders of his pasha without understanding right from wrong.

Sheridan understood, but he did not care. Like a demon child, he could lie with his heart in his eyes.

Twenty

Fitzhugh took afternoon tea.

That about summed the man up, in Sheridan's opinion. He answered an invitation to the state cabin the next afternoon and found a table set with lace and delicate porcelain—and a bowl of pink and white tulips, of all the damned things. Three gilded French chairs sat in a waiting semicircle overlooking the bank of stern lights. The place looked like a bloody drawing room, except for the way the flowers swayed with the motion of the moving ship and the damask drapings didn't quite obscure the shapes of the four cannon mounted at the closed gunports.

Olympia and Fitzhugh were already there. She turned at the sound of the cabin door, and Sheridan's heart seemed to take a silly and painful leap at the sight of her.

It took a savage intellectual effort to quash the emotion. He put it down to a sudden attack of seasickness and focused on Fitzhugh, who strode across the carpeted deck with his hand outstretched.

"Good afternoon! Sit down, sit down—Miss Drake was about to pour." The captain looked like a man who'd just run a footrace, breathless and red-faced as he pumped Sheridan's hand and grinned. He lowered his voice to a murmur. "And she tells me that you've spoken to her. I'm so glad, sir. Thank you. I'm the happiest man alive."

Before Sheridan could answer, he was drawn forward by the enthusiastic grip at his elbow. He kissed Olympia's hand, looking quizzically into her wide green eyes.

She smiled at him blandly.

"Perhaps you'd like to give your brother the news," Fitzhugh said.

She clasped her hands in her lap, still smiling steadily up at Sheridan. "I think he may have already guessed," she said.

"News?" Sheridan hid his consternation and tried to look paternal. Things had apparently moved faster than he'd expected—and he'd never had time to instruct her on how exactly to handle Fitzhugh, blast the luck. But she seemed to be doing all right; the fellow certainly appeared happy enough so far.

She looked modestly down at her lap. "Captain Fitzhugh has asked me to marry him."

"Ah." Sheridan nodded wisely and cursed the fellow for an impetuous puffball. Did he suppose he was such a catch he'd not even have to put in some lengthy courting first?

She looked up, meeting Sheridan's eyes again. "And I've accepted."

Sheridan felt his features freeze.

"Accepted?" The word came out a croak. He could not help it. Not by any mortal effort this side of hell could he have held a natural expression on his face in the split second after her words sank in.

"Yes," Fitzhugh said eagerly. "If it seems a bit hasty to you, sir, I beg you to remember that your sister and I have known one another for a considerable time."

Sheridan felt as if someone were sitting on his chest. Air was suddenly a scarce commodity. He looked from her flushed and smiling face to Fitzhugh's expectant one.

"Well, I—" He couldn't find words. They simply weren't there. Bewildered, he returned to Olympia's guileless green gaze. What the devil did she mean by this? Play Fitzhugh along, yes, keep him dangling and appeased—but surely Sheridan hadn't given her the notion it would be necessary to go to this length? "I suppose I—" He strove desperately for a normal voice. "I'm happy for you, of course. A formal engagement does seem a little—precipitate—to me, if you can understand."

''Certainly.'' Fitzhugh made a quick nod. ''Quite a natural reaction, from your point of view. You can't be expected to fully realize how well we came to know one another in our months together.''

Sheridan looked at him. Like sudden midnight, a veil of suspicion came down over his heart, clutching with black fingers. He had a vision of them—alone together—in this very cabin all those weeks: Fitzhugh talking to her, touching her . . .

''We had tea together every day,'' Olympia said, with a smile at Fitzhugh that seemed to Sheridan to prove his darkest forebodings.

And last night, just last night, she'd been delicious fire in his arms, begging him to take her. To marry her, the little slut! And here she was—

''We've been discussing a date,'' Fitzhugh said with a fatuous smile down at his bride-elect. ''Of course, the sooner the better. But I want to do it right. I insist on that. I daresay a fortnight would be long enough for us to make some special preparations—perhaps a velvet canopy for the poop deck, and the cakes will take a bit of time. And Miss—'' His smile broke into a grin and he took her hand. ''*Olympia* must decide on a gown.''

''Yes,'' she said faintly. ''I have an ivory silk, but I'll wish to add some trim.''

Fitzhugh kissed her fingers. ''Of course. I thought of that. Look.'' He drew her quickly to the map chest and opened a drawer, lifting tissue with a careful rustle. Inside the paper was a quantity of silver lace and seed pearls.

''Oh!'' She touched the airy silver and then put her hand to her lips. ''Oh, dear, you didn't—''

''I bought it in Buenos Aires. I thought—I hoped that when I found you—that is . . . do you like it?'' He laid it down and grasped both her hands. ''My dear Ollie, are you crying? But you're safe now. Safe with me. I'll never let you out of my sight again.''

She bowed her head. Sheridan stared stupidly at their clasped hands. He kept waiting for a withdrawal, for coyness, delay, a secret signal—anything to tell him this was not real.

"A fortnight," she said softly.

Fitzhugh's ruddy hands tightened around hers. "November third. Shall we set it then?"

Sheridan stood still, taut. Now was the time, now—she would begin to postpone and waver and prettily beg for a moment to think. He ought to open his mouth and help her, put in some foolproof excuse for delay, but his mind seemed numb.

"Yes." She looked up at Fitzhugh. "November third."

Sheridan stopped breathing. He felt sick and dazed. He turned away suddenly and walked to the table, fumbling among the tea things. Behind him, Fitzhugh called her his darling Ollie and said they should celebrate tonight with one of the chef's best specialties, and have all the wardroom officers up at the captain's table.

"And I hope you'll honor us by making the announcement, sir," he said, coming to the table as Sheridan lifted a cup.

The porcelain cup seemed to disintegrate in his hand, bouncing against the edge of the table and rolling across the Turkish carpet, the handle shattered. Sheridan swallowed, full of rage and misery and baffled despair.

"Sorry," he said.

Fitzhugh retrieved the broken cup. "For shame, old man." He put a hand on Sheridan's shoulder. "You haven't got your sea legs back yet."

Sheridan moved. Fitzhugh's friendly hand fell away as he turned to beckon to Olympia. Sheridan glared at his back in a fury of contempt and loathing.

Olympia came, a quiet rustle of skirts, the picture of modest womanhood. She might have been made of wax. Sheridan tried to meet her eyes, but she poured tea for them all and sat down without once looking at him. The sense of frustration built to agony. He didn't believe it. He did not. Not after last night. Not after . . . everything.

The tea tasted like acid in his mouth. He held the saucer in both hands and gazed at her, wretchedly aware that he must look like some unhappy dog starved for a kind word, aware too that it made no difference, that she never looked at him, that he might have been one of the draped cannon for all the interest she showed in his sentiments.

With a sluggish, terrible clarity, he began to realize that he'd made a fatal blunder. All that affection, all that sweet warmth—the love that had seemed to grow with aching slowness out of her hatred for him . . . it was all a misinterpretation built of hope and isolation.

He should have known. He should have realized. It had been so hard for him to believe it was happening. That she could come to know him for what he was, fully, and understand what he'd done by opening the circle of himself and including her. They'd fought together, survived together, shared the miseries and the laughter and the disasters, and each small morning victory of waking up alive.

He'd thought that meant something. That was love, that was the only name he had to give it. Last night, when in the midst of his whining concern for his own skin she'd said she loved and trusted him, he'd been so certain of it. He would have died for her then, he would have killed every man on board to protect her—except this was civilization, not a battle, and all he'd been able to do was make some brainless joke to cover the raw surge of emotion and then retreat before he embarrassed himself beyond recovery.

She loved him.

It had been hard to believe that; it had gone against every instinct built up in years of solitude, but he'd convinced himself.

Aye. And he was wrong.

"You know," she was saying shyly, "I never thought to be married on the deck of a ship."

Fitzhugh patted her hand. "I think we can make it quite lovely and memorable, with a little effort. You didn't have your heart set on a church wedding, did you?"

She hesitated. "Well," she said, stroking her fingertip against the edge of her cup. "No. Not really, I suppose."

" 'Not really'?" Fitzhugh gave her an indulgent smile. "That has an equivocal sound. Aren't you sure?"

"It's silly," she said with a faint blush. "I've always

dreamed of—" She shrugged. "But it's not worth mentioning. A childhood fancy."

"Tell me," Fitzhugh insisted, like the simpleton he was. "What did you dream?"

"Oh—I daresay you'll think me a hopeless romantic." She gave him a little sideways glance.

"But that's what I love about you," Fitzhugh said, leaning toward her. "You've such an intelligent grasp of worldly matters like politics, and yet sometimes you can be so . . ."

Arousing, Sheridan thought. *Tantalizing breasts, hips, sweet ankles— Oh, God. I know what you're looking at, you randy little goat.*

". . . so innocent. Tell me what you've dreamed of, and I'll give it to you if I can."

"Oh, no," she said. "It would be impossible. It would be asking too much."

"Nothing is too much. If it's in my power."

She took a breath. "Well—you'll think me silly. But ever since I was a little girl and read about the Seven Hills, I've always wished . . . to be married . . ." She glanced up timidly. "In Rome. At Santa Maria—in the moonlight."

The sounds of the ship seemed to grow loud in the pause.

"Rome," Fitzhugh repeated in slow surprise.

Sheridan just stared at her.

Rome.

Of course.

Rome was where she'd intended to go, and Fitzhugh would be her new ticket to get there.

Sheridan had let down his guard, and he'd been conned. Neatly, wholly and properly conned. There were lessons he'd learned the hard way, and he'd forgotten them; neglected to be wary and not ask too much of fortune.

He was barely aware of Fitzhugh's fumbling answer. As the young captain stammered that he'd have to consider going as far as Rome, Sheridan stood silent.

He felt unreal. It was strange and frightening: he thought he should be angry, but instead he felt displaced, as if he were there and yet not there. He looked at Olympia and she seemed like someone he had never seen before. He looked at his cup and his own hands were strange to him. He felt himself quietly exploding, like glass that shattered and made no sound.

Very carefully, he set down the cup. He had to think of each move—hand here, foot there—he had to plan his turn like a battle as he shifted and walked toward the door. Fitzhugh asked him something, but Sheridan ignored it. He could not have answered if he'd tried. He left, closing the door behind him, and stood in the passage.

He looked around uncertainly. There was a weird skewness to everything—as if that door wasn't where it should be, that ladder out of place. He felt peculiar. A voiceless panic hung at the back of his throat. He forced himself to walk forward.

His head hurt. He could hear his own pulse in his ears.

The panic in him rose suddenly to cold-sweat terror. He clenched his teeth against a moan of dread and walked on—down the ladder and out into the open cavern of the gun deck.

There were two sailors and a midshipman working at the tackle on a cannon. He looked at the sandy hair of the boy bent over the gun carriage.

"Harland," he exclaimed.

All three looked up. "Sir?" asked one of the older men in surprise.

"For God's sake, Harland—" Sheridan felt excited irritation rising in him. His belly tightened and the throbbing sound in his head intensified. He scowled at the boy with the sandy hair. "What the bloody devil are you doing down here? Where's the signal book?"

The boy stared at him. "Sir," he said. "Excuse me. I'm Stevenson, sir."

Sheridan glared at the boy. It was hard to orient himself amid the pounding in his ears. He put his hands to his head, wanting to block out the noise. It hurt his brain, it made him angry and it would not stop. He squeezed his eyes shut and then recognized the sound. "The shore battery!" They were firing, they were close—and Sheridan wasn't ready. He turned sharply. "Harland! Pass the word to Mr. Wright. All hands clear for action!"

The boy stood there, gaping at him.

"Move, blast it!" he shouted. "We're in range. Mr. Wright—" The ship had to turn; they had to turn back. She pitched beneath him while the sound of the guns became thunder. "Mr. Wright!" he ordered. "Wear the ship." But she wouldn't turn; she wouldn't turn—with a nightmare alarm he felt them in the teeth of the guns, the blast growing louder and louder. "Mr. Wright!" he yelled over the sound of them. "Come about—that's an order! Wear ship, damn you—"

The rush came up through him, the powerful surge of bloodlust and frenzy. He lunged at the first officer, furious at the way the man stood dumbfounded, ignoring his direct command as they lay under certain destruction. The noise was unbearable, terrifying; it exploded in his head as his hands closed in killing rage and excitement on the officer's throat. Someone grappled him from behind. Sheridan whirled, bellowing outrage. He went for his knife with enemies in a kaleidoscope around him, fighting for his life amid a rush of attack that sent him sprawling backward. His head cracked brutally against a barrier.

White light flashed over his brain, drowning him in pain and panic.

He came to awareness on the deck, flat on his back, with a burly form on top of him and a sailor holding down his wrists. The man on top was panting in his face. The dead weight made it hard for him to breathe.

He stared at the face above him in slow confusion. The fury and terror ebbed away like the thunder of the guns, dissipating into the normal sounds of a ship under peaceful sail. His fist opened. He turned his head to the side and realized that the knife in it was imagination.

The seaman held him in a tight grip, watching suspiciously. Sheridan closed his eyes. He made his body relax, suffering the painful vise of the sailor's rough fingers with what dignity he could muster. At length, the man softened his grasp.

"Right in your head now, sir?" he asked.

Sheridan took a breath. He nodded. The man let go. They both stood up, slowly, the center of a silent crowd of onlookers. Sheridan glanced at the midshipman, a boy he'd never seen before. The youngster was watching him with round eyes, wary and curious.

Hot shame washed over him. He tugged at his sleeves, refusing to look at the others. He wasn't sure what had happened, but his guts felt like jelly.

"Is he crazy?" the boy asked hopefully.

The man who'd been on top of Sheridan grabbed the young midshipman by the collar. "Listen, whelp—you'd better hope you make as good a man yourself when the day comes. He ain't crazy," he added gruffly.

The boy looked puzzled. But he said, "Aye, sir," quickly enough when the other gave him a shake.

"And don't let me hear this tale from nobody else, you got that?" the man demanded, and glared around. "Keep your mouths shut."

The midshipman nodded. "Aye. I won't say anything, sir." Some of the others murmured.

"There." The seaman gave the youngster a cuff. He was a midshipman himself, one of the old ones—older than Sheridan, a case of failed hopes and broken rungs on the promotion ladder. "You're a good 'un, then. Maybe you'll command a ship through a real action someday, and then you'll understand."

The boy stood a little straighter at those words. He looked at Sheridan with a new respect. The familiar dawn of hero worship in those young eyes made Sheridan feel physically ill. He knew what he was expected to do; he ought to stand straight and nod commandingly and walk away with some of the image intact. But he could not. He felt helpless and shaky. He was afraid he could still hear the guns when he knew they weren't there; he was afraid the world around him was going to dissolve into something else again.

He moved abruptly past the others and then came to a halt, his hand on a gun breech. He could see where he was, he knew the way to his cabin, but there was another ship hovering behind his eyes. His fingers slid on polished metal, seeking cold reality.

Something warm touched his other hand. The boy slid his fingers around Sheridan's fist. "I'll take you to your cabin, sir," he said.

Sheridan stared down at the tawny hair, so familiar and so strange. He jerked his hand away. "Let me be," he snarled. "Christ—oh, Christ, let me be."

He plunged down the companionway, leaving them to think what they would. He found his cabin and shut himself inside. He sat down and stared at the door, breathing hard. With a low moan, he pressed his palms over his eyes to blank out the picture there.

He could feel the anger; it moved like a living thing inside him. He fought it, but it was there. It terrified him. His heart hurt. His throat and his heart and his chest; he was so full of rage and pain. He wanted to kill. There was an old woman in a shattered town who'd cursed him in Arabic with her last breath, told him she'd send demons to consume him, and he hadn't believed it; his rational mind had rejected it, but with a sense of horror he felt them here—he felt them now, breathing in his soul. They would take him over if he let them loose.

"No," he moaned, pressing his arms to his head and rocking back and forth. "No." He couldn't let that happen; he didn't want to hurt anyone; he'd do anything to not hurt anyone again.

He wanted peace. He wanted it so badly. For a little while, he'd had it. His princess, sweet mirage of happiness—he reached out for her, touched her, and she changed like the silver promise of water turned to desert. It made the demon inside him scream for blood.

He sat on the berth with his head in his hands. He could feel himself shaking. He concentrated on control, and when he felt he could stand up, he went to the door and locked himself inside.

Olympia struggled between reason and guilt. She knew she ought to feel guilty about Captain Fitzhugh; it was beneath contempt to manipulate him the way she was doing. But she would keep her promise—she *would* marry him . . . if he still wanted her after she told him the truth.

It seemed unlikely. Francis Fitzhugh was upright and conservative; he would never understand the sequence of events that had brought her to this. He would never understand how she could stoop to lies and subterfuge to accomplish a worthy goal, how she could put practicality before ethics, how she could make a commitment she didn't plan to keep . . . in short, how much she'd become like Sheridan.

Somewhere, so slowly that she hadn't noticed it herself, she'd lost her innocence. It was odd, but she felt infinitely older than her fiancé. She didn't want to hurt him, but he made himself such an easy victim that she found herself taking advantage before she could stop. He seemed so naive—everything was black or white, and he never caught the undercurrents that moved around him. He'd stood in the cabin with Sheridan, spoken with him, and never even noticed the play of emotion on that dark face as Francis gushed about their coming marriage.

Olympia had.

Her fingers twisted as she thought of the way Sheridan had looked when she'd announced the engagement. Stunned. Disbelieving. And then miserably hurt.

But she couldn't let herself fall for that. She'd expected him to be angry, to try to bully her out of her chosen course and back under his control. But Sheridan was a master manipulator, and much too smart for that. Instead of heavy-handed outrage, he instantly chose a far more effective method to reach her—playing on her deepest emotions—and the power of that alone was enough to arouse her distrust.

He wasn't hurt. He probably wasn't even all that surprised.

It's a game, Princess, he'd told her once. *There aren't any rules.*

No—there weren't any rules. And if Francis got hurt, it was because he was foolish enough to give his heart in blind trust. The same way Olympia had been, before she'd learned better the hard way.

It had been almost a week before Francis had agreed to take her to Rome to be married. He'd promised to ask for a matrimonial shore leave as soon as he completed this mission to Arabia. He was being brave and noble about it, but Olympia detected a slight increase in his demands to see her, and just a trace of stiffness in his manner if she said something he didn't quite approve of. She hadn't seen Sheridan since he'd left the state cabin so abruptly. He didn't come to meals, and never walked on deck. He was sulking, down in his own lair—no doubt expecting her to think he was devastated, waiting for her to come begging forgiveness and hot kisses.

But she would not go. No matter how much she wanted them.

When Sheridan closed his eyes, he would dream. So he didn't close them—except when he passed out cold on Fitzhugh's brandy.

Being awake wasn't much of an improvement. He thought of corpses in a Burmese mudbank, or of his father's vicious amusements, or of an old man the thugs had murdered while he stood by and watched. There seemed to be something splintered inside him, some barrier that had kept these things at a distance and let them rush in on him now.

He tried to drink himself senseless, but it didn't help. He dreamed, bad dreams, and every time he woke the images were there, more vivid than before. He kept seeing the broken remains of Midshipman Harland on a shattered gun deck, and hearing the soft ceaseless mutters of Mr. Wright, who'd been all night and another day dying. *Bring me some water, Mama. Mama, I'm so thirsty. Please, Mama, please—I won't cry.*

Sheridan wanted to cry. He wanted to kill. He seemed to have disintegrated into bewildering pieces of a man: someone he didn't know . . . and yet he did know.

Oh, yes . . . he knew.

This was himself, yes—this was the part of him that lived below the surface, the wolf that answered everything with slaughter. He embraced death. He was good at it. He survived.

He didn't dare leave the cabin. He made Mustafa lock it from the outside. He drank and stared and huddled in his borrowed berth in confusion and misery. He despised himself; he was lost; he couldn't put these pieces into a person anymore. He could not understand what was happening to him.

Sometimes he thought disjointedly about his life, bits and fragments of hopes and illusions. All he'd ever wanted was his music. It was comical, the way he'd clung to that for so long. He'd waited and waited for the moment, the day he could leave behind the existence he'd led and begin again. Then his father had died, and that had seemed like the time.

Only it turned out to be too late. Decades too late. He was a fool—and worse, an old fool—to have thought there was soul enough left in him to make music anyone would want to hear. There was music in him, yes, but it sounded of guns and smelled of death and powder smoke, and no one would want to listen, any more than they wanted to hear the truth of the ghastly scenes that made a man a hero by mistake.

Sometimes he dreamed of his princess, and thought that any normal man would cry.

But he could not cry.

Mustafa came and went, tending him as if he were a child. It all seemed like a dream. Once, someone knocked on the door and said the captain wished to see him. They left, and came again, with a louder demand, and then an order.

Sheridan looked at the door and looked away, uninterested. He touched the barrel of the pistol that lay on the pillow beside him. He slid his hand beneath the butt and caressed the trigger.

It was comforting. One fractional move, and no more nightmares. No more flashes of black fear and anger that made him terrified of himself. No more waking from restless half sleep to the smell of burning flesh that filled his brain and his nostrils, more real than the ship around him.

Far more real. Living and dying blended into one another; he was dead already, he'd been gone for years, what difference did it make?

But he was hanging on.

Why, he could not fathom. But he reckoned it to be his only real talent.

Twenty-one

Another week passed, and Olympia hadn't seen Sheridan for a fortnight. She walked the deck, watching the sailors or staring at the water. Pressure was growing inside her. She tried to keep her feelings under control of her mind. It was a game, and she did not dare lose. She would not break first, not this time.

Between the strength of her desire to rush to Sheridan's cabin and the frequency of her imagining that she would find him outside hers, contrite and begging to marry her, Olympia was becoming highly suspicious of her own motives. They began to seem much less pure than she'd originally thought. Instead of the high-minded goal of reaching Rome and Oriens under Captain Fitzhugh's protection, she feared she might have been equally interested in the mean hope of making Sheridan madly jealous. Perhaps even more interested.

Oriens and its problems seemed so far away, and the emptiness of days without Sheridan so piercing—she could not seem to keep the relative importance of them in proper proportion.

She stood with her hands on the polished rail, braced against the plunge of the ship, watching the bow wave arch outward, shatter with a cascade of white on green and then slide past her in a foaming roll. She preferred this forward spot to the sheltered captain's deck, a disagreement which was escalating into an actual argument with her doting fiancé. Francis became more possessive and restrictive daily.

She tried to imagine being married to him and felt a deep uneasiness. But she'd promised, and it would be his choice once they reached Rome and she confessed. If he still wanted her, she would have to do it.

"Excuse me, ma'am?" A young voice spoke beside her. "Miss Drake?"

Olympia turned. One of the midshipmen stood at her elbow, dressed in tight blue ducks with gold trim, his cheeks pink in the chilly breeze. She always marveled at how young they were to be so far from home—this boy was no more than thirteen at best. Olympia thought he ought to be home with his mother and family, going to school instead of sailing on a warship to battle slavers.

She smiled warmly, reading the name stitched on his collar. "Good morning, Mr. Stevenson."

"Ma'am," he said quickly, "I hope you don't think I'm impert'nent for asking—but—me and . . . and some of the others was wondering—is Sir Sheridan going to get better, ma'am?"

Olympia looked at him. "I'm sorry . . . I don't quite understand."

He locked his hands behind his back. "Well—we'd noticed, ma'am, that he hadn't come on deck no more since . . ." He bit his lip. "Well—a fortnight ago. And we heard he didn't take meals in the cabin with you an' the captain, and we was worrited, you see. After we saw the way he was an' all, ma'am."

Olympia frowned at him. He wet his lips.

"I know it's a secret, ma'am," he said in a rush. "You don't got to worrit that I'd say anything, nor Barker nor Mr. Jackson nor the gunner's mates neither, and we was the only ones that saw."

"Saw?"

"Well—" He shifted his feet. "One of his . . . fits . . . you know. When he thinks he's somewhere else, fighting some battle. He went after Barker, calling him Mr. Wright and all, and got real mad because we wouldn't call 'All hands.' " The boy raised wide eyes to Olympia. "I was frightened at first, ma'am, but Mr. Jackson made me understand what it was. And we—we just was hoping he would be getting better now. Mr. Jackson told me all about all the things he's done, and I wanted to say—well, ma'am—" He touched his tongue to his upper lip. "I don't guess he 'members me at all, but I'd be obliged if you could tell him I was very stupid to ask if he was crazy, and I'm sorry, and I hope he feels better, and I think he's the best, ma'am. Would you tell him that for me?"

Olympia looked silently at the towheaded boy. Her fingers tightened on the rail.

"He called me Harland, ma'am," the boy said after a pause. "Would you know who that is?"

"No," she said faintly. "I'm afraid I don't."

"Oh. Well—I thought maybe it was somebody who'd—you know—done something . . . grand."

She managed a smile. "I'm sure it is."

He ducked his head. "Will you tell him what I said, ma'am?"

"I'll tell him. Yes. I'll go and tell him now."

Mustafa sat against the bulkhead outside Sheridan's cabin. Olympia dismissed the sailor who'd led her belowdecks and glared at the huddled servant.

"Why didn't you tell me he was ill?" she demanded, reaching for the door.

He stood up, blocking her way, and looked at her with unfathomable eyes. "He will not see you, *Emiriyyiti.*"

"Yes," she said. "He will." It was the command of a princess. "Open the door."

Mustafa looked at her beneath his lashes, dark and speculative. His thin face seemed thinner, drawn with weariness, but Olympia did not cease her commanding stare. After a moment he shrugged and stepped aside. The door swung inward.

For an instant, she thought she must be in the wrong cabin. There was someone there, but it wasn't Sheridan. The man who lay on the berth was a stranger in a black beard and rumpled clothes. He didn't even look at her, but lay gazing blindly at the bottle propped on his raised knee until she closed the door and spoke his name.

It came out a questioning whisper. He did look toward her then—a gray stare that lasted five beats of her heart before he turned away. He put his fingertips over his eyes and sighed. His hand seemed to shake a little.

"Sheridan," she said. "My God—what's wrong?"

There was a silence. Then he said, "Nothing."

"You're ill." She stepped forward, lifting her hand to touch his forehead.

"No." He pushed her arm away. "I'm not ill. Leave me alone."

She bit her lip, stepping back. "I'm going to call the surgeon."

"*No.*" He sat up, a move that seemed swift and healthy enough. "Don't call anybody."

Olympia stood uncertainly. He sat, not looking at her, his gaze focused somewhere off at the floor in obvious avoidance. The sweet smell of brandy mingled with sea salt.

"Just go," he said. "I don't—I'm not—" He spread his hands on the edge of the berth. "Hell! Just go away. I'm not in the mood for tea and polite conversation."

"What's wrong?" she asked again.

He frowned angrily, still not meeting her eyes. He shook his head.

"You cannot expect me to believe that you're all right." She moved closer again, anticipating that he would pull away. But instead he pressed his fist against his mouth and drew a shuddering breath. He closed his eyes briefly, then reached for the brandy and drank a long swallow from the bottle.

As he lowered it, Olympia took it out of his hand and set it aside. She started to sit down next to him, but first had to pick up a pistol that lay on the berth. She stood, holding it gingerly out to Sheridan. "Expecting an attack?"

He stared at the weapon. After a moment, he lifted it from her hand. His fingers fitted around the handle and trigger with a natural move. He hefted it, and for one startled instant she had the notion that he actually wanted to fire—at what, she had no idea.

"I was cleaning it," he said tonelessly.

He held the gun in a loose grip, looking down the interior of the barrel as if it fascinated him. His voice sounded strange, but the ragged beard made it hard for her to interpret his expression.

"Why are you hiding down here?" she asked abruptly.

He shrugged.

"Is it—" She hesitated. "Is it because of Francis and me?"

He turned the gun over, smoothing his fingers down the bore. "Who the hell is Francis?" Then he looked up at her sideways. His eyes glittered. "You mean that bloody little bastard Fitzhugh?" He cocked the pistol and aimed it lazily at the brandy bottle. Olympia drew a breath as his finger tightened suddenly on the trigger.

The hammer fell with a harmless click.

"Bang," he said indifferently. "There's dear Francis with his brains all over the wall."

As soon as he said it, a queer look came into his face. He wet his lips and stared at the bulkhead. His breathing quickened.

"Oh, my God," he whispered. He groaned softly. "Oh, my God."

"Sheridan?"

He jerked his head, turning back to her as if she'd startled him. It seemed to take him a moment before he focused, and then he said aggressively, "Just keep that strutting little cock away from me. Or I'll kill him."

Olympia looked down at him in astonishment. She hugged herself. If this was another attempt to throw her off-balance, it was certainly succeeding. The beard made his face look pale and strained. Fierce tension marked his mouth. She wanted to touch his cheek, to smooth her fingers down the rough beard and hold him as she used to do, for comfort and warmth. But there was Julia. She had to remember that. Julia, and all his perfidy. "Why are you locking yourself up down here?" she demanded again.

"I have to," he said.

"Of course you don't. Sheridan, if it's because of me, if you wanted me to come to you, I—"

"No!" He rose suddenly. "No, I didn't want you to come! Go away, leave me alone." He grabbed her by the shoulders. The pistol dug into her arm as he shook her. "It's dangerous, don't you see? You don't know—you don't understand. I didn't want—" His voice broke. Suddenly he pulled her hard against him, his hold so tight it hurt. "What am I gonna do?" he whispered. "What'm I gonna do, what'm I gonna do?" He muttered a slurred litany into her hair. "I didn't want you to see me. She wouldn't turn, do you understand? I only wanted to live. I only wanted to live. Oh, God, I'm so sorry. I'm sorry, I'm sorry, I'm sorry."

He was trembling, crushing her against him cruelly. The cold barrel of the pistol lay against her ear. She had the feeling he hardly knew she was there, that he was only holding on, mumbling unconnected phrases over and over.

She didn't know what to do. Her suspicions of him evaporated in that desperate and painful embrace. This was real, this was no game—he was distraught and rambling incoherently, and she didn't know why or how to help. If only she were Julia. Julia could have handled this; Julia would have known what to do. Olympia felt frightened and confused and helpless.

"Sheridan." She stiffened against him and tried to sound firm. "You're hurting me."

He made a peculiar moaning sound, as if the litany of words had sunk under his breath.

"You're hurting me." She said it louder, pushing at him.

He let her go so suddenly that she stumbled backward. "Go away," he said.

Olympia gulped a needed breath and stood leaning against the door. "Not until you tell me what's wrong."

He would not look at her. He sat down on the berth and took a slug of brandy. "Nothing's wrong."

"Sheridan." She bit her lip. "I want to help." She felt her defenses crumbling, the fatal words rising. Because her discipline could no longer contain what her heart cried out—in spite of Julia, in spite of everything—she said in a whispered rush, "I love you."

His gray eyes lifted. He stared at her a moment, and then he began to laugh. It had a crazy, frantic sound, halfway between a chuckle and a sob. He lay back on the berth and put his arm across his eyes, holding the pistol loosely. "You don't love me. You don't know me. You don't know what I am. If you did, you wouldn't—" His voice caught on one of the peculiar chuckling sobs. He took a breath. "You wouldn't even be in here with me, take my word."

What would Julia say? She wouldn't be kind; she would be firm. She'd state the case in measured tones and expect reason to speak for itself.

"I think," Olympia said slowly, "that I know you quite well." She looked down at the deck and added in a carefully mild voice, "You can be a scoundrel; I know that. You stole from me and betrayed me and lied to me. You have no morals and no ideals; you think of yourself first and you're a coward sometimes on that account." She hesitated, chewing her lip. "What people call a coward, anyway. I don't know what cowardice is anymore. I don't know what heroism is." She looked up. "But I know one thing, and I learned it from you. I know what courage means. It means to pick up and go on, no matter what. It means having a heart of iron, like they say. You have that."

He stayed the way he was, his face hidden. She watched the rise and fall of his chest as the sounds of the ship filled the silence.

"A heart of oak, I think you mean," he said suddenly. Rationally. "This is the navy, my dear. We use iron for ballast."

He lifted his arm—and it was as if the baffling stranger had vanished. The same cynical, self-contained Sheridan she knew so well gave a twisted smile and added, "Sorry to disappoint you, but on top of being a scoundrel and thief and liar and coward, I can't claim that kind of courage, either." He sat up and shoved his hand through his hair. He shook his head. "You don't love me. You'd be a god-awful fool if you did. We had a fine time for a while, but you're doing the right thing. Believe me. Marry Fitzhugh. Go to Rome and start your revolution. I'm quite all right." He looked into her eyes, abrupt and intent. "Go on living, Princess. You've barely even started."

There was something . . . but Olympia could not fathom what lay behind that look. He sounded reasonable again. At least he sounded sane, even if what he said made her chest ache. "Are you certain you're all right?" she asked.

"Yes."

She considered him. "Then—will you come up to dinner tonight?"

His dark lashes fell. He shrugged. "If you wish."

"Will you come on deck and walk with me now?"

He looked down at the gun, toyed with it. After a moment, he said, "Let me get cleaned up."

"In an hour?"

"Yes." Still he looked down at the weapon. "In an hour."

"All right." Olympia felt a surge of relief. Perhaps she had done the right thing by simply talking to him as if he'd made sense all along. She opened the door. "I'll wait for you in the saloon."

He glanced up at her. Beneath the unshaven beard, she could see the familiar, beloved outlines of his face.

"In an hour," she repeated with schoolteacher sternness, and stepped out the door.

Just before she closed it, she heard him say quietly, "Goodbye, Princess."

Sheridan sent Mustafa on a long errand. Then with careful patience he re-primed the pistol and lay back on the berth. He rested the barrel against his temple.

It would not misfire this time.

He realized he'd been waiting for her to come. He knew now why he'd delayed so long. He'd wanted to see her one last time. He'd wanted . . .

What?

To make her understand why?

She would never understand. He didn't want her to. He never wanted it to touch her. Why had he ever touched her? He was poisoned. Contaminated. He was so angry, he hurt so much—but he had to lock that up. He couldn't tell her. She had to be protected. He loved her ignorance; he cherished her for it; silly, innocent princess, talking bravely of violence in her cause and having no notion of the reality.

Her revolution—it would be no different from any other war. Friends and enemies and humanity: they all died on their knees in the smoke and blood.

But how could he tell her that?

Fitzhugh would keep her from it, anyway, shield her dreams from the savage truth.

He thought about that, lying there with the cold metal comfort against his skin. And slowly, he became aware of the paradox.

He frowned faintly. A sense of irritation moved through him, as if it were an annoying delay in some critical journey.

He wanted to keep her from violence. But if he did this—here, now—he would bring it into her life with a vengeance.

There was no way they could keep the secret from her. Fitzhugh might try; he might lie about ways and means and try to soften the picture, but someone would tell her enough of the truth. And worse . . . Sheridan swore softly . . . worse, he'd stupidly promised he'd join her in an hour. What if she came back looking for him?

He spent a despairing moment imagining that. The gun slid slowly downward, cool steel on his cheek.

He could not do it to her. He could not take the risk that it would be she who discovered him.

He'd have to find another time and place.

He held up the gun and looked at it with dark longing. But he had this one last responsibility he could not evade.

He thought of other ways—less bloody, quieter—and slowly, reluctantly, discarded them all. He found that he was truly a coward right down to the bone, because he could not face the idea of leaving her with the smallest scar. He wanted too badly to think of her as whole and untouched by his shadow. And too . . . God forbid—what if she should conclude it was her fault? And she might.

She might think it was because she'd chosen Fitzhugh, and live all her life a martyr to misplaced guilt.

The irony of it almost made him laugh.

He was the guilty one. He was the one who ought to suffer. He could not think of any reason why he'd survived all that he had, unless it was to be punished.

He laid the gun down. Then, because he could not help himself, he reached for the nearest vulnerable object—a well-thumbed copy of *Steele's Original and Correct List of the Royal Navy*—and began methodically to tear the pages out and shred them into tiny white pieces. When he came to the end, he held the cover between his shaking fists and ripped it apart.

Olympia waited in the state saloon, frowning out at the ship's wake. The steward came in with a tin of sugared biscuits for tea and offered one to her. She took it absently, nibbled a bite and then held it while she puzzled on the things Sheridan had said. She barely heard the sound of the door closing behind the steward, and when Francis spoke, she jumped.

"Ollie, my dear." He smiled when she turned, doffing his hat, his cheeks apple-red from the wind. "You're early for tea. I hope you've taken my advice and been here all morning instead of displaying yourself on the foredeck."

She held back a retort. Instead she merely said, "Good afternoon, Francis," and ate the rest of the sugar biscuit.

She knew it would annoy him. He had decided that he preferred her newly slender waistline and had begun a campaign of "advice" on what she should eat. He frowned slightly as she finished the biscuit, but only pursed his lips and turned to the table. Olympia eyed his stout, straight profile and had the sudden desire to puff up to the size of an elephant just to spite him.

"How have you been occupied this morning?" he asked.

She hesitated. "I've been to see my brother."

Francis glanced over at her. "I see," he said. "I hope you had a pleasant visit. Has he decided to forgive you?"

"I don't know what you mean," she said stiffly.

He looked down, his lower lip moody. "Why, for accepting my offer, of course. It's clearly caused a rift between you. You haven't seen him for weeks." He frowned again, rattling silver among the tea things. "I've tried to speak with him myself, but he's refused to see me either. I must say, I think it's quite churlish, the way he's acting. He did give his permission, after all."

She sat down, staring at her hands. "I believe—he has much on his mind."

"Well, he won't find a better family than the Fitzhughs, if that's what concerns him." Francis's voice held a trace of belligerence. "Our lineage is spotless."

Unlike the bastard Drakes, was the unspoken end to that sentence. Olympia felt a rise of resentment on Sheridan's behalf. She considered inquiring where the *Fitz* in Fitzhugh had come from, if the family was so perfectly legitimate, but decided—once again—to avoid a confrontation. Instead she said, "Sheridan is going to walk with me this afternoon."

"Ah." Francis looked up, all his pouting dissolved into childlike satisfaction. "He has forgiven you, then!"

"Well—I suppose so."

"Perhaps I'll join you."

She shifted uneasily, thinking of the odd things Sheridan had done and said. Somehow it seemed very important to hide that from Francis. "I think—just now—it might be best if you didn't."

The animation faded from Francis's ruddy features, replaced by the faint scowl. "I see." His voice rose a little. "I'd like to know just what the dickens it is that concerns him about my suitability. I expect you'll ask, will you?"

It was more a demand than a request. "I'm sure he thinks you're quite suitable," Olympia said, trying to soothe. "It isn't that."

"Well, I can't think what else makes him behave like a yahoo," he said peevishly. His face was growing redder. "I asked him to come up and speak to me. I asked him twice. I passed a direct order for him to present himself, and he ignored it! I'll tell you, if anyone else on this ship were to disobey me like that, they'd have three hundred stripes before they could say Jack Tar!" His fist clenched. "Do you know what it does to discipline, his treating me so? They laugh at me! I've already got four men in irons, awaiting—" He broke off, muttering. "And you insist upon walking the foredeck, too. I don't know what I'm expected to do—have them flogged in front of you?" He sighed and poured a cup of tea. "It's enough to make a man shoot himself."

Olympia looked down at her lap. "I'm sure we never meant—" she began, and then suddenly raised her eyes.

Make a man shoot himself.

She had a vision of Sheridan, staring down the barrel of a pistol as if he were bewitched. She heard his quiet voice as it said goodbye.

She put her hand over her mouth. "My God!" she whispered. "Oh, God."

Then she was at the door, grabbing the frame against a sway of the ship and pushing off, lifting her skirts to climb down the steep ladder, while Francis's exclamation drifted after her. She hurled herself down another ladder, fell against a startled seaman at the bottom and pushed past a marine into the passage.

Mustafa was not sitting outside the cabin. She grabbed the knob and threw herself against the locked door. "*Sheridan!*" She shook it frantically, her eyes blurred with terror, her heart in her throat. "*Sheridan!* Oh, God, open the door—please, God, please—*open the door!*"

The brass knob turned under her palm. Olympia shoved the door wide, stumbling forward.

Sheridan stood aside, bare to the waist, wiping the last of his shaving lather away with a towel.

Olympia took a breath. Relief and emotion spun around her. She could hardly see him for the dizzy blackness that rose before her eyes.

He caught her arm. "It's all right," he said softly. "Sit down."

She fell against him instead, holding tight. "Sheridan." Her voice was hoarse and broken. "Oh, God, you frightened me!"

He stroked her hair. "It's all right," he repeated. "Everything's all right, Princess."

She felt the warm, solid, living shape of him, so familiar, so loved, and pressed her face to his chest. She was crying. He caressed her hair with gentle fingers. When he took his hand away, she clutched him harder, but he was only closing the door against the fascinated glances from a small audience of sailors outside.

She pushed away from him suddenly and looked around the tiny cabin. "Where is it?"

He leaned against the washstand and regarded her. Shaved, he looked like Sheridan again—but so different, so dark and distant.

"Wha-wha-where *is* it?" The stuttering of a sob broke her demand. "Do you think I'm going to let you keep it?"

He only looked at her. He was so beautiful and somber, her fallen angel: his winter eyes, his midnight hair, the shape of his face and his mouth and his body. She turned away and began to search the berth with shaking hands.

She found it under a pile of shredded paper and cardboard. She didn't even want to touch it, but she lifted the gun carefully and held it against her breast in both hands, facing him, ready to fight if he tried to take it from her.

He didn't. "Princess," he said quietly, "if I decide to kill myself, there are a thousand ways to do it on this ship."

She stared at his impassive face, trying to make herself believe he had said that. Then she closed her eyes, feeling the tears well from beneath her lids. "What is it?" she whispered. "Is it me? Have I done this to you? I'll leave you alone, or come back to you; whatever you want; what can I do? If only—"

If only I were Julia, and not fat and stupid and myself. I love you so much, and I don't know what to do.

"It's not your fault," he said.

She licked the salty liquid from her lips. "What's wrong, then?" Her voice was pleading. "Sheridan—what could be so wrong?"

A look came into his eyes, an expression of such silent

pain that her fingers softened their grip on the gun and she took a step toward him.

He turned away. "It's not your fault," he repeated harshly. "It's nothing to do with you, do you understand?"

She stood there, helpless. "I can't believe this. I don't believe this is happening."

He leaned against the bulkhead, his eyes closed wearily, his hand spread over them like a shade against hot sun.

Olympia's lip trembled. "Promise me," she said, "that you won't do this. That you'll never, ever hurt yourself. Promise me."

He made no answer. She gazed at him in growing horror.

"*Sheridan,*" she cried when she could not stand it any longer.

"All right, for God's sake!" He turned toward her sharply. "All right. I promise."

He rubbed the towel across his face roughly and threw it down, reaching for the shirt that hung on a hook beside the door. He pulled the linen over his head. As if she were no longer there, he turned away to the washbasin, tucked in the shirt and began to tie his neckcloth.

Olympia watched him in the mirror. She wanted to feel relieved. She wanted to believe that promise with all her heart.

But Sheridan was a liar.

He'd probably never kept a promise in his life.

Twenty-two

Hot wind blew off the coast from Aden, faintly perfumed with incense. If Olympia closed her eyes, she could imagine shaded gardens and fountains in the desert, but when she opened them, she still stood on the familiar deck of *Terrier* between Francis and Sheridan, watching the sun rise over the glassy water and silhouette the hundreds of small boats that moved serenely out from the trading town.

It had taken four months to reach Arabia around the Cape of Good Hope, more than three of them spent wrestling strong currents and contrary winds up the east coast of Africa. Now Francis was in a fret because he'd missed his rendezvous with the other British warships and *Terrier* lay alone at anchor off Aden, becalmed in the growing heat of day.

Olympia glanced at the men beside her. A trickle of perspiration already made a faint glistening trail down Sheridan's temple and jaw, and Francis—lobster-red, the edges of his hair plastered to his skin in coppery tendrils—was dripping so that he looked as if he'd had a bucket of water splashed against his face.

Poor, stupid Francis—he'd never admit it, but he'd probably be secretly relieved if someone *would* splash him, mired as he was in his officer's dignity. Olympia looked enviously at the sailors who were scrubbing the decks white with seawater and holystones and getting a cooling bath in the process. In the heat, with the ship at anchor, every one of the two hundred crewmen was allowed on deck, even those off watch. Her own gown felt hot and damp at the base of her throat, though the sun was hardly above the horizon.

Sheridan said something sharply in Arabic to the pilot who'd supervised the towing of the ship to anchor amid the calm water. The man lifted his arm and began talking rapidly. His white burnoose fluttered as he indicated the clustering boats with an expansive wave. Olympia could see the baskets of fruits and hear the squawks of trussed roosters as the boats and their brightly colored occupants approached.

Sheridan moved behind her. While she was leaning over the rail, imagining the taste of fresh fruit after weeks since their last landfall at Mozambique, he said softly to Francis, "Have a care, Fitzhugh. Fire a warning shot, and tell 'em to come alongside one at a time."

Olympia looked over her shoulder. She saw Francis stiffen instantly at this advice—the first she'd known Sheridan to give since they'd come aboard. From that strange day she'd found him with the gun in his cabin, he'd acted quite his normal self, attended every meal, walked with her on deck, made his old dry jokes . . . but there was a wall a thousand feet thick around him. She looked into his eyes and saw no one there.

Francis had developed a profound case of injured pride, certain that Sheridan didn't approve of him, but no matter how her fiancé baited, he could not draw Sheridan into the slightest statement of disparagement. Sheridan was eerily agreeable to everything—"patronizing," Francis claimed, but Olympia doubted it.

Sheridan's compliance haunted her. There was something uncanny in it. He'd never been a tractable automaton; she knew him far better than that. But in three months there had not been a crack in his facade. She requested, and he accommodated, whether it was a game of cards or a walk on deck or a cup of tea, until she could hardly bear to be near him for the unnatural pleasantry of it.

This soft warning was the first real statement she'd heard

him make for the whole of the voyage. She turned, looking up at his face.

He was squinting at the crowd of light trading craft, his expression unchanged while Francis frowned.

"Why the devil bother with that?" Francis wiped his forehead with a limp handkerchief. "You aren't afraid of this trash?" He paused, and then added with stiff formality, "Sir."

Olympia glanced at the Arab pilot, who stood impassively a few feet away. She looked at Sheridan and sensed a new alertness in him. It was nothing tangible, but the wall was gone. He was *there*. And he thought there was danger in this ragged trading fleet. "Francis," she said, "perhaps you should consider—"

"Pardon me, my dear," Francis interrupted. "You need not take it upon yourself to advise me as to how to conduct my duties."

She shut her mouth. The first of the trading dhows came alongside with a thump. Two robed merchants began shrilly touting their wares in a broken mixture of English and Portuguese.

They looked innocent enough. And *Terrier* was an eighty-gun warship, after all.

Another boat slid alongside. The sound of hawking doubled. Within a few moments a swarm of the fragile-looking dhows had pulled up under the gunwales, and the British crew was lined along the rail, shouting and haggling. Mustafa was among them, tugging at a sailor's sleeve and pointing down into one of the boats. Ropes went over the side, and a basket of dates came up for inspection.

Sheridan's hand closed on Olympia's elbow. She looked up and felt him exert a steady pressure, pulling her away from the rail. Her heart started to beat faster.

She let him guide her. Francis glanced at them, and Olympia said quickly, "It's so hot. I think I'll go below."

Her fiancé wiped his face and nodded absently. "I'll join you when we've cleared this nuisance away."

As they moved toward the stairs, she saw that the Arab dhows had crowded around the other side of the ship, too. They seemed perfectly peaceful, interested only in selling, but the purposeful grip on her arm sent a message. The motley fleet, increasing in size by the minute, appeared to press in on the ship with ominous fervor, filling the air with shrieks of excitement.

She and Sheridan had reached the companionway ladder when the first gaudily robed trader came over the side. The swift slide of color made Olympia pull back, startled, but the Arab only stood shouting and waving his arms at the purser, alternately pointing to a wooden cask that had been hauled on deck and lifting his eyes as if beseeching heaven to reason with this foreigner.

The pressure on her arm grew tighter. Sheridan pushed her toward the ladder. With her heart pounding in her ears, she went down just ahead of him. On the empty, sweltering gun deck, he strode to the nearest cannon and reached toward the weapons stored in brackets overhead. A sword slid from its brass rack with a metallic hiss. He took a pistol, and then another, while the noise on deck increased steadily. With expert efficiency, he loaded them both, shoving a ramrod down the barrel and checking the fire-lock before he held one out to her. "Stay with me," he said.

She stared into his eyes and saw the old Sheridan there, the man who'd saved her life more than once. She nodded, asking no questions.

He turned, gesturing her to go ahead of him into the cramped, dead-end passage behind the ladder. He took up a station just beneath the open rungs, his hand resting on the sword, his head tilted back slightly, watching above.

The sounds from the deck were merry, full of eager, incoherent argument and the occasional shout of laughter. Olympia leaned against the bulkhead, perspiration trickling down her neck and into her bodice. The weight of the gun in her hand seemed unreal. It made her think of the scene in Sheridan's cabin. She gazed at his back, wondering what was in his mind.

What had he seen out there? She could feel his tension, the way she'd felt it that day—tension that seemed to have no rational source. Long minutes passed, and she began to wonder if it had a rational source this time. There was not the least sound of threat from above, only the loud babble of men trying to make themselves understood in an alien tongue. She pushed back her sagging hair, trying not to let her fingers slip on the handle of the loaded gun.

"I'm going crazy," Sheridan muttered suddenly.

Olympia straightened, watching him.

"I'm going mad." His voice sounded anxious. "There's nothing wrong. Why did I think there was something wrong?"

She touched his shoulder tentatively. He started, gripping the sword, and turned as if he'd forgotten she was there.

"Do you think it's safe?" she asked.

"Jesus." He closed his eyes and slumped against the bulkhead. He bit his lip. The tension and alertness had vanished. He looked vulnerable, uncertain. "What's wrong with me?"

She laid her hand on his arm. "Tell me why we're here."

He lowered his head and shook it with a defeated move. "I'm sorry. I—sometimes I think . . . I could have sworn . . ." He looked at her, almost childlike in his earnestness. "It's a bad position, can you see that? We aren't armed; we can't retreat, can't bring the guns to bear—it's a bad position. It's an ambush." His voice rose. "Can you see that? I have to know. I have to be ready. I'm responsible, do you understand?"

She wet her lips. "Sheridan—"

"I know," he said bleakly. "I know. I'm not in command here." He covered his eyes and shook his head. "God, I can't explain it . . . sometimes it seems like I am." His hand fell. He tilted his head back, resting it against the wall. "Sometimes it seems like I'm just . . . losing . . . my mind."

She slid her fingers into his and gripped hard, saying nothing. The din of trading went on above them, as if no one up there could come to an agreement over a miserable basket of melons. He stood there in the dim light from the companionway, his face sweaty, his eyes still closed, a figure of shadow and glistening heat.

A shriek of laughter drifted down to them. Sheridan opened his eyes, stiffening. The steady noise seemed to waver, and suddenly there was a shout that was not laughter at all. Feet began to pound on the deck above; men's voices rose; Olympia heard a pop and a cry, and then the noise erupted into a roar.

Sheridan jerked free, turning. Just as he faced the ladder, the bare feet of a sailor appeared at the top. The man made it down three rungs and then fell free to hit the gun deck with a terrible thud. Around Sheridan's back, Olympia could only see an outstretched leg—but the sailor did not rise, or cry out, or stir.

Sheridan seemed to ignore the fallen man; he was looking up. She sucked in her breath as she saw the bright swing of a trader's robes begin the descent, and then Sheridan was crowding her back into the cramped passage, lifting the sword. The trader came down facing them—his sandaled feet, a drape of green-and-red robe, a flash of light on the dagger in his hand as he gripped the ladder—and Sheridan moved.

His sword winked, thrusting upward. It seemed to Olympia to merely disappear into the man's voluminous robes and reappear instantly, carrying a thin sheath of red silk with it. But the red was blood, and the trader was dead, with nothing but a strange choking sound and another heavy fall onto the deck in front of them.

Olympia could see the Arab's face. There was blood in a scarlet dribble at the corner of his mouth. The screams of combat rose to a deafening echo.

Two sailors came then, in a half scramble, half jump, and leapt for swords. There was a commotion of movement on the ladder far down at the other end of the gun deck. Armed, the seamen ran to engage the invading Arabs. Another robed figure started to come down in front of Sheridan. The sword poised, drove upward, and the pirate screeched. He scrabbled and fell sideways, clutching his torso. Sheridan glanced up and then stepped out from behind the ladder. With a deliberate move, he thrust his sword through the writhing man's heart, picked up the pirate's dagger and stepped back into the passage in front of her.

She could not see Sheridan's face, but she could see the blood pumping through the veins on his hand where he gripped the sword.

At the far end, the gaudy robes were pouring down, surrounding the two sailors. They fought frantically, but a tide of color seemed to flow over them. Sheridan's back grew taut; he lifted the pistol and aimed it through the ladder rungs. Olympia could see the dark, wild faces of the Arabs rushing upon them. In a strange distortion of time she seemed able to note every detail: she could see the jewels on their scimitar hilts, the gold thread shot through one's sash, the brown stains on their teeth.

Sheridan fired.

The explosion hit her ears, echoed amid the shouts, and two pirates were down. Suddenly Sheridan was no longer in front of her; he was beyond the ladder, the handguard of his sword glistening with the blood of a man he'd taken upward under the ribs. The others closed, but the reach of Sheridan's sword far exceeded their curved scimitars, and he cut down one, and then another, with an economy of motion like a dancer's.

Suddenly a wash of white obscured the scene, and Olympia looked up to see another enemy descending their own ladder. He howled and leapt free of the last rungs, his weapon lifted to plunge at Sheridan's back.

Before any logical thought had crossed her mind, Olympia raised her pistol and pulled the trigger.

The white robe crumpled soundlessly amid the din. The pale cloth settled and began to turn crimson.

She put her hand over her mouth. She could feel herself shaking. Sheridan slashed at the last man standing, cut his forearm, feinted aside and then drove for his heart. Olympia watched the sword point go in—halfway to the hilt—while the pirate grabbed the blade with his hand as if he could stop it as he fell.

Sheridan knelt swiftly by the man Olympia had shot. For an instant he slanted a look back at her, and in that moment she knew for certain she had killed a man. Sheridan's face was frightening: fixed in calm, and yet alight with a cold flame of excitement. His mouth curved, almost a smile. It was as if the devil stared out of his eyes, not a human being at all. He turned back as though she didn't exist and stepped over the body.

With a casual move he bent over another robed figure that lay curled and groaning on the deck. Sheridan jerked back the pirate's head and cut his throat.

She watched him rove among the bodies like an avenging angel making sure of retribution. Olympia realized the noise from above had ceased sometime when she hadn't noticed. There were a few shouts—not in English—and she began to shake worse than ever.

Sheridan stood at the foot of the ladder, looking up. His chest rose and fell, and his face was still a devil's face—his eyes light gray and inhuman. He waited. The shoulder of his coat gaped, showing a long slash of bloody white shirt, but he gripped the sword as if his hand were welded to it.

Olympia felt as dizzy as if she'd been wounded herself. Her ears hummed. She saw Sheridan raise the sword and yell at someone above, but could make no sense of the words. She had to concentrate on each breath to keep herself from fainting.

It seemed that a long time passed with just the rushing sound in her ears and a haze with Sheridan at the vague focus of it in her vision. The next thing that came clear was Sheridan in the passage with her, taking the pistol from her cramped fingers. There was blood all over his hand; it smeared on her skin; she could smell it. She shrank back, looking up at him in horror.

He met her eyes. The weird calm suddenly vanished, and confusion seemed to overtake him. "What is it?" he asked.

"Don't!" she cried. "I don't want you to touch me."

As soon as she said it, she wanted it back. It was wrong; it was unfair—and she saw by his face that the words were deadly.

He turned white. His hand dropped.

"You're all bloody," she said, in weak and desperate explanation. "Please—I'm afraid!"

A scowl made his face into a mask. His teeth showed in a terrifying grimace. "Afraid of *me?*" he shouted. "I'm protecting you! I killed 'em for you; I slaughtered those bastards! What do you think I did that for?" He grabbed her arm and hauled her out of the passage. "Look at me, damn you!" His shout echoed all over the gun deck. "Christ, you can't even look at me—what's the matter?"

Olympia stood trapped in his crushing grip, aware that they were surrounded by a gathering audience of silent Arabs, and that Sheridan's voice had gone to pleading. He didn't even seem to see the pirates, but stood there with his back to them, shaking her.

"What—do—you—want?" he cried in time to his jolting clench. "I had to do it. That wasn't me, do you understand? *That wasn't me!*"

In her numbed haze, she saw that the *teskeri hilaal* had appeared around his neck. Now it was flashing gold, swinging free against his chest. "It wasn't me," he moaned, and then suddenly let go of her and dropped to his knees. He took an awful, sobbing breath, trying to wipe the blood onto his breeches with furious moves. One of the Arabs came forward, speaking quietly as he reached to take Sheridan's arm.

Sheridan lashed out instantly, up and swinging the gun. It was empty, but he aimed a murderous blow at the pirate's head. The man ducked, and suddenly the circle had closed, arms clutching Sheridan from all sides as he fought bare-handed. Olympia was past screaming, expecting at any second to see him cut down and slashed to death by the jeweled daggers.

But the Arabs had not drawn their weapons. By sheer number, they fought Sheridan to a standstill and held him. When he stopped struggling, the multiple grip on him relaxed to a surprising gentleness. He closed his eyes and threw back his head, panting.

"You are the princess," said the man who'd reached for Sheridan first.

Olympia turned toward him with a start, astonished to

hear him speak English. She wet her lips, making no response.

"This ship is mine," he said. He grinned, displaying gold-capped teeth. His dark eyes were feminine soft beneath kohl-black lashes, but his face was old with sun lines. He nodded toward Sheridan. "He has announced that he takes you as a gift to the Sultan Mahmoud. Is this true?"

She stared at him, at a loss to know what was the safest answer. She didn't dare look toward Sheridan.

The pirate leader waited patiently. At length he said, "An English ship. An Englishman. I first say no, it is not true. But he wears this *teskeri*. He speaks the tongue of Allah like a brother. He fights as a whirlwind and then turns his back on the enemy to dispute with a woman. It is a puzzle. I dislike a puzzle." He reached out and lifted her chin with one long finger. "I like an answer."

She turned her face away.

Sheridan spoke suddenly, something in Arabic. It caught the pirate's attention. There was a rapid exchange, and Sheridan tried to shake off the hands that held him.

The pirate leader laughed. "Let us speak in your tongue, my friend. Our beloved sister should hear that you wish to sell her into the Sultan's service. My experience is that English ladies do not consider it such an honor."

"What does a female's preference matter?" Sheridan snapped. "Take us there, and you'll have the Sultan's reward."

"Perhaps." The Arab turned his head and spat. "What good does the Sultan's reward do to me? The great Mahmoud holds little sway here—the Wahhabis fight him. We take this ship in *jihad*, to kill the infidels and purify our land and water—not for the paltry honors of a Turk."

"Kill these English, and others will come to level the town and hunt you with their warships until there's no one left."

The pirate jerked his chin upward. "The English are less than grains of sand."

"Aye, and the number of their guns is greater," Sheridan said grimly. "They have no honor. They'll stand off in their ships beyond reach of your little boats and rain fire on you until ten of your women and children have died for every one of these sailors you kill. And then they'll come ashore and kill the rest. Aden will not exist. It will burn to the ground. I know this." He set his jaw. "I've done it."

For a long moment, the pirate leader regarded Sheridan. Then his dark gaze slid over the bodies sprawled on the gun deck. There were seven that Sheridan had killed, not counting the one Olympia had shot. A slow grin grew on the pirate's face. "Join us instead," he invited. "You are a good fighter. We will give you enemies to the ends of the earth and all the blood you wish to drink."

Sheridan's mouth grew queer and tight. "I don't want that."

The Arab chuckled. "Allah has truly touched your head, O killer of women and children. I will call you Il-Magnuún—The Crazy One—who slays like ten devils and then shows us his back merely to plead with a woman as if this were his hareem." He waved toward Olympia with a negligent, graceful flick of his bejeweled hand and looked aslant at Sheridan. "Why did you do that?"

Sheridan stared at him coldly, not answering.

"Why did you turn your back?" he persisted. "Are we so little and weak to you, warrior? Can you kill us all with one sweep of your sword?"

"No."

"You thought we loved you so much, then. You were unafraid. We are such women, you expected no revenge for the deaths you have dealt us."

"No!"

"Why, then?" The pirate tilted his head speculatively. "I would know what makes a man so brave."

Sheridan wet his lips. "It doesn't sound brave," he said, as if he were talking of someone else. "It sounds stupid." He moved uneasily in his captor's hands. "I don't know why I did it."

The pirate looked at Olympia. "He is mad, is he not?"

The question seemed utterly serious. She sensed an underlying point, some issue that the pirate leader was turning over in his mind. With the dark, soft eyes holding hers, she made a headlong decision to tell him the truth. "He has bad dreams. Sometimes he talks strangely," she said, "and seems to think he's somewhere else."

Sheridan glared at her.

The pirate nodded, as if it confirmed his own opinion. He glanced around at the other men and spoke in Arabic. A debate broke out. Sheridan said nothing, but she saw his body grow stiff as he listened. Suddenly he jerked, freeing himself on one side, and flung himself toward a blue-robed pirate a few feet away.

"No!" he shouted. He seemed to disappear under a tangle of robes and then broke away, sending one man sprawling with a vicious kick. Somehow he'd gotten a dagger, and before they could catch him he had his blue-robed quarry backed up against the mast, the knife tip pressed beneath the pirate's ear. "You sell her and I'll butcher you." Sheridan's face was a calm devil-mask again. "I'll cut you apart and feed you to the jackals, and all your friends with you; don't touch her, do you hear me?" The pirate's head jerked as the dagger pressed harder, drawing a bright trickle of blood. "Do you hear me, you son of a bitch?"

The man's lips were drawn back in a tight grimace. He might not have understood the English words, but the intent was clear enough. Anyone could see that Sheridan was fully capable of driving the knife into the man's neck at any instant, right in front of all his comrades.

The leader called out a question in an amused voice. The trapped pirate answered, short and gruff. Sheridan flung him aside and faced the others with the dagger at the ready. "Who else?" he snarled.

"Be calm," the Arab leader said. "Leave the sound of battle and the groans of the dying and let your enemies breathe, O father of assassins."

Sheridan's fingers squeezed restlessly on the knife hilt. He lowered it a fraction, but he did not move. He stood in front of Olympia as if he could single-handedly protect her from the horde of armed men. The pirate looked around at the company and spoke an inquiry in Arabic. The others murmured assent.

He glanced aside at Olympia. "We are agreed—we will not kill these English sailors or burn the ship—not because we are *afraid* of their revenge, but because we honor Allah, who speaks in this mad Englishman's voice. Nor will we sell you away from him, since all have just witnessed here that it is not the will of God that we do so."

Thank you, she thought. *Thank you, thank you, God—whatever name you go by here.*

Sheridan still stood taut, the knife in his hand. He showed no sign of recognizing the truce that had been called, so Olympia summoned her courage and said steadily, "I think that is very wise."

The pirate gave his quick, gold-capped grin. "Little dove, do you know who you meet here?" He tapped his chest. "Salaa'ideen, who is called the Scorpion of the Sea, and I have not heard you wailing yet."

"I have not seen where it would help," she said honestly.

He gave a bark of laughter, though she'd hardly meant it as a joke. When he spoke to his men, she had the feeling he was relaying the comment, for they all looked at her and nodded, and several of them grinned like wolves. Salaa'ideen gestured toward Sheridan. "You have traveled far with him?"

"Very far."

"He is your protector. So he said."

She bit her lip. "Yes."

"Yet he fears you."

Olympia looked at the pirate in confusion. "Fears me? I'm sure that's not the case."

"He does." Salaa'ideen said it matter-of-factly. "A woman. And he such a fine killer. But the ways of Allah are inscrutable, blessed be His Name." The pirate leader shook his head and went on talking to her, turning from Sheridan as if he weren't there. "If it is so willed that we give up our victory, we obey, but there are still the affairs of men to attend to. Now I ask you, English princess—you have seen that we honor the instructions of God through your protector—tell me, how can these English sailors be prevented from turning on us when we release them?''

She automatically looked toward Sheridan. ''I'm sure he could tell you that better than I.''

''When he speaks, we will listen, of course. But I am no magician who presumes to put questions to Heaven.'' Salaa'ideen smiled slightly. ''Then I could not dispute the answers.''

Olympia glanced uncertainly toward Sheridan, expecting him to take over the discussion. He didn't. He just stuck the dagger in his belt and looked back at her, his expression completely unreadable.

It seemed she had no choice but to provide an answer. The whole scene became more and more like a bizarre dream, to be consulted by pirates on the most prudent move for them to make in a delicate situation. She felt, absurdly, like laughing. But Salaa'ideen was waiting, his hand resting on the golden handle of his scimitar, and the rest stood around her like a ring of sun-browned lions.

She tried to think of it as a political problem, separating wishes from reality.

''Have many men been killed?'' she asked tentatively.

Salaa'ideen waved his hand. One of the robed figures swept up the ladder, spoke rapidly to someone on deck and returned to report to his leader.

''Thirty-five infidels,'' Salaa'ideen informed her. ''Nine of the faithful—eight of them called to Paradise by the wrath of Il-Magnuún,'' he added with a touch of pride.

She took a deep breath. ''And the captain?''

''He is alive. Injured. But not badly, I think.''

Olympia closed her eyes and let out the air slowly. Then she looked up at Salaa'ideen. It felt treasonous, what she was about to suggest, but she could think of no other way to avoid more killing. Certainly, if the pirates simply released the ship, Francis would exact revenge, and she wouldn't put it past him to bombard the innocent residents of the town as Sheridan had predicted.

''Does anyone else know that you speak English?'' she asked.

Salaa'ideen considered. "No. I think not."

"We were supposed to meet other British warships here. Have they come and gone?"

His face darkened. "Yes. It is unfortunate I had business in another place then. They demanded water, but we have none to spare. Ships must go to Mocha for water." He waved his hand. "The sultan here is a simpleminded fool; he might have brought water from Mocha and made a good profit, but instead he becomes like a timid gazelle when the English threaten, and he gives them all we have. Ha! I shall have to make myself sultan, all praise to God, but it is a confounded nuisance."

Olympia bit her lip, feeling a half-hysterical giggle well up at this pirate with his jeweled scimitar and exotic robes dismissing the desk job as a confounded nuisance.

"When his body is skinned and hanging at the gates, we will have no more bowing to infidels," Salaa'ideen added casually, which brought Olympia out of wondering where he'd learned his English and back to the reality of his character in an instant. "He has a wizard who protects him, but I have no fear of the meager demons that one can summon. And now I have the sign—Il-Magnuún has come to me. That is proof enough. I have only to send word of it and the sultan flees me like a sheep." He looked at Olympia. "But we must pacify these English, or they will bombard the city and the people will lose their proper respect for me."

She stared at him, and finally let the dreamlike quality of everything submerge the protests of reason. She did not argue with this preposterous mixture of superstition and Machiavellian politics, but only said, "You'll have to convince Captain Fitzhugh it was all a mistake, then."

Salaa'ideen nodded. "Tell me what I must do."

"Well—" She chewed her lip. "I think if you are very humble, and say that you were warned by the other ships that a French warship might come in disguise to take the port . . . say that you were only trying to defend yourselves . . ."

"And give him gifts," Salaa'ideen suggested. "We will give them the freedom of the city and have the officers to the palace as guests. We will abase ourselves. We are sorry. We meant to drive off the French. The English are welcome; blessed is the hour of their coming.'' He shook his head. ''It is a pity they would not like to own slaves—I have a very good lot from a Dutch brig out of Zanzibar, which I would be willing to sacrifice in this cause.''

''Do not offer them slaves,'' Olympia said.

''No. I have an understanding of the English. They do not care for slaves.'' He gave her his sly smile. ''The Sultan Mahmoud, who fancies himself ruler of all the earth—he is a different matter. He will be pleased with you, my fresh white dove.''

Twenty-three

Olympia sold for fifteen thousand gold piasters.

She knew, because Sheridan told her. He himself had cost a Turkish pasha twice that, Salaa'ideen being not only a pirate but a shrewd businessman who made sure the merchandise was sold in the direction it would be most appreciated. He bypassed the poor and rebellious Wahhabi Arabs in disgust and conveyed Olympia and Sheridan by a fleet of dhows to Jidda, where they were bought by a female slave trader who sent them by merchant caravan to a Persian at Basra who planned to turn a profit by persuading a lieutenant of the caliph to take them to Baghdad, where word of the prize had already begun to spread to the Great Sultan's minions.

It was a strange and wondrous progression, luxurious by one turn and grueling to the point of heartbreak by another. Olympia tried to fathom the idea that she was being bought and sold like a prize mare, but it was not at all what she would have expected. Lost in a world so different it seemed utterly implausible, surrounded by an unknown language, by dazzling brightness in the robes and the sea and the flaming desert, she found it hard to believe anything was real at all.

It was hard, too, to find any degradation in the manner in which they were treated. For merchandise, they received royal consideration, lodged in rich houses in rooms that overlooked gardens, transported on swift white Syrian dromedaries, guarded by armed and mounted Bedouin warriors, protected by bribes from the bandit-tribesmen who ruled the desert routes.

But all the guards in the world could not protect them from the desert itself. In the day it was hot, hot—searing hot inside the caparisoned tents, and frigid at night when they traveled. She was thirsty all the time, though even the water she drank smelled of camels. Food was rice with rancid butter and fried camel meat coated in grease, cooked by Abyssinian servant girls with exceedingly dirty fingers.

Amid the dust and rock, her tent was a colorful green blossom with a gilt crescent at the peak. When they traveled, she rode closed in a litter with scarlet and brass trappings, slung between two dromedaries. It was airless and cramped and swayed like *Terrier* in a heavy sea.

She complained of it to Sheridan when they brought him to her tent, which had been pitched just as the morning heat was rising on the third day of caravan. They always kept him near her, his guards escorting him reverently to the opening of the tent and backing quickly away, bowing with each step. He said little about it, except to remark dryly that there was a certain advantage to becoming somebody's tame madman. But even with no other interpreter Olympia could tell that superstition was building around him daily. The way a rumor would ferment at home in an English village, so Sheridan's reputation as a fighter and a prophet was growing without encouragement as they passed from hand to hand.

In brief answer to her complaints about the litter, he simply said, "Then get out and ride a camel."

She'd really only been trying to draw him into conversation. He'd walled himself up again, saying nothing to her beyond what was necessary, though he spoke Arabic and even laughed with the others congenially enough.

"They wouldn't allow that, would they?" Tugging self-consciously at the *sarwal*—the dark silken trousers she'd been given to wear beneath a light tunic—she curled her feet under her on the soft divan. The months of confinement aboard *Terrier* had filled out her figure to plumpness again, in spite of Francis's strictures. "Don't women have to stay hidden?"

"Respectable women. I'm sure you'd prefer to be eliminated from that category."

"Thank you," she said tartly, and turned away from him to sip at the tea the servant girl had brought, trying to hide the way her eyes burned from the casual cruelty of the remark.

After a few moments of heavy silence, he muttered a tired curse and said, "I didn't mean it that way."

She bit her lip, staring down into the tea. They were like strangers now; he came to the tent and lay down on the far side and slept without touching her, without speaking if she didn't put a question to him. It was worse even than the long months of polite pleasantries; they were thrown together in mutual isolation in this strange land, and she wanted to turn to him as she had on the island, in companionship and love—but she knew without trying that any move to reach out would be furiously rebuffed.

She needed him. She needed to talk to him. Questions and fears and regrets tumbled together on her tongue—*Is there danger? What are you thinking? What are you feeling? Why can't I find you anymore? Do you hate me? . . . Do you love me?* But even the least of them seemed beyond her courage to voice.

If only she were Julia.

"I meant," he said suddenly, "that if you act like a slave and a woman, they'll treat you like one. If you want to ride outside, just do it." His mouth curled a little and he drew on the chibouk the servant had lit for him, blowing fragrant smoke. "Bravado is everything here."

"I see," she said shortly.

She didn't bother to pursue the subject, though she would have liked to learn more of what he knew. But there was no hope of that now that the pipe had come. She sipped tea and watched him in bleak frustration, knowing that soon the tension would fade from his face under the influence of the sweet fumes. The wall she so badly wished to break down would dissolve and he would smile at her, his dark lashes would relax and lower . . . and he would ignore everything she said with benign patience, until she felt like a gnat trying to annoy a sleepy elephant.

She stared at the long-necked chibouk as he drew deeply on it. She hated the pipe, hated that it could bring to his face the same expression of peace and pleasure he'd always worn after loving her.

She looked at him wistfully. In the green-and-gold light that filtered through the tent, he sat cross-legged in desert robes, his hair dark and tousled where he'd pulled the flowing red *kufiyah* off his head. The tasseled scarf lay like a pool of dark blood on the rug beside him.

She thought of other days, another place, when it had been different between them.

"Sheridan . . ." she whispered. "Oh, Sheridan . . . I wish we'd never left our island."

The spell of the smoke had not quite taken him. His eyes met hers. "Princess." He sounded so tired. Defeated. "Don't. Please don't."

Suddenly her throat closed and her eyes went blurry. The silent tears spilled down her cheeks. Through the haze she saw Sheridan watching her. He slowly bent his face into his hands and stayed there, hidden, his feelings and his thoughts a mystery.

In late afternoon, the servants struck the tents. As usual, the Abyssinian girl covered Olympia from head to toe in a swath of dark cotton, with a white *yashmak* drawn across her face. The camels and litter awaited her.

Through the slit in her headdress she looked around at the caravan. Behind and ahead of her the Bedouins and traders milled, a barbaric splendor of colorful rags and glinting armor. Some of the horse-mounted warriors tilted at one another, wheeling and evading playfully, while hundreds of camels moaned and grunted under their renewed loads. All around, long afternoon shadows moved in alien shapes.

She squinted at Sheridan. He was waiting a few yards

off, mounted on a camel and looking quite as wild as the Bedouins in his white robes and cloak and drifting crimson *kufiyah*, with a silver-handled dagger in a sash at his waist and a sword and a matchlock slung behind his back. In the desert, even a madman and prophet-slave was armed against bandit attack. No one worried much about attempted escape, apparently—the desert itself was wall and bar enough. He did not glance toward her, but talked casually to two of the contingent of fierce-looking tribesmen who seemed to be their particular guards.

Olympia watched him a moment. He'd not said another word to her in the tent, but lay back and closed his eyes and drank the smoke until she knew he had forgotten her and the guards and the desert—forgotten everything, until the pain passed from his face and he contemplated her with dreamy disinterest, his eyes unfocused and his hands relaxed on the silken divan.

It made her angry to recall it. How could she fight that? How could she ever hope to reach him when he could retreat behind that smoky stupor whenever he was with her? And now that he was awake and alert, here was this silly litter waiting to coop her up like a mummy in the few hours of coolness before they stopped again at midnight.

Julia wouldn't have stood for it.

One of the Bedouins waited with a servant by the litter. He spoke sharply to Olympia, gesturing toward the open door. Seized by a sudden passion, she flung up her chin in negation and strode over the rocky ground to the nearest camel.

She reached up to pull off the *yashmak*, shook out her hair over her shoulders and glared up at the shocked man on the dromedary.

"Get down," she ordered in English, and pointed to the ground.

"*Allaah!*" he muttered, staring at her.

Olympia heard a sudden quiet descend around them. She quelled her tremor with a vision of Julia facing down a bellicose groom in the stable at home. Instead of arguing, she grabbed the single rope rein attached to the camel's halter and yanked downward. *"Nak'h! Nak'h!"* She managed a decent rendition of the guttural command she'd heard the merchants use.

The camel gave a pathetic moan and went down to its knees with the Bedouin aboard. The man emitted a shriek of objection and kicked at the dromedary's shoulder. The camel hefted its hindquarters again, but before it could rise, she reached up and grabbed the pommel, got a foot on the beast's neck and let the momentum of the upward pitch put power behind the shove she gave the rider.

More from shock than from actual force, he slipped off balance. With Olympia hanging onto the rope, the camel made a swift, sharp turn, and suddenly the Bedouin was on the ground and she was clinging to the caparisoned saddle. Without much grace, she scrambled over the pommel, settled into the saddle, crossed her legs, readjusted her *yashmak* to protect her face from the sun and turned toward Sheridan.

"Well?" she asked.

There was dead silence, except for the low moans of the camels and the sound of a distant quarrel in the rear of the caravan.

One of the Bedouins began to laugh.

No one else did—but then, no one came to pull her off the camel, either. The dismounted Arab glared at her as if the mere heat of his look could make her wither to ashes and disappear. She inclined her head politely and said, *"La mu'axsa"*—no resentment, I hope—which was a phrase she'd learned from Salaa'ideen.

The man looked around at his impassive companions as if he thought they ought to do something. No one moved. He took a step toward her, looked around again and stepped back. After a moment, he lifted his head and muttered, *"Magh'liss,"* and then stalked off toward the horses.

"Excellent choice," Sheridan said. He guided his mount up beside her as the straggling group began to move. To her surprise, he was grinning. "They all think the fellow's gotten above himself ever since he robbed the Damascus caravan and made off with an emir's camel.''

She looked down at the animal's braided and tasseled harness and realized belatedly that it was far richer than any of the others. As the camel took up its rolling gait, jerking her painfully backward against the high cantle, she had a feeling that she might regret commandeering an open-air seat. But Sheridan rode beside her, the air was dry and sweet and pure, the sun was just setting behind a range of mountains across the vast, empty distance of blue-and-purple hues—and for the moment, though her heart was hammering with belated reaction, she was glad to be alive and where she was.

Hours later, the moon rose, silvering the white washes of mineral salts that covered the barren ground. The huge body of men and animals moved along in eerie, shuffling silence, broken only by the occasional quiet conversation between the Bedouins as they scouted up and down along the column. Olympia had drifted in and out of light sleep, kept in place by the tall back of the camel's saddle. She woke up once to find that Sheridan held the braided rope attached to her mount's halter, leading the dromedary beside his own.

''Sorry,'' she muttered, embarrassed to think she must have dropped it in her sleep.

''It's all right.'' He spoke softly, more easily than he'd spoken to her for a long time. Olympia glanced at him. The moonlight washed his figure, turning his white cloak to a dim glow, lighting only his mouth and jaw beneath the shadow of the *kufiyah*.

They rode in silence for a while, bathed in the sterile moonlight and the warm, sharp scent of sweat and camels. On the horizon, the distant black mountains seemed to float above a faint halo of mist.

''Do you feel different,'' he asked suddenly, ''now that you've killed a man?''

She looked toward him. The question ought to have seemed brutal and abrupt, but the tone wasn't. It was odd—almost hesitant.

She let the camel rock her along for a few steps and then answered honestly, "I just try not to think about it."

"Yeah," he said, and sounded strangely melancholy. "Yeah."

She was close enough to touch him. She wanted to, but she was afraid. She tried once again to think of what Julia would do, but imagination failed her. She felt stupid and helpless, paralyzed in her chubby ineptitude.

"I wish I were dead," he said hollowly.

The despair in his voice touched a place in her that responded instantly, without thought or logic; it simply went past all the longing and hesitation and fear of rejection into the action. She put out her hand and rested it on his arm—one moment of contact—and then the motion of the camels broke it. "Sheridan," she said gently, "tell me what's wrong."

"I'd like to." His head was lowered, his face completely hidden from her.

"Tell me."

His words were almost a whisper. "I'm afraid to tell you. You'll despise me. You won't understand." He raised his face to the sky and said in a painful rush, "How could you understand?"

She said nothing. She wanted to argue, to claim that she would understand anything. But life had humbled her lately, and she kept the declaration to herself.

The wooden saddles creaked in awkward rhythm. She watched the silvery, shadowy ground move past beneath the camel's feet.

"I'm not real," he said suddenly. "I mean—I don't feel . . . I don't know; I can't explain it . . . I'm not alive. I walk around and I talk and I eat and I'm dead. I'm not here." He took a deep, ragged breath. *"I'm not here."*

She looked at him, confused by the words, torn by the anguish in his voice.

"I never could go home," he said, speaking faster, as if a dam had fractured and the words were pouring from the break. "I wanted to go home, I wanted out of it so much—God, I despise the navy; what's the point? We haven't got a war, we haven't got an enemy worth the name, and still we have to—'' He made a peculiar noise, halfway between a breath and a sob. ''Damn 'em all; they sit up there at Whitehall smoking their pipes and getting fat and tell me to stop the slavers—so I chase slavers, and I catch 'em, and the bastards abandon ship and set fire to it to destroy the evidence.''

He stopped. Silence reigned.

Then he whispered, ''Those people chained in there . . . I can still hear it; I can still hear it; I can still hear it . . .''

Olympia held onto the saddle. There was a shivering in the pit of her stomach. She waited without speaking.

He kept his head down. ''I wanted to go home after that.'' His voice wavered. ''So I went on half pay. I thought—what the devil, even being destitute would be an improvement on this nonsense. And I went back, but you know, hell, I don't have a home; I don't know what made me think—''

He broke off. In the moonlight, the camels rocked relentlessly forward in their long-limbed gait. He paused for a long time, and then when the words came, they came in a gush again, as if he'd tried to hold them back but could not.

''I hated 'em all!'' he exclaimed. ''I hated their starched collars and their beaver hats and their stupid smart-ass aristocratic assistants who came in at noon because they'd been waltzing half the night with Lord Somebody's daughter and whoring like billy-o the rest. I found out the facts. I found out medals don't buy the time of day, not when it comes to getting a position you can live on. I found out you don't tell a duke's son that he doesn't know a halyard from a hole in the ground, even if he doesn't and it's going to drown a ship full of decent sailors. I found out the only paying post I was fit for was kept lover to any ladylike trollop who'd birthed enough little barons to earn her diamonds. So I did that, because it seemed better than sleeping in a gin palace. Those stupid sluts; I hated them, too—the way they'd try to tell all their friends what a hero

I was . . . and they'd ask me what it was like—they'd ask me if I was ever afraid—and did it hurt very much to be shot—" He laughed bitterly. "God, they were idiots. They'd ask how many ships I'd sunk and how many men I'd killed hand to hand . . . as if I kept a damned running account. They always wanted to know how it felt . . ." His voice had begun to shake. "But I never told them. They didn't want to know the truth. Not really."

Olympia twisted one of the saddle's silken tassels between her fingers, wondering how many of those same questions she'd asked him herself. She knew a little of what the truth was like now—she remembered that white robe crumpling, splotched with crimson. She wondered if the man she'd shot had been a father, if he'd been cruel or kind—and then quickly retreated from the thought. She was glad she'd never seen his face.

But to save Sheridan's life, she would have done it again.

In the dim light, she saw him gaze out over the stark landscape. He shook his head and muttered, "I'm a friggin' failure at civilization. I spend half my life trying to get there, and when I do, I just walk around wanting to strangle somebody."

She thought of how he'd seemed to change when they left the island and boarded *Terrier*. "Is that what's wrong?" she asked softly. "Civilization?"

"No. It's me. I'm what's wrong." He sounded tense. "I shouldn't hate them; I've got no reason to be angry. They're just . . . normal. It's normal to live the way they do. They don't feel strange; they don't have dreams or see things. They don't—" His voice took on a peculiar note. "They don't . . . want to do the things I want to do."

She bit her lip, sensing the strain in him nearing a break. "What things?" she murmured.

After a hesitation, he whispered, "You won't understand."

She saw him turn his face away from her. "What things?" she asked again, as gently as she could.

For a long time he didn't answer. Then, low and rapid, he said, "I want to fight. I wish we'd be attacked, so I could fight. I'd feel better if I could kill somebody." He made a queer, anxious moan. "Maybe they'd kill me. That would be better . . . that would be good."

"Sheridan—" Olympia put her fist to her mouth. "Why?"

"I knew you wouldn't understand."

Her heart was beating so hard it made her voice quiver. "Explain it to me."

Again a silence, so long that she feared she'd lost him.

"I feel so strange!" he burst out. "I should have died. It's not right that I'm alive. They all died—all my men. All my friends." That low moan escaped him, a wordless sound of agony. "Oh, God, I'm going to hurt someone. That's the only time I'm real now. I want to kill somebody."

The words drifted in the still desert air—so simple, and so terrible to comprehend.

"I knew it was here," he said. "It got out—I let it out, there at Aden . . ."

She remembered the way he'd looked up at her over the bodies of dead men, his eyes a ghostlike calm amid the violence. No fear, no disgust, no reason—only the bright gray flame of destruction.

He whispered furtively, "That's me; that's what's real—I want that back, but I can't have it. I can't have it, can I? No—I can't; I don't want to hurt anyone. But I'm dead, I'm dead . . . I don't know what to do . . ."

She was aghast. Distantly, she recognized that she ought reasonably to be afraid for herself, listening to what he was saying, that he wanted to kill someone—but it was Sheridan she was terrified for. He would turn this on himself. She had a clear and dreadful vision of him gazing down the barrel of a pistol in his cabin aboard *Terrier*.

"I don't know what's happening to me," he mumbled. "I don't understand."

Olympia didn't understand either, but she knew when it had begun. She'd become engaged to Francis, and she would never forget Sheridan's face when he heard it. Somehow—though he'd denied it and said it wasn't her fault—something inside him had gone dreadfully wrong from that moment.

"Sheridan," she asked shakily, "do you want to kill me?"

"No!" The single syllable held absolute horror. He turned to her, grabbed her shoulder. "Not you—I swear—dear God, Princess—never you; I'd never hurt you!"

She remained quiet under the cruel grip of his fingers. With sudden resolution, she said, "No . . . of course not. But you have a right to be angry with me. After what I've done. I said I loved you and trusted you, and then I turned to Francis."

"I have to protect you," he said intensely.

She bowed her head. "If I were you, I'd be furious at me."

His hand left her shoulder. "I have to protect you," he repeated. But a faint note of anxiety had crept into his voice.

"You're not angry?"

He hesitated.

"Sheridan? Are you angry with me?"

"Why are you asking me that? I'm tired of it," he said explosively. "I'm tired of hurting and killing people."

She shivered in the cool night air, struggling to make sense of it all. "You just said it would make you feel better."

"Somebody else!" he exclaimed. "The enemy. Not you. I'll protect you; Princess, I don't want to hurt you. Never. Never."

"Yes," she said honestly, "I believe that. I only want to know if you're angry at me."

"I told you I won't hurt you!" The agitation in his voice mounted. "How can you even think it?"

She looked at him intently. With slow thoughtfulness, she said, "They aren't the same thing. You can be angry without hurting and killing."

He didn't answer. She watched his silhouette and saw him put his hand to his temple.

"You can be angry with me, Sheridan," she repeated

softly. "Do you understand? I won't be happy, but I'll survive it."

"My head aches," he said fretfully.

She almost pushed him. But a newly awakening intuition stopped her. She felt like a flower opening petals before a thunderstorm, sensitive to each shift and play of wind. It was a risk; she might end up torn and beaten—but the storm wouldn't dissipate; it could only grow until it broke with furious intensity. She would have to spread and bend, though it meant opening to enfold depths of pain and violence she'd never imagined.

She thought again of Julia, tried to imagine how she would act, what she would say and do to give him comfort. After a frowning moment, Olympia realized with a sense of wonder that Julia wouldn't do anything at all, except put as much cool distance between herself and the hazard as possible. Perhaps she'd been his lover, but she would not stand by him at peril to herself—Olympia felt that in her bones.

For the first time in her life, she was proud she wasn't Julia.

There in the desert moonlight, she came to the truth, and a sense of infinite calm spread through her. Julia was more beautiful, Julia was slender and sophisticated and everything Olympia was not—but she didn't love Sheridan. Olympia doubted she'd ever loved anyone. In fact, growing up with that icy perfection, Olympia knew that if Fish Stovall had never taken pity on a lonely child and spent those warm, silent hours with her in the Norfolk marshes, she would never have known anything about love or friendship or faithfulness at all.

She could turn away from Sheridan and this darkness inside him; she could say he was dangerous—that he had a killing demon in him that was struggling for control . . . but she'd met that same demon face-to-face on the bloody gun deck of *Terrier* and it had defended her—with unselfish, single-minded, savage loyalty.

Love might exist in strange shapes, and demand more than simple commitment. A wolf was not a lapdog, not after a lifetime in the wilderness—but still it might long for a hearth and home.

The moon was setting, silhouetting the bleak mountains in an unearthly glow. On a hill ahead, the dark shapes of camels stalked in slow rhythm across the silver disc of light and then disappeared into shadow beyond: so lovely and majestic and alien they were like a dream of an unknown world. Their own mounts reached the top by steady steps—and there, spread before them, was a valley of frosted light, the long column like faint smoke winding through it.

"I wish this night would go on forever," Sheridan whispered. "I wish I never had to live in the world again."

The ache in his voice made her throat close. Her camel swayed down the slope next to his. They took up the trail behind the others.

"Would you sing for me?" she asked.

He looked at her, but she couldn't see his face. They were in shadow now, the night pressing closer as the moon disappeared.

Softly at first, his voice hoarse and faintly uncertain as if he'd half forgotten the words, the melody of "Greensleeves" rose above the shuffle of sand. The quiet conversations around them hushed. As midnight enveloped them, his fine voice gained depth and rhythm, drifting out over the silent desert: sweet reminder of home and love sung in time to the camels' march.

They made camp in the dark, pitching tents for the few hours of rest before the pre-dawn signal to move again. Sheridan stayed with her of his own will, and when they were together in the tent, he did not call for the chibouk, but dismissed the servant girl and doused the lamp.

In the chilly dark, he lay down on the carpet beside her and drew her into his arms. He touched her cheek, and her hair, drifted his fingertips across her forehead and down the line of her chin.

She turned her face into his hand and kissed his palm. There was no passion in this embrace, only the need to be close, as they'd been in the long months of hardship on the island. With a sense of warm familiarity, she did now what she'd often done then: turned on her side and settled into the curve of his body with only the soft desert robes between them.

"You're so beautiful," he said in the darkness. "You're the most beautiful thing in my life."

Twenty-four

I can see it coming," Sheridan said to her under his breath as the magicians consulted their pans of burning charcoal. They were ponderously determining the proper moment to conduct the mad English prophet into the presence of Ishak Pasha, the mighty vizier of all eastern Anatolia. "He's got an ailing wife, or a son with a cast in one eye, and I'll be expected to foam at the mouth and say 'The whale weeps at midnight' twenty-nine times before anyone's allowed to go to bed."

Olympia bit her lip, watching three white eunuchs pad by, soft-footed and long-limbed like graceful insects. She and Sheridan stood beneath an archway that opened into a garden, surrounded on all sides by fabulous tiled walls of blue and green and gold designs.

Sheridan was right—a wild performance always seemed expected of him, though in reality all he ever did was bow smoothly in the eastern manner and converse with his "hosts" in Arabic while Olympia sat without headdress or *yashmak* in the presence of men who'd never seen a woman's face outside the hareem. As he'd predicted, his polite sanity and her calm flouting of convention created more sensation than any fit of mania—fits being pretty common stuff among the wandering *darwayshes* and holy men in any case.

The magicians determined that they must wait four more hours before the auspicious moment. Olympia's shoulders fell at this news—she was tired, having ridden all night and morning down from the foothills of Kurdistan and then been bathed and perfumed and dressed and fussed over by the hareem servants for the rest of the day. Even the magical sight of Ishak Pasha's palace, its domes and minaret floating up out of the haze like a vision from the Arabian Nights, with the vast plain below and Mount Ararat's peak of snow in the purple distance—not even that wonder could erase the cumulative exhaustion of weeks of weary travel.

But she sighed and nodded when Sheridan told her, trusting him to know the proper etiquette. He looked at her for a moment. She smiled tiredly. Something came into his face: his mouth hardened and his eyes took on a cold, fixed light—he spoke abruptly to the magicians and grasped her arm.

Without waiting for the usual attendant to slink ahead, or the eunuchs to whisper their arrival in the vizier's ear, or any of the other points of procedure that had been followed at every stop from Jidda to Ha'il to Baghdad, he led her swiftly beneath the arch and into the antechamber, past the little fountain and right up to the startled figure of Ishak Pasha on his cushioned divan.

Sheridan did bow—cursorily—but she was horrified to see that he didn't slip off his footwear before he bypassed the guests and petitioners who sat hunched on low stools before the dais. He stepped up onto the carpeted platform and seated a bewildered Olympia on the divan next to the plump, old vizier. With a disinterested air, Sheridan sat down himself on the other side. She saw that the *teskeri hilaal* had appeared, to lie conspicuously against his chest like a glinting warning. They'd dressed him in Turkish clothing: tight trousers and a deep red velvet tunic encrusted with embroidery, but instead of slippers he wore European boots, which he raised casually to rest on the vizier's divan as he clapped his hands.

Ishak Pasha turned white beneath his plumed turban. Olympia held her breath. She'd learned enough of oriental etiquette to know they'd just delivered a series of murderous insults. But as a moment of silence passed and the other guests began quickly to stand and perform their greetings, bending low—not toward the vizier, but to Sheridan and then herself—she understood with astonishment that the governor of the whole territory was trembling with fear instead of fury.

She looked at Sheridan and saw the fixed expression there still, the calm lit by a cold excitement in his eyes. He could have been a real prophet—he had that look of inhuman intensity, that flame of passion locked in ice that she'd seen in the battle with the pirates.

The demon had woken again.

"We call this inspiring respect and striking terror." He used English in a tone that sounded as if he were pronouncing some sentence of doom. "This little tub of butter thought he'd bought some nice expensive playthings to pass along and ingratiate himself with the Sultan." He smiled with sweet menace at the hapless pasha, caressing the *teskeri* as if it were a weapon. "But it's not quite that easy, is it, my fine basket of tripe? We're not going to await your pleasure. We're tired; we want to go to bed. We're going to be such overbearing bullies that even Mustafa couldn't find fault with the way we insult our inferiors. Too bad he ain't here to do it in our behalf, but we'll have to muddle through by ourselves. Here are the pipes." He stared with magnificent gloom at the riveted faces around the room, still speaking English. "Pretend to try yours, and then push it away. Show us some royal disgust."

He nodded, and the silent servants stepped forward together from the lower end of the room, each one placing a long-necked pipe before an individual guest. Olympia looked down the five slender feet of modeled clay to the glowing bowl, and then at the jeweled mouthpiece presented to her lips.

She touched it delicately to her tongue, and barely suppressed a cough at the flood of sharp tobacco smoke. "*Kikh!*" She thrust it away with the expression she'd heard a Bedouin use upon startling a rat out of a grain bag.

The servant before her looked horrified. Instantly he removed the pipe, disappeared and brought another, more exquisitely decorated than the first. Olympia repeated the refusal. The vizier sweated miserably and addressed anxious questions to Sheridan. After two more rejections, when the servants and the vizier appeared almost beside themselves with stress, Sheridan allowed her to settle for tea.

He monopolized the conversation, asking sharp questions of the vizier and receiving voluble answers. When at last they rose to leave, Ishak Pasha leapt to his feet and personally ushered them down the single step and all the way to the anteroom, cooing a single phrase over and over. When they'd been led to a chamber and left alone with bowls of figs and pastries stuffed with cheese, Olympia asked what the vizier had been saying so earnestly.

" 'Go with the fortune of a prince,' " Sheridan interpreted, smiling grimly. "The highest compliment for a departing guest. We have him on the run, anyway."

She drew a breath to calm herself. Her heart was still beating painfully fast after the ordeal of defying a vizier in his own palace. "You have the most amazing nerve."

"We're out of Arabia and amongst the real Osmanlis now." He touched the *teskeri*. "This buys me any damned thing I want—including Ishak Pasha's fat head. That's what I hope he thinks, at any rate."

"It's not true?"

For a moment he didn't answer, staring pensively down at the rug they sat on. "I don't know. I'd reckon odds are against it." He shrugged. "Ishak says a message has gone out from the Sultan already to all the provinces. The Great Mahmoud has a wish to see the crazy Englishman who wears his crescent. That could mean anything—good or bad." He looked up at her, his eyes a cool gray, giving away no emotion. "And it seems Fitzhugh hasn't wasted any time taking his gripe right to the British ambassador at Stamboul, demanding his fiancé and restitution for the attack on his ship. We're a wanted pair in the Ottoman Empire."

She dropped her eyes. Then she glanced around at the chamber, so serene and simple and lovely, carpeted with myriad soft rugs, the walls glowing with painted tiles and the air filled with the whispering of fountains. "Are we in much danger?"

He laughed and stretched out to his full length, his shoulders propped against the low divan. "You haven't changed a bit, have you? Christ, yes, we're in danger. D'you think just because this Ishak sweats and scrapes that he's actually developed any affection for us? As long as we've got the nerve to wipe our boots on his divan, he'll ooze charm and generosity. But just wait for the word to come through that we don't have the Sultan behind us, and we'll pay for every insult. With interest."

She looked at him dubiously. "It seems a risky way to go on. Can't we just be customarily polite?"

"I was under the impression you didn't care to stand around for hours waiting on a bunch of constellations to converge."

She sighed. "I suppose not."

"Ripping slack stars they've got in this place," he muttered, adjusting a tasseled pillow beneath his head.

Olympia tried to smile, but didn't quite manage to banish her uneasiness.

He reached out and touched her cheek. "Princess . . . I'll take care of you."

She bent her head. An eastern silence fell between them, full of rustling leaves and the soft sound of water. He lowered his eyelashes, sliding a glance along her body. A distant muezzin called the faithful to evening prayer with a singsong drone.

"They've rigged you out enticingly," he murmured.

It was the first time since they'd left the island that he'd mentioned her appearance. Without thinking, she'd slipped off the hot and heavy brocade robe she'd worn into the audience room, and now she felt her cheeks grow scarlet as she looked down at the thin rose-colored trousers, embroidered with flowers and covered with a gauzy smock that showed her breasts right through it. The open caftan that matched the trousers was somewhat more modest, but the cut fitted so closely to her body that she squirmed in embarrassment. "I've gotten much too fat."

He clasped his hands behind his neck and shook his head with a silent smile.

Olympia sat with her legs crossed. She slanted a look toward him, wondering if he was going to call for the pipe and hashish. Since the desert, he'd continued to retreat into that sleepy asylum daily, silently forbidding any effort to speak of troubling things. Olympia had chosen not to push at the wall, but she watched him.

He made no move to summon the chibouk. He reached out and ran his fingers over her hand and across the thin silk that covered her thigh, his touch warm and sensual. "I haven't forgotten," he murmured. "I think about you . . . every day."

She closed her eyes. Like one of the fountains in the courtyards outside, instant warmth sprang up inside her. It had been so long . . . just the lazy, rhythmic stroke of his hand along her thigh was enough to spark excitement.

She wanted him. She wanted him so much.

She put her hand over his, caught it and stilled it. "Sheridan," she asked softly, "how do you feel?"

She thought he might pretend to misunderstand the question. But he seemed to think about it; he stared soberly into space for a moment, as if checking inside himself, and then said, "I feel all right." He looked up at her. His hand pressed her thigh. A slow smile lit his face. "I feel pretty damned good."

Olympia took a deep breath. This was the moment, the opening in the wall. With no notion of whether she was right or wrong, with only love and instinct as a guide, she held out her hand to the savage wolf hidden in the silver depths of his eyes and asked it to take a step toward civilization.

"How did you feel in the vizier's chamber?" she asked, playing with his fingers on her thigh, stroking and caressing the sun-darkened skin. "Did you feel good in there?"

Instantly, his hand curled into a fist. He was silent. After a moment, he said abruptly, "I don't remember."

All along his arm, the muscles had gone tense. She stroked his hand, slipped her fingers into the taut curl, asking it to open. "Yes, you do," she insisted gently. "It wasn't that long ago."

"I felt fine." He pulled his hand away.

Olympia reached out and took it again. "Alive?" She stroked the back of his palm with her thumb.

The sinew beneath her fingers tensed and relaxed in restless rhythm. He stared upward, into the shadows of the domed ceiling, where painted tiles made a gold-and-blue sky of stylized flowers and Arabic script.

She went on stroking his hand, waiting, not knowing what more to say if he would not answer.

"Yes," he whispered. "I guess so." He frowned at the ceiling. "I guess so. Taking us in there like that . . . it was a hellish risky thing to do. But they wanted to make you stand there for hours, and you looked so tired—you looked like a flower wilting—all pretty in your new clothes, and wilting, and I couldn't stand it. So I made 'em stop." He glanced at her. "I had to. Sometimes that feeling just . . . comes over me, and I can't stop. I would have killed 'em all if they'd tried to hold us."

His face tensed, as if his own words jarred him. Then he turned and stared into space—and she saw the wolf in his eyes, the pleasure at the thought of carnage.

"Thank you," she said, in an impulsive attempt to communicate with it. "I'm glad you're on my side."

He looked back at her warily.

She slid her fingers through his. She would not be afraid of him. He was too afraid of himself. What if he struggled to control this thing inside, to keep it trapped until it turned and destroyed him?

Come to me instead. She lifted his hand and kissed the back of it, feeling the weight of hard muscle and bone—and his eyes watching her. *I believe in you. I believe you can learn another way.*

For a long moment, the wariness held. Then one corner of his mouth curled upward. He made a sound, an awkward chuckle. "Glad?" He sounded hopeful and doubting . . . and so very, very vulnerable.

"Yes." She squeezed his hand. "Very glad."

"It did feel good," he said, "It feels like—a rush . . . like everything is so clear, and I know exactly what to do and say. I know what I want, and I can get it. I can keep you safe, and I can make 'em take care of you." He glanced at her, a sideways look, quick and shy. "It makes me . . . proud of myself."

She smiled and leaned over him. She kissed his mouth, tasting the hard warmth. "I'm proud of you, too." She held back a little, looking down into his eyes, wondering if she was talking to Sheridan or his demon—and if she could reach either with words of reason. "You've kept us safe. But you didn't hurt anyone. You didn't kill anybody."

"I would have," he said with instant ferocity.

"No, Sheridan, you wouldn't have. Because that wouldn't have made any sense. It wouldn't have gotten you what you wanted. It would have been wrong, and you'd have felt bad afterwards."

His breathing quickened. "I wouldn't want to do it. But there's something inside me . . . I can't help it. I can't let it out. I have to keep it under control. If I let it out—" He groaned. "Oh, God, if you knew me—what I've done, what I am . . . you'd hate me."

She laid her hand against his cheek. "I won't hate you, Sheridan. I promise. With all my heart, I promise you that."

He closed his eyes. With a sudden move he pulled her down against him, burying her face in his shoulder. "Why did you leave me? Why?"

"Because I was a fool," she whispered. "A fool and a coward."

"You're afraid of me."

"No!" She raised herself, forcing him to look at her. "No. Listen to me. I'm not afraid of you. I'm afraid of Julia."

He stared at her.

"I'm afraid because she's beautiful. I'm afraid because she always knows what to say. That's why I went to Francis, because I know I'll never be what she is"—Olympia bit her lip —"and you've loved her, and I'm jealous."

He just looked at her with a faint, blank frown. "Julia?"

She shrugged, ashamed of her weakness.

"Julia," he repeated slowly. An expression of incredulous comprehension came over his face. "Are you talking about Julia Plumb?"

She buried her face against his chest and nodded.

"Good God. You really do think I'm a hopeless lunatic."

Olympia kept her face hidden, wondering if she'd understood him correctly.

"I despise that witch. She's the worst of 'em all."

"Mustafa said—" She took a breath, still keeping her face against his chest. "Mustafa said she'd been your . . . lover."

"Much he ever knew about it."

Her heart thumped in her throat. What if his servant had been lying again? She waited, and when she couldn't stand it any longer, asked, "Was she?"

He turned on his side and stroked her hair. His hand trembled. "You're jealous? You're jealous of Julia?"

She lowered her eyes, pressing her lips together. "Oh—how could I not be?"

"Poor, blind princess. Jealous of Julia." He shook his head. "She'd love to hear this. She'd be in raptures. The icy slut, I'll wager she's been bleeding the heart out of you since you came under her control."

Olympia made an effort to smile. "It wasn't so awful as that. But I never thought she cared for me very much."

"She doesn't know the meaning of the word. And she has bled you, Princess. She's made you believe you're not beautiful; she made you dislike your own body, so that you wanted to hide from me." He put his hand on her waist and slid it down to her hip, watching her breasts through the translucent fabric. "Never believe her. You're perfect. You're so lovely."

She wanted to believe him, but it was too hard. She

moved a little, so that his hand fell away. "You seem to know her awfully well."

"She was my father's mistress." He smiled bitterly as she sucked in her breath. "Ah—I've shocked you. I know Julia damned well. She first seduced me when I was sixteen and home on leave. At the time I thought it was my idea—by way of spiting my father, y'know—but the wisdom of age has enlightened me. On that point and a few others."

"Your father's mistress?" Olympia echoed numbly.

"Well—ex-mistress," he said. He moved his hand in a careless gesture. "Apparently the old man turned her off a considerable time ago and she had to go to work for a living."

Olympia could hardly comprehend the idea. Julia? That severe black elegance and obsessive concern for Olympia's reputation hid a rich old man's mistress? "M-Mustafa said—"

"I can imagine what Mustafa said. And yes, she came to me when I got back. And I took advantage of it. I've always told you I'm no saint, and God knows she owed me, considering the way she was planning to trap me into—"

He broke off suddenly, frowning.

She put her hand on his arm. "What is it?"

He looked down at the rug. "It's nothing. Nothing important."

Then he rolled over onto his back, his jaw set moodily. His features were grim and dark above the scarlet tunic, shuttered in thought. Abruptly he turned again. Without a word he took her in his arms and held her hard, pushing his hand into her hair.

Olympia closed her eyes and pressed herself against him. Through her light silk costume, his body felt hard beneath the velvet coat, his arms taut. His fingers moved restlessly in her hair.

"Christ, I'm such a sorry bastard," he whispered against her throat. "I love you." His voice broke in hoarse intensity. "Princess, I love you so much."

She stroked his cheek. "I love you, too."

He moaned, shaking his head. His arms tightened, and then suddenly he let her go. He stood up and began to prowl the room. "You can't," he said. "You can't. You just don't know . . ." His voice trailed off hopelessly.

"About your father's will?" She sat up. "And that it was Julia who forced you to propose to me? Yes, I do know. Mustafa told me." She looked down at her knees. "I think I knew it must be something like that all along."

"It was worse than that," he said.

She looked up.

"I wrote a letter to your uncle. I figured I could sell you to him when we got to Rome. But that was before. Before we—"

She held his eyes, keeping her chin steady. It was growing dark, the shadows in the little garden outside their room lengthening.

He leaned back against the tiled wall with a sigh. He pressed his hands over his face and shook his head.

"I still love you, Sheridan."

He lowered his hands, staring at the floor. "That was why you took up with Fitzhugh, wasn't it? Because I've been such a blackguard."

"That's what I told myself," she said honestly. "But I think . . . I think it was mostly Julia. When I heard that you and she were—lovers . . ." Olympia shrugged and rubbed at the silk on her trousers. "How could I think I ever meant anything to you?"

"For what it's worth," he said gruffly, "you mean everything to me."

She lifted her face, gazing at him.

He bent his head and avoided her eyes. "You're the reason I'm alive. I'll get you to Rome. I'll keep you safe. I'll never let anything hurt you."

She stood up and went to him, taking his hands between hers. "What does that mean—I'm the reason you're alive?"

He stared down at their hands. She smoothed his hair, touched the little scar across his eyebrow.

He spoke quietly. "I went to sea when I was ten, Princess. My father told me I was going to Vienna to study music, but it was a joke. He liked to play jokes. I think he meant to come back and get me. I really do.'' His jaw worked. ''Sometimes I do, anyway. But I was just a kid—another midshipman—there must have been ten thousand of us, and there was the French war . . . and he didn't come, or he couldn't find me, and the ship sailed.''

He rubbed his thumb over hers, frowning deeply. Olympia gripped his hand. ''It isn't fair,'' she said. ''It isn't right, to take children and send them to war.''

''It wasn't so bad,'' he said slowly. ''I don't know if you can understand how it is, how you . . .'' He seemed to search for words. ''. . . make a bond with the others. It's more than friendship. It's as if—as if something happens to them, it happens to you. The first time we were fired on, I was so scared I couldn't cry—I wet myself—all the noise—and the way it smells; you can hardly breathe, the powder smoke burns your throat . . . every time we took a ball, I thought the ship would sink. And there was another middie, who'd been aboard a few years—and he saw me. I was standing there about to fall down; I was so paralyzed and terrified and ashamed of myself—and he yelled some stupid joke to me—I don't even remember what it was—but I just started laughing, and he laughed—in the middle of all that hell.'' His throat worked. ''His name was Harry Dover.'' He pulled his hand away from hers and rubbed his ear. ''Harry Dover. I don't know what happened to him.''

She watched his face. It held distance: space and time . . . memories.

''The first few months,'' he said, ''whenever I was off watch, I used to get under a blanket in my hammock, no matter how hot it was, and cry. Maybe it was longer than a few months. Maybe it was years. I wanted to go home. I was so lonely and scared and helpless.'' He bit his lip. ''I was really scared.''

She touched his cheek. ''Of course you were scared. You were ten years old.''

''I've always been scared. I don't want to die. Not that way. Not all torn to bits by bullets and canister shot.'' He shook his head. ''But after a while, something happens to you. All that fear—the bodies, the noise . . . you just get numb. You see a man's head shot off, and you think: that's an amazing sight—and you don't feel anything. Nothing.'' He swallowed. ''Except . . . you keep seeing it. Maybe not for a while. Maybe not for a long, long time. But then someday you lie down and dream about it. And then you keep seeing it, over and over.'' His voice trailed off to a whisper. ''I can still see it.''

She put her arms around him and rested her cheek against his chest wordlessly.

''I don't know what's gone wrong,'' he said in a shaky voice. ''I used to be all right. I had dreams, sometimes, but it wasn't like this. It wasn't with me—waiting for me; I didn't look in the mirror and remember . . . these thoughts didn't come to me in the middle of trying to hold a conversation, or dress, or just eat. I didn't wake up in the middle of the night and see things. They get hold of me, and I can't make them go away. I push one off and there's another—worse.'' He rested his mouth on her hair with a soft moan. ''I think I'm being punished. I think I was supposed to die—I'm supposed to be in Hell . . . but I can't go yet. I have to protect you.''

''Sheridan. Oh, Sheridan.''

''Don't cry.'' He held her tight. ''Don't be afraid. I'll take care of you. I won't fail this time.''

''It's you I'm afraid for!''

He took her face between his hands and kissed her. ''Don't be afraid for me. I don't even care where I am, except you're here, and I love you—'' He kissed her nose, and her forehead. ''I love you.''

She gazed up at him, her eyes leaking tears. ''I w-wish I knew what to do.''

''You can't do anything. It's me. It's not your fault.''

''I love you, Sheridan!''

He put his forehead to hers. ''Don't love me, Princess. I just want to hold you, just for a little while. I think about you all the time while we ride out there—I was so proud of you when you got mad and took that damned camel; you're so beautiful and brave and clever—and I just want to have a little while, like it was on the island.'' He held her close, burying his face in her hair. ''But you can't believe in it, Princess, you can't. Life isn't like that. There's now, and there isn't anything else, and if you let yourself believe, if you take it for granted, it'll crush you into little pieces and there won't be anything left when you lose it.''

''No,'' she said, ''that's not the way life is.''

He held her to him. ''Innocent princess. Beautiful, sweet princess.''

''You can't go on like this. We have to—''

A quiet voice broke in on her, foreign words that made Sheridan look up. His arms loosened.

Three tall, soft-skinned eunuchs in rich brocade tunics and fezzes stood just within the chamber. The foremost bowed toward Olympia and gestured at the door with the whip that was his badge of office as keeper of the seraglio. She picked out the word *hareem* from the flow of Turkish.

''No. She stays with me,'' Sheridan exclaimed, and took a step in front of her. He jerked his chin and gave a sharp order.

The servant bowed again, apologetic, profuse in his salutations, but firmly repeating the gesture for Olympia to accompany him.

She grasped Sheridan's arm, unwilling to leave him for the sequestered hareem while he was in this uncertain mood. She felt his muscle grow taut and looked up at his face. He seemed to pale in the dimming light—she could see the change come in him, the wolf spring to life. His eyes locked on the servant. He didn't move, but his balance shifted and his body went fluid in anticipation.

''Sheridan,'' she said, tightening her hand on his arm.

He ignored her.

The eunuch walked forward, his beardless face serene. He bowed again to Sheridan.

''I'm sure there must be some mistake,'' Olympia said, shaking her head to get the notion across. She could feel the tension in Sheridan's arm grow with every inch the servant moved forward. She silently countered the force, pressing his arm downward with her fingers as she pointed to herself and to the ground. "I always stay with him."

The eunuch bowed again, and reached out to guide her away.

Sheridan moved. The power pulled her forward like a dangling stake jerked free of the ground. His first blow sent the servant staggering back with a shrill cry, plump arms lifted to fend off his attacker. But Sheridan didn't stop. The other two ran forward with high-pitched shouts as Sheridan went after the first, hit him again and knocked him to his knees. Olympia threw herself forward, ducking the whips, trying to drag Sheridan back before he could kill the man.

Suddenly there were stronger hands than hers hauling at his arms, the clatter and shouts of real guards. While he wrestled in their hold, the limp eunuch was carried bodily from the room, his pale skin already showing bruises. Sheridan still struggled, his face marked with red welts, his breathing harsh and furious as he strained like a chained dog to reach the remaining two eunuchs. He swore at them in English and Arabic and languages Olympia had never heard, while they stood near the door, speaking in wild, palpitating voices.

"Sheridan," Olympia repeated, over and over. "It's all right; I won't leave—Sheridan, listen to me—please—I'm here; I won't leave." But he never even seemed to hear her. He simply fought himself into exhaustion, imprisoned at every point by fresh guards. His curses turned to grunts, and then to painful gasps. Finally, the guards were holding him up instead of holding him still. They pulled him against the wall and let him slide down to his knees.

He knelt there, his head hanging for a moment. Then he looked up, searching the room with a quick sweep. He saw her, seemed to register that she was still there and safe, and then with a weary heave sank back against the wall.

The guards left, one by one. The last one bowed to Olympia, rolled his eyes at Sheridan and closed the door.

He sat hunched against the wall as darkness fell, his

arms crossed on his knees, staring ahead: a shadow lost in shadows. Sometimes a shudder racked him, but he stayed there, awake and unpredictable, keeping his own vigil against whatever dangers he saw in the black night.

Olympia did not dare to disturb him. She'd thought she could tame the wolf. She'd thought she might reach that part of him with reason and love. But she hadn't.

She hadn't even come close.

Twenty-five

Sheridan treaded warily through the days and nights as they journeyed from Ishak's palace on the hill above Douubayazit to Stamboul. He felt detached, riding behind Olympia along the forested mountain paths of Anatolia, noting the way the winter wind lifted her *yashmak* and made it flutter, watching the splendid caravan Ishak Pasha had assembled—occupying his mind with small and harmless details.

It had snowed often in the mountains, and at night he held her, supplying warmth with his body that was lacking in Turkish notions of luxury. He wondered what she thought of him—that he made no move to spark the passion between them. He wanted to. But that would require coming back to reality, living in the world instead of on the floating plane of apartness. How long had it been? It seemed like a moment ago, and forever, the last time he'd made love to her—and even then he hadn't been free to take her fully.

She'd asked him to . . .

He shifted in the saddle, feeling disquieting emotions rise to threaten his drifting equilibrium. He wasn't ready to think about that yet. He blinked, and he could see her face, tilted back in glorious ecstasy, her warm naked body arched in invitation—as vivid as the evergreens around them, as sharp as the scent of pine smoke from a nearby camp. Flashes of the image lit his brain, powerful and tantalizing. He felt himself slipping away into it.

"Sheridan."

He blinked again, like waking from a sound sleep, and found that the surroundings had changed. They'd left the woods and entered a village: far ahead, downhill, he could see the blue glint of water among the budding cypress trees. The air had warmed—there was a scent of spring blossoms on the breeze blowing inland from the coast.

"What do they want us to do?" Olympia's quiet voice directed his sluggish attention.

He listened to their attendant's excited babble of information. All along the caravan behind, voices began to lift in excited chatter.

He looked up at Olympia. "We're to go ahead to Beykoz tonight. On the Bosporus." He paused. His heart began to beat harder, feeling reality coming, like something far away on a vast horizon that had just begun rolling toward him, picking up speed as it went. "Wc'rc to stay there," he added slowly. "The Sultan comes . . . to receive us in person."

He stood on the terrace of their rooms in the waterside palace, making a concerted effort to shake off the mental lethargy and focus on the situation at hand. Below, in a grove of plane trees at the water's edge, a group of women filled earthen water jars, bright silhouettes against the blue water.

As he waited for Olympia to be returned from her bath, he gazed at the colorful boats and the exotic white domes and minarets of the palaces on the European side. He found it hard to believe Mahmoud was coming—it was good news, too bizarrely good. He was uneasy. He'd expected a weeks-long wait in a crowded chamber at Topkapi Palace before he was even summoned. How well he remembered that magnificent warren of tiny rooms and endless ceremonies and delays. He'd learned Turkish patience at Topkapi, but the slow oozing away of time and life had always chafed. He'd been younger then.

Now he wished time might drift on endlessly in this lovely spot where the dark green trees overhung the fabled sweet waters of Europe and Asia. He didn't even know whose palace this was: one of Mahmoud's summer residences, perhaps, or some gift awarded to a Grand Vizier. The owner wasn't in evidence. If only he and Olympia could stay here, in peace and solitude, maybe he could find himself again.

For the thousandth time, he thought of things she'd said. That she would not hate him. That she was glad he was on her side. That he could keep them safe without violence, without hurting anyone. He tried to believe those things. He repeated them to himself. But he was afraid.

He heard her enter the room behind him and dismiss her attendants. He closed his eyes, waiting. Her scent came to him, then the soft song of her belled slippers on the carpets, a warmth at his side. He opened his eyes and looked down at her.

She twisted one of her golden braids beneath the sheer, tasseled scarf that covered her head. "It's a very great thing, isn't it?" she asked without preamble. "The Sultan coming to meet us here."

He blew out a breath. "It's the devil of a thing. I don't know what to make of it."

"It's all the servants can speak of. There was an interpreter waiting here for me, did you know that? A lovely Greek girl. She translated everything—and very odd it was, too—to hear that my hair must surely be a wig and I certainly ought to be shaved in the most—" She broke off, coloring scarlet.

"Private places?" Sheridan found his mouth curving in a slow, secret grin.

She put her hands on the terrace railing and gave him a pert glance. "I understand it's *de rigueur.*"

"Most certainly."

"And did you follow the custom?"

"No. But I'm a well-known madman and prophet. If you don't like it, I'll consult some entrails and see if I can't get the thing changed." He leaned on the rail, turning lazily to look at her. "In fact—when I think of those pretty blond curls, I believe that saving 'em clearly ought to count as a divine mission."

"They're . . . safe so far." Her cheeks were pink with

embarrassment, but she parted her lips and held his eyes steadily. Hopefully. He realized where he'd taken the conversation, and the sudden ferocious depth of his desire for her seemed to make a roaring in his ears.

He stood where he was, frozen. She still looked at him, the tasseled scarf a transparent, graceful curve over her shoulder, the flowing Turkish dress splendidly seductive. He could see her nipples, and the shadow beneath her breasts, all hazed into mysterious roundness by the gauzy fabric. They'd dressed her simply, not at all in the extravagant Turkish idea of a houri, but to Sheridan she was intolerably alluring.

He curled his fingers, wanting desperately to reach out and hold her. But another part of him wasn't ready—it held back, like a stubborn child in the shadows, fascinated by the glitter of a wonderful toy and still afraid to touch. He stood still, watching the hope fade from her face, until finally she turned away, clasped her hands and gazed out across the water.

Her plump chin took on a resolute stiffness as she coolly changed the topic. "I think, since we're to meet the Sultan tomorrow, it's time you told me how you come to wear that crescent."

He lowered his eyes. After a moment, he said, "I did him a favor once. A deuce of a long time ago."

"What favor?"

He shrugged. "Along with several other people . . . helped to save his life."

She turned to him slowly, questions burning in her expression.

He squinted out over the sparkling water between the dark green hills. "It was just a stupid palace revolt. I really don't want to talk about it."

She tilted her head and smiled a little. "Oh. Just a stupid palace revolt. Just a minor matter of saving the Sultan's life."

"Leave it alone, will you?" He felt anger gathering in him. He didn't like this topic; he didn't like the way his throat and belly tightened on the edges of memories. "Quit trying to pretend I'm a bloody damned hero. I'm not. I'd think you'd have noticed by now.''

She bit her lip, and then said quietly, ''All right. You're not a hero. But I'd like to know why the Sultan's going to so much trouble to do us all this honor. I think that's a fair question.''

He looked away from the blaze of sun on water. His head hurt. But she was right, it was only reasonable to let her know where they stood in this situation. What he knew of it, anyway. And he had a feeling she'd demand an explanation until he gave her one.

''Mahmoud was the old sultan's half brother,'' he said. ''Next in line to the throne. They're not overly nice-minded when it comes to politics around here—'' He moved his hand negligently. ''It's the custom to keep all the extraneous princes locked up in some palace apartments they call The Cage so they won't be tempted to start any trouble.'' Sheridan frowned, remembering, and then went doggedly on, wanting to get the tale over with. ''Without boring you with all the Byzantine details, so to speak, there was a revolt and Mahmoud's cousin took control from his brother.'' He locked his hands and leaned on the rail. ''The Ottomans also have the delightful habit of murdering all the rival heirs whenever a new sultan takes charge—which is expedient, but damned messy, and plays hell with your afterlife. The new fellow had a bit too much sensibility to stomach it, y'see; he just locked Mahmoud and his brother together in The Cage.'' Sheridan looked toward her. ''And there lies a lesson in politics for you, Princess,'' he said bluntly, ''because somebody came along and decided to put the proper sultan back in his place. The softhearted upstart got butchered . . . but not before he'd seen his mistake—too late—and sent his minions to The Cage to strangle Mahmoud and his brother. They got his brother, but Mahmoud escaped.''

She was watching him, her eyes wide and expressionless. ''Exactly what was your part in this?''

He rubbed his fist on the marble rail. ''Not all that much. I was pretty young—I used to lurk about and figure out ways to spy around—mostly in the hareem. Anyway,

I saw them coming with the bowstring. They went after Mahmoud's brother first—there was a lot of confusion—fighting, which I made sure to stay out of—a slave threw a pan of burning charcoal in the way—and I knew how to get out, and I took him. Over the roofs."

"Ah," she said.

They both gazed out at the water. Somewhere below, a nightingale called in the trees.

"How old were you?" she asked.

"God knows. Eighteen. Maybe nineteen."

"Why," she said in a careful, quiet voice, "were you in the palace at all?"

He'd understood it would come to this, of course. He took a deep breath. "Well, I was a slave, you know. I couldn't leave." He didn't look at her.

"I thought—"

"Yes, very true. I made Mustafa lie. I don't like it spread about. Would you?"

"No," she said in a small voice. "I suppose not."

He pointed out a pretty yacht working up into the wind to anchor in the bay across from their palace, hoping she would drop the matter there. His head was throbbing. It made his ears ring like the sound of guns.

"It's beautiful," she agreed, and then went right back to worry the issue. "But it wasn't your fault—being a slave. And you saved the Sultan."

"Who gives a damn? Can we go on to some other stirring chapter in my heroic life?"

She looked pointedly at the *teskeri,* which he wore openly all the time now. "The Sultan obviously thought much of it."

"He was young, too. And lonely. Looking for friends. Willing and able to buy 'em."

"He bought you for his friend?"

Sheridan shifted restlessly. "More or less."

"Then—when you helped rescue him, did he reward you with your freedom?"

"The gratitude of sultans," he mused with a touch of scorn. "They don't offer you three wishes and a genie anymore. He wanted me there. He liked me. He had all kinds of reasons to keep me, and none to let me go."

"How did you get away?"

"I escaped. That was how I knew the way over the roofs—I'd been intending to use it. But after I brought Mahmoud over that route, I had to find another. It took me a year."

"How did you finally get out?"

He studied her eager face, and imagined the story going in impetuous innocence to the Greek girl and from there all over Stamboul. "I don't think I'll tell you that."

She looked offended. "Why not?"

"I might need to use it."

"An escape route? Now?"

He shrugged.

"But surely this Mahmoud can't call you his slave anymore! You're as free as I am!"

He looked at her meaningfully. Her eyes widened in horror.

"I don't believe it," she said. "There's a British ambassador. He wouldn't let that happen."

He nodded, unwilling to argue the point. There was no use in frightening her beyond this gentle warning. She plucked a flower from a pot of carnations and sniffed it, then absently began to bruise it between her fingers.

"How were you taken as a slave in the first place?" she asked.

He'd hoped he'd exhausted her curiosity on the subject. He dropped his head, staring down at his arms on the rail. He rubbed his aching eyes and thought of not answering at all.

"Were you captured? Were there others taken off your ship?"

"No," he muttered.

"Just you?"

Sheridan chewed his lip. "There was a storm," he said suddenly. "There was a storm, and our captain was a fool, and she went on the rocks at Imroz. Lost with all hands." He paused. He felt her look up, felt her gaze on him. "Except me."

She reached out and took his hand. She squeezed it.

He closed his eyes. The safe dullness was slipping. It seemed as if something inside him was tearing apart: a slow wound, old pain: grief and guilt and the way his head kept pounding, noise and noise and noise. "I should have died," he whispered. "I shouldn't have left them."

She touched his arm. With gentle insistence, she put her hand to his cheek and made him look at her. "I need you here." She stared up into his eyes, steady and unblinking. "I'm *glad* you're here."

"You don't understand," he said. "They were mates. My crew."

"I don't care." She gripped his hands. "Is that selfish? Is that so wrong of me? I don't care, Sheridan. I didn't know those men—I know you. I love you."

He let her hold him: his anchor to earth and life. Her eyes caught the green of the landscape, so earnest—like the nightingale in the tree, like all the small, ordinary, beautiful creatures of the world. There was peace in her, and part of him wanted it, cried out for it, but he was afraid to reach past the barrier. If he opened himself to that, other things would come for him.

He had to contain that part of himself, cram it down and keep it hidden. He could not risk letting it out, not for any hope, not for joy or forgiveness or love.

He drew his hands deliberately from hers.

She pressed her lips together and bent her head. Without another word, she turned in her embroidered slippers and walked back into the room, the bells a faint music fading with her into shadow.

Olympia had been wakened at dawn, bathed and perfumed and dressed until she felt like an oversized doll painted for presentation. While she'd been at her endless toilette, a whole fleet of battleships had come into the little bay: they lay at anchor in silent rows across the narrow water, the yards manned. Below, in the palace garden by the shore, tents had blossomed in gay colors and troops in European and Turkish dress milled with scurrying servants.

Sheridan was splendid—not in native dress, but in the glittering blue-and-white uniform of the British navy they'd provided him. His gold epaulettes sparkled as the two of them were escorted beneath the trees to the tents in the garden. They were received, coolly, by one of the Sultan's ministers. This caimacan lifted a hand and motioned toward a little barrel-shaped velvet stool at his feet.

Sheridan ignored that silent assumption of authority and led her up to the divan as he had before, though this time he left out the insult of wiping his boots on it. No one seemed to take notice. The stool was quietly removed, along with a screen which Olympia had a feeling she'd been expected to hide behind.

The most extravagant exchange of compliments between attendants followed, their translation whispered in Olympia's ear by the Greek girl, who kept her head strictly bowed before the Sultan's minister. After Olympia had heard herself described as the most royal Princess of Oriens and all Christendom, beloved from China to India to the Falkland Islands, daughter of the Conquerers of France, sister of the Kings of England and cousin of all the Lords of Europe; heard Sheridan called the Savior of the Sultan, Lord of His Oceans, Scorner of His Enemies, Bearer of His Standard across the vast face of the Earth, Prophet of Allah, Friend of the Poor and Abuser of Traitors; then been made to understand that they were welcome, their coming was blessed by Allah, the list of their honors covered the ends of the earth, her beauty outshone the moon and stars and planets, Sheridan's glorious deeds would be known unto the tenth generation and it was hoped they would both live a thousand years—they were allowed to retire and eat.

The thirty-two different platters had scarcely been removed when the ships' guns boomed out their salute. A great cheer rose from the mob that had gathered outside the garden walls. Sheridan and Olympia stood at their tent as the salute boomed again, echoing around the bay, and from behind the nearest headland came the Sultan's gilded caique, rowed by silver oars that flashed in the sun.

From a tent by the water steps, a white Arabian horse

was led forth: the loveliest mount she'd ever seen, its back covered with trappings of gold and jewels. The moment the Sultan's boat touched the shore, the view was blocked by rows of pages with tall, peacock-plume headdresses.

"It is to protect him from the Evil Eye," the Greek girl whispered to Olympia as they watched the Sultan proceed in slow, concealed state on the splendid Arabian. The troops salaamed and the crowd let out a tremendous cheer.

She'd been warned that he would repose for a lengthy period of time before they were summoned, but there was no such wait. Just a few moments after he'd disappeared into the largest tent, a black eunuch hurried to escort them to the royal presence. Someone threw a transparent scarf over Olympia's head, another precaution against the Evil Eye—*hers!*—and then they were inside for their audience with Mahmoud, the Sultan of All the World.

In the midst of the pomp, Mahmoud was a simple figure. He wore only a western-style military cloak and breeches with spurred Wellington boots. There was a single diamond in his blue fez. He stood before the cushioned throne, not tall, not imposing, not much older than Sheridan: alone except for two armed attendants.

For a moment after they entered, he stared at them, his dark eyes and fine, pale features intent. His eyebrows and hair seemed very black. Olympia was wondering if she should bow or kneel or just stand silently when suddenly he gave a low cry and walked rapidly forward.

He fell on Sheridan with a hard embrace, gripping his shoulders and kissing his cheeks with an enthusiasm that amounted to violence. Then he stood back, still holding Sheridan's shoulders, and bared his white teeth in a grin as he bestowed a quick, fierce shake. Neither spoke. Mahmoud was weeping—the tears slid openly down his smooth cheeks and into the glossy, pointed beard.

"My friend," he said finally, in hoarse, heavily accented English.

Sheridan put his right hand over his heart and bowed. Mahmoud smiled. He turned and went back to the throne. As he sat, he nodded at his feet. This time, Sheridan took the plump, embroidered stool that waited there, lowering himself on it cross-legged, his ankles resting on the floor.

Olympia stood uneasily, feeling conspicuous. Mahmoud glanced at her, clapped his hands and spoke to one of the servants. She was led forward and seated on the carpet beside Sheridan. A moment later, the Greek girl knelt silently behind her. "I am to interpret everything that is said for you, madam," she whispered.

Olympia looked up at the Sultan to nod her thanks, and then realized he could not really see her through the veil. "Please tell him I'm much obliged," she said.

The Greek girl, her voice shaking, made a little speech. Mahmoud grinned, looking at Sheridan, and asked a question.

"He wonders if you belong to the Man of the Sea, madam," the interpreter whispered.

Sheridan answered affirmatively, to Olympia's bewilderment.

"May I see her?" Mahmoud's request came through the Greek girl.

It was only after Sheridan put his hand on her shoulder and lifted the scarf that she realized that he himself was apparently this Man of the Sea.

"A rose of dawn," Mahmoud was understood to say. "A pearl. Very beauteous, cheeks as blossoms, and hair as the rising sun. The Man of the Sea has always been a judge of the fair sex."

She felt her face burning.

"I am well inclined to your gift," was the next bland translation of the Sultan's words. "I will take great pleasure in her."

Olympia looked at the Greek girl with a start.

"With respect and sorrow," the girl translated as Sheridan answered in Turkish, "I cannot give her to you. We are married."

Mahmoud's amiable expression altered a little. He looked puzzled. "I was told that you brought me a gift."

There was a tension around Sheridan's mouth. "I come empty-handed," the girl translated him. "I own the air that I breathe, and nothing else."

There was a silence in the tent.

"You have not prospered since you left me."

"I have not."

Mahmoud smiled. "And you have come back. That is very well. I have work for you, and rewards in plenty."

Sheridan said nothing.

"Tell him," Olympia whispered to Sheridan, "that you're escorting me to Rome."

He didn't glance at her, nor did he say anything else to Mahmoud.

"I lost much of my navy in the conflict at Navarino," the girl interpreted as the Sultan continued. "It is the will of God—a perfect time for complete reform. I wish to take the opportunity to rebuild on the English model. You will tell me what is best, inspect my new ships—teach strategy and seamanship to my capitan pashas. I will make you Grand Admiral."

The matter-of-fact assumption that Sheridan would be staying made Olympia jump to her feet. "Tell the Sultan," she said, to the Greek girl this time, "that he's already the Lord High Admiral of the Navy of Oriens, and isn't available for the Sultan's service."

The girl looked horrified.

"Tell him," Olympia insisted.

In a barely audible voice, the girl spoke rapidly, ending the speech with a series of bows with her forehand to the floor.

"Did she tell him?" Olympia demanded of Sheridan.

He flashed a look sideways at her. "Yes," he muttered. "Now sit the devil down!"

She hesitated a moment and then lowered herself onto the rich rugs. But she kept her gaze leveled at Mahmoud. She wasn't the foremost Princess of Oriens, the Falkland Islands and Points In Between for nothing. She hoped she gave him the Evil Eye. "And tell him—" she began.

"Olympia," Sheridan murmured, without looking at her. "Do you see those guards?"

She glanced at the impassive guards who stood on either side of the divan. Their curved scimitars gleamed dully in the delicate blue light of the tent.

"If he raises his hand," Sheridan said in a soft, neutral voice, "all our heads will go out of here in silver bowls."

Olympia bit her lip. She glanced again at the silent guards. Then she lifted her chin and said to her interpreter, "Tell him that I don't wish to insult him, but I am a princess, and if he executes me, it will create an international incident."

The Greek girl fumbled out a squeak of translation.

Mahmoud tilted his head. A wry smile curled in the trimmed beard. He spoke.

"He says Madam reminds him of his mother," the girl whispered.

Olympia lifted her chin. "Thank you," she said clearly.

Mahmoud laughed even before he heard the translation. "The Man of the Sea has taken a lioness to wife."

"A sultana," Sheridan responded, which sent Mahmoud into a great howl of amusement.

"Yes, I know the like," he said. "Daughters and sisters I have in plenty. I will bestow another such upon you, and they can growl at one another and leave you to your pipe and God's peace."

Olympia stiffened, but Sheridan answered by gently skirting the topic. "You make me feel old, Mahmoud. Do you have grown daughters?"

"Beautiful daughters. You have none?"

"No. No children."

Mahmoud looked with vague disapproval at Olympia. She felt like announcing that it was certainly no fault of hers, but decided the subject was beneath her dignity to recognize.

Mahmoud sighed. "Life is fleeting. You should have children, my friend." He looked at Sheridan, his dark eyes wistful. "You would not be a beggar if you had stayed with me. Your life would not be barren of family and friends."

Sheridan said nothing again. Olympia reached up and took his hand. For a long, long moment he didn't react, and then his fist tightened firmly around hers. He spoke—paused, and spoke again.

"I have what God has seen fit to give me," came the

girl's whispered interpretation. "I am more fortunate than I deserve."

Mahmoud's dark eyes rested on them. "You are modest, but that is good; it is God's grace in you. I have recently been told of your deeds with the English." He tilted his head quizzically as the Greek girl quoted him to Olympia. "You were a favorite with me, always. I searched for you many years, do you know that? I sent out pursuit. But no one knew the name the English call you, and I had no word of the man who wore my crescent."

The girl sucked in a dismayed breath at Sheridan's answer, making Olympia listen anxiously to the quiet translation.

"With respect," the girl interpreted him, "I did not wish you to have word."

Mahmoud sat still, his hands on his knees. Only his eyes moved, flicking toward Sheridan and away and back again, almost shyly. "Do you remember the day I found you?" the girl translated his murmur. "The first day I ever dared venture outside the palace, I found you hiding from your owner and the dogs in the Street of Nafi. Do you remember how I felt compassion when I saw how you had been beaten, and put off my disguise, and ordered him to give you up to me?"

Sheridan bent his head in silent assent.

"And I do not forget," the girl whispered as Mahmoud spoke. "I do not forget how the crowd in the street gathered when they recognized their prince, and howled and pushed, and I was stupid with fear of them—and you were clever and calm and showed me the way to safety. That was the first time. Many times after that we went outside together in secret masquerade. Outside The Cage. And then when the upstart's dogs—may they burn for eternity—came for Selim and I, you showed me safety again. I have not forgotten. We are the same, you and I. We like to roam outside the walls."

"We are not the same," came Sheridan's answer. "Mahmoud—the walls belong to you."

The Sultan sat silent for a moment. Then he looked at Olympia and spoke suddenly.

"He asks—do you enjoy this palace at Beykoz?" the girl murmured to her.

"Oh, yes. It's magnificent," she said, relieved to go on to a neutral subject. "Truly superb."

His dark eyes slid to Sheridan, rested on him intently. "I will give it to you."

Sheridan's hand tightened almost imperceptibly on hers. Before he could answer, Mahmoud spoke again.

"The Grand Admiral of the Fleet must have a worthy residence. The Chief Eunuch will see that it is staffed properly, and a household purse dispensed with regularity. It is a post of many gifts, my friend. You will prosper. The capitan pashas will be diligent in pursuing their favor with you."

"You would do better to have them diligent in pursuit of the enemy's ships." The girl's murmured translation was serious, but Olympia caught the slight curl at the edge of Sheridan's mouth. "If it is a navy you desire."

Mahmoud gave his quick, white grin, unoffended. "That is your task."

Sheridan lifted his chin. He said something—soft and even.

The smile faded from the Sultan's face, and the Greek girl moistened her lips without translating. Olympia glanced toward her, and in a barely audible voice, she muttered breathlessly, "No, he says; no, it is not his task. Oh, madam—he says his loyalty is to you, madam."

Olympia glanced back, to find Mahmoud's eyes on her. He stroked his beard, the light flashing off three huge diamond rings. When he spoke, his voice was equally as soft as Sheridan's.

Olympia felt Sheridan go taut beside her. She had to pinch the trembling girl before she would interpret the Sultan's words. "The Sultan says—the Sultan says—" She ducked her head even farther down. " 'I hold her in my hand . . . therefore your loyalty is ultimately to me.' "

The whisper of the English words died away into silence. Mahmoud tilted his head with another low comment.

"Is that not true?" the girl mumbled, hastily interpreting his words.

Sheridan answered, his voice slow and inflexible.

"As long as you hold her safe . . . it is true," came the quivering translation. "For that long only."

Mahmoud stared at Sheridan, his lips pressed in a faint, peculiar expression, petulant and wistful. For a moment he looked more like a small, sad, thwarted boy than the Sultan of All the World. The Greek girl was shaking visibly now, the only indication that this somber man had the power to take their heads with just the lift of one diamond-studded finger.

Mahmoud raised his hands and clapped. The girl made a tiny moan and Olympia sucked in her breath. There was a rustle behind them at the door of the tent.

Sheridan rose. Olympia turned her head.

On the carpet behind them, each person held strictly at the right elbow by a eunuch, stood a small European delegation. It was composed of a tall, elegantly dressed blond man, two shorter male strangers, Captain Francis Fitzhugh . . . and Mrs. Julia Plumb.

Twenty-six

When Sheridan lay down, he was shaking inside. He stared into darkness, and all he could think was that they had taken her from him—and he'd let them: Julia and Fitzhugh and some beef-brained blond Prince of Somewhere; the British ambassador had been there, all the big guns, too much power, too much civilized muscle; there hadn't been a chance—not a chance, if Mahmoud wouldn't stop them. And he hadn't.

Now Sheridan was trapped, made by the wave of a hand into a Grand Admiral and a slave, because every one of Mahmoud's ministers, right up to the Grand Vizier, was the Sultan's slave in Ottoman eyes. They ran the country, but they were slaves, their lives circumscribed by the whims of absolute sovereignty. Not that it had ever been a whole devil of a lot different in the British navy. Here they just called a spade a spade.

His bloody big show of defiance with Mahmoud had got him nowhere. Sheridan hardly knew what he'd meant by it anyway. It was all so pointless—why hadn't he known they would be waiting, Julia and the ambassador, with a writ for Sheridan's arrest and their own schemes for his princess? Why hadn't he been planning for it, all those drifting days in the desert and mountains? Where the hell had he been?

He got up from the rich pile of bedding and paced out onto the terrace. The Bosporus gleamed faintly under the starlight, the lights of fishermen scattered like more stars on the surface.

Now they were going to marry her off to that great blond hulk, that was what Julia had announced. Prince of God-Knew-Where; the politics were all different; Sheridan was no longer the topping wonderful choice he'd appeared to be a year ago—this other chap was going to bring law and order to the entire European continent if only they could get him leg-shackled to Princess Olympia, and thank God there'd never been a Christian ceremony with Sheridan, how fortunate, no need to treat him to a knife between the ribs in order to free her up after all.

And Fitzhugh—Fitzhugh had called him out five times already, poor, hysterical bastard. The upright captain wasn't having any of Olympia herself now that he knew the truth, of course, but he was panting to avenge her honor. He seemed to have got it all mixed up with patriotism and public spirit and a whole barrel of other unrelated rot, carrying on like bejesus until Mahmoud got tired of it and had him removed.

Sheridan ran his palms down his face and sighed. It had been one deuce of a day.

But it all had a certain inevitability. He found balance in it. He stood there in the darkness, furious and miserable and alone—and strangely comfortable with himself. Things were just as they'd always been before his princess had come along: he was solitary, expecting nothing, giving nothing, no demands and no dreams and no contact. Just survive—one day at a time.

Angry as he was, at Julia and Mahmoud and the rest of those diplomatic snakes, he was in complete control. There was no chance he'd wake up and find he'd started some lunatic one-man battle with armed guards. Not now. Something had happened to him when he'd seen them whisk his princess away so fast that she hardly even had a chance to change expression before she was gone. Something had fallen back into place.

In that instant, he'd been brutally compelled to face life again as it really was and see his proper place in it. He despised himself for being a pawn, but it was a familiar spite. It fitted like a well-worn shoe.

He could quit trying, because there was no way he'd win. They were taking her away from him, and he could relinquish this haunting fantasy of love at last.

He was meant to be alone; he understood that now. It felt hard and real and right. It was bitter, yes, but solitude was an old, old friend. He was not meant to be close to another human being; that was the source of this mess inside him. She was the source. He'd been weak and a fool: wanting, wanting . . . *believing* in that dream, but it just made his feelings into mayhem, believing things like that.

He should have known better. But their time on the island had made him forget that some doors were shut and locked for damned good reasons. Where there were unicorns, there were tigers, too. He couldn't open to one without letting out the other.

He felt better, safer, now that he'd sealed it all away. He was himself again. In control. His future didn't look so bad. Mahmoud wanted a Grand Admiral—Sheridan was willing to do that. He could live like a king, keep a hareem, smoke a *narguile* and spend his days plotting for honors and riches and licking the Sultan's slippers.

Right in Sherry's line.

He stared into the shadows of the trees. The turmoil inside him was gone. He wasn't exactly at peace, but he was empty, at any rate. Better to be a desert than a maelstrom.

He thought of Olympia, of her round breasts beneath the gauzy fabric. It occurred to him suddenly that she would be gone tomorrow. They'd take her from this country palace down to Stamboul and put her and her new fiancé on a ship for the royal wedding in Upper Burgomeisterstein or wherever. Sheridan's one regret was that he'd gone through all that frustration to save her maidenhead just for some Teutonic bastard who walked around with his medal-laden chest stuck out like an oversexed rooster.

For a few moments, he brooded on that injustice. Behind him, the palace was silent and dark, just the constant whisper of fountains and the wind in the trees. Slowly, a hard, intent smile curved his lips. He turned back to the room. Armed with a slipper lamp and a satin robe trimmed with sable pulled on over his breeches, he began a midnight prowl of his new home.

Olympia dreamed she was running. The Sultan's eunuchs chased her with whips and scimitars, and she kept trying to find Sheridan, but she couldn't, not in all the halls and courtyards and gardens. Then as she despaired, he was there, whispering her name in the darkness, his arms pulling her close, hiding and protecting her . . .

She clung to him. It was his kiss that brought her to full awareness: deep and demanding; she opened to him with a cry of gladness as she realized he was really there.

She tried to say his name, but he pressed her back against the cushions. Dim lamplight touched the side of his face. "Don't talk." His breath was a heavy warmth at her throat. "Do you want me?"

"Are we—"

He stopped her question of escape with another kiss. There was something different about him, something purposeful. Instead of whispering a plan of evasion for spiriting them both to safety and freedom, he fingered the pearl buttons that held her caftan. They sprawled open, and he cupped her naked breast. His body moved over hers.

She felt his urgency. He was rough, spreading the silk away from her with primitive moves, capturing her hands and pinning them together above her head. The golden lamplight caught the hot intent in his face.

"Sheridan?" she whispered in confusion.

"Love me," he muttered, pressing a line of swift kisses down the side of her face to her lips. "Open for me."

Then he forced her to it without waiting, made her accept his tongue seeking deep in the kiss. He wore nothing; everywhere he'd bared her, his skin touched hers. His weight spread her legs, a burning warmth against her thighs.

Olympia whimpered a little under the aggressive power of his body. His maleness pressed her, sparking the eternal urge to arch upward into the demand even as he hurt her with his ruthless hold. Then shock and animal excitement flowed through her. She understood at last what he wanted: the stiff swell of his body pushed hard, seeking entry.

Of course—of course! She made a wordless sound of passionate accord. She'd wanted him this way forever; now she'd be his, utterly; protected from this crazy new marriage to a stranger that they'd planned for her. The humiliation of the doctor's examination she'd suffered that afternoon evaporated under Sheridan's possessive touch.

"Oh, yes," she whispered, and unfolded like a flower. "Oh, please . . ."

He responded, thrusting strongly into her warm invitation. She tilted her head back and drew a sharp breath, surrendering to his conquest, reveling in the pressing burn of his body forcing hers. It hurt a little, yes—but it felt so glorious. This prince would never want her now—she'd seen enough of his icy blond pride to know that. Sheridan's kiss was like a flame against her throat, his hands a brand around her wrists.

Soft moans escaped her. His invasion filled her. Her body tightened and moved beneath his. He seemed to fill up the whole world, the sounds in his throat filled her ears, the glistening curve of his neck and shoulder filled her sight—he was everything, every inch of her belonged to him, joined with him.

She buried her face in his shoulder as he thrust again and again, taking full possession of her in power and mindless passion. Something in her responded as it had not before: before, when he had always been in control; before, when he had put her pleasure ahead of his own, never forgetting himself, never losing himself to the ecstasy that drove them now—satin and silken rug at her back, his breath in her ear, heavy with the low sob of fervor as he pressed deep within her and held there. Her body was full of him, molten with him, rising beyond thought into pure sensation. It was so different, so vivid—this was real, and all that had gone before a dream.

She touched him, slid her hands downward and caressed him in places she had not dared. She felt his shuddering response; he groaned and whimpered and crushed her against him—and her soul laughed with joy at the freedom to give him that pleasure: so deep, so full and luxurious to feel him inside her, his body trembling as he took her, thrusting with potency instead of control.

Her own climax washed through her again and again, an endless miracle, waves and waves of singing consummation until she felt him burst within her and his body moved hard against hers in that explosive tremor that she loved. It was solace; it comforted her to feel his arms go taut around her and hear his breath rush in her ear. It felt good to taste the salt of desire and satisfaction on his skin.

As he relaxed heavily, she held him in a quivering grip. She ached everywhere they touched; she burned where his hard intrusion still pinned her. She thought of his body and seed within her . . . part of her. She was ruined. Ravished. Violated.

At last.

She closed her eyes and laughed.

For a long time, Sheridan was nowhere. Just breathing. Breathing was effort enough; it seemed his chest could not hold sufficient air to allow his brain to think or his body to move. So he simply let himself lie lost and euphoric, unconcerned about where he was or why.

Slowly, small realities intruded on his consciousness. His body was hot, but cool night air fanned across his skin. A light feather-touch moved up and down his back and shoulder. There was something wet beneath his cheek.

The sensations crystallized into a thought. *Princess.* He mumbled the word, turning his head. With an effort, he lifted himself onto his elbows and looked down at her.

So beautiful. So utterly beautiful. He put his hands on either side of her face and felt the wetness again.

"You're crying," he muttered.

She looked up at him in the lamplight. He wondered if there was another green in the world like the green of her eyes.

"It hurt a little," she whispered. Then she bit her lip and smiled, and fresh tears welled up and made silver swim with the green.

"Jesus," he said as comprehension dawned.

She shook her head vigorously. "It doesn't matter."

"I didn't realize; I never meant—"

"I know." She lifted her hand and tugged at his hair. "I know. Don't say you're sorry. Please."

He frowned down at her. "I am."

"Well, I'm not. Not at all. I'm glad, Sheridan." She pulled him down and kissed him, the softness of her lips mingling with the taste of tears. "I'm so glad."

He brushed away the moisture with his thumb, carefully finding each wet track. By the time he'd tenderly wiped them away, another drop was sliding down her temple. Something very raw and painful moved in his chest.

He shifted, lifting himself off her. His body was still firm; he saw her features tighten as he withdrew, though she bit her lip and smiled quickly to cover it. He looked down.

The satin robe beneath her showed a small, dark stain. He closed his eyes. It made him feel weak inside, as if he held something delicate and precious in hands that would be too clumsy to preserve it.

He concentrated on watching her as she levered herself into a sitting position with a series of winces. The smooth curve of her buttocks reflected pearly light. Her breasts bobbled a little as she moved, awakening instant and desperate heat in him. He hated himself, thinking of that again. Already. She sat with her legs drawn up.

"There," she said, looking down matter-of-factly. "I've bled a little. That should help." She smiled at him. "I love you."

He swallowed. He was past speaking, simply past it. He wanted to pull her into his arms and hold her against his heart, hold her safe from everything that could hurt her—knowing in the same instant that he was going to hurt her, that he contained in himself the cruelest weapon to wound her of all.

She hugged her legs and rested her cheek on her bare

knees, gazing at him. He looked down, unable to cope with the particular view she presented—not in his current precarious state.

"I can't wait to break the news to Julia," she said. "And that beastly Prince Harold. Do you know, on his orders they actually had a doctor examine me yesterday to see if I was *pure?* I kicked him." Her lower lip set in aggression that looked more like a pout. "Where it hurts, I hope."

Sheridan managed a faint smile. "Vicious mouse."

Her mouth flattened. "They examined me anyway. But this will change everything." She reached over and lifted his hand. Her lips warmed the back of his palm. "Thank you. Thank you."

He felt as if he were going to fall into a hundred crazy pieces. "Don't be a fool, Princess." He drew his hand away.

"I'm not. This will work. It's perfect. You should have seen the look of relief on Prince Harold's face when they reported I was still a virgin. His Royal Snottiness won't take soiled goods."

Sheridan scowled. "You're not 'soiled goods,' damn it. Don't talk rubbish like that."

"Yes, I am." She smiled at him impishly and patted the stained satin. "I can prove it."

He caught her arm and gripped it hard. "Princess—don't tell anyone about this. And don't tell Prince Harold anything. Not even after your wedding."

"What wedding? I thought that was the point, to get out of the wedding. It has to be something drastic like this, Sheridan. Plain escape isn't good enough. They have my grandfather's permission and everything. You know they can marry me off without me even being there!"

He was back to himself now, finding cold sanity in her talk of the usual manipulations by greater powers. She still believed in him, and saw this ravishment as a gallant plan to rescue her instead of what it was—just a last, selfish indulgence in the pleasure of her body and a thumbing of his nose at the victors. But everything had its price, and the price of this time together was facing her loving innocence and betraying it one final time.

"What do you think you're going to do, then," he asked with deliberate indifference, "if you manage to escape this marriage they've planned?"

She looked up at him quizzically.

Before she had time to think about it, he added, "Now that you're 'soiled goods,' as you put it."

She tilted her head, naked and luscious. "Well—I thought—perhaps . . . that you would take me to Rome. Or to Oriens."

"Why the devil would I want to do that?"

He said it carelessly, and watched the cut go deep. Her eyes widened a little, but she did not move. After a moment, she said quietly, "You don't?"

"Mahmoud's given me a palace and a rich post. Servants. Women. Power. What do you have to offer?"

She stared at him silently.

"A revolution?" he asked dryly. "More travel? What little's left of your bloody jewels?" He let his eyes slide along the length of her curled body. "Or maybe you thought I couldn't live without the pleasure of soiled goods?"

He saw the glaze of pain in her eyes. He wished she would get angry. There was something in his throat—but he forced his voice past it. Harshly, he said, "You're nothing, Princess—you couldn't run a revolution even if you got yourself to Oriens somehow. Look at the mess you made of a paltry little mutiny. They'll never let it happen anyway—the British or Julia or your uncle. They're far too smart. Out of your league entirely. You won't get away from them and you can't stay here; I don't want you. I have other things on my mind."

She'd begun to tremble, a faint shudder that ran the length of her naked body.

"You've got nowhere to go but where they tell you," he said. "Be a good girl. Be clever instead of stupid for once, and go."

Her lips parted a little. The glaze had gone to vacancy, as if she stared at him and saw nothing. He felt like nothing. Worse than nothing. But his mouth somehow kept working, saying the necessary words.

"I'm leaving now. I won't see you again. You're leaving for Stamboul tomorrow, but there's a fleet inspection ordered and I shan't have time to say goodbye." He gathered up the fur-trimmed robe and stood, pulling it on. She didn't look at him.

He gazed at her, long and desperately. Her eyelashes, her shower of hair, her hands and waist and feet.

Then he picked up the lamp and turned, striding for safety. He locked the wooden door behind him. The glow lit blue-and-red tiles and intricate arches in a fluttering globe around him as he walked back to his apartments—back to security, back to isolation, back to where nothing touched him.

He doused the lamp and sat cross-legged, staring into blackness. Inside him was a heaviness. It seemed unbearable. He thought he was going to cry. He was surely going to cry now.

But he looked into the empty dark and didn't.

In the days after she was gone, he felt the last of his humanity slipping. Sultan Mahmoud gave orders for a purge, in preparation for the new, updated navy. The first time Sheridan went out to the flagship and ordered the trumped-up accusations read, then watched a hapless capitan pasha marched below and saw the head come up on a tray a few short minutes later, he had to make a conscious effort to busy his hands with writing a report, because they had a slight tendency to tremble.

The second time he smoked a chibouk, and his hands didn't shake. The third, he shared the pipe and a careless joke with the new captain as the loser's head was presented to them before being sent on to the Sultan's palace as proof of the deed.

That was the way the Osmanlis did things—cold-bloodedly and efficiently. It backfired on them in the occasional revolt, but for the most part it had held an empire together for five hundred years.

The trick was to keep one's own head off that platter.

He had, besides the admiralty, the governorship of four towns in Anatolia. Mustafa was in his element after leaving Fitzhugh's party, strutting up and down the corridors of the waterside palace, brandishing a hippopotamus-hide whip, inspiring respect and striking terror in the hearts of every slave and supplicant he could find. He complied enthusiastically with Sheridan's order to fill the hareem, presenting a selection of veiled females daily for perusal. When Sheridan returned from assisting at the Sultan's divan, he had the ritual of inspection to go through: he commanded the veil removed, the hair taken down, the cheeks wetted and rubbed to reveal painted artifice.

He felt very strange, as if he were watching himself from outside. He chose the dark ones, with black, lustrous hair and slender limbs. One time, with a sly, sanguine air, Mustafa presented a plump Russian girl, blond and green-eyed, taken from an Afghan trader who claimed to have bought her from a Chinese magician at Kabul. She spoke French with the manners of a gentle, frightened aristocrat, and when Sheridan ordered her sent on to the Russian consulate, she threw herself at his feet and wept. He couldn't tell if she was joyous or terrified, and he didn't care. He only wanted her away from him.

He had Mustafa caned with his own whip for that trick, and for two weeks the little servant came crawling into his master's presence on hands and knees. That was the extent of Mustafa's quailing; he was too full of his status and his own new riches as the savior of the Sultan's favorite Englishman to be chastised for long.

Sheridan never visited his hareem. He sat on his palace terrace overlooking the water at sunset, smoking hashish and thinking about going. Sometimes, on his orders, Mustafa had a graceful group brought out for examination, and Sheridan selected one to be prepared for his visit. But he never went.

He just watched himself with a mild curiosity, functioning coolly, flattering the Sultan with perfect subtlety, forming alliances and identifying enemies, bestowing gifts in the right places, never tasting food until his servant had tasted it first, consolidating wealth and power and feeling the crack in his reality widen into a rift.

It was all right. It was strange, but it was detached and undemanding.

He lost none of his survival instincts. He honed them. The impersonal way he felt about himself made it easy; no distractions, no emotions or desires interfered with his perception. So he knew instantly when he left his audience chamber one afternoon and someone followed him.

It was Mustafa's duty to prevent that kind of thing. The audiences were full of petitioners who'd been carefully sorted and screened as to the merits of their pleas and the depth of their purses. It wasn't cheap, buying a captaincy in Mahmoud's new navy. Sheridan's authority as Grand Admiral would have plummeted if it had been. But he insisted on a few elements of seamanship and a commitment to an arduous course of study to make up the deficiencies, and so he gave even the richest ones a brutal interview session.

A few proud sons of pashas he turned down, in spite of their generous offerings, and he thought this shadow in the empty corridor might be in the service of one of those who held a grudge. He made no change of pace, but walked through the doors his guards held open and wondered idly how this chap intended to get into his private apartments.

The doors shut behind him. A Negro servant rose from the corner. Sheridan dismissed him with a wave as usual and then looked around the silent room. He pushed back the latticed screens himself, stepped out onto the terrace and waited.

A full quarter hour passed. Then, through the lattice, he saw a movement beyond the archway that led directly from his rooms to the hareem. He raised his eyebrows. This was brazen indeed—to invade his women's quarters for access; a true leap of ingenuity for a Muhammadan mind. He wandered deliberately back inside, allowing his back to face invitingly toward the arch.

The bait was taken. He heard the faint hiss of silk behind him, ducked and came up with his dagger ready and his boot hooked in the intruder's robed legs. The figure went down with a soft curse, and Sheridan registered two things as he flung himself on top of his attacker: the curse was in English, and the enemy passed up an instant when Sheridan's guard was open in order to protect his own throat.

The effort failed. Sheridan held the dagger at the man's windpipe, a rush of speculation in his brain. *Not an assassin, not a Turk—who, then? What?* But he stayed quiet, his weapon ready, staring down into the man's dark eyes.

"I'm a friend," the intruder whispered hoarsely in English. "I have a message."

For a fleeting, shattering moment, Sheridan thought of Olympia. The dagger pressed into the man's skin.

"Wait—wait!" The frantic petition was no louder than before. "Hear me out, for God's sake! You sent a letter—Claude Nicolas—I've brought word from him."

Sheridan relaxed with an explosive breath. "You crimson idiot. Is that all?" He lowered the knife and rolled upright. "You might have brought it to an audience and waited in line like the rest of 'em. It's a damned year after the fact anyway."

The man looked sullen. He sat up on his elbows, glancing carefully at the dagger still resting in Sheridan's hand. He had dark, Italian eyes and olive skin that would allow him to pass easily as a Turk. "I've been trying to get by that bloody little eunuch of yours, but he wasn't having any of it. He wants you here."

Sheridan looked at him. "And you want me somewhere else?"

"Briefly."

Sheridan lifted his eyebrows in question.

"Briefly," the man repeated. "Then come back here." He waved his hand at the room around them. "Enjoy all this in perfect peace. Claude Nicolas can remove a great nuisance for you if you do him this one small favor."

"I can remove my own nuisances." Sheridan turned the knife lazily in his hand. "If and when I find it necessary."

"Are you sure?"

Sheridan ignored the pointed question. He shook his

head with a dry smile. "Just how far behind the time is old Claude Nick, anyway? I can't do any favors for him, even if I wished. He doesn't think I've still got control of the princess, surely?"

"No. He's got control of her. This marriage the British have planned, to Harold of Braunfels—he's going along with that because the wedding's to be in Oriens. As soon as she crosses the border, she's in his hands."

The mild amusement Sheridan had been feeling sharpened into something else suddenly. He ran his thumb across the knife blade and drew blood. He stared down at the red drop, concentrating on the sting. After a moment, he said, "Well—what else does he want, then?"

"To stop the wedding itself. To be rid of her once and for good. She's become a rallying point for all the rebel factions—they'll fall apart in squabbling once she's been neutralized."

Sheridan touched his finger, drew a smear of blood down his thumb and across his palm. "What does he want from me?"

"Nothing dangerous. Only come to the wedding. Stand up and refuse to allow the ceremony to go forth. Announce that she's been living with you for a year and has a bastard planted in her belly."

Sheridan looked up. "Oh, is that all?" he asked mockingly.

The man frowned. He sat up, and as the light fell on his face, Sheridan saw that he was younger than he'd seemed at first. "Well, it's damned distasteful, I know. But it spares her life. The people won't have her once she's discredited like that, and neither will Harold, so she can toddle off and lose herself. Nobody will care."

"Claude's a real altruist, ain't he? Heart of gold."

"Come along, Drake—you know the stakes. You must have, or you'd never have written that letter to him in the first place. You've managed to make yourself a nice little nest here now; you may think you don't need what he's got to give, but there's something you may have forgotten."

"Such as?"

The man looked sideways at Sheridan. "One of these nights, you'll be lyin' there on your back—bare naked and gloriously ruined, if you take my meaning—being fanned by all those ladies next door, and one of 'em will slip a yellow noose around your neck and strangle you before you can say billy-o. Because under all those veils, she won't be a lady a'tall."

Sheridan gazed at him, fascinated by this stupidity. "I take it you're talking about the *sthaga?* That's your notion of what they would do?"

"How do I know what they'd do? But they're professional killers, and they're after you, Drake—and Claude Nicolas has them on his leash. If you go to the wedding and do this little favor, he'll take care of 'em for you."

The room grew quiet. Sheridan pressed his forefinger against the cut on his thumb, making it sting with his own salt. "Why should I believe that?" he asked softly. "The *sthaga* don't answer to anyone."

"These do. Look." The man produced a primrose scarf from beneath his robe, held up an Indian rupee, blessed it in the *sthaga*'s secret language and looped it swiftly in a knot at the end of the scarf. "Is that proof enough? Where else would I have learned it but from his tame thugs? After they lost you in Madeira, they reckoned the next place you'd pop up was Oriens—seeing as you were so cozy with the princess and all. But Oriens isn't a very big place. They couldn't lurk around there for long before Claude Nicolas sniffed 'em out. Now he has 'em on a string—their sect's wiped out in India and they blame that on you. And he knows where you are. They don't." He tossed the scarf in Sheridan's lap. "*So far* they don't."

Sheridan lifted it. "You know how to kill someone with this?"

"Not I. I'm just a messenger."

Toying with the silk, Sheridan smiled at his companion. "I do."

The other shifted uneasily. "Well, no need to look at me that way. I'm trying to do you a service."

"For a price."

"Very small. Very easy. Risk-free. Just ask the Sultan

for leave to attend the wedding of a dear friend. Two months and you'll be back here getting yourself tickled in all the right places.'' He looked around the rich chamber. ''You're no fool, Drake—that's clear enough. I wouldn't have bothered to bring you this offer if I hadn't thought there was enough in it to be worth your while.''

''Your consideration is heartwarming.''

He shrugged and grinned. Sheridan saw a flash of the roguish charm that he knew would be this fellow's stock-in-trade. The visitor said, ''I reckon we don't think so differently. You've a pretty position here, and I'd really hate for you to turn up floating in the Bosporus one morning. I was hoping that when you got back, you'd remember me kindly.''

Sheridan held the dagger, one finger pressing it lightly at each end. He wasn't afraid of the *sthaga.* He felt a certain black fondness for them. There was appeal in the idea of sudden and silent death that came upon him out of the darkness. He leaned on his crossed legs.

''I see,'' he said.

''Good.'' The other man nodded amiably. He smiled. ''Besides, I've never liked the idea of that pretty little chit being shot in the back at her wedding by her own damned uncle's brutes. I try not to be squeamish, but that seems a bit too beastly to me.'' He rubbed his chin. ''I've only seen her once. She seemed like a nice tidbit, but I don't know—maybe she's a harpy or something. You'd know better than I.''

Sheridan kept his voice level. ''I thought he wanted to marry her himself.''

''Not anymore. She's too much of a handful—all this running off around the world with unwholesome chaps like you.'' Again that charming grin. ''And me. Perhaps I'll be waiting in the wings to comfort her when she gets booed off the stage, mmm? That a good notion?''

Sheridan turned the knife in his hands, over and over. ''Maybe,'' he said.

The other man waited a moment, and then he stood up. ''The date's set for a month from today, Drake. Will you do it?''

The dagger caught the afternoon sun, gleaming red on silver. Sheridan locked his hands around the handle, holding the blade pointed straight up. "Yes," he said, staring at the killing edge. "I'll do it."

Twenty-seven

In the very last row, in a cathedral that seemed half as large as Oriens itself, Sheridan sat in the seat next to the center aisle. He had a small pistol in his pocket and cold purpose in his soul. He might not walk out of this church alive—he doubted it—but his princess would.

The glittering congregation was subdued, their murmurs and rustlings overwhelmed by the uneasy grumble of the mammoth crowd outside. Sheridan hadn't counted on that—it appeared that every able-bodied citizen in the country was gathered in the streets. They were watching for their exiled princess, waiting for this wedding. They'd never seen her, but she'd become a symbol to them: her name consolidated feuding factions, her invisible presence stimulated conservative merchants to subversion, the romance of this wedding brought peasant women from their villages with garlands of flowers and laurel.

If Sheridan were to do what Claude Nicolas hoped, they'd tear him apart.

Behind him, stationed on either side of the door, he felt the presence of the two *sthaga*. Claude Nicolas had them rigged out in scarlet uniforms as part of an honor guard of Bengal lancers. Sheridan would have laughed at the idea, until he saw them. They looked at him and never moved, but he knew the faces—as they knew his.

They were Prince Claude Nicolas's reserve plan. He'd do nothing so clumsy as have Olympia shot in the church. Sheridan had been briefed on the details. If his public denouncement somehow didn't work, if the wedding went forth, he wasn't to be concerned that Claude Nicolas would go back on his promise. The *sthaga* would go with the coach as it headed for the honeymoon castle in the mountains. Neither Olympia nor her new husband would come back. The thugs knew how to conceal bodies. And Claude Nicolas knew how to dispose of thugs.

Sheridan stared at the gold braid on the cuffs of his dress uniform. The man was thorough, there was no denying that. He had everything anticipated, all the rational contingencies covered.

Except Sheridan wasn't rational, not by Claude Nicolas's sane standards. His life and the *sthaga* meant nothing. He wasn't going to stand up and speak out. The wedding ceremony was going to be celebrated. The music would fill the church and the party would pass him—first Olympia and her husband, then the bridesmaids, then the groomsmen, and then Prince Claude Nicolas would follow them down the aisle.

And Sheridan would kill him.

He had an escape plan, and Mustafa supposedly waiting with horses at the vestry door, but the crowd jamming the streets outside made an already unlikely prospect into mere futility.

He didn't care. He'd seen this end coming upon him for a long, long time.

If he could only make her safe from her enemies. Protect her, and through her, all the best things in the world, the good things, the simple, beautiful, guileless things. That was all he asked now. That was worth his life. He owed it to her, and to all the men who'd died when he hadn't.

Why them? he'd always asked; *why them and not me?*

He had an answer now. He wanted this to be the answer.

Olympia heard the organ begin, and the rising cheers from the crowd outside. Ladies-in-waiting fluttered around her, plucking here, arranging there, nervous fingers and high, giddy voices that pierced through the rumble and music. They'd all been smuggled into the church, one by one—to prevent a riot, her uncle said—and Olympia believed him.

She'd found Prince Claude Nicolas unexpectedly kind. He was tall and thin and gentle with her grandfather's querulous complaints. He wore spectacles, and peered around like a shy schoolboy at the ministers who attended the court. He'd spent many patient hours explaining the political situation in Oriens and never chided her for running away.

A year ago, she would have been astonished and relieved and taken him for what he seemed. Now she just listened, and watched, and drew her own conclusions.

There were lies everywhere—people who seemed made entirely of falsehoods. Julia smiled, Claude Nicolas smiled, Prince Harold and the British diplomats smiled; everyone was all joy except her irritable old grandfather, who looked at her sideways from underneath his brows and complained of his digestion. He was the only one she trusted.

Olympia herself was a lie, dressed in a maiden's wedding white, and they all knew it. She'd told them, but they pretended not to hear. This marriage would take place; nothing could be allowed to stop it. Prince Harold would swallow his pride and accept what had belonged to another man, or the country would explode. And still he smiled, but in his eyes she saw that he would make her pay.

She held the bouquet over her stomach, pressing her fingers to the sick distress that hovered there. It was only nerves—she'd prayed and prayed it would be more, that she carried part of Sheridan with her, but two months had passed, and the hope grew dim as the signs failed her.

It was hard to think of him. She wanted to, and didn't. In a queer way, she felt he was still with her—that it had been some stranger who'd said those things and left that night, and she would turn and find him here, watching over her with silent tenderness.

To think so gave her courage. She remembered the cliff on the island, the way he'd only looked at her, not tried to encourage or bully or cajole her into going down. He'd simply expected her to do what she had to, and believe that he would not let her fall.

She knew what she must do now. The tide had carried her far enough. She made her shaky limbs obey her and walked with her bridesmaids to the vestibule of the cathedral, took her waiting uncle's arm and faced the huge, arched doors as they opened to a cascade of triumphal notes.

The congregation filled the church in a blur of color—aristocrats, royalists—her uncle's friends and supporters. They all rose as Olympia and Claude Nicolas passed amid the deafening music and noise from outside. She looked from side to side, but the mass of faces seemed to dim before her eyes; everything focused into the magnificent sweep of stained glass and stone, upward and upward above the tiny figures at the altar to the glorious wheel of color in the rose window, where dyed sunlight streamed through shadow to hurt her eyes.

She was still gazing at it when she felt Claude Nicolas release her arm. She focused again, and found the altar in front of her and Prince Harold at her side. The great organ fell silent, and so did the crowd outside.

The Protestant ceremony was in French, but she barely heard it. She was waiting for the moment. She'd planned this for weeks: they had her trapped from all sides, they could marry her off by proxy if she managed to run away, but no one could stop the public announcement she was about to make.

The church was quiet, but the sound of her heart filled her ears. Through it, she saw rather than heard Prince Harold's lips move in his vows. Like a faint whistle through a loud wind, the clergyman's voice came to her, asking if she, Olympia Francesca Marie Antonia Elizabeth, took this man . . .

"*No!*" She raised her voice. "I will not!" Then she realized that in her excitement she'd spoken English. She tore her hand from Prince Harold's and faced the crowd. "*Non! Nein—Ich will es nicht!*" she exclaimed in French and German and then in Italian, too, covering all the languages of her people. She gathered her dress and threw down the bouquet, tossed the huge train back as she started down the stairs, still making the statement, louder and louder with every step, until she was proclaiming at the top of her voice into the stunned silence. "I'll lead my people if they want democracy," she cried, "and I won't marry to uphold a throne."

Let them try to conceal that vow, the way they'd covered up everything else. If the people of Oriens wanted revolution, if they wanted her, then she was here. Let it start now.

She heard movement behind her and began walking faster. In front of her, the elegant congregation stared, frozen, as her trembling voice echoed in the church and repeated her declaration all down the aisle.

Behind, the sound of footsteps on stone made her pick up her skirt in haste. People began to lean forward as she passed, turning toward her. Hands reached out to catch her. She could see her goal—the great doors to the vestibule. Her uncle's voice shouted something, close behind her, a sharp order that vibrated through the church. Next to the doors, the scarlet coats of lancers began to converge on her escape. She felt her lungs laboring with the weight of the train, and panic began to rise in her throat.

She wasn't going to make it. The lancers were going to stop her. The congregation in the pews was still not quite believing, catching at her but not holding, but the lancers—

"Princess." The familiar voice cut into the blur of fright. She did not stop; she could not tell if it was real; she tried to sweep the crowd through the growing frenzy, but there were so many people—so many—*there*—one man standing, stepping out to catch her arm, not to hold her but to pull her with him another way, a figure of blue and gold shimmering so that she could not see his face . . . but she heard his voice above the others, steady and beloved, felt his white-gloved hand grip her arm with familiar strength, and she went with him—in blind panic and faith while everything around seemed to erupt and collapse in on her in a blaze of noise and light.

They burst out of the vestry door on the side of the

cathedral. Sheridan saw Mustafa on one of the horses, riding it, trailing the other like a boat on a sea of humanity. The crowd shrieked as they recognized their princess—a sound that blossomed into a roar through the narrow street. Her train caught in the door; Sheridan shoved it closed in their pursuers' faces and pushed her down the steps. He saw the fabric rip, though he couldn't hear the sound above the thunder of the crowd.

The mob surged toward them. The door exploded open behind. *Sthaga* lancers charged out, swords unsheathed. Sheridan tried to hold onto Olympia, but the crowd was pulling at her, dragging her down among them. She clutched at him; he saw her mouth open in a scream he couldn't hear. Something struck heavily on his arm, a sting and then numbness, and there was blood on a lancer's sword before the crowd closed them off, roaring with fury.

Someone went down next to him in the push. He felt his fingers slipping from Olympia's arm and shouted in panic and rage. He could barely see her, white amid the swirl and press of faces and arms just ahead. Fear drove him through; they would kill her—he caught at the flash of white and lost it, and then suddenly she was above him, swept on up the shoulders of the howling mob.

Sheridan plunged forward. He could see Mustafa working for them, striking with his whip to clear a path, and somehow the crowd was helping, pushing Olympia and the horses together—while behind, at the cathedral door, everything was struggling chaos. Hands rose above the mass, shoving her onto the horse, and she clung, reaching back toward him, her face white and frightened. She was crying something—his name, he thought, but he couldn't reach her. The crowd surged backward, sucking him like a wave as the tumult rose to a new shrill. He saw her look up, beyond him, toward the door, and amid the turmoil her eyes seemed to fix on the scene—her lips parted and something terrible came into her expression. He turned, trying to see what she saw, but at his level there was only the uncontrolled crush and shove of people.

He turned again, and she was farther away, the crowd and Mustafa carrying her along the street. Her face appalled him—she'd seen something; he knew that ghastly look and what it took to bring it. He lunged forward, thrusting with his shoulders and knees and wounded arm, using all his strength and balance to keep upright and moving in the surging crowd.

He had to stay with her. She would need him. When the shock evaporated and the specter of whatever she'd witnessed was still there, she'd need someone by her who knew that kind of nightmare.

"I don't want it!" Olympia's voice was sharp, irritated. Before Sheridan could move with his unwounded arm to stop her, she swept her hand at the chocolate, and the cup went clattering off the table.

Mustafa caught it with a quick duck before it hit the floor. Dark liquid splashed his loose trousers, but he only bowed and murmured, "*Emiriyyiti,*" in a passive voice.

Sheridan glanced at the neatly dressed woman who'd given them shelter from the coming night and the icy mountain drizzle at her farmhouse-inn. He wanted to apologize, but she didn't speak French and explanations in Italian or German or whatever language prevailed here were beyond him—he'd only managed to convey their need for food and rest with a show of his purse. The woman had been kind—she'd taken one look at Olympia, bedraggled and blank-faced, and waved the gold aside, insisting they come inside instantly.

From this elevation, they could still see smoke from the fires in the main city on the far side of the pass. God knew what their hostess thought. While binding up the sword cut on his arm, she'd asked Sheridan a few anxious questions, but he had no idea if his mimed explanations reached her. Then other refugees had begun to straggle by, and Sheridan caught the important news. "Claude Nicolas!" came the excited word. "*Morto! Morto*, signora!"

Dead. He relaxed back into his chair. Pursuit would not be very hot in that case.

The Signora, with the natural canniness of a border innkeeper, kept Sheridan's party out of sight of these passersby. He had a notion that what was left of Olympia's rich gown and his dress uniform told its own story. It was probable that the proprietress had guessed the identity of the princess—which was a danger, but one that could hardly be avoided. He listened to the way she dealt with the other travelers, the natural chatter she used to draw information from them and pass it on in sign and drawings to Sheridan, the Gallic shrugs with which she shook her head and sent the others on their way instead of filling her rooms—and he knew they'd been lucky and found a friend.

Olympia sat at the table, her hands twisting in her lap. Her face still held that dull glassiness, and when he could get her to speak at all, it was only in angry, childlike responses—refusing food, refusing dry clothes, refusing to be touched at all.

He wanted to hold her. He looked at her pinched and bloodless face and wanted to cradle her and rock her and soothe her until the pain went away. But he did not try, not yet. Best to get through to safety while she was still in this stunned and defensive state.

"Olympia," he said, kneeling beside her chair, "I want you to eat something and change out of that dress. You have to rest."

She frowned at him. He'd already exchanged his own uniform for a nondescript coat and breeches.

"Where are we?" she asked in that biting, half-frantic voice.

"We're on the way home."

"No. I have to go back."

He took her hand. She pulled it away.

"I have to go back," she repeated. "I have to stop it."

He broke a piece of bread from the loaf on the table, laid cheese on it and handed it to her. "Eat this."

"My uncle—"

"Claude Nicolas is dead," he said. "Eat this."

She stared at the bread and then looked at him. Her eyes were haunted.

"Do you understand?" He touched her hand, stroked it lightly and then took his away before she could pull back. "You don't need to be afraid of him anymore."

"I'm not afraid of him," she said.

"Do you understand that he's dead?"

"Yes." She blinked and stared. "And my grandfather. And the others."

Sheridan looked at her sharply. "Your grandfather?"

"Leave me alone." She pushed at the bread. "I'm not hungry."

He summoned patience. In a little while, perhaps, he could cajole her into eating. Mostly he wanted her out of the damp wedding gown and in bed. He rose and went into the kitchen to confer with Mustafa and the Signora and see if there was any laudanum to be had.

When he returned a few minutes later, Olympia was gone.

He swore, yelling for Mustafa. The stableyard door was open, letting in gusts of chilly breeze. Sheridan strode outside into the mud, swore again at the inky darkness beyond the farmhouse light and ran into Mustafa as he turned back for a lantern.

He didn't dare call her name. Armed with lights, the two of them split—Sheridan took the barn and Mustafa the yard. The horses were both there, their damp backs steaming gently in the chilly air. He met Mustafa at the stable door, alone. New panic began to rise in his chest.

"Check the road." He gestured. "That way." Then he turned down the steep, slippery track in the other direction. Mountain mist swept around him, clinging to his coat and hair, driving chill into his muscles. His heart was pounding and his wounded arm ached like the devil. Every step was treacherous in the rutted mud and rock.

A hundred feet down the hill, he finally caught sight of her, a white blur in the dark. He gripped the lantern and moved faster, skidding dangerously on loose stone, jarring his arm with each rattling slide downward.

She made no move to wait for him, though she must have seen the light gaining on her. He hissed her name, but she only caught at another tree trunk at the edge of the road for balance and kept moving blindly downward from stone to stone.

He grabbed her arm. "Where the blazes are you going?"

She turned her head toward him. Mist had plastered her hair to her face. She looked like a white corpse in the lantern light. ''Oriens.''

''Well, you're headed in the bloody wrong direction.'' He pulled her toward him, setting his jaw against the sharp pain in his arm. ''Unless you're going by way of Calcutta.''

She jerked away. ''This is the right direction,'' she snapped. ''Just leave me alone.''

He caught her again, bracing himself with one knee against the muddy slope as she tried to struggle away. ''All right, Marco Polo—maybe it is. But let's wait till daylight before we go falling off mountainsides on our way back to the revolution, shall we?''

Between the lantern and his injured arm, she didn't have to fight very hard to free herself. He lost his hold and she started away. ''You don't need to come,'' she said cuttingly. ''I don't want you.''

He pushed his knee out of the mud and caught her again. This time he didn't bother to argue, just transferred the lantern to his bad arm and took her around the waist with his good one, hauling her with him up the slope.

She fought. He felt her slipping, tightened his hold and scrambled another step before she got free. He fell on his wounded arm with a grunt. The lantern rolled and went out.

He still had hold of her dress. Treating the air to a rush of nautically enlightened swearing, he hauled her back. She fell into his lap and they skidded together downslope a few feet. Once they stopped, Sheridan just sat there, with his arm firmly around her and his back against the mountain, feeling the mud soak into his clothes.

His arm was agony. The sword had caught him high, near the shoulder, intersecting the healed scratch he'd taken at Aden. This one was much more serious—it needed stitching, and he could feel fresh blood now beneath his shirt. But he held onto Olympia, listening to her tell him in no uncertain terms how unwanted he was.

''You've bloody well got me, wanted or not,'' he muttered.

"I just want to be alone!" She moved jerkily, desperately. "Go back to your sultan. Why did you come? Why won't you let me alone?"

He didn't answer. He put his face to her nape and rocked her gently.

She kept trying, kept struggling and condemning him, until they wore each other out. Sheridan won, through nothing but inertial strength, and they sat there in the mud and mist and dark. Finally, after a length of time he couldn't even count, the gleam of a lantern fell on them, and Mustafa's soft voice came out of the gloom above.

With light for guidance, Sheridan resumed his mission. She was too tired to struggle now, but she gave him no help: he had to carry her, stumbling upward a few feet, resting, nursing his throbbing arm and starting again. Mustafa picked out the easiest route, but still it was four hours after she'd disappeared before Sheridan staggered through the farmhouse door with her.

He let her go. She suddenly found the strength to stand on her own two feet and used it to glare at him as he leaned back against the door, holding his arm. There was a deep shivering growing somewhere low in his chest. The light in the room seemed too bright.

"Go to bed," he ordered. "Or I'll take you there and tie you down."

She was a pathetic figure, standing straight in the muddy remains of her wedding gown, with hate and desolation vying for control of her features. He tried to reconcile himself to that—he understood she needed anger now to protect herself from whatever reality she'd seen from atop that horse in the mob. But it was hard. He found himself wishing things had gone as he'd planned, so that he'd be alone and on the run, but knowing at least that she was safe—instead of floundering here, not sure what to do for her, trying to offer his futile comfort.

He knew what she was suffering, he recognized the signs of horror that went beyond a soul's ability to withstand, but he didn't know how to help; he'd never known how to help himself, except to close his heart to everything but death: to be a machine that fought and survived.

He didn't want that to happen to her. He would not allow it. Somehow, he would prevent it.

But he didn't know how.

"I mean it," he said, taking a step toward her as she stood frozen. "I'll tie you down."

She stepped back. "I hate you," she said, very cold and very sane. And then she turned and went up the stairs.

He sent Mustafa after her, with orders not to leave her for an instant. When they were gone, he turned to the Signora.

She gestured at his arm. He shook his head and sat down heavily at the table. She had new information from Oriens since they'd been gone. On the table was a paper with the word *morto* at the top. Beneath it were names and numbers. Fifty-two was the highest count, and the name of Olympia's grandfather had a question mark beside it.

He wondered if that was what she'd seen from the horse. She'd never really known the old man, but it would be a shock to witness his murder amid all the other turmoil.

He sat at the table, his forehead in his hand, staring down at the body count. His head ached. His arm burned. His own demons hovered, flashing in and out of his mind with disturbing vividness.

He sneezed into his muddy sleeve and waited with the silent Signora for more news.

By morning he was thoroughly ill, feverish and confused at waking from a fitful sleep to find his head on a wooden table and his arm in agony. The first thing he saw was a face he thought he ought to know: roguish and smiling—and then he thought of ordering tea and seeing the Sultan and how he needed to take a sextant reading if the weather had cleared, but he hurt, and he couldn't seem to find the will to lift his head.

Foreign voices spun around him. A strong hand dragged him back and he made a sound of anguish, breathing hard and trying to hold his arm still.

"Tallyho," a male voice said. "You'd best fall in bed until the doctor comes, old fellow."

Sheridan hauled his eyelids open. He stared into the face that confronted him.

"Yállah," the other said, not unkindly.

Sheridan's brain flashed him a sudden spark of reason, and he pulled his head up. "You," he said, and fumbled for his dagger.

"Here, now." The dark-eyed man caught Sheridan's good arm, showing a familiar, charming grin. "Don't be rude to an old friend. I've got nothing against you—even if you did let Claude Nicolas down and keep your mouth shut at the wedding. I got paid for my part. But that's ancient history, eh? Goodbye and good riddance and long live the revolution, that's what I say. If you're on your way back to Turkey, I'll be damned if it looks like you'll get there without my help."

Sheridan frowned through a haze. Laboriously, he tried to think. He felt as if he were on the edge of a cliff and falling. This man—trustworthy?—no, not that, but . . . predictable. Looking for advantage. Reward. Not likely to be welcome in Oriens now, having lately been in Claude Nicolas's pay. Knew the language; but smart . . . too bloody smart . . .

"Name?" he grunted.

"Randall Frederick Raban. Count of Beaufontein. Your servant, sir."

Sheridan tried to lift his right hand, but he could not do it. He spread his left on the table. "You have . . . funds?"

Raban nodded. "Certainly. You needn't worry I'll make off with yours. I look forward to a long and satisfying friendship between us, and that's no way to start." He grinned. "The lady of the house guards your purse like Cerberus at the gates of Hell, in any case."

Sheridan closed his eyes and let his head fall back. He heard Raban speaking to the Signora. They seemed to be having an argument, but when someone touched him again, it was Raban.

Sheridan used him for the support he offered, stumbling to his feet, his head reeling and his arm in flames. He swung toward the stairs, willing to try—but no . . . from somewhere a pallet had appeared, and fortunately all he had to do was make it across the room. He nearly fainted when Raban jostled his arm in the process of helping him down.

He reached up with his good hand. "Raban—" he muttered. "Princess—"

The grin turned into a grimace. "Yes, I know all about her. She's a harpy after all, ain't she? Pity."

"Don't let her go . . . back."

"Oh, we'll have a discussion about that. I'll tell the little puffball she's not wanted. Revolution and all that. Princess—an embarrassment—completely *de trop.*" He shook his head sadly. "She's an idiot."

Sheridan gripped his sleeve. "Don't let her go back," he said through clenched teeth.

"Right-ho. Count on me, old man. I've got my eye fixed on the main chance." The white grin flashed. "And you're it."

"Why are you interfering?" Olympia demanded. She paced the tiny, low-ceilinged room, holding her arms crossed tightly over the peasant costume she'd been given to wear. "What right do you have to imprison me?"

"Admiral's orders," the young count said calmly. "Do sit down. If you'd show the slightest bit of rationality, I'd be happy to kick you out at the side of the road to fend for yourself. But he seems to harbor a morbid obsession for your safety, and I expect you'd just march off to Oriens and get yourself guillotined."

She put her hand to her mouth. She was shaking all over with hate and fury. "Let me out." Her voice rose. "Let me out; let me out!"

"No."

She whirled around, grabbed the tray Mustafa had brought her and hurled it to the floor. Pottery and wood splintered with a crash. *"Let me out!"* She reached for the rough cotton curtains at the window, tore at them and suddenly found herself jerked backward. *"I have to go back!"* she screamed.

"Listen here, you little bitch—" He shook her violently. "Don't pull your silly tantrums with me! Maybe you've got that poor blighter downstairs wrapped around your finger, but I won't put up with it. Got that?" He shoved her against the wall, his dark eyes hot. "You aren't going back, not if he says you aren't."

She beat at him with her fists. "I have to stop it!" she cried, panting. "I have to go back."

"Stop what? The revolution?" He evaded her hand and caught her by the wrists. "You couldn't stop it if you tried. It's over. Done. The moderate committee's taken control, and the British moved in this morning to support them. Your throne's gone, ma'am. Oriens is a republic. You aren't a princess anymore."

She froze and stared at him. "Is that true?" she whispered.

"Why do you think you can't go back? If you were smart, you'd be running from this place like a rabbit. The last thing anybody wants in a new regime is one of the old royals hanging about collecting sympathy. You go back, and they'll be polite and hospitable and kind, and pretty soon you'll have an accident, and nobody will have to worry about that problem anymore."

Her muscles went limp. Like in a collapsing balloon, air left her. "I don't want sympathy," she said feebly.

He let go of her. She sat down in a rough wooden chair. All the anger had gone out of her. She felt sick and upset. Bewildered. She looked around the room and had a difficult time remembering how she'd gotten there. She could recall the wedding, and her announcement, and after that . . .

She hugged her stomach, feeling uneasy.

"Did you bring me here?" she asked.

"Of course not." The dark-eyed count looked at her with exasperation. "Didn't I just introduce myself? I'll be helping Drake get back to Constantinople—trying to make sure he doesn't die before he can write me into his will. And for the moment you seem to be an unpleasant but unavoidable part of the task."

She chewed her lip. She couldn't remember how she'd come here—all she remembered was how she'd needed to go back, to stop what she'd begun.

But it was over. This count said the revolution was over. Oriens was a republic.

It all seemed so confusing.

"You're helping Sheridan?" she asked vaguely. "Is he with the Sultan?"

The man gave a snort. "Not a bit of it. What's wrong with your head? He's downstairs—half dead, by the looks of it. He'll be lucky if he doesn't lose that arm."

"What?" she whispered.

"I see that your gratitude doesn't extend to paying much attention to the condition of your faithful supporters. He took a devilish bad sword cut that's not been seen to properly—and from what they tell me, you've had him out rolling in the mud and rain half the night. It's no wonder he's nearly run through."

"He's here?" Her voice was shaky and hoarse. "He's ill?"

"Damned ill. Thanks to you."

She moistened her lips "It's my fault?"

"Of course it's your fault. He'd be eating sugarplums and having his back rubbed in Constantinople if it weren't for you, wouldn't he? I've been talking to that servant of his, and you wouldn't credit the crazy notion he had to save your neck from Claude Nicolas. Damned lucky he's not shot through the heart or locked up for hanging right now."

"It's my fault," she whispered, gripping her hands in her lap. "It's my fault."

"Right. So just behave yourself and take orders, understand?" The count moved to the door.

She looked up. "Please—" she said in a small voice. "May I see him? I won't say anything, I promise. I won't do anything."

He leaned on the door handle, frowning at her speculatively. Then he shrugged. "It might calm him, I reckon. To see that you're still here. You can come for a few minutes. But I warn you—one move to bolt and you'll be back up here before your head's stopped spinning. He can't take any agitation."

"No." She could barely speak. "No, of course not."

She let him take her arm, preceding him submissively down the narrow stair. In the farmhouse kitchen, Sheridan lay on a low cot near the fire, his hand moving restlessly from his raised knee to his bound arm and back again.

The count gave her a little shove in the direction of the cot, but Olympia stopped a yard away. Sheridan's face was pale, with bright color burning on his cheekbones. The tendons in his hand stood out as he gripped his thigh.

My fault, she thought. *My fault, my fault, my fault.*

"Here she is, old chap," the count said cheerfully. "Right as rain. Sound as a drum."

Sheridan turned his head. "Princess," he said, so low she could hardly hear it. He coughed, and the flush left his face as he reached toward his wound, curled his fingers before he touched it and let his hand fall against his chest. "Hurts," he muttered, closing his eyes with a parody of a smile: an upward curve of his mouth that strained his whole face. He opened his eyes again and turned his head, searching.

"Move over closer—" The count gave her a poke. "Where he can see you."

She moved a step. But she could not go farther. She stood there, held to the spot, her hands locked together. Her tongue was too numb to speak.

Sheridan bit his lip. His lashes lowered and lifted. He watched her, but his eyes were dull pewter, hazy, and she couldn't tell whether he really saw.

"Is he going to die?" she whispered.

"Not if I can help it," Count Beaufontein said, peering over to examine the dressing. "Won't do me a bit of good that way. And we're going to save this arm, too—so he can write me a commendation to the Sultan . . . I say, ain't that correct, dear fellow?"

Sheridan's eyes drifted. He mumbled something unintelligible.

"Right-ho," the count said. "Nothing to it."

Dear Sheridan,

I have waited to write this until your fever has broken. Count Beaufontein promises me that he will make certain you receive it, but I've given Signora Verletti a gold crown from your purse to make sure he does it, as I do not entirely trust his promises.

Mustafa has told me what you did for me: of my uncle's plan and how you intended to stop him. I'm glad that didn't happen; I'm glad you didn't have to kill anymore for me. It's very odd, but I can't seem to remember you in the cathedral, or leaving, or how we made our way through that great crowd, but Mustafa says you brought me out of there, and I believe him.

You've brought me through so much.

I understand that my uncle and grandfather were both killed in the riots. The count says that I must go somewhere and live very quietly, so as not to disturb the new government in Oriens, and I am sure he is right, but I feel a bit lost just now. All my life I've been thinking of Oriens and what I would do here, and now everything has turned out differently than I expected.

I wish I could stay here forever and watch you sleeping. But I have been praying and praying while you've been so ill because of me, and I made a promise that if you could be all right, I would never again be the cause of hurting you or anyone else, and so I have to go away. I really didn't intend to write this letter before I left, but I wanted you to know that I'm grateful.

How I wish there were a better word than that! You taught me what courage and loyalty really are. You're the best friend I ever had, or ever will have.

Mustafa tells me you are doing very well at the Sultan's court, and I wish you all the honors you deserve. Please do everything the doctor says about your arm, as he is a very good doctor. We were afraid you would die. And please be generous to this nonsensical count, even if he seems like a terrible rascal, because he really has taken care of all of us, and he found the doctor, and he's made all the arrangements for me to travel safely. He's hoping you will have him made into a pasha. He talks often of the dancing girls he looks forward to keeping in his hareem.

I will not forget you, Sheridan. I wish I could change

the mistakes that I made, all the stupid mistakes that hurt you and other people. I wish I could have helped you when you needed help, but I don't seem to be very good at that. I wanted to. I wanted to so badly. I just didn't know how.

I don't want to kiss you now, because I don't want you to wake. Think of Vienna, and a grand staircase and music, and remember me when you go there. That was the best time. That is my kiss goodbye.

I'm sorry. I'm sorry I failed at everything.

Olympia

Twenty-eight

Sheridan folded the letter carefully once again, staring into the campfire. Around them, the trunks of tall trees seemed to tremble and shudder in the light of the leaping flames. The tin implements their Tatar guide had hung out to frighten demons clattered tunelessly under a gypsy servant's tireless hand.

Raban gave him a dry look. "Haven't got it by heart yet?"

Sheridan stretched his right arm, testing and exercising it against the soreness. "Be damned to you," he said with abstracted venom. He couldn't summon much resentment for Raban's gibes. It required too much concentration, and against his better judgment, he'd actually developed a certain degree of attachment to the rogue.

"A fool in love." Raban tossed a twig into the fire. "Poor devil."

Sheridan watched the flames. Was that it? Was he just another miserable sod dumped by a woman? He remembered a carpenter on one of his ships—one face among hundreds at the first mail call in months—stricken, stunned; bullied and stuck in the ribs by the others. "Come along, Chips, cheer up like a man. You'll never see *her* again; square yards and don't let a petticoat make a fool of you."

But it shook everyone; they all depended on one another—it was bad for morale if the fellow took it too hard, so he was hounded for his weakness with unfeeling cruelty. There wasn't room for sympathy. Sympathy was poison; it reminded everyone they were out there watching their lives slip away in hardship and boredom and battle while the world went on unheeding.

Not me, Sheridan had always thought. *You'll never catch me with that look on my face.*

But it stung. It upset him that she'd left him while he could not think.

He had nightmares every night now, woke up in a whimpering sweat that had nothing to do with the fever he'd contracted in the mountain drizzle. He felt as if he were riding deeper into the bad dreams; that with every step his mount took on the road back to Stamboul, he went a little farther toward destruction, stretched the barrier that protected him from crisis a little thinner.

He was going the wrong way.

He knew it. He did not know where she'd gone, but whatever direction it was, it wasn't this one.

But he was afraid to turn back. He'd made a choice. The nightmares were bad, life hurt: the things life made him do. The anger hurt. The fear and defiance and survival cunning—all of it. But that was his choice. That was what he was going back to. Deliberately, the way he'd always chosen to go back to the navy, even though he despised and feared it. Because he knew how to live in that world; he trusted nothing, and felt safe; he knew how to numb and isolate himself there—while he was adrift and exposed in hers, and that vulnerability was more terrifying than the worst of the dreams.

And yet he remembered her eyes: glazed . . . frightened and angry, her face wild in the mountain rain—and God, how he knew what it felt like inside that look.

How could he leave her alone with that?

The most precious thing in his whole existence; and he was deserting her. He was running away.

He moved a stone with the toe of his boot, looking down, watching shadows lick it haphazardly in the firelight. "Raban," he said suddenly, "do you know what courage is?"

There was a little silence. The young count looked up

from a chip of wood he'd been whittling idly. "Are you going to tell me?"

"I'm asking."

"What courage is." Raban held up the wood and turned it in his hand. "As Socrates so succinctly put it: 'That's certainly not a thing that every pig would know.' "

Sheridan pushed one stone next to another. "I don't suppose he said anything more to the point than that?"

"Of course he did. Have you completely forgotten your Plato, old man? To hear him tell it, the lads were constantly chewing it over on every bloody street corner in Athens."

Sheridan nudged a third pebble into the pile. "Never read Plato," he said in a low voice.

"Ah." Raban closed his eyes. "How does it go? 'And now, Laches, try and tell me—what is that common quality called courage?' . . . and Laches replies: 'Well, Socrates—I'd say courage is a kind of endurance of the soul.' Which seems a damnably good answer to me, but of course it isn't good enough for Socrates; nothing ever is, and he's got to argue. 'But what would you say of a foolish endurance?' he asks. 'Isn't that evil and harmful?' And poor slow-top Laches turns red and shuffles his feet and says, 'Well, yes—can't argue with that, I s'pose.' 'So'—Socrates reckons it's time to drive in his big point—'then according to you, only a wise endurance is courage.' "

Sheridan watched the fire.

"Is that Greek enough for you?" the young count asked.

"Quite."

Raban chuckled. He went back to idle whittling.

Sheridan closed his eyes. He thought of living out his life in Stamboul, of the inevitable nightmares, the numbed fortitude it seemed to require simply to face each day. And then he thought of his princess, of what it would be like to face those nightmares with his heart open, without the numbness to protect him.

Courage and loyalty. You taught me what courage and loyalty really are.

But he was afraid. He wasn't brave. He'd endured, yes—he hadn't killed himself, he hadn't taken that final escape, but he'd wanted to. He still did. His fearless involvement in the brutal intrigue of the Ottoman court was nothing but another kind of suicide—slower, somewhat more interesting, but just as surely fatal in the end. He knew it. He'd known it all along. He wasn't brave.

Only a wise endurance is courage.

He didn't know what that meant. He didn't know what was wise or foolish. He only knew that she needed him. Her face had said it. The letter said it.

"Raban." He spoke quietly. "I'm going back."

"Back? To Oriens?"

"No."

Raban flung the wood aside. "You bloody born fool. Are you going to look for that damned princess?"

Sheridan worked his arm restlessly. He didn't bother to answer.

His companion rolled his eyes skyward. "God save us. Where're you going to start?"

Sheridan slanted him a look. "You're sure she never said anything? Nothing at all about where she might go?"

"Not a peep. I told you—after she found out she'd lost her throne, she just sat there in the corner for three days and sulked. Didn't offer to help, didn't say anything—just wrung her hands and stared at you as if you might disappear any minute. Wouldn't even eat, the silly chit. And then all of a sudden, the minute you start to regain your senses, she wants to leave." He shook his dark head. "Women!"

Sheridan rubbed his lip. "If I go to England, I'll be arrested for debt."

"Will you really?" Raban sounded interested. "And here I thought you were rich."

"Your greed's made you overly optimistic. I'm down to the tune of a half million at home. It'd take about twenty more summer palaces from the Sultan to pay that off."

Raban retrieved the chip of wood and began whittling at it again. "You're too modest. We'll do well enough in England."

" 'We'?" Sheridan asked mockingly.

The charming grin was guileless. "Certainly. Do you think I'd desert you now?"

"I can't reckon why not."

"Act of Parliament, entered into the record March 18, 1828, or thereabouts. I won't quibble over the date."

Sheridan frowned at him.

"Birmingham to Liverpool railway, old chap. Remember?"

His jaw tightened. "What are you saying?"

"Only that I made the acquaintance of a certain Mrs. Plumb a while ago, who can be quite talkative when plied with a proper excess of champagne and romance. Charming woman. Apparently Parliament had a heavenly visitation in the form of certain irate merchants who were quite impatient for the railway to open. So Parliament opened it. The first half year's profits paid off your debt. And you own it *all*, my friend. Every bleeding share. It had the lady in a blue funk, I'll tell you. Seemed to take it as a personal affront."

Sheridan sat still, trying to let the information sink in. The railway. The debt. He was rich, and he didn't care. After a long silence, he said disgustedly, "She would."

Raban lay back against a carpet-roll, grinning.

"Confound you. You knew I didn't know," Sheridan said.

The count shrugged. "I'm regularly vexed to postpone our trip to Stamboul. I'd really prefer dancing girls as a reward for my faithful service. Plain cash is so—unimaginative. Not that I'd be churlish enough to question whatever you might choose to offer . . ." He trailed off hopefully.

"Bastard," Sheridan said, and rolled over to sleep.

It was raining in Wisbeach, a gentle spring rain that made silver circles on the calm surface of the river and weighted the heavy heads of daffodils with transparent drops. Sheridan stood in front of the closed house. The knocker was gone; the shades were drawn. The housekeeper next door said no one had lived there for half a year.

He walked along the muddy road. He had not thought it would leave him so empty, this defeat. He had not realized how certain he'd been that she'd come home.

There was some hope still: that Mustafa would find her in Rome, or Raban in Madeira—those had seemed the next likeliest places to Sheridan, but in his heart, he'd been so sure he'd find her here that he'd hardly given the possibilities any thought, beyond their value as excuses to be quit of his helpful, diligent and undesired companions.

He'd even been to see Fish Stovall. That had been hard—to admit to the silent old man that he'd failed her, lost her. He'd stood in the neat, poor cottage in the fens, his hat gripped between his fists, and asked if she'd come to Fish. And Fish had looked at him for a long time, and then said slowly that she hadn't.

Sheridan had fumbled in his pocket and pulled out the harmonica. He'd held it out to the fenman.

"Keep it," Fish Stovall said.

It seemed to Sheridan that there was an infinity of condemnation in those simple words. He put the harmonica back in his pocket and left. He kept walking. The misty fens spread out on all sides below the elevated cart track.

He supposed, vaguely, that he ought to go back to Wisbeach in time to catch the Norfolk coach. Mud sloshed beneath his boots. He stood on the edge of a dike and saw the grim towers of Hatherleigh Hall in gray outline across the flats.

He walked with his hands in his pockets, his head down. More mud. Matted grass and a burst of sound as his passing frightened a nesting bird into flight. He found gravel beneath his feet; then stone steps. He looked up at his father's black granite monstrosity.

He had no key. There was no reason to go in. He wandered along the perimeter of the house, the crunch of his boots the only noise. He stopped outside the stained-glass window of the little study. Inside, he could just see the withered fuchsia plant she'd brought him, a sad skeleton on the windowsill.

A whiff of smoke came to him on the heavy air. He hunched in his cloak, feeling damp to his bones. It made him think of the island: the peat smoke and chill. He closed his eyes and imagined the sound of the surf, the wind in the tussock grass and her body, warm and waiting for him, innocent passion and infinite quiet peace.

He walked onto the grass, the sound of his footsteps dying into muffled stillness. The house sat like a great sphinx in the mist, ponderous, full of absurd corners and pointless projections. He circled it slowly, trying to think, trying to formulate some plan for what he would do next. But his mind seemed lost in memories and fog. He stopped and leaned against the dark bulk of a flying buttress. At his feet, the dewy grass was crushed down in a little path some other intruder had made. He gazed at it indifferently.

The scent of smoldering peat grew stronger. He frowned, looking up as a waft of smoke drifted past the buttress. There was wet mud on the little track in front of him, freshly smudged across the rain-soaked grass. He hefted himself off the wall and followed the trail, around the corner to the back of the house, where the servants' wing made a gloomy bay between two overhanging ramparts.

Far back in the corner, white peat smoke swirled and rose sluggishly out of the shadow. He walked forward, staring at the little camp huddled in a dry space beneath the intersecting eaves. Next to the fire was a carefully dressed catch of plovers, spread on a bed of fresh rushes. To one side a stack of peat had been laid to dry next to a pile of faded blankets.

As he looked at the blankets, he realized they were occupied. The bundle showed the lonely small outline of legs and torso and shoulders, head and face buried beneath damp wool. At one corner, spilling out between the drab folds, was a limp curl of reddish gold.

Sheridan walked closer, his footsteps soft in the grass. He stood looking down at her, his back against the wall. Slowly, unsteadily, he sank to his knees. He sat next to her sleeping form. Not touching. Not speaking. His vision blurred. His throat had a desperate block in it, pure fury, an ache like a wound that made it hard to breathe.

What was she doing here? Who had sent her to this? As

if no one cared for her. As if she were no one, nothing—scrounging in the open like an orphaned animal.

His hands closed. He bent his head between his knees. This was it; this was what he feared—the flood of raw feeling, rage and love and despair with nothing between himself and the torrent.

He sat there a long time. The peat smoke curled upward. She'd built a good fire, banked it well: it kept going through the mist and drizzle.

Olympia woke with her feet cold. She had her fingers curled beneath her chin, her nose buried in the musty, smoky smell of the blankets.

She spent a careful time uncurling her fingers, then her legs and arms. She had found that if one concentrated on things like that, on the simple physical motions of existing, it kept other thoughts at bay. But it was necessary to be very thorough about it, to focus, and not allow anything else to slip into consciousness.

She peered out from under the blankets and sat up, brushing her hair back. It was a little mad, she knew, to live like this. But she didn't know what else to do. The British consulate in Naples hadn't wanted her; they'd seemed embarrassed and advised that she go to London and inquire there. She left the consul ashamed of her boldness. Why should they wish to help her? She sold the last of her jewels to pay passage, but when she arrived back in England, the bustle of the city and crowds frightened her. She'd been scared and alone, and glad to find a mail coach to Norfolk and then Wisbeach.

The fens had comforted her in their familiar desolation. But something held her back from going to Fish, or to the house where she'd lived all her life. She felt better here, alone, not talking or thinking or planning. Just existing.

She stayed hidden in the shadow of Hatherleigh Hall and only went out in the early morning and at dusk, carefully avoiding the rounds she knew Fish and the other fen tigers would take. She wasn't afraid of them. She just wanted to hide. It felt safe, hiding. She didn't want to answer questions.

Fumbling the blankets aside, she shifted stiffly into a cross-legged position, reaching toward the stake she used to tend the fire. It was then that she perceived her company, jerked back with a startled cry from the unexpected sight of a muddy boot behind her.

She thought he was a hallucination at first, like one of the intrusive images that jarred her sometimes at the edge of twilight, the upsetting flashes of something she didn't dare remember. But he didn't disappear. He sat against the wall, his arms on his raised knees, watching her.

"Why?" he asked in a husky voice.

His face was fierce. Anguished. That confused her. The question confused her.

She ducked her head.

"Why are you living like this? Princess—" Something seemed to catch in his throat. He lifted his hand toward her.

"I'm not a princess," she said quickly, moving away. She picked up the poker, pretending she'd meant to stir the fire. She didn't want to be touched. She wanted to run away.

Sheridan watched the instant withdrawal, the wild, spooky look in her eyes. He rested his head back against the wall. He could not breathe right; his chest hurt. His vision swam again.

"Where's Julia?" he asked, and heard himself: guttural hoarse with the barrier in his throat, while she stared at him dry eyed.

She blinked, looked away as if she'd heard something frightening in the gloom behind her and then looked back at him with a small frown. "I don't know."

"What about the damned government? Don't they know where you are?"

She bit her lip. "Why should they wish to know?" Her hands clenched nervously in her lap. "Do you think they're looking for me?"

He thought of the way things had gone: the fresh treaties and stable rapport between the new republic of Oriens and the British diplomats. With disgust and a sense of violent shame for his country's callous politics, he said, "No.

They'd probably just as soon you disappeared from the face of the earth."

She bent her head. "I can understand that. I was afraid they might be looking for me."

She seemed to shrink, to grow smaller at the idea, her shoulders hunched and her arms crossed tightly. He scanned the little camp, and what he saw was fear. Fear in the way it huddled back in the shadows; fear in the modest snare of birds and the ragged pile of nondescript blankets; fear in the isolation and the daytime sleep that meant at the edge of dark and light she would go out to forage like a slinking stray, trying not to draw attention.

"Afraid," he repeated, in the grating way his voice wouldn't seem to work right. "Why?"

She hugged herself. "Well—it was my fault, you know. If I hadn't . . . if I hadn't—tried to interfere, and do what I thought was best, when I didn't know . . ." She shook her head quickly. "I really didn't know," she said in a quavery voice. She lifted her eyes. They were haunted, deep with shadow in her white face. "I never did. You tried to tell me, but I never knew what it would be like."

Rage and grief seemed to press with a physical pain in his chest. "I wanted to keep you from that," he whispered. "I never wanted you to know." He reached for her, to cradle her in his arms and stroke her hair and comfort and protect her and make his own sweet princess whole again, make that terrible dull shadow go away—but she wouldn't let him touch her; she moved back, sitting anxiously up on her heels, like a deer ready to take flight.

"Please," she said. "I don't—I can't . . . I can't bear it."

He stared at her, feeling himself crumbling. There was something crushing him, forcing its way through the spreading cracks in his reason, like an ocean slipping and pouring and surging over a dike as it gave way.

He lifted his hand toward her, palm open, an offering—a plea—and she did not take it. He held it there until it began to shake. Until he could not see it for the blur in his eyes—he couldn't see anything at all; he couldn't hear; there was only a noise like a giant confusion in his head, splinters and twisted metal flying, his balance gone as the world pitched. He felt himself falling, hurled forward with faces in a tumbling mayhem around him, their features set in contorted screams. He curled into himself, and he had to get up, but he couldn't, he couldn't, he could hear his men shrieking but he couldn't help. The eruption of noise lasted on and on. He moaned and begged and buried his head, wanting the end of it—and then he somehow made his feet, still surrounded by the noise and confusion and torn bits of human beings. Sons and fathers and husbands and friends. He walked the streets of a desert town; angry, furious, his surviving crew like enraged wolves in a pack behind him, taking anything, anyone—they shook a frightened, dark-eyed woman, their dirks in her unveiled face: *Who mans the shore battery? Where do you hide them?* He cut her hair with savage strokes while they held her, chopped it off in blue-black hunks. He was crying as he did it. He was stalking through the dark, a predator with a personal grudge against his prey, a killer to his soul. When he found them, there was no quarter, only the sound of gunfire and the flash of bayonets. He was on his knees, his fists curled against the baked desert walls . . .

He heard himself. He sounded like a madman, yelling and sobbing and swearing. His hands were bleeding, torn by the rough granite of his father's house. He pressed his forehead to the wet stone, hiccuping, still whimpering curses under his breath.

She sat unmoving while he leaned against the wall on his knees. Her eyes were squeezed shut, her arms tight around herself. It made him cry to see her; he could not seem to stop crying.

He bent his head, his palms flat against the granite. "I don't know why," he said. "I don't know—why." He swallowed, trying to take control of his voice and failing. "Why?" He turned, slumped against the wall, tilting his head back. "I need you, Princess. Oh, Jesus Christ, I need you. What can I do to bring you back? What can I do?" The tears got in his mouth, filling it with salt, making the world swim around him in a shapeless blur. "I don't know what you saw back there . . . outside the cathedral—'' He spoke blindly, to the muddy colors that sparkled before his eyes. ''I know it must have been bad. I know you want to hide from it. But please—'' He turned toward her, reached toward the dark wavering patch, blinking to make it into a human shape, and then let his hand fall back when she didn't move. ''I don't have any right to ask, but come back to me. Can you come?''

She did not answer. He squeezed his eyes shut and opened them, wiped with his fist to clear them. When he could see her, the pinched and set expression on her face was answer enough. He lowered his head, held it between his hands.

''I'll tell you,'' he said to the ground. ''I'll tell you something I've never told anyone.'' He took a choked breath. ''I've tried not to think about it . . . I never could stand to think about it, but it keeps coming to get me now—I haven't got control of it anymore.'' A shudder seemed to take him, catching in his throat. ''I've got all these commendations . . . a damned knighthood—and I shouldn't. I shouldn't. I should have been court-martialed.'' He squeezed his eyes shut, leaking tears. ''I've lied to you. I told you I lost my men to a lucky shot—a corsair—do you remember what I told you? It's a lie. I made it up.'' He hesitated. He was shaking deep inside. ''I've lied about it so long I've got to where I believe it myself. It gets all mixed up in my head. But it wasn't a lucky shot. It wasn't even a goddamned battle.''

He chewed his lip, tasting blood and tears, concentrating on what he needed to say. She had not opened her eyes. He didn't know if she was listening, but he had to tell her. He had to make her understand that she wasn't alone in that wilderness, that he was there; he knew what it was like. He wiped at his face, wiped it again and then gave up as the blur kept coming.

''The town was called . . . Salah,'' he began carefully. That was true. That detail was true. He searched for another, feeling around the memory as if it were a festered wound. ''Coast of Algiers.'' Another small truth. He tried to work up to larger ones. ''It was supposed to be simple. I had orders to land a pair of diplomats. They were going to be diplomatic, y'see, and get a—'' He attempted again to press the tears from his eyes with the heel of his hand. ''A promise from the local bey to release his slaves and stop the trade. If that didn't work, and nobody was fool enough to think it would, my orders said I was to knock out the shore battery.''

He stopped, searching for her again amid the blur. She seemed to be a small, motionless shape, a darkness with a pale oval above it.

''But you know,'' he said to her in a voice that held a tremor, ''I was like you. I thought I knew best. Maybe I wasn't so naive as you, Princess—I knew what it would be like to go in under those shore guns—and I was bloody sick of guns. It just seemed to me those orders would get us all killed for no good reason. And it wasn't as if it was a real war; we weren't up against line-of-battle ships, where you could use some tactics. Where your brains might be good for something besides a target. But that was the way it was—we didn't have an enemy—you couldn't tell a pirate from a fishing boat out there, so they sent us against whatever they could see, and that was the shore batteries. Who cared if we sat there like a duck in the water until we were blown away? There were too damned many of us left over anyway after the French war. We were just a pin on some admiral's map so he could say he was fighting the Barbary pirates on his way to a peerage and a house in the country.''

He chewed his knuckle and took a deep breath, staring into space, seeing memories in the shadows. He could hear the bitterness building in his voice, but that was only fear—only a way to protect himself, to make excuses.

''We went ahead, though,'' he said. ''What else are you going to do?'' He shook his head blindly. ''Argue? I wish I'd had the sense. I wish I'd resigned my commission right there. But I had a good crew; my second command, been with 'em at Baltimore and Lake Erie—I doubt the thought even crossed my mind. That's the worst of fighting—you hate what you're doing, you hate what it makes of you . . . and you love the men beside you. You don't want to leave them. You think about who might be put over them in your place, and whether he'd be a gentleman fool and sacrifice your men for nothing; whether he'd see that they got fed properly and kept onions against the scurvy and smoked the hold for rats.'' He stared silently into space. ''You think a lot on a ship. Day and night, sitting there by yourself in the captain's cabin and trying to plot some way to carry out your orders and keep your bloody crew and yourself alive.''

He bit his lip. The tears rose again, and for a few moments speaking was beyond him. He was ashamed; he ought to have some semblance of manhood left, but the mask was just more than he could summon.

''I failed,'' he said explosively. Another truth. ''I lost them. Two hundred out of three. I made a mistake. I went ashore with the delegation, to translate. I shouldn't have; it's against regulations, but I thought I could move things forward. And I did. We came off with an agreement and an invitation to anchor in the harbor and oversee the release of thc Christian slaves personally.'' He bent his head. ''I was pretty proud of myself. I'd done it: I knew how to talk to those orientals, y'see; I knew how to put the fear of God in 'em. I'm such an expert,'' he said bitterly. ''So I bring her in . . . right under the gun battery like a deuced fool. I know we can take it out at that range, the battery and the whole town, too. I'm not worried they'll fire on us.''

He looked up at the dark bulk of the house, seeing another place. The scene began to pour in on him: the heat rising from the water and shore in pale waves; the little city itself, mud-colored, huddled on the bank above the harbor.

''It's dawn,'' he mumbled. ''I'm not quite asleep; it's too hot to sleep. The first shot sounds like pistol-fire.'' He stopped. ''That's what I thought: pistol-fire.''

He shivered suddenly, wetting his lips and staring.

''It's not. There's another, and a whump and a splash, and that's a sound I know—that's a ball hitting water. And them I'm on deck—I'm not even dressed; I've got on breeches and boots and everything's chaos; they're clearing the decks and rolling out the guns—I think I gave that order; I must have—and the watch officer keeps shouting at me and pointing at the shore—but I know that; I know they're firing, does he think I'm deaf and blind? I want him to run out the guns on the seaward side for ballast, to raise the angle of fire, but he's not listening, he's just pointing; and finally I take the glass and look . . . and I see it . . ."

He swallowed. His vision clouded.

". . . what they've done. In the night, they've brought the slaves and staked them out under the gun battery. Like dogs. There are hundreds of 'em—women . . . children . . . chained along the bank: oh, Jesus, some of 'em trying to pull away, some of 'em trying to dig trenches with their hands, some of 'em just sitting there with their heads on their knees, and those guns a yard above them, so I can't open fire."

He stared at nothing.

"I used to be a slave." The shivering in him had become a shudder. "I used to wear that crescent . . . that filthy damned crescent . . ." He locked his hands against the tremor. "God help me, I used to be one of them."

He could feel himself cracking, the boundary between remembrance and reality wavering, letting in the nightmare.

"We have to turn back," he moaned. "We have to get out of here. Can't fire. Can't fire." He took a trembling breath. "I just can't. But they've got the range; they're walking in on us from both sides, sighting all those guns together—spray all around . . . while we drift down on the anchor they hit the foremast and take out half the men at the capstan. And the bos'n's just got another crew heaving on it, we've got the stuns'l set, but she won't turn; she won't turn; there's no breeze—we've got no way on . . . and they hit us. Everything at once. Everything; every gun in the battery."

He put his hands over his ears, feeling again the lunge and stagger of the ship as it hurled him down in an explosion of splintering sound. He fought to keep himself anchored in reality instead of that hallucination. He had to hang on. This time he had to keep a grip on the present, the place he wanted to be. Had to be. But he could see his men as they died, and he cried again and swore a little and saw himself trying to count who was still standing amid the wreckage . . . one, two; six; nine—fumbling, like a child trying to reclaim scattered marbles.

The trembling numbness twisted into something else. "Goddamned bloody cowards." He swallowed a sob. "I'll kill 'em all." In his mind he was screaming it. He lifted his arm and wiped his face. "I didn't care then. Didn't give a damn for the slaves or the ship or anything—I just wanted to pound that battery to ribbons. We did it—put her back in position, and opened fire with everything we had left. I couldn't see anything for the smoke; I don't think we even had a gunner—we didn't aim; we just fired and kept firing; three men at each gun, and I carried powder until we ran out of ready cartridges."

He fell silent. Tears ran down over his hands as he held them, fists against his mouth.

"Two hundred killed," he said at length. His voice cracked. "My men." He groaned softly. "But we'd dismounted every gun in that battery, and the slaves . . . oh, God." He closed his eyes. "There were a few left. Maybe ten. I don't know; I didn't care. When we went ashore I was looking for the Algerian gunners, but there weren't any. Not a single corpse at those guns. They'd all run when we started to fire back. And the townspeople hid them." His jaw grew tight with anguish. "But we found 'em." He gulped a sobbing breath. "I wouldn't leave until we found them."

He laid his head on his arms, rocking gently, grieving. He couldn't see anything; the tears made a shimmer of dark and light in his eyes, wet his lips and his hands and his sleeves. His body ached. His chest seemed full. Every breath was a jerky effort to push past the jam in his throat.

But he made himself stand up. She still sat huddled in the same place, her head bowed—not looking at him. He fell on his knees in front of her and took her face between his hands.

She lifted dull, dry eyes.

"Princess." His voice had a plea in it. "Do you understand? I don't know why the world is like this; I don't know why we go out to fight something that's wrong—something so much bigger than we are, something that ought to be fought—and end up creating a thousand little horrors to stop a huge one. Slavery's wrong. Tyranny's wrong. You weren't stupid or naive or trivial to believe that. You're right. Maybe your revolution was right. You just . . . didn't understand how real it would be."

He pressed her skin, spread his wet fingers against her delicate cheekbones and looked up into her eyes with his face close to hers. He wanted her to listen, to hear him through the wall.

"You can be a coward like me, Princess. For thirteen years I've been running from this; I've been hiding from what I did. From myself. I wish I could say it wasn't my fault . . . that it would have happened anyway; any other ship and captain would have done the same. And maybe that's even true." He swallowed. "But it was me, Princess. I gave those orders; I made those choices, the same way you made yours. People died for it—and I did. I wished I had. I couldn't see why I'd been allowed to live after that." His voice fractured and failed. He took a breath, straining for control of it. "Then you came—and our island—and I started to feel again. I started to think there was a reason I'd survived—that you were my reason. I thought it was to protect you. But nothing's so simple, is it? I didn't protect you. Here you are hurting so bad, living like this, and I can't even help. I'm just here, and I need you. That's all it comes to. I need you to be brave when I haven't been. I know how hard it is. Look at me. Look at what's happened to me, facing this and telling you—I'm a shambles; Jesus, I feel like I'll be crying for the next century." He bent his head, pressed his tear-wet cheek to her dry, cold skin. "But I'm here. I'm not hiding anymore. Princess—I'm asking you. Come back to me. You're my life."

Beneath his hands, he felt a faint quiver begin to grow in her. She stayed still, but the trembling intensified. She bit her lip. A single tear tumbled down her cheek.

Sheridan pressed his mouth to the shining drop. He held

her face cupped in his hands, just held her, not speaking, not looking into her eyes.

"They killed Julia," she said in a squeaky voice. Her whole body was shaking. "I saw it."

He stroked his thumbs across her skin, feeling the tears begin to spill down her cheeks.

"And my uncle and my g-grandfather." Her body shook in a hiccuping breath. "That crowd—my people . . ." She sounded like a child. "I never thought they could be like that. Like . . . animals. They just . . . swept over everyone. The lancers. They trampled them. Took their swords." She pulled back, looked up at him, her green eyes swimming. "And Julia came out of the door, and they killed her. She hadn't done anything. Not anything."

He pushed back the wet tendril of hair that clung to her temple, his hands gentle.

"I was always so jealous of Julia," she whispered. "Sometimes I wished she was dead. And look what I did. I was the cause of that—mob—and they killed her." She looked at Sheridan helplessly. "Do you think I killed her?"

"I don't care," he said. "Listen to me. I won't say it would have happened anyway if you hadn't walked out of that church. I don't know what would have happened. Maybe I'd have shot Claude Nicolas and be hanging for it now. Julia's no loss to me; she was a scheming, selfish bitch, but Princess, I wouldn't care if she'd been Joan of Arc—I can't find a moral in it and say the blame lies here or there or with somebody else. I just don't know. We're dominoes—we fall one way or we fall another." He kept stroking her cheeks. "I don't care. I only know I'd love you whichever way it fell out."

She bit her lip. "I don't deserve that."

"Oh, Jesus . . . If we all only got what we deserved . . ." He shook his head and squeezed his eyes shut against new tears. "Pray God to spare me that," he whispered.

He let her go and sat back, cold and drained and aching. The chilly mist drifted down around them, sinking like midnight into his bones. His arm hurt, and his heart felt like an open wound in his chest. He stared at the crushed grass beneath his knees.

Please—spare me that, he thought, and wondered what would happen to him if she didn't. He couldn't go back now to the numb denial; he'd put himself in the open with no way to retreat. He was too tired to move; if she turned away from him, he would just give up. He would sit here on his knees with the rain and the gray mist and the sky and never get up again.

He gazed up into the low clouds above him, pale gray between the black towers, his hands locked gently together, resting between his legs. With clean rain and salty tears sliding down his temples he waited for his fate.

A long time passed.

A long, long time.

He felt himself vanishing, fading away like the mist that drifted over the gargoyles and monsters carved on his father's house.

And then something touched him: a soft touch on his hand, and then on his face. He turned toward her, trying to swallow down the emotion. She came into his arms. He couldn't speak; he knelt on the ground and held her against him.

"Sheridan." Her lips were trembling, her voice a feeble breath next to his ear. "My terrible lonely wolf." Her arms tightened, and he could feel the wetness on her face against his throat.

He stroked her hair with shaking hands.

"I'm here," she said into his shoulder. "I'm here, and I love you. I love you no matter what."

This book is dedicated to
the combat veterans of Vietnam
With respect, and love,
and hope for healing